Touchstone

ALSO BY MARK ALPERT

Final Theory

THE
OMEGA
THEORY

A NOVEL

MARK ALPERT

A Touchstone Book
Published by Simon & Schuster
New York   London   Toronto   Sydney

Touchstone
A Division of Simon & Schuster, Inc.
1230 Avenue of the Americas
New York, NY 10020

This Touchstone export edition February 2011

For information about special discounts for bulk purchases, please contact Simon & Schuster Special Sales at 1-866-506-1949 or business@simonandschuster.com.

The Simon & Schuster Speakers Bureau can bring authors to your live event. For more information or to book an event contact the Simon & Schuster Speakers Bureau at 1-866-248-3049 or visit our website at www.simonspeakers.com.

Designed by Akasha Archer
Map by Bryan Christie Design

Manufactured in the United States of America

10 9 8 7 6 5 4 3 2 1

Library of Congress Cataloging-in-Publication Data

Alpert, Mark, 1961–
   The omega theory : a novel / Mark Alpert.
     p. cm.
   "A Touchstone book."
   1. Physics teachers—Fiction. 2. Nuclear terrorism—Fiction. 3. Women physicists—Fiction. 4. Historians of science—Fiction. 5. Women intelligence officers—Fiction. 6. Einstein, Albert, 1879–1955—Influence—Fiction. I. Title.
PS3601.L67O64   2011
813'.6—dc22
2010043737

ISBN 978-1-4516-2849-4
ISBN 978-1-4391-0008-0 (ebook)

For my parents and my brother, who taught me how to dream

Science without religion is lame, religion without science is blind.

—ALBERT EINSTEIN

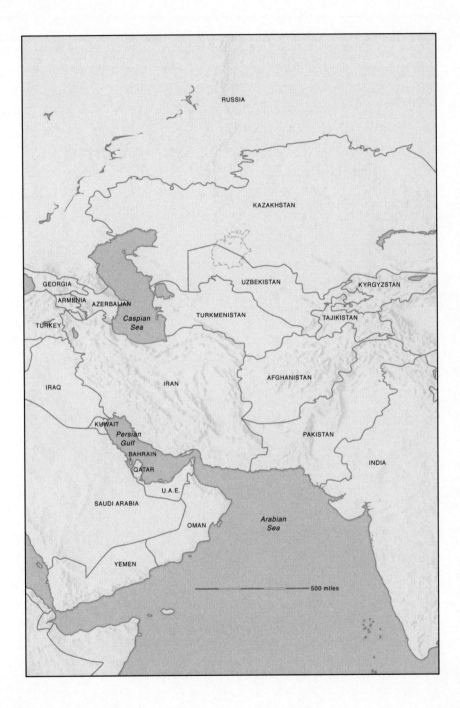

1

IT HAPPENED ON A TUESDAY, JUNE 7TH, AT 4:46 P.M. WHILE MICHAEL GUPTA
was in his behavioral therapy session. There was a knock on the door and
Dr. Parsons went to answer it. Just before he got there, the door opened
wide and Michael heard a quick, muffled burst. Dr. Parsons tumbled
backward and his head hit the floor. He lay motionless on his back, a jagged black hole in the center of his polo shirt. In less than a second, the
hole filled with blood.

They were in the computer room of the Upper Manhattan Autism
Center, which Michael visited every weekday afternoon. He was nineteen years old and his teachers had said he'd made great progress over
the past two years, but he still needed to improve his social skills so that
he wouldn't get nervous on a crowded sidewalk or start moaning if someone bumped into him. So Dr. Parsons had found a computer program
called Virtual Contact that presented simulations of people and places,
animated figures walking down realistic-looking streets. The point of the
program was to teach Michael that ordinary social encounters weren't
dangerous. The doctor was just about to show him how to launch the
simulation when they heard the knock at the door.

About one and a half seconds after Dr. Parsons collapsed, a man and
a woman stepped through the doorway, both dressed in baggy, dark blue
jumpsuits. The man was tall and his hair was a black crew cut and he had
a long, curved scar on the side of his neck. Michael didn't look at the
man's face. He usually avoided looking at faces because he didn't like to
make eye contact, and most of the time he couldn't figure out the meaning of facial expressions anyway. The woman was also tall and her hair
was almost as short as the man's, but Michael could tell it was a woman

because her bosoms puffed out the front of her jumpsuit. Her left hand had bandages on three of the fingers, and in her right hand she held a gun.

Michael knew about guns. He'd seen them before, and not just in video games. The woman's gun had a silencer, a fat gray cylinder attached to the muzzle. That was why the gunshot had sounded muffled. The woman had shot Dr. Parsons and now she was going to shoot him, too.

She took a step toward him. Michael let out a moan. He slid off his chair and curled up into a ball on the linoleum floor. He closed his eyes and started calculating the Fibonacci sequence, which was something he did whenever he was frightened. Michael had inherited excellent mathematical abilities; in fact, he was a great-great-grandson of Albert Einstein, although he wasn't supposed to tell anyone about that. And the Fibonacci sequence was easy to calculate: each number in the sequence is equal to the sum of the two previous numbers. The digits flashed on the black screen of his eyelids, swiftly streaming from right to left like the words at the bottom of a television screen: 0, 1, 1, 2, 3, 5, 8, 13, 21, 34, 55, 89 . . .

The woman took two more steps and stood over him. Michael opened his eyes. Although his forehead was pressed against the linoleum, he could see her shadow.

"It's all right, Michael," she said. Her voice was quiet and slow. "I'm not going to hurt you."

He moaned louder, trying to drown her out.

"Don't be afraid," she said. "We're going on a trip. A big adventure."

He heard a jangling noise. Out of the corner of his eye he saw two pairs of wheels. The man with the black crew cut had rolled an ambulance gurney into the room. He pulled a lever that lowered the gurney to the floor. At the same moment, the woman grabbed Michael by the wrist. He tried to scream but she clapped her hand over his mouth. Then she turned to the man. "Get the fentanyl!"

Michael started thrashing. He kicked and squirmed and flailed so violently that all he could remember afterward was a sickening whirl. They strapped him into the gurney, tying down his arms and legs. Then they put a plastic mask over his face, an oxygen mask. Michael couldn't scream, couldn't breathe. All he could do was bang the back of his head against the gurney's mattress, pounding so hard that the guardrails on either side of him vibrated. The woman turned the valve of a steel canister that was connected by plastic tubing to Michael's oxygen mask. He felt air pumping into the mask, air that smelled sweet and bitter at the same time. In a few seconds all the strength drained out of his limbs and he couldn't move at all.

It was like being halfway between awake and asleep. He could still see and hear but everything seemed very distant. The man and woman in blue jumpsuits pushed the gurney down the corridor toward the emergency exit. Then they slammed through the door and headed for an ambulance that was parked at the corner of Broadway and Ninety-eighth Street. Michael saw a crowd of people on the sidewalk, all of them stopping to stare at the gurney. He was so groggy he could barely lift his head, but he forced himself to look at the faces in the crowd. He was looking for David Swift. The last time Michael had been in trouble, two years ago, David had saved him. Ever since then Michael had lived in David's apartment, sharing a bedroom with David's son, Jonah. They were Michael's family now, David and his wife, Monique, and Jonah and Baby Lisa. He was certain that David would come running down the street any second.

But David wasn't there. All the people on the sidewalk were strangers. The man with the black crew cut opened the rear doors of the ambulance and then he and the woman hoisted the gurney into the vehicle. The woman got inside, too, and shut the doors while the man walked to the front of the ambulance and got into the driver's seat. The woman sat down in a jump seat beside the gurney. Her knees were just a few inches to the left of Michael's head. Then the ambulance started moving.

Michael stared straight up at a control panel on the ceiling and began to count the number of switches there, but the woman leaned over him, blocking his view. She removed his oxygen mask. "There, that's more comfortable," she said. "You're not hurt anywhere, are you?"

He took a deep breath. With the mask off, his head began to clear. He tried to turn away from the woman, but she grasped his chin with her bandaged fingers and pulled it back. Her grip was very strong. "I'm sorry we had to rush you," she said, "but we don't have much time."

She leaned over some more, bringing her face so close that Michael couldn't help but look at it. She had gray eyes and a slender nose. Her eyebrows looked like black commas. Her lips curved into a smile, which was confusing. Why was she smiling at him?

"My name is Tamara," she said. "You're a handsome boy, you know that?"

She let go of his chin and stroked his hair. He wanted to scream again but his throat was so tight he couldn't make a sound. Her bandaged fingers moved slowly across his scalp.

"I'm taking you to Brother Cyrus," she said. "He's looking forward to meeting you."

Michael closed his eyes. He tried again to calculate the Fibonacci sequence, but instead of numbers he saw words in his head now, scrolling rapidly from right to left. They were German words: *Die allgemeine Relativitatstheorie war bisher in erster Linie . . .*

"You'll like Brother Cyrus. He's a good man. And right now he needs your help. It's very important."

He kept his eyes closed. Maybe if he ignored her long enough, she would stop talking and go away. But after a few seconds he felt the woman's hand on his cheek.

"Are you listening, Michael? Do you understand what I'm saying?"

He nodded. The German words kept streaming through his head. Then the equations scrolled past, a long string of Greek letters and mathematical operations, with symbols shaped like snakes and pitchforks and crosses. They were his secret, his treasure. He'd promised David Swift that he'd never reveal the theory to anyone.

He opened his eyes. "I won't help you," he said. "You killed Dr. Parsons."

"I'm sorry, that was unavoidable. We have to follow orders."

Michael saw the doctor in his memory, tumbling backward with the bloody hole in his polo shirt. David had warned that something like this might happen. There were bad people, he'd said, who wanted to use the secret theory to make weapons. Michael had asked, "What kind of weapons?" and David had replied, "Weapons that are worse than atomic bombs. Guns that could kill half the people on earth with a single shot."

The woman named Tamara tried to stroke his hair again, but he shook his head. "I won't tell you anything! You want to use the theory to make weapons!"

"Are you referring to the unified field theory? The equations you've memorized?"

Michael pressed his lips together. He wasn't going to say another word.

"Let me set your mind at ease. We already know some of the equations in the unified theory, and if we'd wanted to use that knowledge to build weapons, we could've done so a long time ago." Her strong hand cupped his chin and held him still. "Listen closely now. Brother Cyrus is a man of peace. Like the prophet Isaiah. Have you ever read the Book of Isaiah?"

Michael felt sick. Tamara's hot breath was on his face. She was too close and he couldn't turn away. "Let go of me! I want to go home!"

The wolf shall dwell with the lamb, and the leopard shall lie down with the kid. And a child shall lead them. " She smiled. "That's you, Michael. That's why Brother Cyrus needs you. You're going to help us fulfill the prophecy."

He started screaming. There was nothing else he could do.

Without letting go of his chin, Tamara stretched her other hand toward the steel canister and turned its valve. "But now you need to rest. We have a long journey ahead of us."

Then the oxygen mask came down again.

2

AT 4:52 P.M., LESS THAN TEN MINUTES BEFORE DAVID SWIFT WAS SCHEDULED to open the Physicists for Peace conference, the Islamic Republic of Iran announced that it had just tested a nuclear bomb. One of the conference organizers got an alert on his iPhone, and the word quickly spread to the hundreds of scientists and journalists who'd gathered for the event. They made a beeline for the nearest television set, which was in the lobby of Pupin Hall, Columbia University's physics building. David went with them and watched the story unfold on the flat-panel screen. Somber CNN reporters stood in front of the White House and tirelessly repeated the few facts that were available. A grainy video showed the celebration in the Iranian Parliament, bearded men in black turbans embracing each other. Then a map of Iran stretched across the screen, with a red X in the Kavir Desert marking the site of the underground detonation.

"Officials at the State Department had no comment," the anchorman intoned, "but intelligence analysts said the nuclear test was apparently successful. They estimated that the strength of the explosion was between ten and fifteen kilotons, about the same as the bomb that destroyed Hiroshima."

No one could say it was unexpected. For almost a decade all the experts had predicted that Iran would eventually manufacture enough highly enriched uranium to build a nuclear weapon. But seeing the predictions come true on CNN was still a shock. David stared at the television and wiped the sweat from his brow. He felt empty and anxious and sick to his stomach.

"The president is meeting with his advisers in the Oval Office. White House sources say he will address the nation at nine o'clock tonight."

David shook his head. All his efforts over the past two years had been aimed at preventing this. Officially, he was still a professor in Columbia's history of science program, but his work with Physicists for Peace took up most of his time now. He'd used his contacts in the scientific community to create an organization with more than two thousand members around the world. As the director, spokesman, and chief fund-raiser for the group, David had appeared several times on CNN himself, a hopelessly earnest forty-six-year-old activist in a threadbare tweed jacket, preaching about the need for international friendship and cooperation. All along, though, he'd suspected that no one was taking him seriously. To the networks and newspapers, he was just another oddball, another eccentric professor with unkempt hair and impractical ideas. Good for an occasional quote, but ultimately irrelevant.

"In a brief statement, the secretary of defense said the Pentagon was studying its options. A carrier group led by the USS *Theodore Roosevelt* has reversed course and is now heading toward the Persian Gulf."

He stood there, paralyzed, for the next few minutes, listening to the newscasters' breathless reiterations. At 5 P.M. he was supposed to give the welcoming address for the conference, but he made no move toward the lecture hall. It was pointless, he thought. How could he talk about peace when the whole world was preparing for war? He wished he could cancel his address and go home to his apartment. Maybe take Baby Lisa for a stroll in Central Park. Or toss the softball with Jonah and Michael.

Then he heard someone nearby clear her throat. He turned around and saw Monique. His wife cocked her head and smiled. One of her lovely eyebrows rose slightly, arching a few millimeters higher on her forehead. Her face was dark brown and shaped like a heart. "Isn't it time for your speech, Professor?"

David was delighted to see her. Although Monique was also involved in Physicists for Peace—she was one of the most highly regarded theorists in the country—she'd told David she couldn't attend his opening speech because she was working at the computer lab that evening. She and another physicist from Columbia's department were running a particle-collision simulation program on the university's supercomputer, which was so much in demand that the time slots for using the machine couldn't be rescheduled. "What happened?" David asked. "Did your computer break down?"

She shook her head. She wore her usual work clothes—faded jeans, old sneakers, and a Bob Marley T-shirt—but she still looked better than anyone else in Pupin Hall. Her hair was braided in gorgeous cornrows that trailed down her back. "No, it's just a delay. They bumped our run by twenty minutes. I had just enough time to swing by and wish you luck."

He smiled back at her. "Well, I can use it." He pointed at the television screen. "You see the news? The Iranians tested a nuke."

Monique's face turned serious. She pressed her lips together and narrowed her eyes. "Forget the news, David. You have—"

"How can I forget it? No one's gonna be interested in anything else."

"No, you're wrong. These people have come from all over the world to hear you. They want to hear about peace, not war."

"That reminds me of an old saying. Peace activists can't put an end to war, but war can put an end to peace activism."

"I don't believe that. Not for a second."

A thin vertical line appeared between those lovely eyebrows. David knew what it meant. Monique was a fighter, born in a rough housing project in the Anacostia section of Washington, D.C. Although she'd suffered all the disadvantages of poverty and neglect, she'd fought her way out of the ghetto and into the Ivy League, becoming a professor at one of the best physics departments in the world. It wasn't in her nature to give up. She hadn't even considered it.

David leaned over and kissed her forehead, brushing his lips against the vertical line. "All right. I'll start herding the crowd. Thanks for the pep talk."

"Anytime, baby." She slipped her hand under his jacket and gave his waist a surreptitious squeeze. "I'll come home as soon as I finish the computer run, okay? I'll give you a little reward for all your hard work." She winked at him before heading for the exit.

He watched her leave, his eyes fixed on her jeans. Then he gave a signal to one of his grad students, who began directing the conference attendees toward the stairway. Within ten minutes everyone had reassembled in the lecture hall, settling into rows of varnished seats that hadn't been renovated in half a century. David had chosen this venue partly for its symbolism. On the same floor of Pupin Hall was the labora-tory where the atomic age had begun. Seventy-two years ago a team of scientists led by Enrico Fermi had used Columbia's cyclotron to split uranium atoms. Although the scientists later relocated to a bigger lab in Los Alamos, New Mexico, the effort became known as the Manhattan Project because that was where it had started. The cyclotron was gone now, dismantled and carted away and sold for scrap, but David still felt its presence. He couldn't think of a better place to have this discussion.

Striding toward the lectern at the front of the room, he noticed that every seat was filled. Still more people crouched in the aisles and stood behind the last row. He recognized most of the physicists in the crowd and many of the journalists as well. The Physicists for Peace conference had suddenly become quite newsworthy, and the reporters in the first two rows eyed David intently.

He placed his notes on the lectern and adjusted the microphone. "Welcome, everyone," he started. "Welcome to the first annual confer-ence of Physicists for Peace. I have to admit, I'm a little overwhelmed by the turnout. I know from personal experience how hard it is to gather so many physicists in one room, especially when no one's offering free beer or pizza."

There were one or two laughs, then silence. The crowd was too dis-tressed to respond to the usual jokes.

"As most of you know, I'm not a physicist. I'm a historian of science, which makes me something of an outsider here. My work has focused on the founders of modern physics—Albert Einstein, Niels Bohr, Erwin Schrödinger, and so on. I've studied how their discoveries have changed the world, for better and for worse."

David paused. He spotted two Nobel Prize winners in the middle of the third row. Dr. Martin Chang, the discoverer of the tau particle, sat next to Dr. Leon Hirsch, who'd developed the theory of superconductiv-ity. Their presence was a little intimidating.

"Over the past fifty years," he continued, "the advances in physics have triggered a technological revolution. They led to the invention of lasers and computers and MRI machines and iPods. But at the same time, military leaders have used these breakthroughs to develop ever more sophisticated weapons. Ballistic missiles, satellite killers, Predator drones, Hellfire rockets. And, of course, nuclear weapons, which unfortunately have just spread to yet another country. The human race seems determined to invent new ways to destroy itself, and many scientists are appalled that their work is being used this way. That's why we started Physicists for Peace."

David reached for the glass of water on the lectern. The audience was dead quiet, waiting for him to go on. Of course, he couldn't give them the full explanation for why he'd devoted himself to this cause, because that would mean telling them about the unified field theory and the ordeal that had nearly killed him two years ago. And David knew that if he wanted to promote world peace, revealing the existence of the unified theory was the last thing he should do.

He took a sip of water and set the glass down. "Our work at Physicists for Peace is based on the premise that people are more alike than different. We all want to lead long, happy lives and ensure the same for our children. It's a universal desire, just as strong for Iranians and Russians and Palestinians as it is for Americans and Italians and Israelis. And yet our governments keep saying that we're different, that we're in conflict. The American government tells its citizens to be afraid of Iranians, and the Iranian government teaches its people to hate Americans." He shook his head. "Well, I didn't believe what my government was saying. I wanted to talk to people in other countries and see for myself. And I discovered that many of my colleagues felt the same way. So we started to build an international network of scientists, opening new lines of communication that bypassed our governments. We have members in more than fifty countries now, including Pakistan, Syria, and, yes, Iran. And despite today's disappointing news, I firmly believe that our efforts are more important than ever."

He scanned the audience, trying to gauge their reactions. Physicists were a tough crowd, notoriously skeptical. They were adept at finding the weak points in any argument. But as David studied his colleagues, what he sensed was impatience. They weren't interested in the historical perspective. They wanted to hear about the immediate crisis. So he decided to switch gears. He picked up his lecture notes and waved them in the air. "This is the speech I was going to deliver this evening. Unfortunately, the events in Iran have rendered it obsolete. So I'm going to do something different. I'm going to listen rather than talk. One thing I've learned in my new career as a peace activist is that everyone ought to listen more and talk less."

He crumpled his notes into a ball and tossed it aside. Then he leaned forward, propping his elbows on the lectern. "We all saw the news about the Iranian nuclear test. I'd like to know what all of you are thinking. How should we respond to this development? How does it change our mission?" He held out his hands, gesturing to the whole crowd. "Please, anyone can start the discussion. I want to hear from as many of you as possible."

A murmur rose from the audience, but no one spoke up. The physicists shifted in their seats. The Nobel laureates in the third row leaned their heads together, and it looked like Dr. Hirsch was about to raise his hand and make a comment. But then David heard a deep, gravelly voice from the standing-room-only section at the back of the lecture hall. "Yes, you should change your mission. What happened today proves that your organization is a failure."

David had heard this voice before. He peered beyond the heads of the people in the last row and recognized Jacob Steele. He was dressed very conservatively, in a blue three-piece suit that draped loosely over his gaunt frame. David hadn't seen him in five years, not since Jacob left Columbia to head the Advanced Quantum Institute at the University of Maryland, and it was shocking to see how much his old friend had deteriorated since then. He and David were the same age, but Jacob looked at least fifteen years older.

"Your international network didn't stop the Iranians from building their nuke," he continued. "They seem to have ignored all your marvelous outreach efforts."

Jacob stepped past the other standees and walked down the central aisle of the lecture hall, banging the end of his cane on the varnished floor. As he came closer David noticed his sunken eyes and hollow cheeks, and the liver spots on his nearly bald head. Jacob had leukemia, diagnosed shortly before he went to Maryland. What made the sight even sadder was the fact that twenty years before, when he and David were grad students in Columbia's physics department, Jacob had been a phenomenal athlete. He'd demolished David every time they'd played basketball, even though he didn't really care for the sport. The only thing he cared about was physics.

"Don't get me wrong, David. I admire your ideals. But ideals are useless when you're dealing with terrorists. While you've been making your declarations of peace and friendship, the thugs of the world have been sharpening their knives."

David took a deep breath. Even before Jacob left Columbia, their friendship had died. They'd drifted apart after David flunked out of the physics program and decided to pursue a Ph.D. in history instead. But they'd once been quite close, and now this made it difficult to respond to him in a professional way. "Today was a setback, no question about it," David said. "But peace is a long-term project. Right now we're trying to make connections and establish relationships. And we hope that in time our members will become advocates for peace in all countries."

Jacob came down the aisle until he stood just a few feet in front of David's lectern. Then, without changing his pained expression, he let out a loud, derisive "HA!"

"That's heartwarming, David. A beautiful dream. But unfortunately we can't sit around and wait for your utopia to materialize. Now that the Iranians have tested their weapon, they're going to work on miniaturizing the warhead until it's small enough to fit on one of their ballistic missiles, or in a suitcase carried by one of their jihadis. By the time you finish assembling your network of enlightened scientists, half of the Middle East will be a radioactive wasteland. And maybe parts of the United States as well."

The lecture hall went silent. David sensed that the crowd didn't know what to make of Jacob Steele. He was a loner, a professor who rarely attended academic conferences and never collaborated with other physicists. His published papers—primarily in the fields of quantum computing and information theory—were brilliant but not very well known. And his unhealthy appearance was enough to give anyone pause. David felt a pang of sympathy for the man. Although he opposed Jacob's political views, David didn't want to argue with him. "Well, what should we do, then? Abandon all attempts at communication? If that's not the solution, then what is?"

Jacob turned around, pivoting unsteadily on his cane, so that he could address the audience directly. "We should eliminate the threat. Launch an immediate strike against Iran's uranium-enrichment complex in Natanz. At the same time, destroy all their nuclear labs and missile installations. Decimate their air force and decapitate their military leadership. It's the only solution that makes sense. We should've done it years ago."

This was too much for the other physicists. Dozens of them jumped out of their seats and started shouting. For a crowd of peace-loving scientists, their reactions were remarkably harsh. The Nobel laureates seemed particularly incensed. Dr. Hirsch, the superconductivity expert, pointed at Jacob.

"That's insane!" he yelled. His face had turned pink. "The whole Muslim world would rise against us! Not to mention the Russians and the Chinese! It would start World War Three!"

Soon the lecture hall was ringing with denunciations. But Jacob, to David's surprise, didn't say anything in his own defense. Instead, he turned away from the crowd, pivoting on his cane again. He stepped up to the lectern and leaned toward David.

"We need to talk." Jacob had lowered his voice to a whisper. "Right now."

"What?" David was bewildered. "What are you—"

"I'm sorry for instigating this little scene in front of your pacifist colleagues, but I had no choice. I arrived here just as you started your speech and I couldn't wait for you to finish."

"Dr. Swift! Dr. Swift!" It was Hirsch again, waving at David to get his attention. He'd barreled his way past the other scientists in the third row and now stood in the aisle, still pointing at Jacob. "I want to respond to this madman!"

David held out his hands, palms forward, like a traffic cop. "Hold on! Everyone will get a chance to—"

"And I want to make an announcement, too!" Hirsch held up his iPhone. "I just received word that the Union of Concerned Scientists has issued a statement about the Iranian nuclear test. Could I borrow the microphone so I can read it to everyone?"

David sighed. It was impossible to run an orderly meeting of physicists. There was too much intellectual entropy in the room. Meanwhile,

Jacob leaned a little closer. "Let the old fool read his statement," he whispered. "We can talk in the hallway."

For a moment David just stared at Jacob's ruined face. Then he turned back to Hirsch. "Okay, go ahead. I'll be right back."

While the Nobel laureate approached the lectern, David and Jacob retreated to the left side of the room. They came to an exit and Jacob grunted as he pushed the door open. David followed him into the dimly lit corridor that separated the lecture hall from the lab that had once housed Columbia's cyclotron.

Breathing heavily, Jacob leaned on his cane in the center of the corridor. "I find it odd that you've become a peacenik, David. You certainly weren't one in graduate school. In fact, I can recall several occasions when you were downright belligerent."

Back in grad school Jacob had been fond of practical jokes, and now David wondered if his old friend had interrupted the conference for his own amusement. But on second thought, it seemed unlikely. Jacob played tricks only on his friends, and he and David weren't friends anymore. "So this is what you wanted to talk about?" David asked. "This is why you interrupted me?"

"I remember one night in particular when you got into an argument at the West End Bar with someone from the mathematics department. We had to pin you to the floor to stop you from killing him."

David didn't remember the incident. He'd had a drinking problem in graduate school and his memories of those years were spotty. He'd hit bottom after Columbia kicked him out of its physics program. He spent three agonizing months in rehab before he sobered up and switched to the history department. Although he couldn't recall the details of his long drinking binge now, the feelings of shame and failure had stayed with him. He'd done far worse things than throw a punch at a mathematician. "In case you didn't notice, Jacob, I'm in the middle of running a conference here. We can talk about the good old days when I'm done, all right?"

"No, this can't wait. Did you listen carefully to the news reports of the Iranian test?"

"Of course. I—"

"Then you must've heard what the Pentagon said about the timing of the explosion. It occurred this afternoon at one o'clock Eastern Daylight Time."

"Yes, yes, I heard. They probably detected it with their seismic monitors. A nuclear explosion produces a distinctive seismic rumble. Very different from an earthquake."

"Well, I also detected the explosion this afternoon, at exactly one o'clock. But not with seismic monitors. That's why I'm here, David. After I saw the data from the Caduceus Array, I caught the next flight to New York. This isn't the kind of thing we can discuss over the phone."

"Caduceus?" David knew what the word meant—it was the ancient symbol of Mercury, the Roman messenger god, who carried a staff with two snakes twined around it—but he had no idea what Jacob was referring to. "What the hell is the Caduceus Array?"

"I need to speak with Monique Reynolds, too. You're both involved in this. "

"Whoa, wait a second—"

"I told you, this can't wait." His voice echoed in the hallway. "Where's Dr. Reynolds? You do know how to locate your own wife, don't you?"

"Yeah, she's in the computer lab, running a simulation."

"Get her on the phone. Tell her to drop whatever she's doing and come here immediately."

"I don't understand. Why do you need us?"

"You know why." Jacob's eyes locked on him. "You and Dr. Reynolds have information that no one else has."

David felt an uneasy prickle in his stomach. "Look, what are you trying to—"

"You can't keep it a secret forever, David. The physics community is like a small town, so there's always going to be gossip. Especially about the *Einheitliche Feldtheorie.*"

David froze. At first he wondered if he'd misheard Jacob, but the sound of the German was unmistakable. *Einheitliche Feldtheorie* meant "unified field theory." Jacob was referring to Albert Einstein's last discovery, the elegant, all-encompassing Theory of Everything that the great physicist had formulated near the end of his life but never revealed to the world because he'd realized how dangerous it was. David and Monique had unearthed the theory two years ago and then, for the sake of humanity, buried it again. Somehow, despite all their precautions, Jacob had gotten wind of it.

David shook his head. "I don't know what you're talking about."

"Please don't play dumb. Especially not now. The event that took place in Iran this afternoon was much more than a nuclear test. The Caduceus Array detected a disruption in spacetime, originating at the test site in the Kavir Desert and spreading outward at the speed of light. In layman's terms, it was a rip in the fabric of reality. It severed the continuity of our universe, tearing apart the dimensions of space and time for the briefest of instants and then splicing them back together. Needless to say, this hasn't occurred in any previous nuclear explosion. In fact, it hasn't occurred anywhere in the universe before, not since the Big Bang started fourteen billion years ago."

David's stomach was roiling now. He still didn't understand what Jacob was saying, but he could hear his dismay. And Jacob wasn't easily dismayed. "Wait, slow down," David said. "If there was a rip in the fabric of the universe this afternoon, how come I didn't notice anything?"

"Fortunately, the anomalies were fleeting. They lasted less than a trillionth of a second, which is why no one felt the disturbance and no laboratory but mine detected it. But a larger disruption could trigger a catastrophe. It could bring down the whole system." Jacob was motionless, absolutely still. Even his eyes had stopped moving. "Someone is deliberately tampering with spacetime. We need to pool our knowledge to have any hope of stopping this."

David felt dizzy. This was the moment he'd been dreading for the past two years. The *Einheitliche Feldtheorie* revealed the fundamental nature of reality, showing how all the particles and forces in the universe originate from the convoluted folds of spacetime. But the theory also showed how spacetime could be manipulated to release the immense energies contained in those folds. If someone had managed to rediscover the equations . . .

"All right," David said. "You got my attention. I want to know everything about this Caduceus Array. What did you—"

A loud thump interrupted him. The doors to the lecture hall burst open. David expected to see Dr. Hirsch come running into the corridor to report that open warfare had broken out at the Physicists for Peace conference. Instead he saw a heavyset, sixtyish woman in a red jacket, accompanied by a man wearing a gray suit and sunglasses. FBI special agent Lucille Parker's face had grown a little more weathered since David had last seen her, with a few more lines across her forehead and wrinkles around her eyes. But she still moved like a Marine going into battle, rushing forward under her helmet of platinum-blond hair. "Swift!" she shouted. "You're coming with us."

Lucille and the other agent cornered David, each grabbing one of his elbows. He tried to break free, but they held on tight. "What are you doing?" he shouted. "What's going on?"

She frowned. "Bad news. About Michael."

LUKAS STOOD AT THE BACK OF THE LECTURE HALL, BLENDING IN WITH THE crowd. He'd bought a suit for the occasion, a cheap blue pinstripe, and under the jacket was a Heckler & Koch pistol in a shoulder holster. The assignment was simple enough. There were no security guards or metal detectors in the building. The only problem was the timing. Lukas was supposed to complete his mission at approximately the same time the other teams finished theirs, but he couldn't take out his target in front of all the scientists in the lecture hall. So he had to wait. To pass the time, he recited the Lord's Prayer, mouthing the Latin words under his breath: *Pater noster, qui est in caelis, sanctificetur nomen tuum . . .*

Luckily, after a few minutes his target left the room. Lukas slipped out a different exit and took up position near the staircase, flattening himself against the wall and peering down the corridor. It was a good place to do the job. The hallway was dark and there was only one witness who needed to be eliminated. Lukas reached into his new jacket, removed the Heckler & Koch, and quietly attached the silencer. But just as he raised his gun, the doors to the lecture hall opened and two more people stepped into the corridor. One was a standard-issue FBI agent. The other was some kind of supervisor, a big ugly brute of a woman. Lukas quickly stepped backward, retreating into an alcove.

This is unfortunate, he thought. He didn't want a firefight. But he was a veteran of the Delta Force, the U.S. Army's elite counterterrorism unit, so he was ready for combat. Over two decades he'd taken out dozens of targets in Somalia, Bosnia, Iraq, and Afghanistan, and he'd lost none of his skills in the three years since he'd heard the Lord's call. The FBI agents stood with their backs to him, so he knew he could kill both of them before they drew their guns. He raised his pistol, lining up the gun sights with the old woman's hairdo. Always eliminate the commander first, that's what they'd taught him.

A second later, though, his luck changed again. The FBI agents marched off with the witness, a trim, dark-haired professor in khaki pants and a tweed jacket, leaving the target alone in the hallway. Lukas waited until he couldn't hear the agents' footsteps anymore. Then he aimed his pistol at the bald man with the cane.

3

MICHAEL COULDN'T MOVE HIS ARMS OR LEGS—THEY WERE STILL STRAPPED
to the gurney—but he could turn his head to the right and stare at the
clouds through one of the airplane's oblong windows. He'd never traveled in a plane before and the first few minutes were terrifying. The floor
shook and the gurney jangled and an impossible roar filled the airplane's
cabin, which was a tube about twelve feet long and six feet wide. Then
Michael's feet tilted upward and his head sank down and the horrible
roar drilled into his skull, tearing through his eardrums. It was so loud he
couldn't even hear himself screaming.

He closed his eyes and kept them closed for a long time. When he
finally opened them, the gurney wasn't tilting anymore and the roar
had died down to a steady rumble. Michael lifted his head and saw two
people sitting in the cockpit at the front of the plane, the man with the
scarred neck in the copilot's seat and the woman named Tamara in the
pilot's. It reminded him of a computer game he used to play, Eighth Air
Force, which simulated the cockpit of a B-17 flying over Germany during
World War II. But in the computer game the pilot and copilot were both
men and they never left the plane to kidnap or shoot anyone. Confused,
Michael turned back to the window and focused on the clouds, which
glided past in great white domes tinged with orange from the sunset. It
was a pretty view and after a while he felt calmer. He made a point of
memorizing how the clouds looked, every ridge and hump and billow.

He continued studying the sky for about an hour. Then the noise
from the airplane's engines subsided and his gurney started to tilt again,
dipping at the feet this time. In a panic, he closed his eyes as tightly as
he could. The tilt grew steeper. Michael felt like he was sliding, feetfirst,

into a deep hole. Against the black of his eyelids he saw hundreds of red stars, all moving in unison from right to left. Then, for the second time that day, he saw the *Einheitliche Feldtheorie*, written by Albert Einstein, his great-great-grandfather. Michael had memorized the equations when he was thirteen, and they'd burrowed in his mind for the past six years. Their odd symbols glowed as they streamed through the darkness.

After another fifteen minutes Michael felt a jolt and opened his eyes. He looked out the window and saw a flat, empty field crisscrossed with red and white lights. The plane was coasting down a runway, raising the flaps on its wings just like the B-17s did in Eighth Air Force. The sky was dark now, almost black. As the plane slowed he glimpsed a building on the far side of the field, a hangar with a curved roof and giant doors. But there were no other buildings in sight and no other aircraft. At the end of the runway the plane turned and came to a stop. Then the engines shut down and all the runway lights switched off and Michael couldn't see anything outside.

In the cockpit Tamara rose from the pilot's seat. She'd taken off the jumpsuit she'd worn when she was pretending to be an ambulance attendant; now she wore camouflage pants and a brown T-shirt. Because the cabin's ceiling wasn't high enough for her to stand up straight, she hunched forward as she came down the aisle and squeezed into the space beside the gurney. Michael turned his head away, but a moment later he felt the scrape of her bandaged fingers on his chin. She pulled his face toward hers and bent down low. Her lips were wet and her teeth glistened. "How are you doing, Michael?" she asked. "Everything all right?"

He strained his eyes to the left and right, frantically trying to look past her. He caught a glimpse of the cabin door and imagined David Swift bursting through it. Oh, where was David now? Why wasn't he here?

"Are you uncomfortable? I'm sorry about that. I wish I could let you get up and stretch your legs, but I can't." She reached into the pocket of her camouflage pants. "But I have something if you're hungry. A little snack. I bought it this morning." She pulled a candy bar out of her pocket, a Milky Way Midnight bar. "Here, I'll unwrap it. I can hold it up to your mouth and you can take a bite."

Michael shook his head. He usually liked Milky Way bars, but this one was crooked and the wrapper was wrinkled. He wouldn't have eaten it even if David had offered it to him.

Tamara shrugged, then slipped the candy bar back into her pocket. "We're just making a quick stop here. The longest part of our journey is still ahead. Angel is going to refuel the plane and pick up supplies." She glanced at the cockpit, where the man with the scarred neck was pressing buttons and throwing switches. Michael took a deep breath, relieved that she'd turned away from him. He wanted to close his eyes and slide into the darkness again, but Tamara was too close. He was afraid she might bend a few inches lower and bite him.

"And while we're waiting here, we're going to have a visitor. Brother Cyrus is coming to see you, Michael. He'll be here any minute." She let go of his chin and ran her fingers through his hair. The bandages made a crackling noise as they moved behind his ear. "Please be respectful in his presence. Don't say anything unless he asks you a question first. He's our leader and he deserves respect."

Smiling, she gripped Michael's chin again and brushed the fingertips of her other hand against his cheek. "You're going to help Brother Cyrus," she said. "And he's going to help you, too. No more pain, no more suffering." She slid one of her fingers across his forehead, soft and slow. "Just peace. Everlasting peace."

He opened his mouth to scream, but at that moment the man with the scarred neck called out, "They're coming!" Tamara instantly let go of Michael and rushed to the door at the front of the cabin. With one hand she grasped the door's handle and swung it open, and with the other she pulled a gun out of her pants, the same gray pistol she'd used to kill Dr. Parsons.

She waited in the doorway, pointing her gun outside and peering into the darkness. After about fifteen seconds Michael heard the sound of a car approaching, then screeching to a halt. After another ten seconds he heard footsteps. Then Tamara stepped back from the doorway and a man without a face entered the plane.

He wore black pants and a black jacket, and his head was wrapped in a thick black scarf that covered everything except his eyes. Michael stared at him, transfixed. It was like a man-size piece of the darkness outside had drifted into the plane's cabin. He wasn't very tall—in fact, he was shorter than Tamara—but he had a broad chest and bulky shoulders, and the narrow confines of the cabin made him look enormous. His eyes glinted within the slit of his head scarf as he approached Michael's gurney.

Tamara followed a few feet behind. "This is Brother Cyrus," she announced. "Say hello, Michael."

The strange thing was, Michael wasn't afraid. This is a game, he told himself. He imagined he was immersed in a computer game, one of the first-person shooters he used to play all the time on his Game Boy. David had convinced him to stop playing the more violent programs—Warfighter, Desert Commando, America's Army—but Michael remembered them clearly. In all those games the enemy soldiers looked like Brother Cyrus. They wore black uniforms and helmets, and their faces were usually masked or obscured so you wouldn't feel bad about shooting them. And if this was a game, Michael reasoned, there must be a strategy for winning. He didn't have a gun, unfortunately, and his avatar was immobilized. But he wasn't defenseless.

He avoided looking at the man's eyes. Instead he focused on the black creases where the scarf wrapped around his jaw. "Hello, Brother Cyrus," he said.

The man folded his arms across his chest. He wore black gloves, Michael noticed. Not a single square inch of his skin was exposed. It was impossible to tell whether he was white or black or something in between.

"Hello, Michael," he finally said. His voice was low, muffled by the scarf. "Please forgive my appearance. I suffered a disfiguring accident a few years ago. I've found that it's less disturbing for everyone if I keep my face hidden."

For a moment Michael wondered what kind of accident it was. A fire? An explosion? But in the end it didn't matter, he thought. He disliked looking at faces anyway. "Where are you taking me?" he asked.

"All in good time, Michael, all in good time. It's a pleasure to finally meet you. When I was a young man I once met Amil Gupta, your grandfather. He was an assistant to Albert Einstein during the 1950s, correct? And he married the great man's granddaughter?" Brother Cyrus moved closer. The creases in his scarf shifted as he cocked his head. "Amil was a genius himself, one of the finest physicists of his generation. I was very sorry to hear about his death."

Michael didn't want to talk about his grandfather. Amil Gupta had broken his promise and tried to reveal the *Einheitliche Feldtheorie*. David had told Michael that he shouldn't think too badly of his grandfather; the old man had gotten sick, David said, and the sickness had made him do all those terrible things. But Michael didn't believe it. He decided to repeat his previous question, which Brother Cyrus hadn't answered. "Where are you taking me?"

Tamara stepped forward. "Michael! Show some respect!" Then she leaned over his gurney and slapped him in the face.

The pain and surprise were so sharp, Michael's eyes watered. Still, he didn't turn away from Brother Cyrus. It's just a game, he told himself again. Nothing but a game.

Cyrus uncrossed his arms and pointed a gloved finger at him. "I've spent the past two years observing you, Michael, and I've learned that you're a remarkable young man. In some ways, you're even more remarkable than your illustrious great-great-grandfather." He moved his hand closer, aiming his index finger at the center of Michael's forehead. "I'm not talking about your mathematical abilities now, all the numbers and equations you can cram into that brain of yours. No, I'm talking about your innocence. Your purity of spirit."

Michael wanted to ask for a third time, *Where are you taking me?* but he was afraid that Tamara would slap him again, maybe harder than before. Or Cyrus would hit him with that big, gloved hand.

"God gave you a wonderful gift," Cyrus continued. "Yes, your autism is a gift. You can't lie or cheat. You can't be deliberately cruel. Your mind lacks all the evil impulses that make the human race so despicable. In a sinful world, you point the way to our salvation." He opened his gloved hand, splaying the fingers. They hovered just a few inches above Michael's eyes. "You're a herald of the world to come, my child. A world without sin and rot and corruption. The Kingdom of Heaven we will soon bring to earth."

"Amen," Tamara whispered. She lowered her head and stared at the floor.

To Michael's relief, Cyrus withdrew his hand and took a step backward. His eyes still glinted, though, within the slit of his head scarf. "The Lord has given us a great task, Michael. After Amil Gupta died, I heard the rumors about the theory he'd uncovered. Through my informants in the FBI and the other American intelligence agencies, I confirmed that it was Einstein's *Einheitliche Feldtheorie*. And I saw that the Almighty was giving me a sign. The Lord was telling me to pursue the unified theory because it held the keys to His holy kingdom." He extended his arms, gesturing at the airplane's cabin. "Luckily, I have significant resources at my disposal. I hired experts to assemble the bits and pieces of equations that had been picked up by the intelligence agencies."

Michael's stomach jumped. Although he and David Swift had tried to destroy every hard drive and computer disk that had held the formulas of the unified field theory, it was possible that they'd missed some. Amil Gupta had been very careless with the equations.

"We couldn't reconstruct the entire theory," Cyrus said. "But we learned enough to put us on the path to the Redemption. We conceived a plan to carry out the Lord's will and open the gates of His kingdom. And just a few hours ago, the Almighty gave us another sign. The results from our test prove that we're on the right course. Now all we need are the missing pieces of the theory, the parts we haven't been able to reconstruct." He pointed at Michael's forehead again, his gloved hand trembling. "I know you have the equations, Michael. Einstein bequeathed the *Einheitliche Feldtheorie* to his young assistants, and fifty years later they passed it on to you. Once you give it to us, we can take the final step."

Tamara raised her head and looked at Michael. She leaned over his gurney and grasped his left hand. "Don't worry, it'll be simple. I'll show you what to do when we get to our camp."

Michael tried to pull his hand out of her grasp, but his arm was strapped down too tightly. The cords dug into his wrist as he struggled. "I told you, I won't help you! You killed Dr. Parsons!"

Brother Cyrus nodded. "Yes, and there will be more deaths, unfortunately. But in the end we will triumph over death. The Lord has given me His promise, whispering the holy words in my ear. There will be no death in His Kingdom, only eternal life. All of God's subjects will be resurrected, and we will live forever in His loving embrace."

Tamara whispered "amen" again. Then Cyrus stepped sideways, moving behind her. He put a gloved hand on her shoulder. "Sister, I'm afraid I must leave you now. But I'll meet you at the rendezvous point the day after tomorrow." He walked to the front of the cabin, heading for the door. "Before the plane takes off, make sure that Angel gives the boy a sedative. We want him to be well rested when he arrives."

"Yes, Brother. Go in peace."

Tamara let go of Michael's hand. She watched Cyrus leave the plane and continued to stare at the cabin door after it had swung shut behind him. Then she turned to the cockpit and shouted an order at the man with the scarred neck. Several seconds later he came toward them, fitting a shiny silver needle into a syringe.

Michael couldn't pretend that this was a game anymore. He rolled his head from side to side and began to scream.

4

DAVID SWIFT AND HIS FAMILY WERE IN ONE OF THE INTERROGATION ROOMS on the twenty-third floor of Federal Plaza, the FBI's field office in Lower Manhattan. While David paced across the linoleum, Monique cradled their one-year-old daughter in her arms, rocking Baby Lisa to sleep. Jonah, David's son from his first marriage, sat at a table in the center of the room and stared at his iPod Touch. The screen was blank—Jonah had taken the device out of his backpack half an hour ago, but he hadn't turned it on. Normally, he was a cheerful, blond, blue-eyed nine-year-old, but now his eyes were red and his cheeks were wet. He'd been crying ever since the FBI agents had picked him up from his after-school karate class.

David stopped pacing. He came up behind his son and placed a hand on his shoulder. "Go ahead, turn on the iPod," he urged. "It'll help pass the time."

Jonah didn't move. He kept his eyes on the small, dead screen.

Monique swayed toward them, bouncing on the balls of her feet. Baby Lisa's eyes were half closed, her caramel face pressed against her mother's shoulder. "Hey, Jonah, I can show you a new app," Monique offered. "It's a 3-D model of the Milky Way galaxy. You can zoom in on the spiral arms and everything. It's very cool."

After a few seconds the boy looked up at David. Another tear slid down the side of his nose. "Dad, are we under arrest?"

David's heart constricted. He would've preferred to tell his son the truth—that the FBI was protecting them from any further kidnapping attempts—but he didn't want to frighten the boy. "No, we're not under arrest. We're safe. Everything's all right."

Jonah scowled. He dropped the iPod, which hit the table with a clunk. "Then what are we doing here? And where's Michael?"

This last question was harder to answer. All David knew for certain was that Michael had been kidnapped from the Upper Manhattan Autism Center and that one of his teachers, Dr. Irwin Parsons, had been shot to death. David could guess the reason for the abduction—the kidnappers wanted the *Einheitliche Feldtheorie,* the equations locked in Michael's head—but he had no clue who the bastards were or where they could've taken the boy. "There's nothing to worry about, okay? Michael is missing, but the police—"

"Missing? What do you mean, missing?"

"It looks like he might've wandered off from his school." It was a pitiful lie, but David was too anxious to come up with something better. He couldn't stop thinking about the kidnappers and what they might be doing to Michael. "But don't worry, the police are going to find him. Sooner or later they'll—"

"What happened? Where did he go?"

Jonah furrowed his doughy brow, trying to look defiant, but his lower lip trembled. He and Michael had grown close since the autistic teenager had moved into their apartment two years ago. Even though Jonah was a full decade younger, he'd taken charge of Michael, introducing him to the customs and rituals of the Swift household. They'd played countless games of Stratego using special rules that Jonah had devised to keep Michael from winning every time. Jonah got frustrated occasionally by Michael's lack of responsiveness—the boy couldn't understand jokes, much less laugh at them—but he'd learned to live with it. He'd always wanted a brother, and now he had one.

While David stood there, not knowing what to say, his wife handed him Baby Lisa, who squirmed for a moment before nestling against his chest. Then Monique sat down in the chair next to Jonah's. "Look, Michael's going to be all right," she assured him. "He's made a lot of progress over the past two years and he knows how to take care of himself now. He'll find his way home. You just have to be patient, okay?"

"Where is he?" Jonah's face crumpled and the tears began to flow again. "Where did he go?"

Instead of answering, Monique wrapped her arms around the boy. At first Jonah fought her, furiously twisting in her embrace. But after a while he gave up the fight and sobbed against her T-shirt, shaking uncontrollably. And as David watched them, his own eyes began to sting.

He and Monique had also fallen in love with Michael. In the beginning it was more of a charitable impulse, a simple desire to help this poor kid who'd been abandoned by his family. David had enrolled him in the best autism program in New York and conferred weekly with his therapists. As the months passed, Michael's behavior improved: he no longer screamed if you accidentally touched him, and he started reading science textbooks instead of playing computer games all day long. The veil of autism seemed to lift a bit, allowing David to catch a glimpse of the boy's essential nature, which was sweet and curious and trusting. Although he understood that Michael would never fully emerge from his isolation, there was already more than enough of him to love.

After a couple of minutes Jonah stopped crying. Monique stood up and took hold of Baby Lisa, who was fast asleep now. She carried the child to an adjoining room and laid her down in a portable crib that the FBI had provided. Just as she returned to David and Jonah, the door to the interrogation room opened and Special Agent Lucille Parker stepped inside.

She wore the same outfit David remembered from two years ago, a bright red jacket over a loose-fitting white blouse and a matching skirt. A pair of reading glasses hung from a beaded chain around her neck. She looked more like a librarian than an FBI agent, but David knew she wore a shoulder holster under her garish jacket, and tucked in the holster was a Glock 17.

"We found Karen Atwood," she announced in her familiar Texas drawl. "Our agents in Philadelphia picked her up and they're bringing her here."

David let out a sigh of relief. His first wife, who shared custody of Jonah, had gone to a lawyers' conference in Philly and hadn't returned any of the frantic phone calls David had made after he learned of Michael's disappearance. He couldn't imagine why anyone would want to kidnap Karen—unlike Michael, she knew nothing about the *Einheitliche Feldtheorie*—but it was still good to hear she was safe.

Jonah leaped to his feet. "You found my mom? Is she okay?"

Lucille gave the boy a smile. Her lipstick was the same shade of red as her jacket. "Yes, honey, she's fine. We got her on the phone right now and she's itching to talk to you." She pointed at another agent standing in the hallway, a stone-faced woman in a gray pantsuit. "This is Agent Carson. She'll take you to my office. Go on, you can use the telephone there."

Jonah looked uncertainly at the pair of agents. David squeezed his son's shoulder. "It's all right. Go ahead."

The boy walked toward Agent Carson, who took Jonah's hand and briskly escorted him down the hallway. Lucille waited a moment, watching them go, then closed the door and turned to David and Monique. She wasn't smiling anymore. Dozens of creases etched her forehead and the skin below her eyes.

David swallowed hard. "What's going on? Have you found Michael?"

She shook her head. "We sent alerts to Homeland Security and every police department in the Northeast. But so far we haven't heard anything." She walked over to the table and pointed at the chairs. "Have a seat."

David was too anxious to sit. "How could this happen? How could they just walk into the autism center and take him?"

Lucille pulled out a chair and sat down. She winced as she stretched her legs under the table. "The kidnappers were professionals. They disguised themselves as paramedics, driving a real ambulance they'd stolen from Lenox Hill Hospital. It looked like a genuine emergency call."

"Were there any witnesses?"

"We interviewed some folks who were on Ninety-eighth Street at the time, but they didn't give us much in the way of ID for the paramedics. That's typical—when people see an ambulance crew, they're usually too busy gawking at the guy in the stretcher to notice anything else."

Monique stepped toward the table. She stood shoulder to shoulder with David. "What about surveillance cameras?" she asked. "There must be some at the autism center."

"Yeah, about half a dozen. And every damn one was disabled just before the abduction. Like I said, these guys were professionals."

"Well, what about the ambulance? That should be easy to track down, shouldn't it?"

Lucille frowned. "The New Jersey State Police found it an hour ago. The kidnappers dumped it near an abandoned warehouse in the Meadowlands. They must've switched to another vehicle."

Shit, David thought. The New Jersey Meadowlands was next to I-95, the Newark shipping terminal, and two airports. Michael could be anywhere by now. "So what are you saying? You don't have anything?"

"Calm down, Swift. We're pursuing every lead. We got the ballistics from the two homicides at the autism center and the—"

"*Two* homicides? Someone else was killed there besides Dr. Parsons?"

Lucille nodded grimly. "One of our undercover agents was stationed on the first floor, just down the hall from the behavioral therapy room. The kidnappers shot him and threw his body into a closet. Then they went into the therapy room and shot Irwin Parsons." She curled her upper lip, baring clenched teeth. "That's how we found out about the abduction so quickly. We knew something bad had happened when our undercover didn't radio in."

Monique looked confused. She tilted her head and stared intently at Lucille. "Wait a second. Why was one of your agents at the autism center?"

"You can probably figure it out. We've had Michael under surveillance for the past two years."

David told himself he shouldn't be surprised. After the Amil Gupta fiasco, Agent Parker had thoroughly interrogated everyone involved. Lucille knew they were hiding something from her, and although neither David nor Monique had said a word about the unified field theory, she'd obviously deduced where the equations were hidden.

"It's my fault," Lucille added. The creases under her eyes seemed to deepen. "I went easy on you. I let you keep your secrets. But I knew there were people who wouldn't be as kindhearted if they discovered what was inside Michael's head. I knew they'd do anything to get the information. So in the interest of national security, I ordered protection for the boy. We put him under surveillance to prevent any foreign operatives from getting their hands on the unified theory. Unfortunately, I underestimated the threat."

She lowered her head and stared at the tabletop. All of a sudden she looked old. Although she was still in her early sixties, at that moment she seemed at least ten years older. When David looked at her, he saw a stiff-jointed, overweight agent who should've stepped down from active duty a long time ago. It was a little jarring to see her this way. Two years ago Lucille had pursued him relentlessly, chasing him halfway across the country. He'd never noticed her age because he was too busy running away from her. But this time was different, he thought. Agent Parker was trying to help them now. And they needed her help.

David decided to trust her. He'd already told Monique about his conversation with Jacob Steele. Now it was time to tell Lucille. "I have a lead for you," he said. "I can't say for sure if it has anything to do with the kidnapping. But it might."

Lucille raised her eyes. They narrowed, instantly alert. "What?"

"Just before you came to get me, I talked to Jacob Steele at the conference. He's the director of the Advanced Quantum Institute at the University of Maryland. We were talking about the Iranian nuclear test and Jacob said he'd detected a spacetime disruption at the exact moment of the explosion."

"Spacetime is the coordinate grid of our universe," Monique added. "It's the three dimensions of space—length, width, and height—plus the dimension of time. Einstein showed that space and time are joined together in a continuum that changes its shape near massive objects, bending around stars and planets and—"

"I know what spacetime is." Lucille pulled a notebook and pencil out of the inside pocket of her jacket. "I've had to learn a lot of this physics crap because of you two." She jotted something in her notebook, then turned to David. "Tell me more about this disruption. What did Steele say exactly?"

"Well, we didn't get a chance to talk for long. He said the disturbance spread from the nuclear test site, mangling the dimensions of space and time as it moved outward. And he detected it with an instrument he called the Caduceus Array, which is a strange name for a physics experiment. A caduceus is the twisting-snakes symbol that you usually see at hospitals and doctors' offices."

Monique shook her head. "I never heard of this instrument. Jacob's never written about it in any of his papers. It must be something new."

"Anything else?" Lucille asked.

David searched his memory for the exact words Jacob had used. "He said the disruption was like a rip in the fabric of reality, a break in the continuity of the universe. And it showed that someone was deliberately tampering with spacetime."

Lucille jotted a few more words in her notebook. "You said it occurred at the same time as the Iranian nuclear test, right? So was it like a shock wave from the explosion?"

Monique stepped forward. She was better than David at explaining the physics. "It wasn't just an explosion. The universe has big explosions all the time, novas and supernovas and gamma-ray bursts that are trillions of times more powerful than atomic bombs. The energy they release can change the shape of spacetime, but none of these events can tear the fabric apart." She shook her head again. "No, you'd have to know the unified theory to do that. The theory is like the blueprints for the universe—it shows the whole structure of spacetime. And if you have the blueprints, you can see how to change the structure." As she spoke she gestured at the walls of the interrogation room. David had seen her do the same thing during her lectures in Pupin Hall. "That's what happened two years ago with Amil Gupta. He used the theory to build a weapon that could focus vast amounts of energy on any point in spacetime. And this event in Iran looks awfully similar."

"So you're saying the Iranians have the theory now? And they're using it to build a weapon?"

"Who knows?" Monique threw her hands in the air. "We thought Michael was the only one who knew the equations. But maybe someone else has figured them out."

Lucille thought about it for a moment. She pursed her lips and tapped the eraser end of her pencil against her chin. "Okay, but what does all this have to do with the kidnapping? If the Iranians already know the unified theory, why would they kidnap Michael?"

Monique opened her mouth to answer, but David spoke first. "Look, it can't be a coincidence. We should talk to Jacob. I want to know what he's working on."

"Yeah, I agree," Monique said. "There's a connection here. The sooner we talk to Jacob, the faster we'll find Michael."

The room was silent for several seconds. Lucille leaned back in her chair, still tapping the pencil against her chin. Then, with a grunt, she rose to her feet. "All right. It couldn't hurt to have a chat with the guy." She headed for the door. "I'm gonna make some calls. You two sit tight."

After she left, David sank into one of the chairs by the table. He was tired. All the stress of the past few hours had exhausted him. Monique sat down in the chair next to his. She put her hand on his shoulder and squeezed it. "This is good, David. I think we're getting somewhere."

He nodded, but he didn't believe her. When he closed his eyes, he kept seeing Michael. Michael in his therapy room at the autism center. Michael crouching on the floor with his hands clamped over his ears. Michael screaming inside an ambulance. The pictures in David's head were so terrible and he couldn't shut them out.

They sat there without talking. David lowered his head and rubbed his eyes. Monique moved her hand to the back of his neck and kneaded the muscles there. Then she started scratching his back. The room became so quiet they could hear the hum of the fluorescent lights overhead.

After several minutes Monique began to talk again. She spoke in a calm, quiet, logical voice, the voice she always used when she talked to herself. "You know what I don't get? Jacob's specialty is building quantum computers, not investigating fundamental physics. He's never written a single paper on the nature of spacetime. So why has he suddenly developed an interest? Doesn't that seem a little strange?" She paused but didn't wait for an answer. "And do you know who provides most of the funds for Jacob's research? The good ol' Defense Department. They awarded him a ten-million-dollar grant to develop his quantum computers. Everyone else in his field is jealous as hell." She paused again. "And that name, the Caduceus Array. That's odd, too. In astronomy, the caduceus is a symbol for the planet Mercury. But what's the connection with spacetime disruptions?"

David finally raised his head and looked at Monique. "We've got to find him. We've got to find Michael."

"Yes, baby, we'll find him . . ."

"We have to be involved in this. We have to convince Parker to let us help."

"We'll talk to her, okay? I'm sure—"

"She won't find him without us. Because this isn't an ordinary kidnapping case. This is—"

The door to the interrogation room suddenly opened. Lucille appeared in the doorway but made no move to come inside. Her face was blank and her eyes showed nothing, but her jaw muscles quivered slightly. "We got problems," she announced. "Two of them."

Monique took her hand off David's back. He stood up. "What do you mean?"

"I tried calling Steele's office at the University of Maryland. I figured some lab assistant might be working late. But I got a message saying the whole university switchboard was down." Lucille's cheek twitched. "I got curious, so I checked with the local police. There was an explosion at the Advanced Quantum Institute an hour ago."

"Jesus." David gripped the edge of the table. "What's the other problem?"

"After I hung up the phone, I saw an e-mail from one of my contacts in the New York Police Department. A Columbia University student found a body in Pupin Hall. In an old laboratory right next to the lecture hall. It's Steele."

5

THE PRESIDENT SAT ALONE IN THE WHITE HOUSE SITUATION ROOM, STARING at a stack of loose-leaf binders on the conference table. He'd spent most of the evening in a meeting with his defense secretary and the Joint Chiefs of Staff. At eight o'clock the Joint Chiefs had headed back to the Pentagon, giving the president a few precious minutes to think about what they'd just told him. The loose-leaf binders they'd left behind contained their plans for eliminating Iran's nuclear facilities.

He leaned back in his chair. His head was splitting and he was desperate for a cigarette. Massaging his temples, he gazed at the flat-panel screen at the front of the room, which showed the positions of American strike forces in the Middle East—aircraft carrier groups in the Persian Gulf, fighter-bomber wings at the air bases in Qatar and Kuwait. And as he stared at the map he thought of his wife and daughters, who'd already been escorted by the Secret Service to the relative safety of Camp David. He pictured his two little girls in the backseat of the presidential limousine, gazing at the Maryland woods through tinted, bulletproof windows.

The Iranian nuclear test was the biggest crisis of his administration. The mullahs in Teheran had rejected all his overtures and flouted all his warnings, and now he had to respond. It was too dangerous to let Iran become a nuclear power—there was too great a chance that they'd use the bomb against Israel, or that Israel would launch a preemptive strike against them. And if he acted quickly enough, he could obliterate their nuclear program, and the whole world could breathe a sigh of relief. According to military communications intercepted by the National Security Agency, Iran's Revolutionary Guard possessed only two more nukes and had moved both to a secure facility near the town of Ashkhaneh, in the northern part of the country. Photos taken by U.S. reconnaissance satellites confirmed the reports, showing the Guard's convoys traveling to the mountain range where the facility was hidden.

He turned in his chair so he could view another flat-panel screen. This one displayed a satellite image of the Ashkhaneh installation: a concrete entrance embedded at the foot of a mountain, leading to a network of tunnels and natural caverns that extended deep underground. Unfortunately, it was a hardened target. Readings from ground-penetrating radar had revealed that parts of the installation were more than a thousand feet below the surface. No conventional bunker-busting missile could reach that far. The only weapon that could destroy the facility in a single blow was the air force's earth-penetrating nuclear warhead, which could collapse the whole underground network. That option was out of the question, of course—the president wasn't going to start a nuclear war. But he wasn't going to let Iran start one, either.

Turning away from the screen, he sifted through the pile of loose-leaf binders. Most of the Defense Department's plans called for conventional bunker-buster strikes on the Ashkhaneh facility, followed by the deployment of commando units to enter the damaged installation and destroy the nukes stored deep inside. The problem was that the Iranians had anticipated this strategy and taken steps to counter it. The facility was located in an inaccessible part of the country, far from the U.S. carriers in the Gulf and the bases in Afghanistan and Iraq. The Iranians also had a sophisticated air-defense system, with dozens of radar stations and missile batteries on their coast and most of their borders. Nearly all of the Pentagon's battle plans predicted hundreds of casualties.

But one plan was different. The president picked up the binder marked *JSOC Operation Cobra.* It was written by Lieutenant General Sam McNair, who commanded the Special Operations forces in Afghanistan. McNair had an impressive record of success, which was a rare thing indeed in the war against the Taliban. He also had a penchant for bold moves. His plan was the only one that offered the advantage of tactical surprise. If the plan worked as promised, the Special Operations assault group would attack from an unexpected direction, and the Iranians would have no time to move their nukes to a different facility. But the best part, in the president's opinion, was the casualty estimate: fewer than thirty men killed or wounded.

He glanced at his watch. It was time to return to the Oval Office. In twenty-nine minutes he was scheduled to give his televised address to the nation.

He stood up and left the Situation Room. As he walked down the hallway, a Secret Service agent and a staff assistant fell into step behind him. He looked over his shoulder at the assistant.

"Place a call to the defense secretary, please. Tell him to give the go-ahead to Cobra."

6

THREE FIRE ENGINES, TWO HAZMAT TRUCKS, AND HALF A DOZEN POLICE cars were parked in front of the University of Maryland's computer science building. David, Monique, and Agent Parker arrived at the scene at 2 A.M., more than six hours after the explosion, but the place was still teeming with emergency personnel. Lucille, who'd spent the past four hours driving the government-issue Chevrolet Suburban from New York to the Maryland campus, parked the SUV behind one of the police cars. From the backseat David gazed at the massive brick building. It looked undamaged—no broken windows, no blackened brick—but a crowd of state troopers, fire marshals, and plain-clothes detectives stood in front of the floodlit entrance, just outside a barricade of yellow crime-scene tape.

Lucille turned to Monique, who sat in the SUV's front passenger seat, and pointed at the building. "It doesn't look so bad to me. Where's Steele's lab?"

"I think it's in the basement." She looked over her shoulder at David. "Isn't that right?"

David had visited the Advanced Quantum Institute several years ago, before Jacob became its director, so he knew the layout. "Yeah, in the basement. That explains why the explosion didn't damage the exterior."

Lucille nodded. "Okay, here's how we're gonna do this. You two are my scientific consultants. And that means you don't talk unless I consult you. Got that?"

She gave them a warning look. Although she'd agreed to bring them along, she clearly wasn't happy about it. Normally, FBI agents didn't invite civilians to a crime scene. But after hearing the news of Jacob Steele's murder, Lucille had acknowledged that there might be a connection to Michael's kidnapping. And the first step in investigating that connection, David and Monique had argued, was figuring out what Jacob had been working on. In the end, Lucille admitted that their expertise in quantum physics might prove useful. So when Karen Atwood arrived at the FBI office to pick up Jonah, Monique pleaded with her to take care of Baby Lisa, too. It was a big favor to ask, but Karen agreed. David's first and second wives had forged a bond during their harrowing ordeal two years ago, and they'd gotten along well ever since.

Now Lucille opened the SUV's door, and David and Monique followed her outside. A tall, red-haired man in a gray suit stepped away from the crowd in front of the computer science building and came toward them. He reached into his jacket and pulled out his FBI badge.

"Agent Parker?" he said. "I'm Dickinson from headquarters. I'll be your liaison with the local field office."

Lucille shook Dickinson's hand. "What's the situation? Can we get into the building?"

"The fire marshals gave the all clear about an hour ago. The explosion pulverized the lab, but there's no major structural damage. Our crime-scene techs are in the basement right now."

"What have they found?" Lucille asked. "Have they done the residue tests yet?"

"Yes, ma'am. Preliminary results indicate that the explosive was C-4. We've alerted the National Counterterrorism Center."

"Who have you interviewed so far?"

Dickinson reached into his jacket again and pulled out a notebook. "Luckily, Steele's lab was empty at the time of the explosion. There were some people still working elsewhere in the building, but none of them saw anything unusual before the blast." He opened his notebook and leafed through the pages. "We contacted the university administration to get more information about Steele. And a few officials came down here to see the damage. One of them said he works with Steele." He jerked his thumb at the computer science building. "His name's Adam Bennett. He's in the basement right now with one of my agents. I told Bennett to stick around because I thought you might want to talk to him. He doesn't know yet that Steele is dead."

David knew Adam Bennett. He was a director at DARPA, the

Pentagon agency that funded defense-related research. Bennett was in charge of awarding grants to scientists and engineers in nearly every field, from robotics and aerospace to communications and computer science. Personally, he was a likable guy; David had met him a year ago at an academic conference, and he'd seemed charming and intelligent. He'd just finished reading David's biography of Albert Einstein and had many perceptive things to say about the book. Nevertheless, David had felt uncomfortable talking to him. Although DARPA was most famous for funding the invention of the Internet, the agency was also responsible for the Stealth bomber and the Predator drone. Bennett regularly visited Iraq and Afghanistan to field-test new technologies such as surveillance robots and laser-guided bullets. David, as a peace activist, found all this a little disturbing.

"Bennett works for DARPA," David told the FBI agents. "He's director of the agency's defense sciences office. He knows everyone in physics, and everyone knows him, because he's the guy who doles out the cash."

"Yeah, he's Jacob's sugar daddy," Monique added. "DARPA's been funding research on quantum computing for at least a decade."

Agent Dickinson stared at them, obviously wondering who the hell they were. They looked nothing like law-enforcement officers—David still wore the khaki pants and tweed jacket he'd put on for the Physicists for Peace conference, and Monique was in her Bob Marley T-shirt. Dickinson turned to Lucille with a quizzical look on his face, but she ignored it. "Well, what the hell are we waiting for?" she said. "Let's say hello to the guy."

She marched toward the computer science building, clearing a path through the crowd of police officers and ducking under the crime-scene tape. David and Monique followed her through the entrance, with Dickinson close behind.

In the lobby they made a quick right and headed down a stairway that smelled of burned plastic. But they saw no tangible evidence of the explosion until they left the stairwell and walked a hundred feet down the basement corridor. Above a gray steel door was a sign that said ADVANCED QUANTUM INSTITUTE: HOME OF THE TRAPPED IONS. Lucille pushed the door open and they stepped into the ruined laboratory.

The room was cavernous and dark, illuminated only by the emergency lights brought in by the fire department and the roving flashlight beams of the FBI crime-scene investigators. The air was warm and acrid and the cinderblock walls were caked with soot. A layer of wet ash carpeted the floor, and thick clods of it stuck to David's shoes. The building's sprinklers had apparently quenched the blaze, but not before it had blackened the lab benches and gutted the storage cabinets and melted every computer and monitor. Chunks of twisted metal were everywhere, thrown across the room by the force of the blast. David looked up and saw that the explosion had pitted the plaster ceiling and smashed the overhead pipes and wiring. Severed fiber-optic cables hung from the ceiling like dead snakes, their glassy fibers bursting through the charred insulation.

Agent Dickinson led them across the room, walking past the jagged hole in the floor that had obviously been the epicenter of the blast. They headed down another corridor, following the string of emergency lights, and as they moved away from the lab the acrid stench lessened. Then they turned a corner and entered an office that the FBI had converted to a temporary command post. The agents had set up their equipment on the office desk: a radio, a couple of laptops, and a portable spectrometer for analyzing explosives residue. An agent with a blond crew cut was fiddling with the radio, while an older man in a black herringbone suit sat in the office chair. David recognized him immediately. It was Adam Bennett.

The blond agent snapped to attention when Lucille walked into the room. Bennett also rose to his feet, glancing first at Agent Parker and then at David and Monique. His eyes widened. "Dr. Swift? And Dr. Reynolds? What are you doing here?"

Bennett was in his mid-sixties. He had thinning white hair and a serious, square-jawed face, with gray eyes and a pinkish complexion, the kind that sunburned easily. He seemed agitated, which was understandable. Several million dollars' worth of DARPA-financed laboratory equipment had just been blown to bits.

Lucille marched right up to him and held out her hand. "Mr. Bennett, I'm Special Agent Lucille Parker of the—"

"What took you so long?" he demanded, ignoring her proffered hand. "I've been waiting in this office for two hours."

She said nothing in response but cocked her head ever so slightly. The agent with the crew cut got the message and left the office with Dickinson.

Bennett scowled at her. David thought it was odd to see them standing face-to-face, because they looked so similar. Bennett was about the same age as Lucille and just as stocky. Even his hair was the same color as Lucille's, although she had considerably more of it. "Where's Jacob Steele?" he asked. "Is he still in New York?"

"Sit down, Mr. Bennett."

He remained standing. His face turned a little pinker. "You're not the only federal official here. This is a DARPA project and I have every right to know what's going on!"

Lucille frowned. Her brow furrowed and dozens of creases fanned from the corners of her eyes. "All right. I'll tell you what's going on. Jacob Steele came to New York this afternoon to see these two." She pointed at David and Monique. "He wanted to talk about a scientific instrument he was working on, something called the Caduceus Array. That name ring a bell?"

"No, I never heard of it."

"I'm not surprised. No one's heard of the damn thing. And unfortunately, Jacob didn't get a chance to describe it either. While he was visiting Columbia University's physics building this evening, someone with a nine-millimeter pistol put a bullet in his head."

Bennett stood there silently for a moment, staring at Lucille, as if waiting for her to say something else. Then he let out a sigh and stepped backward. He sank into the office chair from which he'd risen just a minute ago.

"At approximately the same time, someone blew up Jacob's lab," Lucille continued. "We're obviously dealing with a sophisticated organization, with multiple teams of operatives carrying out synchronized missions. Most likely a terrorist organization. Now you see why we're taking this so seriously?"

Bennett closed his eyes and raised a hand to his forehead. Pinching the bridge of his nose, he muttered something under his breath.

Lucille stepped closer. "To pursue this investigation, I need to know exactly what Jacob was working on. That's why I'm here. And that's why you need to stop bitching and start telling me about Jacob's research." She leaned over his chair. "You think you can do that?"

Several seconds passed. Bennett shrank from Lucille's implacable gaze. Then he opened his eyes and gripped the armrests of his chair. Slowly and unsteadily, he stood up. All the bluster had drained out of him. "Excuse me. I need to go to the men's room."

Lucille pointed at him. "Go ahead. Just don't take too long." She went to the office door and threw it open for Bennett. As he passed through the doorway, she gave another signal to the two agents who were waiting in the hall. Both of them followed Bennett down the corridor. Then she slammed the door shut.

David was surprised. "Why'd you let him go?"

"He'll talk once he gets back." She went to the chair that Bennett had vacated and sat down with a grunt. "He's worried about something. Why else would he come down here in the middle of the night? It's something embarrassing, and because the guy's a mucky-muck in the federal bureaucracy, he knows he has to tell us about it before we find out from someone else. But he's also a chickenshit, see? So he has to go to the bathroom and look in the mirror for a few minutes and work up his courage. It's standard chickenshit behavior. I've seen it a million times."

Shaking her head, she reached into her bright red jacket and pulled out a pair of latex gloves from the inside pocket. Then she rolled her chair closer to the desk and started inspecting the contents of its drawers. She rummaged through a file cabinet and a drawer containing circuit boards and miscellaneous bits of hardware. David watched her, fascinated. She gave everything a quick look, her eyes keen and darting.

After a while she opened another drawer and pulled out a shiny metal canister about the size of a soup can. It had wires coming out of the bottom and a circular pane of glass at the top. Through the glass top David could see two parallel rows of electrodes inside the device. A dark groove ran between the rows, about three inches long and a quarter of an inch wide. Lucille grabbed the reading glasses that hung from her beaded necklace and peered into the device. "Okay, here's your first chance to do some consulting. What the hell is this thing?"

Monique went to the desk and looked over Lucille's shoulder. It took her less than three seconds to identify the object. "That's an ion trap. It's the heart of the quantum computers that Jacob was building. Remember what I said in the car? About what makes quantum computers different from ordinary PCs?"

During the long drive from New York to Maryland, Monique had started to explain the basics of quantum computing. Luckily, Agent Parker was a quick study. "Yeah, I remember," she said. "Quantum computers use atoms to do the calculating. Unlike ordinary computers, which use electrical currents. But what's with the ions?"

"An ion is an atom with an electrical charge. If you add an extra electron to an atom, you make a negatively charged ion. If you strip away an electron, you make it positively charged. The advantage of using ions is that you can move them around easily. You can put positive ions in a vacuum chamber and keep them suspended between positively charged electrodes." Monique took the container out of Lucille's hands and pointed at the dark groove inside. "The positive ion goes here, into the gap between the positive electrodes. Positive repels positive, right? So the repulsion on both sides traps the ion, keeps it in a stationary position. Then you can trap more ions in the gap and arrange them in a line, perfectly spaced. Like a row of beads in an abacus."

"Why would you want to do that?"

"Each ion has a magnetic orientation that can point up or down, like a switch. So it's similar to a bit in an ordinary computer. You know what a bit is, right? As in megabit, gigabit?"

Lucille nodded. "Of course. That's how much data you can put in your computer."

Monique smiled. She loved to explain these kinds of things. "That's right. A bit is a single unit of data, and it has two possible values, zero or one. Putting eight bits together makes a byte, and each byte represents one of the characters on a computer's keyboard." She pointed at one of the laptops sitting on the desk in front of Lucille. "This computer has a microprocessor with four gigabytes of RAM, so it can perform calculations on four billion bytes of data. That's more than enough memory to run a spreadsheet program or display a YouTube video. But a quantum computer could do much more."

"How so?"

"Remember how I said that each ion can point up or down? Well, imagine that the up orientation is zero, and down is one. If you look at it that way, each ion contains one bit of information, because it can be either one or zero. A string of eight ions, some up and some down, contains a byte of information. And we can change the information contained in the string by firing a laser beam at the ions, which flips their orientation. But here's the best part." Monique paused to take a breath. "When you're dealing with individual ions, all the crazy rules of quantum theory apply. Particles are waves and waves are particles, and nothing is completely precise or predictable. And one of the crazy consequences of quantum theory is that we can put an ion into something called a superposition state. In this state, the ion is pointing up and down at the same time."

Lucille made a face. "What? That's impossible."

"It sounds impossible, but it's true. An ion in superposition is like a schizophrenic—it's one *and* zero. It holds two values simultaneously. Now imagine putting two ions into that state. They hold four values at the same time—one/one, zero/zero, one/zero, and zero/one. And a string of three ions in superposition holds eight values simultaneously. You see the pattern?"

Lucille thought about it for a moment. Then she nodded. "Yeah, I do. Every time you add another ion to the string, you double the amount of data the string can hold."

"Right again. The capacity increases exponentially, so a quantum computer with a relatively modest number of ions can hold an extraordinary amount of data. And when those ions interact and start exchanging their data, they're actually performing an enormous number of calculations simultaneously. If you could build a quantum computer with just a hundred trapped ions—and that's definitely feasible within the next decade—it could perform trillions upon trillions of calculations at once. It could accomplish certain tasks billions of times faster than the best conventional computers in the world."

"What kinds of tasks? Anything that DARPA might be interested in?"

"Oh yeah, plenty. A quantum computer would be ideal for searching through large databases, looking for patterns hidden inside gigabytes of noise. Or creating computer simulations of extremely complex phenomena, such as the shock wave that triggers a nuclear explosion. But the thing that DARPA's most interested in is code breaking. A quantum computer could break public-key codes, which are now considered unbreakable. Those are the codes used on the Internet for encrypting credit-card numbers. And the military uses the same encryption scheme on some of its classified data networks."

Lucille nodded again. She retrieved the shiny, glass-topped ion trap from Monique and studied it for a while, holding it up to the light.

David stared at it, too, wondering what the hell Jacob had been doing. Even back in the days when they were in grad school together, Jacob had been unusually secretive about his research projects. It was an extreme case of professional caution: Jacob had been deathly afraid that another grad student or postdoc would steal his ideas. Although he'd freely shared all the details of his personal life, often regaling David with elaborate descriptions of his sexual adventures—he'd been a real Don Juan in those days—Jacob never talked about his research. When it came to his work, he trusted no one.

David stepped toward the desk, intending to tell Lucille about this. Just then, however, the office door opened and the FBI agent with the blond crew cut ushered Adam Bennett back into the room. His face looked even pinker than before and his eyes were bloodshot. David got the feeling that he might've been crying in the men's room. Or throwing up. There were wet spots on the front of his jacket.

Lucille leaned back in her chair and swiveled to face Bennett. "Feeling better?"

He took a deep breath and nodded. It seemed that Agent Parker's prediction had been correct. The man was ready to talk now.

She held up the ion trap for Bennett to see. "While you were gone, we found one of Jacob's toys. And Dr. Reynolds was kind enough to explain how it works." She glanced at Monique, who'd folded her arms across her chest and propped her butt on the edge of the desk. "So how close was Jacob to building his quantum computer?"

Bennett stared at the ion trap for a few seconds, uncomprehending. Then he shook his head. "He wasn't close." His voice was low and ragged. "That was the trouble."

"Really?" She placed the device on the desk and tapped her fingernail on its glass top. "Even after you gave him all those millions of dollars?"

He kept shaking his head. David had never seen anyone look so defeated. "The last prototype he built for us could perform calculations with a string of sixteen ions. That was a record, better than anything built by other research teams. But it was still light-years away from a practical machine."

Lucille gave Bennett a skeptical look. "I thought a quantum computer didn't need a lot of ions. Isn't that the whole point?"

"Well, you need more than sixteen if you want the computer to do something that ordinary computers can't do. You need at least fifty. And Jacob was finding it difficult to scale up his prototypes. He ran into technical problems." He grimaced. "The truth is, the technology isn't ready yet. Sooner or later, physicists will build a practical quantum computer, but it's going to take time. Maybe five years, maybe ten. And Jacob didn't have that kind of time."

"What do you mean?"

Bennett turned to David. The man had ignored him and Monique ever since Lucille began her interrogation, but now he looked David in the eye. "You saw Jacob this afternoon? Before he was . . ." His voice trailed off. "How did he look to you?"

David remembered the sunken eyes and hollow cheeks. "He looked terrible. He had leukemia, didn't he?"

"Jacob had fought it for several years but he was losing the battle. I visited him every six months to check the progress of his research, and he seemed more depressed and bitter each time. He told me that he'd wasted his life. That he'd accomplished nothing of significance in physics, and no one would remember him." He turned away from David and stared at the floor. "Jacob was desperate to do something important before he died. And he knew he couldn't achieve a breakthrough in quantum computing. I think that's why he began diverting his grant funds."

Lucille sat up straight. This was the piece of embarrassing information she'd been waiting for. "You mean he was spending DARPA's money on something else?"

Bennett took another deep breath. "I saw the first evidence of it a year ago. When I reviewed his progress reports, I noticed that he'd ordered the installation of dedicated fiber-optic lines. They were expensive, heavy-duty cables linking his laboratory's server to the phone company's trunk line."

David remembered the severed fiber-optic lines he'd seen in the charred laboratory, hanging from the ceiling like dead snakes. It occurred to him now that the number of communication lines was unusually large, much more than a typical laboratory would need. "What was he using them for?"

"Jacob was vague when I asked him about it. He said he needed a faster Internet connection. But the fiber-optic lines he'd ordered went way beyond his personal needs. They could transmit thousands of gigabits a second. Jacob could send the entire contents of the Library of Congress through those cables in less than a minute." Bennett shook his head again. "I sensed that something was wrong. That Jacob was hiding something, a completely different research project. So I asked him straight out: 'Jacob, are you diverting the grant money from its intended purpose?' He got very upset and denied it vociferously. And though I had my doubts, I took him at his word. Because I liked him, you see. And I felt sorry for him."

"Then what happened?" Lucille asked.

"I noticed more odd things in the report he submitted last fall. And he missed the deadline for building his next prototype, a quantum computer with twenty-four ions. I was almost certain by then that Jacob was working on something else. But I couldn't prove it. I tried talking to one of his lab assistants, but she couldn't tell me much. Jacob kept everyone in the dark."

Monique, who was still sitting on the edge of the desk, tapped her index finger against her lips. "Maybe Jacob changed his strategy. Instead of developing a more advanced quantum computer, could he have been building an array of simpler prototypes? With one quantum computer at this lab and others at different locations, all working together? That might explain the fiber-optic lines. Maybe the computers were exchanging data."

Bennett shrugged. "I don't know. I suppose it's possible."

David tried to picture it, a tidal wave of data coursing from one computer to another. Maybe that was why Jacob had called his project the Caduceus Array, naming it after the symbol of the Roman messenger god. An array of quantum computers and fiber-optic lines could certainly send a lot of messages back and forth. But how could this array do what

Jacob had said the Caduceus Array had done—detect a rip in the fabric of the universe? "Do you think Jacob might've ventured into another branch of physics? Besides quantum computing, I mean?"

"Excuse me?" Bennett looked askance.

"When I saw Jacob yesterday he said the Caduceus Array had detected an anomaly in spacetime. Did he ever express an interest in doing that kind of research?"

"No, I'm sorry. He never mentioned anything like that." Bennett raised his right hand to his forehead. His face was slack. "All I can tell you is that I made a mistake. I should've stopped Jacob when I noticed the first irregularities in his work. But instead I stood by and did nothing. And now Jacob is dead and I don't know why." He raised his other hand to his forehead. His fingers ran through his hair, making it stand up in white clumps.

Lucille got out of her chair and came toward him. Her expression softened a bit. "All right, the first thing we need to do is find out where Jacob was sending all that data. Where did he keep his records?"

Bennett lowered his hands. He was breathing hard. "All of Jacob's records were on his server, and that was destroyed in the explosion. But he was using the phone company's trunk line. And they keep track of all the data traffic."

"Okay, we'll check with them. And I want to see all your documents related to Jacob's research."

He nodded. "Yes, of course. I'll contact my office and make sure you get everything."

Lucille turned away from him. David could tell she was thinking ahead, already planning the next step in the investigation. "We need to talk to whoever was receiving the data," she said. "Because that person knows what Jacob was doing. Maybe we can find a name in one of the reports."

"I can give you one name right now." Bennett's voice was quiet, almost a whisper. "I'm not sure if it's a real name, but . . ."

Lucille spun around. "What?"

"I . . . I mentioned earlier that I talked to one of Jacob's lab assistants? I asked her confidentially if Jacob had been in touch with any other researchers. She said no, but then she remembered a series of phone messages. Seven messages, all in the same day, and all from a computer scientist at the Hebrew University of Jerusalem."

David was familiar with Hebrew University. Ten years ago, while he was researching his biography of Einstein, he'd spent a couple of months in Jerusalem going through the thousands of letters and manuscripts in the university's Albert Einstein archives. The school also had a world-class computer science department.

Lucille stared at Bennett. "What's the name she gave you?"

"It was so unusual, I couldn't forget it—Olam ben Z'man."

"Shit," David muttered. He'd learned some Hebrew during his summer in Jerusalem. "That's very strange."

"Yes, I thought so, too," Bennett said. "I was curious, so I looked it up in a Hebrew-English dictionary. The name means 'Universe, the son of Time.'"

7

MICHAEL AWOKE ON A BARE MATTRESS THAT SMELLED OF PUKE. HE SAT UP to get away from the smell and felt a dull pain in his shoulder. He reached under the sleeve of his T-shirt and touched a gauze pad taped to his skin. Then he remembered the trip in the airplane and the shiny needle at the end of the syringe.

He wasn't in the airplane anymore. The mattress lay on the floor of a dark, stuffy room. It was so dark he could barely see his own feet. He squinted and saw that he was still wearing his jeans and socks and sneakers. No one had undressed him while he slept, and he was glad about this—David Swift had told him many times that he shouldn't let anyone touch his private parts, except a doctor, of course. But his underpants were damp because he'd peed in them during the night, and his T-shirt was sweaty. Also, his throat was sore. He was hungry and scared and wanted to go home.

The mattress was in the corner of the room. Michael touched the walls, which felt gritty. He looked over his shoulder and thought he saw a piece of furniture on the other side of the room, but it was too dark to make out any details. The only illumination was a thin shaft of sunlight that squeezed through a chink in the concrete wall. About an inch wide, the shaft descended at a twenty-degree angle and made a yellow parallelogram on the floor. Michael deduced from the shallow angle of the sunlight that it was either early morning or late evening, but he couldn't tell which. His watch was no help—the glowing hands pointed at eleven, which couldn't be right. The airplane must have crossed several time zones, he thought. He found it very distressing not to know the correct time. It was even worse than not knowing where he was.

He stood up and walked toward the chink. It was nearly six feet above the floor, but Michael was six feet and one and a half inches tall, so he could see through the hole if he stood on his tiptoes. Pressing his right eye against the wall, he peered through the chink as if he were looking through a telescope. At first he saw nothing but an aching brightness. But after a few seconds he saw a landscape of brown hills, rugged and treeless, stretching to the horizon. Two gray Toyota Land Cruisers were parked on the sand below the closest hill, and in front of the cars were twelve men in beige uniforms.

The men stood in a line, shoulder to shoulder. They were soldiers, but they looked different from the animated figures in Warfighter and the other computer games that Michael played. Their uniforms were dirty and didn't match—some were in a desert-camouflage pattern, others were plain khaki. One soldier had a brown beard and a red bandanna. Another wore a black turban. They carried a variety of weapons, too: M-4 carbines, Bizon submachine guns, AK-47 rifles. After a while a thirteenth soldier stepped into view, a large man wearing a black beret. He stopped in front of the others, clasped his hands behind his back, and shouted something Michael didn't understand. The other soldiers turned to the right and marched off. Michael adjusted his head, trying to get a better view through the chink. Then he heard a metallic click and the room behind him filled with light. When he turned around he saw Tamara.

Her left hand gripped the pull chain of an overhead light, a naked bulb screwed into a socket on the ceiling. In her right hand she held a rectangular tray. It was dark brown, like the trays at McDonald's. On the tray were seven packets of Heinz ketchup and a bag of Lay's Classic potato chips, the two-ounce bag that sold for ninety-nine cents. Also a twelve-ounce can of Sprite. This was Michael's favorite snack, which David Swift usually prepared for him as a reward after he'd done a Good Thing, such as walking to the corner deli by himself or going three days without a temper tantrum. It was very confusing to see it here, on a tray carried by Tamara in this room with concrete walls. For a moment he assumed that David Swift had prepared the snack, and his heart beat a little faster—was David here? Had he finally arrived to rescue him? But when Michael looked past Tamara he saw no one behind her. The room was empty except for the bare mattress he'd slept on and a large wooden desk.

Tamara stepped forward, extending the tray toward him. "Dinner-time, Michael. Look, I brought your favorite things."

She was standing too close. Michael backed up against the wall and slid to the left to put some distance between them. Tamara wore a desert-camouflage uniform similar to those he'd seen on the soldiers outside. On her left shoulder several loose black threads hung from the fabric of her shirt, as if a patch had been ripped off there. "Come on," she said. "You like to put the ketchup on the potato chips, right? Exactly two drops of ketchup on each chip? Brother Cyrus said you were very particular about your food."

Michael shook his head. Tamara wasn't his friend. She was his enemy. He turned away from her and stared at the large desk against the opposite wall. "My name is Michael Gupta," he said. "I live at 562 West One Hundred and Tenth Street in New York City." This was the message that David Swift had instructed him to memorize in case he got lost. He was supposed to recite it to a police officer, who would then bring him home. "Please don't touch me. I don't like to be touched because I am autistic. Please contact my guardian, David Swift, at 212-555-3988."

Tamara didn't respond at first. She just stood there. Then she nodded. "Okay, I understand. I won't touch you."

She turned around and went to the desk. It had five drawers, three of which were missing their knobs. Tamara placed the tray on the right end of the desk. On the left end was a computer, a Sun Ultra 27 workstation with a twenty-two-inch monitor. Michael was familiar with this type of computer. The autism center had an Ultra 27 workstation in its recreational therapy room, and he'd spent many hours playing games on it.

Tamara picked up a metal folding chair that leaned against the wall. She unfolded the chair and placed it in front of the desk. Then she backed away, moving toward the far corner of the room. She pointed at the chair. "There you go, Michael. Sit down and eat your dinner. I'll stay far away, see?"

He stared at the bag of potato chips on the tray. He was very hungry. But he didn't want to do anything that Tamara told him to do. Instead, he decided to repeat the last sentence of his message. "Please contact my guardian, David Swift, at 212-555-3988."

Tamara continued to point at the chair. "You haven't eaten anything in eighteen hours. You must be starving."

This, Michael knew, was an exaggeration. He wasn't starving. A human being could survive for three to six weeks without eating any food. He'd read this fact in *The Concise Scientific Encyclopedia,* which was a book that David Swift's wife, Monique Reynolds, had given him for his nineteenth birthday. Michael got confused when people exaggerated; he often thought they were telling the truth when they were actually telling a lie that was supposed to be funny. So he'd found it useful to memorize the scientific encyclopedia, which contained facts on a wide variety of subjects.

"I'm not starving," he told Tamara. But he *was* hungry. And he was thirsty, too. A human being could survive for only three to seven days without water.

"I know you're frightened," Tamara said. "It was a very long trip in the airplane. And now you're in an unfamiliar place. But you need to eat."

Michael looked at the bag of potato chips again. He knew it would be wrong to eat the snack. He hadn't done any of the Good Things that were on the list that David Swift had written, so he didn't really deserve the reward. But he supposed that the usual rules didn't apply if Tamara had made the snack instead of David. And even if she was his enemy, he reasoned that it would be all right to eat her food. It would make him strong, so he could fight her better.

He approached the desk and sat down in the chair. He was so hungry, his hands shook as he opened one of the ketchup packets. He removed a potato chip from the bag and dabbed it with two drops of ketchup, each the size of a dime. Then he put it in his mouth and quickly prepared another. He groaned as he chewed, his jaw humming.

From the corner of his eye he saw Tamara step forward. She was breaking her promise to stay far away from him, but he was too busy eating to protest.

"Whoa, slow down!" she said. "You're going to choke!"

She let out a couple of high-pitched yelps. At first Michael thought they were cries of pain, but then he realized that Tamara was laughing. He had no idea why, and he didn't care. He squeezed ketchup onto two more potato chips and put both in his mouth at the same time. Chewing rapidly, he mashed the chips into a damp doughy clump. Then he used his molars to divide the clump and began swallowing the pieces.

Tamara moved toward him until she was just a couple of feet away. "That's better, isn't it?" she said. "You look happy now. Very happy."

Michael avoided looking at her. He kept his eyes on the tray and put another chip in his mouth. Then he reached for the can of Sprite and took a long drink.

"You have such an interesting face," she said. "Your grandfather was from India, wasn't he? I bet that's where you got that beautiful black hair."

She reached out and touched the side of his head. He felt the bandaged fingers of her left hand running through his hair, just above his right ear. Michael stopped chewing. She'd just broken another promise. He sat there motionless for several seconds. The damp potato-chip clump rested heavily on his tongue. He forced himself to swallow it.

"I know you haven't had much happiness in your life, Michael. Brother Cyrus told me about all the pain and sadness you've been through. Like what happened to your grandfather two years ago. And your poor mother, Elizabeth. You must miss her so much."

He didn't want to talk about his mother. He reached into the bag of potato chips again and pulled out a handful.

"Cyrus told me she was an addict. And a prostitute. And that you lived with her until you were thirteen." She moved her hand lower. Her bandages scratched the back of his neck. "Then your grandfather took you away from her. Which was the right thing to do, I suppose. But it must've been very difficult."

Michael's hands were shaking again. He managed to rip open another Heinz packet, but he squeezed it too hard. Ketchup splattered on the tray.

"It's horrible to watch bad things happen to the people you love. Sometimes you just can't help them. There's nothing you can do." Tamara's hand slid to his shoulder. "Cyrus told me she died of an overdose. Of methamphetamine."

He closed his eyes. His mother had died six months after he'd started living in New York. David Swift and Monique Reynolds had organized a memorial service for her. A minister in a black suit had stood behind a coffin of gleaming wood, so shiny that it reflected all the lights in the church. Michael had wanted to open the coffin so he could look at his mother one last time, and he began to scream when they wouldn't let him. He didn't calm down until David Swift told him the truth. Elizabeth, he said, had been dead for two weeks before they found her. Her body was already half gone. There was nothing left to see.

Tamara squeezed his shoulder. The sensation was unbearable. "I know what it's like, Michael. My little brother Jack was an addict, too. He used to disappear for months at a time. I yelled myself hoarse, trying to get him to stop. But he didn't listen. The last time I saw him, at the Greyhound station in Louisville, his face was yellow and half his teeth were gone. And there were track marks all over his arms."

The grip on his shoulder tightened for a moment. Then Tamara let go. Michael took a deep breath, relieved that she was no longer touching him. He waited about ten seconds, then opened one eye and saw her leaning against the wall to the right of the desk. She stared at the cement floor and shook her head. "The worst part of it was, Jack used to be so beautiful. He had black hair just like yours, Michael. And the prettiest smile."

He glanced at her face, daring a quick peek. Then she suddenly raised her head and looked straight at him. At the same time, she let out another high-pitched laugh. "But I have good news!" she shouted. "Wonderful news! I'm going to see Jack again very soon. And you'll see your mother, and your grandfather, too!"

Her voice was too loud. Michael pushed his chair backward, trying to get away from her. She was smiling and pointing at the ceiling.

"This is what the Almighty has promised! He's called on Brother Cyrus to open the Kingdom of Heaven, where we'll joyfully reunite with all of our loved ones. With every single creature that the Lord has ever created! Hallelujah! *Hallelujah!*" She looked up at the ceiling and stretched her hand toward it. Then she looked down at Michael. "You know about the Kingdom of Heaven, don't you? Your mother must've told you about it, right?"

Michael had heard the word "heaven" before, of course. His mother had often used the phrase "stinks to high heaven." And he once saw a children's book that had a picture of heaven, a place in the sky where dead people wore wings and walked on the clouds. The minister at his mother's memorial service had mentioned it, too, saying that Elizabeth's soul had risen to heaven. But Michael knew that this was another exaggeration. There was no heaven in the sky. Above the earth were the layers of the atmosphere—troposphere, stratosphere, mesosphere, thermosphere—and above those was the void of space. The earth revolved around the sun, and the sun sped through the Milky Way, and all the galaxies hurtled away from one another as the universe expanded at an ever-increasing rate. Michael had seen illustrations of all these things in *The Concise Scientific Encyclopedia*. But the book said nothing about heaven.

"It's not in the sky," Michael said. "If it were in the sky, astronomers would see it with their telescopes."

Tamara laughed again, hurting his ears. "You're right! It's not in the sky. People have so many wrong ideas about heaven—they think it's like Never Never Land, some magical place where their souls will go when they die. But that's not what the Bible says." She reached into the pocket of her fatigues and pulled out a small black book. "The Bible says the Lord will establish the Kingdom of Heaven after the Second Coming, the End of Days. At that holy hour, the Lord shall cast aside our fallen world and replace it with His kingdom. Then the dead shall be resurrected from their long sleep and we shall be at one with God." She opened the small book and pointed to one of its pages. "It's right here in Corinthians, chapter fifteen. *In a moment, in a twinkling of the eye, the trumpet shall sound and the dead shall be raised incorruptible!*"

Michael shook his head. He didn't understand. "Dead people will come back to life?"

"Not just people, Michael. *Everything* will be resurrected. We live in a corrupt world, full of sin and death, but the Lord is giving us a chance now to redeem His Creation. He's called on Brother Cyrus to hasten the coming of the End of Days. And in the Kingdom of Heaven, all the things that have lived and died in our broken world will be reborn. The whole history of the universe will come together in a single eternal moment, and we will live in God's embrace forever!"

He shook his head again. "I still don't—"

Tamara stepped behind Michael and grabbed the back of his chair. With a heave she dragged it to the left, positioning him directly in front of the computer screen. Then she leaned over his shoulder and hit the machine's power switch. "It's easier to show it to you here," she said. "Brother Cyrus says you're very good at mathematics, so you should be able to understand. These are the tools the Lord has given us to remake His Creation."

The computer screen flashed blue, then displayed a translucent yellow sphere that slowly rotated around the word *LOGOS*. After a few seconds the rotating sphere vanished and a row of icons appeared on the screen. Tamara grasped the mouse and clicked on an icon that looked like a hydrogen atom, and then on an icon that looked like a star. Then her hands descended to the keyboard and she typed a series of passwords, moving her fingers so rapidly that they blurred over the keys.

"Here's the first part," she said. "These are the equations that Brother Cyrus pieced together from the FBI reports and the other intelligence sources. I think you'll recognize them. They're the formulas of the unified field theory. Or at least half of them."

The equations came on the screen. At first Michael *didn't* recognize them. Many of the symbols were unfamiliar—squiggles and bull's-eyes and backward *B*s and *Z*s. But he could identify the mathematical operations that the equations were performing, and after several seconds he saw that Tamara was telling the truth. The formulas on the computer screen corresponded to the memorized equations in Michael's brain; the only difference was the notation used to write them down. Brother Cyrus possessed about half of the equations in the *Einheitliche Feldtheorie*. Although they were expressed in an alternative symbolic language, they were essentially the same.

"And this is the second part," Tamara said, typing on the keyboard again. "Brother Cyrus hired a team of computer experts and they've been working on this program for the past year. They couldn't complete it because they didn't know all the equations in the unified theory. But now that you're here, you can finish the job."

She clicked on an icon that looked like an abacus. The computer monitor went black, showing nothing at all for several seconds. Then a block of software code emerged from the bottom of the screen. Hundreds of lines of instructions scrolled upward at a furious pace. The code rose so quickly to the top of the screen that Michael couldn't read very much of it. He saw enough, though, to realize that it wasn't an ordinary program. He was familiar with most of the common programming languages—he'd learned Java, FORTRAN, C++, and BASIC from studying the computers at the autism center—but the code he was looking at now was full of commands he'd never seen before. He leaned forward to take a closer look at the strange operators and variables: qubit, qureg, CNot, Hadamard . . .

"What kind of program is this?" Michael asked. As he stared at the code his forehead began to ache. "What does it do?"

"Brother Cyrus can explain it better than I can. He'll be here tomorrow morning, so you can ask him then. But I can tell you what Cyrus told me." She pointed at the screen and the rising tower of code. "This is the thing that locks the gate to God's kingdom. And you hold the key, Michael. All you have to do is plug the missing equations into the code. Remember the Book of Isaiah? *A child shall lead them.*"

The ache in Michael's forehead sharpened. It felt like a shard of glass had pierced his skull, just above his left eyebrow. He looked again at the lines of code and shook his head. "I can't do it. I don't know how."

"Just think of it as a puzzle. You like to solve puzzles, don't you?"

8

BROTHER CYRUS GAZED WITH WONDER AT THE SUNRISE. HE STOOD ON A
hilltop in the Adraskan district, a desolate part of western Afghanistan
where the Second Marine Expeditionary Brigade was battling the Taliban and the only patches of color amid the arid, stony landscape were
the green fields of poppies being grown for the heroin trade. It was a
no-man's land in the truest sense—Marine Corps convoys sped along the
district's roads during the day and Taliban fighters descended the mountain trails at night, but the land itself belonged only to God. The jagged
ridges and barren valleys were deserted now, and the sinful world of Man
seemed far away. Cyrus shouted, "Hallelujah!" as he gazed at the scene.
It was beautiful because the Lord had fashioned it, folding and crimping
the brown earth with His mighty hands.

But no place in the world was entirely free of Man's taint. The
jihadis hid in their mud-walled compounds in the mountains while
the Americans circled in their fighter jets overhead. Both sides claimed
to be fighting for God, but in reality they were all foot soldiers in
Satan's army, vomiting their foulness on Creation. They'd corrupted this
part of the world so thoroughly that Cyrus couldn't wander alone here.
One of his bodyguards stood on a neighboring hilltop a hundred yards
away, and three more patrolled the surrounding terrain. His bodyguards
were his closest followers, his True Believers. They shielded him every
minute with their rifles and vigilance. He'd chosen them carefully,
selecting only those with the strongest faith. They rejoiced in the
tasks Cyrus assigned, because they knew the reward of eternal life
awaited them.

He turned around and faced west, where the hills snaked toward the

Iranian border, seventy miles away. Even the tools of the devil, Cyrus knew, could be used for holy purposes, and in this manner the Iranians had turned out to be quite useful. Iran's Revolutionary Guards had been so eager to build their nuclear bomb that they were willing to negotiate with an outsider who could speed the development of the weapon. Cyrus had the expertise to help them—before he received the Lord's call, he'd spent many years working with nuclear warheads. He still had friends and informants at the American and Russian military laboratories, so he'd had no trouble supplying the resources that the Iranians needed. And in return he'd received something much more valuable. The Iranian nuclear test had served as a grand experiment, and the results were nothing less than astonishing. Now Cyrus knew exactly how to carry out the Lord's will.

Next, he turned to the north and raised his binoculars, fitting the eyepieces into the slit in his head scarf. About two miles away he saw a long line of Humvees speeding northwest on a two-lane highway. There were also more than forty U.S. Army trucks on the road, including a dozen heavy-duty flatbeds carrying tarpaulin-covered loads. Cyrus smiled as he observed the convoy, which was so long that it took several minutes to pass. He knew that these weren't ordinary American soldiers. He was looking at the First Battalion of the 75th Ranger Regiment, one of the Special Operations forces commanded by Lieutenant General Sam McNair. They were headed for Turkmenistan, the Central Asian country to the north of Iran, where the final battle against Satan's army would begin.

Thanks to his informants in the U.S. Special Operations Command, Cyrus knew about Cobra, the secret plan to attack Iran's nuclear facilities from the north. Unlike the border between Iran and Afghanistan, where the Revolutionary Guards had positioned hundreds of antiaircraft missiles, Iran's border with Turkmenistan was lightly defended. Sensing an opportunity, the Americans had brokered a clandestine deal with Turkmenistan's president-for-life, a tin-pot dictator who was in desperate need of hard currency. In exchange for a substantial payment to his Swiss bank account, the president-for-life would allow the U.S. Army Rangers to quietly enter his country and travel to a hidden staging point near the Iranian border. Once the assault group was in place, it would launch the surprise attack on the nuclear installation.

Cyrus kept his binoculars trained on the convoy until he saw nothing but the cloud of dust in their wake. In less than an hour the Ranger battalion would reach the Afghan city of Herat, where they would hunker down until nightfall. Then they would cross into Turkmenistan under the cover of darkness and advance to the staging point. And Brother Cyrus would follow them, leading his much smaller convoy of True Believers. Everything was proceeding according to the Lord's plan. The path to Redemption lay straight ahead.

Finally, Cyrus lowered his binoculars and turned back to the east. The high peaks of the Hindu Kush were hundreds of miles away, too far to be glimpsed as even a faint blue smudge, but he sensed their presence over the horizon. That was the place where the Lord had blessed him, while he was a prisoner in the bowels of Hades. In a cave underneath Gazarak Mountain, near the Afghan-Pakistani border, Satan's foot soldiers had tortured him with ingenious cruelty. For three long days they'd maimed his body and violated his soul, driving him into a state of such helpless agony that his mind broke and his faith crumbled. Stripped of all hope, he became a man without God, a naked, bleeding animal yearning only for death. And then, during one of the rare intervals when his torturers allowed him a few minutes of sleep, the Lord showed His face. Cyrus saw it floating above him, just inches away. He recognized it instantly. It was radiant with love.

Several years had passed since then, but Cyrus could still see the Lord's face when he closed his eyes. He saw it now as he stood on the hilltop: a face that was neither white nor black, neither broad nor thin, neither young nor old. A face that showed all human features at once. A face that had never appeared in the flesh but would be familiar to even the smallest child.

With his eyes closed, Cyrus unwrapped his head scarf. He wished to stand face-to-face with his God, even though his own features were sinful and hideous. As he removed the black fabric he felt the rays of the early-morning sun on his cheeks. Tossing the scarf aside, he knelt on the stony ground and lowered his head.

"Lord of Hosts, Lord of Glory," he whispered. "We humbly seek Your aid. Give us the strength to carry out Your will. Guide our hands so we can bring Your loving Redemption to this corrupt world. And guide our hearts so we can enter Your heavenly kingdom without shame." His voice cracked. His throat was parched from the desert air. "Oh Lord, You are so close! In a short while we will open the gates of heaven and stand before You! We will kneel by Your throne and behold Your blessed face!"

Shaking with fervor, he bent over until his forehead touched the ground. Then he prayed without words, breathing soundlessly on the warm, brown dirt.

Several minutes passed. Cyrus couldn't say exactly how many; when he prayed he entered a world where it was impossible to keep track of the time. But at some point he heard footsteps, so he opened his eyes. He stood up and saw one of his bodyguards ascending the hill, marching straight toward him.

It was Tamara, his favorite, the truest of the True Believers. Tall and lithe, she wore a desert-camouflage uniform and carried an M-4 carbine. Her hair was so short that none of it showed under her Kevlar helmet. She looked like an ordinary soldier, a young, fresh-faced American infantrywoman, and that was exactly what she'd been until three years ago, when Brother Cyrus had enlisted her to his cause. He'd discovered that the U.S. Army was a good place to recruit his followers. There were so many wounded souls, so many soldiers in desperate need of the Lord's guidance.

Cyrus picked up his scarf from the ground and swiftly wrapped it around his head. Even Tamara, his closest follower, wasn't allowed to view his face. It was too repellent.

She halted and stood at attention about five feet away. Her right hand started to rise, but she stopped herself from saluting. Cyrus had told his followers many times that there was no need to salute him, but they sometimes did anyway. "Peace be with you, Brother," she said. "Are you ready to return to the base camp? I don't like leaving you here in the open for too long."

He nodded. "Yes, I'm ready. I just finished my prayers." He smiled behind his mask, stretching his hideous lips. Then he started walking down the hill, planting his feet carefully on the rocky slope. "How are things at the camp this morning? Has Michael Gupta settled in yet?"

Tamara fell in step beside him. "Michael spent the whole night studying the Logos file. About an hour ago I told him to take a break, but he wouldn't leave the computer. I have a feeling he's going to be there all day."

Cyrus smiled again. He'd suspected that the program would fascinate the child. The young genius couldn't resist looking at it. And with the Lord's help, he would soon complete the task. "Has he made any changes to the file?"

"No, not yet. The boy's been scrolling through the code for hours, but he hasn't made a single change. It's the strangest thing." She stared at the horizon as she made her way downhill. The sun was already scorching the brown landscape. "You know what I think, Brother? I think he's memorizing the code. And he's making all the changes in his head."

"That wouldn't surprise me. What else would you expect from the great-great-grandson of Albert Einstein? Once he completes the program, we'll convince him to write it down for us."

"He's sad, Brother. So sad. His life has been so unfair." She shook her head. "He's suffered so much. And he doesn't deserve it."

Cyrus stopped on the hillside and looked at her closely. Tamara was usually a resolute soldier, a calm and imperturbable Warrior of God, but now she seemed distressed. As she halted beside him, still staring at the horizon, Cyrus noticed that her eyes were wet. She was thinking, no doubt, of her own history. Like Michael, Tamara had survived some fairly brutal events—a father who ran off, a mother who died young, a childhood spent in foster homes in rural Kentucky. So it was no surprise that she felt some sympathy for the boy. But Cyrus worried that this emotion might be a hindrance now. Their plans were at a critical stage, and the Lord needed them to be steadfast.

"Tamara," he said quietly, "you know why the boy has suffered. In this corrupt world, pain and horrors afflict everyone."

She nodded. "Yes, Brother, I know."

"But the Almighty is coming to save us. He's focusing His will right now on this place, this desert." Cyrus swept his arm in a circle, pointing at the lifeless hills around them. "Once the boy completes the code, we can make the adjustments to Excalibur. And then God's holy sword will put an end to this suffering world and lead us all into the kingdom!"

She nodded again but kept her eyes on the horizon. Cyrus stretched his hand toward her and gently gripped her chin. Then he turned her head so he could look directly at her. "The Lord needs you to be strong, Tamara. Can you do that? Can you be strong for Him?"

"Yes, Brother!" she shouted. Her voice was as loud as a drill sergeant's and her gray eyes flashed. "I serve the Lord! I long to see His blessed face!"

"Very good. Now let's get back to camp." He resumed walking down the rocky slope. "I assume everything else is going smoothly? You've made all the preparations for tonight's transit?"

"Yes, we're scheduled to depart at twenty-two-hundred hours." Her voice was confident, but there was still a hint of anxiety in her expression. She bit her lower lip as she marched beside him. "We just received a message, though. From Keller."

Cyrus frowned. Although Keller was one of his allies, the man wasn't a True Believer. He was a bureaucratic underling, a money-hungry assistant in the U.S. Department of Justice. Out of necessity, Cyrus had assembled a network of paid informants in Washington. These men knew nothing of the Lord's plans and their motives were despicable, but by selling their information to Cyrus, they unwittingly aided God's holy cause. "What did Keller say?"

"He intercepted another e-mail about the FBI investigation of the explosion at Steele's laboratory. Agent Parker is continuing to pursue information about Steele's research. She put in a request to travel to Israel, and the Bureau director approved it."

Cyrus nodded. Special Agent Lucille Parker, who'd headed the FBI task force that had done such a poor job of protecting Michael Gupta, was now apparently determined to make amends for her failure. "Well, I was expecting this, but not so soon," he said. "I didn't think the investigation would progress so quickly. Is Parker traveling alone to Israel?"

"No, she's going with Michael's guardians. She made a special request to bring along David Swift and Monique Reynolds. They're scheduled to arrive in Israel this afternoon."

Very interesting, Cyrus thought. Parker was obviously relying on their scientific expertise. And Swift and Reynolds could make things difficult. But it was presumptuous to think that the path of Redemption would be easy. The Scriptures had foretold a great battle. The servants of the Lord would have to fight Satan's army before they could enter the Kingdom of Heaven.

"I have new orders for you, Tamara," he said. "As soon as we get to camp, send an encrypted message to Nicodemus. Tell him about the visitors to the Holy Land and ask him to prepare a proper greeting."

9

THE FBI LEARJET GOT PERMISSION TO LAND AT TEL NOF, A MILITARY AIRFIELD in central Israel. David and Monique sat in the last row of the cabin, behind Lucille. As the plane descended toward the air base, David looked out the cabin window and saw a dozen F-16s lined up on the tarmac. Every thirty seconds, one of the fighter jets took off with a roar and joined the fleet of planes patrolling the country's airspace. The Israeli Air Force was on high alert in response to the Iranian nuclear test. On the other side of the base, several armored vehicles were clustered around a concrete bunker. Tel Nof, David knew, was one of the sites where Israel stored its nuclear weapons. The country had its own nukes and would use them if necessary.

He shook his head. He couldn't worry about nuclear apocalypse right now. He needed to concentrate on the task at hand. He and Monique were in Israel because they'd convinced Lucille that they could help her track down Olam ben Z'man, Jacob Steele's secret collaborator. They had some tangible skills to offer—Monique knew the physics better than anyone, while David knew plenty of Israeli scientists through his work with Physicists for Peace. But their greatest asset was their desperation. If Lucille hadn't agreed to bring them along, they would've come to Israel anyway and begun their own investigation. Michael had been missing for thirty-six hours now, with no word from his kidnappers. Neither David nor Monique could rest until they'd found him.

Unfortunately, the search stalled as soon as they arrived at Hebrew University of Jerusalem. They'd assumed from the start that Olam ben Z'man—a name that didn't appear in any Israeli records—was a fanciful code name that one of the university's professors had adopted. Because

there was a chance that this professor had shared his secret with a colleague at the school, Lucille headed for the computer science department and began questioning the faculty members and students. David
and Monique sat in on the interviews; they'd brought some respectable
suits to Israel so they would look more official. Several of the interview-
ees laughed when Lucille mentioned the name Olam ben Z'man. But no
one had heard it before.

The only other clue came from Verizon Communications, which
had tracked down the phone calls that Adam Bennett had mentioned,
the calls Olam ben Z'man had made to Jacob Steele's laboratory. The
records showed that these calls had indeed originated from a fiber-optic
line in Israel. What's more, the very same line had been used on other
occasions to transmit millions of gigabytes of data, sometimes sending
the information from Israel to the University of Maryland and sometimes carrying it in the opposite direction. But according to officials
at Bezeq—the Israeli phone company—the line didn't connect to any
computer at Hebrew University. Instead, the flow of data seemed to
terminate at a switching station in East Jerusalem, on the Palestinian
side of the city.

By the end of the day Lucille decided to reach out for help. She
called an agent she knew at Shin Bet, the Israeli equivalent of the
FBI. Lucille had worked with this agent a few years before, helping
him identify a Brooklyn imam who raised money for Hamas and other
Palestinian terrorist groups, so he owed her a favor. First, she asked
him to send one of Shin Bet's telecommunications experts to the East
Jerusalem switching station. Then she set up a meeting to talk about
the search for Olam ben Z'man. Because the agent insisted on seeing
no one but Lucille, she headed alone to a hummus restaurant near the
Shin Bet headquarters. Before leaving, though, she asked David and
Monique to go to the switching station to confer with the communications expert.

The station turned out to be a small windowless building located
just outside the walls of Jerusalem's Old City. It was 7:30 P.M. when
they arrived, fifteen minutes before sunset. As David stepped out of the
rental car he shielded his eyes from the sun and gazed at the spires and
minarets of the Old City, which gleamed magnificently in the golden

light. Then he turned around and stared at the ancient, sprawling cemetery that stretched eastward toward the Mount of Olives. Monique, meanwhile, eyed the switching station, paying particular attention to the antennas on the building's roof.

They found the Shin Bet expert, Aryeh Goldberg, in front of the station, bent over a set of blueprints he'd spread across the hood of his car. He was a short, chunky man in his late forties or early fifties, wearing jeans and a gray polo shirt. He'd propped his glasses on top of his balding head so he could scrutinize the schematics. He was so engrossed that at first he didn't hear Monique say, "Hello, Mr. Goldberg." But when she repeated the greeting he stood up straight and smiled. He had a dark complexion and lively brown eyes, and he seemed unperturbed by the fact that they were making him work overtime. Lowering his glasses, he shook hands with Monique and then with David.

"Ah, the Americans!" he said in heavily accented English. "My supervisor says you're from the FBI, yes? The G-men? And now the G-women, too?" He pointed at Monique. "I know about the G-men because I have the DVD of that gangster movie, the one with Kevin Costner in it. You know the movie I'm talking about?"

Monique smiled back at him. "Yes, I do. But right now—"

"I know, you're in a hurry. But I have to tell you, we have a very big mess here. You won't believe what a big mess this is."

"What do you mean?"

"It's such a mess I can't see what happened to your data. I know the signals from Maryland came to this station and were shunted to line number three-seventeen. That's a dedicated fiber-optic line, installed by Bezeq last year. I know the line exists, because I went inside the station a few minutes ago and saw it on the control panel. But it's not on the map!" He slapped the blueprints. "I have to tell you, I don't understand it. Bezeq is supposed to update these maps every week."

Monique narrowed her eyes. Although she wasn't a real FBI agent, she knew a clue when she saw one. "Who ordered the installation of the line?"

"That's another crazy thing. I checked the order and there's no name on it. And the address is a post office box. But the person who ordered the line has been paying his bills, so at least Bezeq is happy, yes?"

"Is there any way to find out where the line goes? Maybe by talking to the crew that installed it?"

Aryeh made a face. "Ah, those guys are schmucks. I know a quicker way." He folded the blueprints and threw them into the backseat of his car. Then he reached into the glove compartment and pulled out a flashlight. "Line three-seventeen is bunched with five other lines inside a cable that runs into the Old City. So we'll just follow that cable. We'll see where your line branches off, yes?"

"Can you do that? Don't the cables run underground?"

"Yes, in most places that's true. But everything is crazy in the Old City. The archaeologists won't let Bezeq dig there, so they string the lines wherever they can." He locked his car and started walking toward the Old City's wall. "Come, this way. The cable runs through the Lions' Gate."

Aryeh walked quickly for a small man. David and Monique followed him, heading for an archway flanked by lions carved into the stone wall. David recognized this entrance to the Old City—he'd seen the Lions' Gate before, when he'd visited Jerusalem ten years ago, but now it shocked him anew with its simple beauty. For a historian, the Old City was truly heaven on earth. Less than a mile across, it was filled to bursting with ancient mosques and temples and churches. David looked to his left and spotted the Dome of the Rock, the Muslim shrine that dominated this part of the city. It sat on an elevated plaza that the Jews called the Temple Mount, because that was where their Holy Temple had stood before the Romans destroyed it in 70 AD. And just below the Temple Mount was the Via Dolorosa, the path Jesus had taken on his way to the Cross. It was enough to inspire even an agnostic like David, who was raised Catholic but hadn't stepped inside a church in thirty years.

They went through the Lions' Gate, then walked down a gently sloping alley paved with stones worn smooth by millennia of foot traffic. The alley was crowded with people headed in the opposite direction, mostly Palestinian women in white head scarves leaving the Old City with full shopping bags. A flock of elderly nuns shuffled past, followed by a pair of Israeli soldiers nervously patrolling the Muslim quarter. Both sides of the alley were lined with shops offering trinkets for the tourists—T-shirts, posters, skullcaps, hookahs, and a wide variety of garish oil paint-ings depicting the Crucifixion. Palestinian men sat in front of the shops, under awnings of rusted iron, drinking tea from slender glasses. They looked suspiciously at Aryeh Goldberg but said nothing as he shone his flashlight down the darkening alley. He pointed the beam at a black cable that ran just above the awnings.

After a few hundred yards they came to a stone wall where the cable passed near a round plaque. A large group of men wearing brown robes and sandals clustered around the plaque, which was inscribed with the Roman numeral I. David recognized this place, too—it was the Via Dolorosa's starting point, the first Station of the Cross, where Pontius Pilate had condemned Jesus to death. The men in robes were Christian pilgrims who assembled at this spot every evening to reenact Christ's suffering, ritually parading down the Via Dolorosa until they reached the famous tomb inside the Church of the Holy Sepulcher. Several pil-grims carried big wooden crosses balanced on their shoulders. Others wore realistic-looking crowns of thorns and read aloud from their Bibles. There were so many pilgrims that they blocked the alley, slowing the foot traffic to a standstill.

Aryeh pushed through the crowd, keeping his flashlight trained on the cable. He looked over his shoulder at David and Monique. "The junction box is over there," he said, pointing at a steel cabinet clamped to the wall a few yards away. "I need to open it to see where line three-seventeen goes. This may take a few minutes. I have to get past all the crazy goyim here."

While Aryeh fought his way to the junction box, David glanced at Monique. She stood with her back to the wall, scanning the crowd. The pilgrims were apparently making her nervous. Many of them seemed overcome with emotion. At least a dozen knelt on the cobblestones, shouting Bible verses and weeping inconsolably. One of the cross-bearing pilgrims flung himself to the ground and almost hit Monique with the bottom end of his giant crucifix. She let out a cry and jumped to the side. "Jesus!" she yelled. "Watch where you're going!"

The pilgrim, whose swarthy, stubbled face was streaked with tears, said nothing in response. He simply staggered to his feet and continued trudging down the alley. Monique glowered at him.

David smiled, trying to cheer her up. "I don't think Jesus heard you."

She didn't think it was funny. Scowling, she kept her eyes on the crowd. "This place is insane. Look at all these wackos."

"It's not their fault. Most of them are probably suffering from Jerusalem Syndrome."

"Is this another joke?"

"No, it's a genuine mental disorder. Israeli psychiatrists have written papers about it. Every year dozens of tourists who visit Jerusalem become convinced that they're the Messiah. The delusion usually goes away when they leave the city."

Monique frowned. "That's great. And we're looking for a guy who calls himself 'Universe, the Son of Time.' Maybe he's a nut job, too."

"I don't think Jacob Steele would have collaborated with a nut job." David shook his head. "Remember what Bennett said? Jacob was desperate to make a significant discovery before he died. Maybe Olam ben Z'man came up with a brilliant idea, a Nobel Prize–winning idea. And maybe Jacob heard about it and started working with him to get a share of the glory."

"Okay, maybe Olam's a genius. But plenty of geniuses are also crazy."

"No, I think he's canny, not crazy. It can't be a coincidence that his fiber-optic line got deleted from the phone company's records. I think he took steps to cover his tracks."

"Why? What was he afraid of?"

"I don't know. But look what happened to Jacob. Obviously someone didn't like what they were doing."

One of the weeping pilgrims let out a particularly loud wail. Monique jumped at the noise. "Damn it, I can't think! This is so fucking distracting!" A look of immense frustration contorted her face. "How the hell am I supposed to think?"

David moved a step closer and put his arm around her. She was shivering. "Hey, it's all right. We're gonna figure this out, okay? One way or another, we're gonna find out what's going on. And then we'll get Michael and bring him home."

She shook her head and started crying. It was a rare moment of vulnerability for Monique, who was usually so steadfast and logical. Like Michael, she'd had a chaotic childhood, growing up with a negligent mother in a bleak housing project, and from a young age she'd developed a fierce self-possession. Very few things could unnerve her like this. Sobbing quietly, she leaned her forehead against David's shoulder. He held her close.

After a little while she began to calm down. David let go of her and she wiped her eyes. She was back to normal by the time Aryeh returned. He was out of breath from fighting the crowd of Christs.

"Line three-seventeen branches off there," he said, pointing to a building just ahead. "Then it goes down a stairway to the Hasmonean Tunnel."

The name sounded familiar. David had read about it somewhere. "Is that the tunnel that runs alongside the Temple Mount? Next to the Western Wall?"

"Yes, the archaeologists excavated it. The tunnel goes down to the big stone blocks at the base of the Western Wall, ten meters underground. It's mostly for the tourists, but the *kippot srugot* like to go into the tunnel to pray."

"*Kippot srugot?*"

"The religious Zionists, the settlers. They have that name because they wear knitted skullcaps, *kippot srugot*."

"Wait," David said. "I thought the religious Jews wear black hats."

"No, those are the *haredim,* the ultra-Orthodox. The *kippot srugot* are religious, too, but most of them are right-wingers, very angry at the Palestinians. They're obsessed with the Western Wall because it's the only surviving part of the Temple. You can see the wall aboveground in the Jewish quarter, but the *kippot srugot* like to pray in the tunnel because it's closer to where—"

"Whoa, hold on," Monique interrupted. "Why does the fiber-optic line go into the tunnel? Are there computers down there?"

"I don't know. But there's a way to find out, yes? Come on."

David and Monique followed him again, sidestepping the pilgrims until they came to the tunnel entrance. Standing by the doorway was a fat bearded man wearing a knitted yarmulke. He held a small black prayer book in his left hand and an Uzi in his right. David knew from his previous visit to Jerusalem that many Israeli citizens routinely carry Uzis because of the ever-present terrorist threat, but the sight was still a little unnerving. Aryeh approached the fat man and said something in Hebrew. The man responded in an aggressive tone, sneering. Aryeh held out his hands and said something else, obviously trying to be reasonable, but the fat man started shouting and waving his Uzi. Then Aryeh pointed a finger at the man and spoke so quietly that David couldn't hear him. Whatever was said, the fat man got the message. He reluctantly stepped aside and let them through the doorway.

They walked into a dark room with gray stone walls. The air smelled damp and ancient. At the far end of the room a metal staircase descended into a rocky, rough-hewn shaft. As they headed down the steps, Aryeh trained his flashlight at the jagged ceiling, following the course of the black cable. He looked over his shoulder at David. "You see what I mean about the *kippot srugot*? They turn everything into an argument. That schmuck at the entrance wanted to charge us for going into the tunnel." He shook his head. "They're always like that, crazy and angry. But that's not the worst part."

"What is?" David asked.

"They're always antagonizing the Palestinians. They stir up trouble by buying buildings in the Muslim quarter and turning them into yeshivas. And then they go marching past the mosques, carrying their Uzis and singing their prayers."

David nodded. "I can see how that might lead to trouble."

"I'm a little surprised, Mr. Goldberg," Monique said. She was just behind David, her shoes thumping on the metal steps. "You work for an Israeli intelligence agency, but you seem pretty sympathetic to the other side."

"I have no illusions about the Palestinians," Aryeh replied. "Their terrorists are worse than the *kippot srugot*. And so are the bastards in Hamas who aim their rockets at our schools and the suicide bombers who try to blow up our buses. And the mullahs in Iran who want to throw atomic bombs at us." He stopped for a moment, as if contemplating this catastrophe. Then he gripped the handrail and continued down the stairs. "But for some reason I get angrier at the crazy Jews."

When they reached the bottom of the staircase, they found themselves in another dark room. Aryeh's flashlight illuminated a vaulted ceiling, where the black cable ran parallel to the wires for the overhead lights.

"The line goes this way," he said, heading for a vertical fissure in one of the stone walls. "The path is narrow here, so we'll have to walk single file, yes? This used to be the aqueduct that brought water to the Temple."

It was now a tunnel designed for tourists, with handrails conveniently bolted to the limestone, but David's chest tightened as he followed Aryeh into the fissure. He didn't like tunnels. He'd nearly gotten killed in a tunnel two years ago, when he was on the run from the FBI, and since then he'd become a bit claustrophobic. After a couple of minutes, though, they came to a wider, better-lit corridor, and David opened his mouth in awe. Running along the left side of the corridor was the underground section of the Western Wall. Stone blocks as big as trailer homes were stacked like monstrous bricks. The edges of the blocks were rounded with age and there was no mortar or cement in the crevices between them. Their weight alone had kept them in place for centuries, even as the detritus of the Old City had slowly buried them.

"Unbelievable," David whispered. He looked down at the smooth paving stones under his feet. "This is the Herodian Street, right? The promenade that King Herod built outside the walls of the Temple?"

"Yes, yes," Aryeh said, but he wasn't paying attention. His eyes were fixed on the fiber-optic line snaking along the tunnel's ceiling. Monique stared at it just as intently.

After walking for another two or three minutes David saw a crowd up ahead, at least twenty-five people jammed into the corridor. They were *kippot srugot*, bearded men in knitted yarmulkes, shouting their prayers as they faced a low archway carved into the Western Wall. Each man held a small black book in front of his nose and rocked back and forth as he yelled in Hebrew. Their Uzis, hanging from shoulder straps, swung like pendulums. As David got closer he noticed that the archway was blocked up with gray stones. The zealots were praying to an ugly, cracked wall glistening with moisture. He caught up to Aryeh and tapped his shoulder. "Why is the archway blocked? What's on the other side?"

"The Holy of Holies," he replied. "The place where the inner sanctum of the Temple used to be. The Dome of the Rock is there now and religious Jews won't go inside the Muslim shrine, so they pray here because this is the closest they can get. There's always a crowd of them here, day and night."

One of the bearded men stopped rocking and glared at them. "Show some respect!" he shouted in English. "Cover your heads!"

"Ah, go to hell." Aryeh shook his fist at the man, then turned back to David. "Look at them with their Uzis. Even when they're speaking to God, they won't let go of their guns."

Monique nodded. "More wackos," she whispered in David's ear. "This city is full of them."

About a hundred yards beyond the crowd of zealots, the corridor widened into a spacious chamber. To the left was another blocked-up archway and to the right was a steel door. Aryeh stopped—the beam from his flashlight showed the fiber-optic line vanishing into a hole above the doorframe. The sign on the door said EMERGENCY EXIT in English, Hebrew, and Arabic.

Aryeh pushed the door open. No alarm sounded. "Ladies first, yes?" he said, gesturing at Monique.

She stepped through the doorway, her eyes still fixed on the cable. David followed her and Aryeh up a staircase. Then they opened a second door and emerged into a cobblestone alley that looked very much like the one near the Lions' Gate. It was narrow and lined with tourist shops, but now the shops were closed and the alley was dark and empty. Aryeh raised his flashlight and found the cable again—it ran directly to the entrance of a nearby building and disappeared into a hole drilled above a massive door. When Aryeh pointed his flashlight at the sign above the door, it illuminated the words BEIT SHALOM YESHIVA.

"Ah, I don't believe it." Aryeh sighed. "This is one of those yeshivas I was telling you about. Full of crazy Jews trying to take over the Muslim quarter."

David stared at the building, squinting in the darkness. The door was steel reinforced and the windows were barred. The place looked like a prison. "Are you sure this is where the line ends?"

"Yes, this is the terminus. I can tell by the markings." Aryeh pointed his flashlight at a pair of white dots on the cable. Then he swung the beam back to the sign. "And look at the name, look what they call this place—Beit Shalom, the House of Peace. Can you believe it?"

David exchanged glances with Monique. He sensed that entering the yeshiva with Aryeh would be a mistake. The man was a little too free with his opinions. David stepped toward him and offered his hand. "Thank you for your help, Mr. Goldberg. We'll take it from here."

"Yes, go ahead. Believe me, I have no desire to go in there." He shook David's hand, then Monique's. Then he started down the alley, heading toward an intersecting street. "Good luck, G-man and G-woman! I hope you find what you're looking for."

Monique watched Aryeh until his flashlight beam moved out of sight. Then she turned to David. "So how do you want to do this? Should we call Lucille?"

He thought about it for a moment. Lucille would certainly want them to contact her before they marched into Beit Shalom Yeshiva. She was the professional, after all. And she'd probably insist on taking the lead in whatever interviews they conducted. But David wasn't sure that approach would be the best. If, as he suspected, Olam ben Z'man was afraid of something, he'd probably feel more comfortable talking with a couple of professors than with an American FBI agent.

"Let's play it by ear," David said. "If we find Olam, we'll try to convince him to come with us and see Lucille."

Monique nodded. She agreed with him. She opened her mouth to say something, but then she jerked her head to the left and peered down the alley. "Shit! Is that . . . ?"

David spun around and looked where she was looking. He saw only the dark cobblestones of the alley and the iron shutters of the closed shops. "What is it?" he hissed. "What's going on?"

"Shhh!" She continued to peer into the darkness. After a few seconds she shook her head. "Damn. I thought I saw someone."

"You saw someone? Who did you see?"

"Remember that pilgrim who nearly hit me with his cross? I thought I saw him down there, just past that pillar on the left. Dark face, black stubble."

"What? You mean Jesus?" David let out a deep breath. In his relief, he couldn't help but smile. "You think Jesus is following us?"

Monique frowned. "Come on," she said, turning to the yeshiva's door. "Let's find Olam."

•   •   •

NICODEMUS WAS TEMPTED TO TAKE A SHOT. THE BLACK WOMAN WAS exposed, an easy target in the middle of the alley, and neither she nor the man was armed. Nico knew this because he'd observed them up close while carrying his cross on the Via Dolorosa. He could've killed them back there without any trouble and escaped into the crowd, but his orders had been very specific. His primary target was neither Monique Reynolds nor David Swift, but the person they were seeking. Nico had followed the Americans across the Old City in the hope that they would lead him to Olam ben Z'man.

Crouched behind a concrete pillar thirty meters away, Nico watched Swift and Reynolds approach the heavy door of the yeshiva and ring the buzzer. The door opened, revealing two bearded men armed with Uzis. They started talking in English. Nico was too far away to hear them clearly, but he could guess what they were saying. After a minute or so, the bearded men allowed the Americans into the yeshiva. Then the door closed with a thump.

Nico reached for his radio. It was time to alert the other members of his team who were scattered across the Muslim and Jewish quarters, monitoring all the exits of the Western Wall Tunnel. Once they assembled, Nico would launch the assault. It looked like the occupants of the yeshiva had fortified the building in case of an attack by Palestinian terrorists, but Nico and his men were well armed and well trained. More important, God was on their side. Brother Cyrus had said the Lord would carry them to victory, and Nicodemus was a True Believer.

10

TWO *KIPPOT SRUGOT* STOOD IN THE DOORWAY OF THE YESHIVA. THEY WERE
tall, solid men with thick necks and muscular arms, but they were also
very young, no older than twenty. Their beards were patchy, with a
few pimples visible under the scruff. They wore jeans and T-shirts and
sneakers, and aside from their knitted yarmulkes and the Uzis hanging
at their sides, they looked like ordinary college students. David felt sorry
for them. They should be relaxing on the beach in Tel Aviv, he thought,
instead of guarding the door of a yeshiva in Jerusalem.

Monique smiled at them. She had a charming smile. "Sorry to bother
you. We're with the Federal Bureau of Investigation, the American law-
enforcement agency. We'd like to talk to the head of this yeshiva. Is he here?"

The yeshiva students looked at each other uncertainly. It was possible that they didn't understand English, although David had noticed that
most Israelis seemed to know at least a little. But even if the students
understood every word she said, the mere sight of Monique was probably
enough to unsettle them. If they were like most yeshiva students, they'd
had little contact with women aside from their mothers and sisters. The
bigger of the two, who wore a yarmulke with a pattern of Jewish stars,
gave her a sidelong glance, then turned to David. "Excuse me?" he said.
"Who are you?"

"We're with the American government," David answered, speaking
slowly and carefully. "We'd like to come inside and ask you a few questions."

He spoke in an authoritative voice, but he wasn't sure it would be
enough. He had no badge or official identification. The yeshiva students
were perfectly free to slam the door in his face. The bigger one shook his
head. "The Rav is busy," he muttered.

"The Rav?"

"Yes, our rabbi, Rav Kavner. He's studying Talmud. And no women are allowed in this yeshiva. I'm sorry." He placed his large hand on the door and started to close it.

"What about Olam ben Z'man?" Monique asked. "Is he available?"

The student froze. He stared at Monique as if he'd just glimpsed a belt of explosives under her jacket. "You know Olam?"

"Yes, I do. And it looks like you know him, too. Can we come inside now?"

He let go of the door and stood there for several seconds, nervously rubbing his scruffy chin. He looked confused, David thought. The poor kid probably wasn't accustomed to making his own decisions. Finally he said, "Okay, come," and waved them forward. David and Monique stepped inside and the student closed the door behind them. "Before you can see the Rav, you must hand over any weapons you're carrying," he warned. "We'll return them when you leave."

"Why?" David asked.

"We have to be careful. The Rav has many enemies in the Muslim quarter. And things are very tense now."

"Because of the Iranian crisis?"

The student nodded. "We've heard rumors that the Palestinians are working with Iran. Hamas and Hezbollah are trying to smuggle one of the Iranian bombs into Israel."

David opened his jacket to show he was unarmed. "Well, I'm not carrying anything. No guns, no bombs."

"Me neither," Monique said. She opened her jacket, too.

They stood in a foyer that had one stairway going down to the basement and another ascending to the second floor. David looked over his shoulder and spotted the fiber-optic cable, which emerged from the hole above the front door and followed the flight of stairs going down to the basement. He took a step in that direction, but the bigger yeshiva student grasped his arm and led him to the other stairway.

They went upstairs to a large study hall. The room had barred windows and creaky floorboards and a long refectory table covered from end to end with massive, ancient books. A dozen young men sat around the table, engaged in the age-old tradition of Talmud study, which involved arguing the finer points of Jewish law by thumbing through the dusty volumes. Sitting at the far end of the table was a tiny old man in black pants and a wrinkled white shirt. He wore oversize glasses and a yarmulke as big as a soup bowl, which made his head look unnaturally small. His beard was long and white, and he smiled beneficently at the students shouting all around him. David was surprised—he'd expected the leader of a militant Zionist group to be more physically intimidating. Instead he looked like a cheerful little beggar.

As David and Monique entered the room, the students fell silent. They stared at Monique in particular, their mouths wide open, ready to start shouting imprecations. But the rabbi seemed neither shocked nor outraged by her presence. Smiling at the pair of students who'd escorted them into the study hall, the Rav said something in Hebrew. The bigger student answered, and in the midst of his rapid Hebrew sentences David heard the words "FBI" and "Olam ben Z'man."

The old man stopped smiling. He rose to his feet and gave David a desperate look. "What is it?" he asked. His face had paled. "What happened to Olam?"

David stepped forward. "Is there a place where we can talk privately, Mr. Kavner?"

"Ach! I knew it!" The rabbi grimaced as if in pain. He balled his right hand into a fist and smacked it against his forehead. "I knew something terrible would happen! I warned him so many times!"

"Please, Mr. Kavner." Monique pointed to a door at the other end of the study hall. "Is that your office?"

"Yes, yes." The Rav lowered his fist. Then he slowly turned around and walked toward the door.

They followed him into a windowless cubbyhole with an old wooden desk and tall stacks of books piled against the walls. While the rabbi settled into the chair behind the desk, David closed the office door. There were two chairs with torn seat covers in front of the desk. Monique sat down in one of them, but David remained standing. "We appreciate your cooperation, Mr. Kavner," he started. "And we—"

"Just tell me one thing," the rabbi interrupted. He slumped low in his chair, looking bereft. "Is Olam dead?"

David shook his head. "We have no evidence that he's been injured or killed, but—"

"*Baruch HaShem!*" the Rav sang out, raising his hands in the air and looking up at the ceiling. "Blessed is the Eternal!"

"But we believe he's in danger, so we need to find him as soon as possible. Do you have any idea where he could be?"

The rabbi frowned. "If I knew where Olam was, do you think I'd be sick with worry like this? He left the yeshiva on Tuesday night and we haven't heard from him since." The Rav sat a little straighter in his chair. "What kind of danger is he in? And why are you Americans here and not the Israeli police?"

Monique gave him an apologetic look. "I'm sorry, Rabbi, we'll answer all your questions in a minute, okay? We just need to get our bearings first. Is Olam a student at this yeshiva?"

"Yes, yes. In fact, he's my most brilliant student. He's older than the others and his studies are more advanced, but he lives in the dormitory upstairs and participates in all the sacred work we do."

"Sacred work?"

"Yes, we're preparing Jerusalem for the Messiah." The Rav spread his arms wide, gesturing at the walls of his cramped office. "That's why we bought this building and turned it into a house of prayer and study. The Palestinians say we're trying to drive them out of the Old City, but that's a lie. The truth is, we don't care about the Palestinians. We care only about God."

David could tell from the look on Monique's face that she was struggling not to roll her eyes. "Let's get back to Olam," she said. "How long have you known him?"

"Let me think." The Rav bit his lower lip and stared at the ceiling again. "Yes, it was four years ago. Olam heard about our sacred work at Beit Shalom and came to see me. We had a nice chat, and a few weeks later he began his studies here."

"You said he's older than your other students?"

"Yes, he's in his fifties. Olam came here after a personal tragedy, you see. You remember the war in Lebanon a few years ago? When we fought the Hezbollah murderers who fired their rockets across our border?"

Monique nodded. "Yes, I remember."

"Many young Israeli soldiers were killed. Olam's son was one of them." The Rav shook his head. "But the Eternal works in mysterious ways. Sometimes a tragedy like this can draw people closer to Him. And that's what happened to Olam. He left his home and his job and went searching for God."

"What was his job? Before he came here, I mean?"

"He was a scientist at Hebrew University, an expert on computers. And he had some connections in the Israeli government, too. He knew people high up in the army and the air force. He didn't like to talk about it much, but he told me a few stories."

David felt a surge of adrenaline. They were on the right track. Bennett had told them that Olam ben Z'man had identified himself as a computer scientist in the phone messages he'd left for Jacob Steele. The connections to the Israeli government also made sense. Olam would've needed some high-level help to make sure that his fiber-optic line didn't appear on the phone company's maps.

"Maybe you can help us with something, Mr. Kavner," David said. "We've already checked the records at Hebrew University. No one by the name of Olam ben Z'man has ever been associated with the school. Is that his birth name?"

The rabbi shook his head. "Oh no! His real name is Loebman. Or maybe Loehmann? It's one of the two. Or something similar."

Monique looked askance. "You don't know his real name?"

"We never call him by that name in the yeshiva. We call him Olam ben Z'man because that's the sacred name he took when he began studying Kabbalah." He leaned across his desk, staring intently at Monique. "I assume you've heard of Kabbalah? It's very popular in America, I hear."

She didn't answer. Her brow was creased. She was probably thinking the same thing David was. With the information they had now, they could figure out Olam ben Z'man's real name. All they had to do was look for a former professor in Hebrew University's computer science department whose son had died in Lebanon.

Rav Kavner turned to David. "What about you? Do you know about Kabbalah? Many people in America think they do, but what they know is just nonsense. They think Kabbalah is some kind of Jewish cult, with secret codes and other foolishness."

As it happened, David knew a few things about Kabbalah. He'd studied the subject at Columbia after he quit the physics program and started pursuing his Ph.D. in the history of science. He'd taken a course called History of Science in the Middle Ages, and Kabbalah was one of the topics they'd covered. "It's a branch of medieval Jewish philosophy," he said. "The Kabbalists were trying to explain the fundamental nature of the universe. They wanted to understand how an infinite, eternal God could create a finite, mortal world."

The rabbi stared at him for several seconds, unblinking. Then he smiled. "Excellent! An American who actually knows something about Kabbalah!" He pointed a crooked finger at David. "But let me give you a little test. Do you know what *Ein Sof* is? And the *Sephirot*?"

David searched his memory. He'd enjoyed the course on medieval science, so he remembered the subject fairly well. "*Ein Sof* is Hebrew for 'Without End.' It refers to the infinite, unknowable God. The *Sephirot* are the emanations of God that were used to create the knowable world. I think the idea is that God had to break Himself up into different aspects to manifest Himself in the physical universe."

"That's close but not exactly right. *Sephirot* doesn't mean 'emanations.' It means 'enumerations.' Like counting, see?" The Rav held out his hands, splaying the fingers. "There are ten *Sephirot* and they're arranged in a pattern called *Etz HaChayim*, the Tree of Life. This pattern has three pillars and twenty-two paths between the *Sephirot*, which correspond to the twenty-two letters in the Hebrew alphabet. You see?"

David didn't. The Rav had lost him. He opened his mouth, intending to steer the conversation back to Olam ben Z'man, but Monique beat him to it. "Rabbi, could we get back to something you said before? You said you'd warned Olam that something terrible would happen. What did you mean by that?"

The Rav let out a sigh. His face turned sober. "The terrible thing came from Olam's studies of the Kabbalah. You see, there are certain Kabbalistic teachings that can be misunderstood. For this reason many rabbis won't teach Kabbalah to anyone under the age of forty. Olam was over that age and brilliant besides, so I accepted him as my student. But he was too brilliant for his own good. After he read all the Kabbalistic books he could find, he came up with some ideas of his own, and those ideas led him into trouble."

"What ideas?"

"Ach, it's hard to explain." The rabbi shook his head. "Olam's ideas didn't come from the traditional books or commentaries. They came from science, his work with computers. He tried to combine his scientific theories with the principles of Kabbalah. But I know nothing about computers. When Olam talked about his ideas, they made no sense to me, and I told him so. So he found someone else to talk to, another scientist he was friendly with."

"Someone at Hebrew University?"

"No, it was someone in America. At a university in Maryland."

David felt another surge of adrenaline. The rabbi was talking about Jacob Steele. "Mr. Kavner, could you try to remember what Olam said about his ideas? Just tell us the words he used, even if they don't make any sense to you."

The rabbi looked at the ceiling again. After a few seconds he closed his eyes, but his head remained in the same position, tilted backward. "He kept using the word *meyda*. In English it means 'information.' He kept telling me, over and over, 'The universe is information.' I asked him, 'What do you mean by this?' and he started talking about particles and forces of nature, and it was all scientific gibberish that had nothing to do with Kabbalah. And so I said to him. 'Olam, you're wrong. The universe is God.' And he said, 'Then information is God, because everything in the universe is composed of information.'" The Rav opened his eyes. "Now tell me, was I wrong? How was I supposed to make any sense of this?"

Monique stood up and advanced to the edge of the rabbi's desk. She bent over and stared at Kavner, her eyebrows scrunched together, but David could tell that she wasn't really looking at him. She was thinking of what he'd just said, her mind working furiously. "What else?" she asked. "Do you remember anything else?"

"Yes, I'm thinking of another thing now. Olam had some strange ideas about the *Sephirot,* the enumerations of God. As I said, there are ten *Sephirot* and they're arranged in a pattern called the Tree of Life. Well, Olam said the *Sephirot* were really computer programs. Like the programs that come on a disk that you put into your computer when you want it to do something. I told him, 'You're crazy, you can't put the enumerations of God on a computer disk,' but he kept saying it was true. He said you could create a whole universe of stars and planets and galaxies with just a few computer programs."

David felt a dull ache in the pit of his stomach. He thought again of the quantum computers that Jacob Steele had built, the strings of ions that could hold inconceivable amounts of data. Then he thought of Jacob's warning about the spacetime disruption, the rip in the fabric of the universe. And now this strange talk of God and computer science and enumerations. What was the connection here? The universe is information?

He took a deep breath. "I'm sorry, Mr. Kavner, but I still don't understand. How did these ideas get Olam into trouble?"

The Rav didn't answer right away. He lowered his head and stared at the floor. "Olam wanted to prove he was right. He said he could do an experiment that would test his ideas about the *Sephirot*. I didn't think he was serious at first, but then he showed me the plans and drawings that the scientist in Maryland had done." The rabbi shook his head again. "I told Olam I didn't like it. I had a bad feeling about this project. It was like chapter eleven in Genesis, the Tower of Babel. Olam was trying to go where no one but God should go. It was an affront to the Eternal. Nothing good could come of it."

The ache in David's stomach grew worse. "But Olam went ahead anyway? He built the experiment?"

The rabbi raised his head. His eyes were glassy. "We were good friends. I couldn't say no."

"And it's in the basement of this building, right? Attached to the fiber-optic line he installed?"

He nodded. "Olam said it was part of something called the Caduceus Array."

NICO RANG THE BUZZER NEXT TO THE YESHIVA'S FRONT DOOR. HE STILL WORE the brown robe that made him look like a pilgrim, but under its folds he carried his combat knife and his Heckler & Koch nine-millimeter. Standing next to him in the alley was Bashir, his second-in-command, who also concealed his weapons under his pilgrim's robe. Bashir was unusually short, barely 160 centimeters, but he was Nico's fiercest soldier. They were both from Beirut, both veterans of Lebanon's long civil war, and neither was particularly fond of Israelis.

After about thirty seconds the door opened again and Nico saw the same two yeshiva students who'd answered the buzzer earlier. They still had their Uzis, but instead of cradling the submachine guns with their fingers on the triggers, the students let the guns dangle from their shoulder straps. This was a sign of either poor training or stupidity, Nico thought. A gun is useless unless you're ready to fire it. The bigger one stepped forward, putting himself within easy striking distance. "What is it?" he asked. "What do you want?"

Bashir, who held an alms bowl in his left hand, moved toward the other student, who wore a skullcap with a childish design of roaring lions. "Donation, please? For the poor?"

The student shook his head. "No, we're not—"

Bashir sliced the Jew's throat before he could say another word. At the same time, Nico rammed his own knife into the bigger student's throat, thrusting it in so forcefully that the tip of the blade emerged from the back of his neck. Nico grabbed the Jew's shoulder for leverage and sawed into his carotid artery. Then he wrenched the knife out and stepped aside. The body fell forward, gushing blood on the cobblestones.

So far, so good, Nico thought. They'd gained entry into the building without raising the alarm. He threw off his robe—he wore black pants and a black shirt underneath—and whistled down the alley. Six more men dressed in black emerged from the darkness and ran toward the door.

11

THE BUILDING THE YESHIVA OCCUPIED WAS HUNDREDS OF YEARS OLD AND full of makeshift rooms and stairways that had been built and rebuilt by generations of tenants. Behind what looked like a closet door in Rav Kavner's office was a spiral stairway that descended to the basement. As the rabbi led David and Monique down the rusting iron steps, he told them that the building had once been owned by Jordanian smugglers who'd dug tunnels for sneaking wine casks under the streets of the Old City. It was pitch-black at the bottom of the stairway, but then the rabbi flipped the light switch and David saw a large room with cinderblock walls. At the far end was a square steel table, more than ten feet across, loaded with laboratory equipment: control panels and oscilloscopes and spectrometers and lasers, all linked by snaking black cables.

"Damn," David whispered. "There must be a million dollars' worth of equipment here."

The Rav nodded. "Two million, actually. Olam got the money from his friend in Maryland."

That was the money from the DARPA grant, David thought, the government funding that Jacob Steele had illegally diverted. U.S. tax dollars had paid for this experiment in Jerusalem.

Monique rushed toward the table and leaned over its edge, surveying all the instruments. There was a look of delight on her face. Her mouth hung open as she examined the lasers, which were enclosed in rectangular steel cases, about two feet long and six inches wide, with tiny circles of glass at their firing ends. She turned to the rabbi. "When did Olam build all this? It looks almost new."

"Let me think. Was it last August? Or last July? Almost a year ago.

For a couple of months he spent all his time down here. We hardly saw him. And even after he finished building the thing, he went down to the basement three or four times a day. The machines were running all the time, you see, and he had to check on them every so often to make sure they were working."

"But the equipment isn't running now," Monique noted, pointing at the table. None of the LEDs on the devices were lit.

"No, Olam shut it down before he left. On Tuesday evening he went to check on his machines as usual, but this time he stayed in the basement for nearly an hour. Then he rushed into my office and said there was an emergency. He needed to visit some of his old friends in the army, he said. He didn't say where he was going, but he promised he'd come back to the yeshiva the next morning." The rabbi frowned. "But he didn't come back. Not the next day and not this morning either. I called the police this afternoon but they said I had to wait another day before I could file a missing-person report."

David approached the table and stood next to Monique. She was examining a small mirror set on a metal stand in front of one of the lasers. The mirror was positioned at a forty-five-degree angle from the laser; if the device were turned on, the mirror would deflect the beam of laser light toward another small mirror on the opposite side of the table. David had seen this kind of setup in other tabletop experiments—physicists used the mirrors to guide the laser beams to their intended targets. The lasers on this particular table were turned off now, but the mirrors were still in their proper positions, so it was possible to trace the paths the beams were supposed to take. And that was exactly what Monique was doing. Her eyes darted from mirror to mirror, following the path to its end. Then she smiled and stepped around the corner of the table.

"There it is!" she said. She pointed at a pair of steel clamps that supported a glass tube, just three inches long. "That's the vacuum chamber."

"What?" David said. "That little tube?"

She nodded. "It's like the chamber that Lucille found in Jacob Steele's office. First you pump the air out of it, then you inject the ions into the vacuum and use electromagnetic fields to line up the charged particles. When everything's ready, you fire the laser beams at the ions."

David craned his neck to get a closer look at the tube, which was propped horizontally between the clamps. Inside were two needlelike electrodes, one at each end of the tube, positioned so that their sharp tips pointed at the exact center of the cylinder. "But this chamber looks different from the one Lucille found," he noted. "This one has just two electrodes. The other one had two parallel rows of electrodes and a gap between them for the ions."

Monique nodded again. "I didn't say they were exactly the same. This chamber is a single-ion trap." She pointed at the tips of the needles. "If both of these electrodes carry a positive charge, they can suspend a positive ion between them through the force of repulsion. But this trap can hold only one ion at a time."

David was still confused. "I thought a quantum computer needed more than one ion. Doesn't the computer perform calculations by getting the ions to interact with each other? If this chamber can't hold more than one ion, how can it calculate anything?"

She nodded a third time. "You're right. It's not a quantum computer. It's something else. But I haven't figured it out yet. Give me a minute, okay?"

While Monique continued to stare at the equipment, David stepped away from the table. He felt exhilarated by their discovery but still anxious. He turned to Rav Kavner. "Are you sure this is a computer?" he asked. "Is that what Olam said?"

The rabbi flung his hands in the air. "I have no idea what it is! I told you, I didn't understand anything Olam said about this crazy business."

"Just think for a second. Did he ever refer to it as a computer?"

"No, he just called it the Caduceus Array. And sometimes he called it his ion clock, but I have no idea what that means either."

David stared at the old man, who was still holding his hands up like a prisoner of war. "He said ion clock?"

"Yes, more nonsense! Does this look like a clock to you?"

David hustled back to the table. Standing beside Monique, he gazed at the electrodes inside the glass tube. He knew, of course, that an ion was far too small to be seen, but in his mind's eye he pictured one of the particles in the space between the electrodes, a charged atom shining within a beam of laser light.

"It *is* a clock," Monique whispered, pointing at the chamber. "If the laser is tuned to the right frequency, the ion will start to oscillate. It'll absorb and release energy hundreds of trillions of times per second. And because the ion acts like a pendulum, swinging back and forth between two energy levels, it can be used as a timepiece." Without taking her eyes off the tube, she grabbed the shoulder of David's jacket and bunched it in her fist. "I read about a similar experiment in *Physical Review*. A team of researchers in Colorado built an atomic clock using a single ion of mercury. It was much more accurate than a conventional atomic clock. Even if it ran for a billion years, the single-ion clock wouldn't fall more than a second behind."

As she spoke, David raised his head. Above the welter of equipment on the table, he saw a black cable running up to the ceiling, where it disappeared into a neatly drilled hole. This was the fiber-optic line they'd followed across the Old City. He realized now why Olam had installed it. "Olam's clock was linked to Jacob's lab in Maryland," he said. "Where there was probably another clock just like it. But we didn't see Jacob's clock because it was destroyed in the explosion."

"And that's why they called it the Caduceus Array! It was an array of clocks containing mercury ions, and the caduceus is a symbol of the god Mercury!" Monique tightened her grip on David's jacket. "Both Olam and Jacob were taking precise measurements of time and sending the data through the fiber-optic line so they could compare their measurements."

"But why go to all that trouble? What were they investigating?"

"Don't you see? An array of very accurate atomic clocks could detect tiny differences in the passage of time. If a clock in one location runs a bit faster than an identical clock in another location, and you know the difference isn't caused by mechanical errors or relativistic effects, then it might be evidence of subtle variations in the fabric of spacetime. And the pattern of those variations would be like a map, revealing clues to the fundamental nature of the universe." She looked David in the eye, trying to make him understand. "That's what Jacob and Olam were looking for, those small but very significant variations. They located their clocks on opposite sides of the globe to improve the odds of detecting the tiny differences. But last Tuesday they detected something bigger, something that scared the hell out of them. A fundamental disruption of time that occurred at the same moment as the Iranian nuclear test."

David shook his head. "It doesn't make sense. How could a nuke alter the flow of time?"

"It wasn't just a nuke. The warhead must've triggered a completely different phenomenon. It's like a hammer came down and smashed the hell out of spacetime and got everything vibrating. And who knows what'll happen if it comes down again? It could—"

She was interrupted by the sound of footsteps on the spiral stairway. As she and David turned in that direction, a muffled burst echoed down the shaft, followed quickly by another. After the second shot, the footsteps ceased and something heavy tumbled down the stairs. The body of one of the yeshiva students thudded to the basement floor, his jeans and T-shirt soaked with blood. Then David heard more footsteps on the stairs, clanging rapid and loud.

NICO AND HIS MEN PUT SILENCERS ON THEIR PISTOLS. WHEN THEY RUSHED into the study hall on the yeshiva's second floor, the commandos spread out and fired at the twelve bearded students sitting around the long table. Nico killed two of the Jews and Bashir killed three. Within seconds, eleven students were dead, most of them still seated in their chairs. But a pale, skinny student at the far end of the table had stumbled backward in the confusion and managed to crawl through a doorway on the other side of the room. Nico and Bashir sprinted after him, both cursing. They needed to kill this Jew before he shouted a warning to the Americans. They followed him into a small office littered with books, but before Nico could line up his shot, the student yelled, *"Rav Kavner!"* and slipped through another doorway.

"Ibnil kelb!" Nico shouted, enraged. He charged forward and found himself at the top of a spiral stairway. It was dark, but when he leaned over the stairway's railing, he could see the Jew running down the steps, going round and round the central pole. Pointing his nine-millimeter at a lower turn of the stairway, he waited for the *kelb* to appear in his sights, then fired twice. The Jew collapsed and fell the rest of the way down the stairs. Nico ran after him, with Bashir close behind.

They stayed close to the central pole of the stairway so that no one below could get a clear shot at them. Although the Americans had been unarmed before, it was possible that the Jews had loaned them a handgun or an Uzi. When Nico was about four meters from the bottom of the staircase, he crouched on the steps and peered down into the basement. An old bearded Jew was running hysterically across the room while the Americans knelt beside the corpse of the student. The Jew must be the yeshiva's rabbi, Nico thought, the "Rav Kavner" that the student had tried to warn. The Americans must've sought out the rabbi because he had a connection to Olam ben Z'man. Now Nico would interrogate the Jew to determine Olam's whereabouts. But there was no need to keep the Americans alive. They'd served their purpose.

Creeping a bit closer to the edge of the stairway, he aimed his Heckler & Koch at the black woman's forehead. It was a shame, he thought—she was quite beautiful. Then he pulled the trigger.

AT THE LAST SECOND MONIQUE MUST'VE SEEN SOMETHING MOVE ON THE stairway because she yelled, "Get down!" and shoved David to the floor. Then he heard another muffled gunshot and Monique fell on top of him, her body shuddering. She let out a gasp of pain and David felt a spray of warm liquid on his face. At the same instant, he saw Rav Kavner speed across the room, moving insanely fast for a man his age. The rabbi dove for the light switch on the wall, and then the basement went dark and David couldn't see a thing.

Several more shots roared in the darkness. The bullets chipped the cement floor and smashed into the equipment on the lab table. There were at least two gunmen on the stairway, and although they were firing blindly now, David knew they would hit him soon enough if he didn't find cover. Monique lay on top of him, unmoving, but he managed to slide free and drag her under the steel table. Bending over her, he reached for her neck and tried to check for a pulse, but his fingers were already slick with her blood and he couldn't feel anything. His chest tightened and his eyes stung, and before he could stop himself, he moaned, "No, God, no!" Then he felt something smash against his lips and heard Monique hoarsely whisper, "Shut up!" She'd slammed her palm over his mouth. It hurt like hell, but David didn't care. He was so relieved that she was alive.

Another fusillade of bullets smacked into the lab table, ricocheting just inches above David's head. Then the gunfire stopped and he heard something worse, the sound of feet descending the final turns of the spiral stairway. David knew that hiding under the lab table would become pointless once the gunmen reached the basement floor and found the light switch. Desperate, he crawled away from Monique and reached up to the tabletop, snaking his hand around the lab instruments until he found one of the laser mirrors. The mirror's stand was fairly heavy, and for a moment he considered throwing the thing at the gunmen. Then he heard a shuffling noise, just a few feet away. David raised the heavy mirror to bash whoever was approaching, but before he could swing it down, he felt the bristles of Rav Kavner's beard in his face. The old man crashed into him headfirst and they rolled under the table. More bullets ricocheted against the lasers and oscilloscopes.

"This way!" the Rav hissed. "Into the tunnel!"

"Tunnel? What do—"

"I told you, the smugglers' tunnel! This way!"

The old man scrabbled forward on his hands and knees. David reached for Monique, but she was already dragging herself in the same direction. Behind him, the sound of the footsteps had changed—now the gunmen were off the iron stairway and on the cement floor, closing in fast. Whirling around, David flung the laser mirror at them. It didn't hit either one, but it made a loud crash against the wall behind them, and the gunmen turned around and fired at the noise. A fountain of sparks lit the air as some of the bullets struck the stairway, and in that flash David saw the Rav in the opposite corner of the room, lifting a metal grate from a manhole.

The sparks died and the room plunged back into darkness, but David remembered where the manhole was. He dashed toward the corner and careened into Rav Kavner and Monique, who'd already lowered her legs into the hole. His momentum knocked her off the edge and she slid into the shaft, gasping in pain again as she hit the bottom. David fell into the manhole just behind her, dropping about six feet and landing in a puddle that smelled strongly of sewage. He scrambled to his feet and stretched his hands up to the rabbi, whose legs dangled over the edge. "Come on!" he cried. "I'll help . . ."

The lights in the basement suddenly came on and David saw the Rav's terrified face above him. He grabbed the old man's hips and started to lower him into the shaft, but the basement immediately echoed with gunfire. One of the bullets struck the back of the rabbi's head. It plowed through his brain and burst out of his skull just above his left eyebrow.

The old man hung at the edge of the manhole for a moment, his mouth gaping as the blood pumped out of his forehead. Then he slumped forward and fell on top of David.

The Rav wasn't heavy but David's knees buckled. He landed on his back and the corpse rolled off him, splashing in the puddle at the bottom of the shaft. David lay in the fetid water, too terrified to move. All he could do was look up at the manhole and wait for the bullets to come raining down.

Then Monique grabbed his arm. She locked her fingers around his wrist and pulled him through a gap in the rocky wall of the shaft. It was a rough oval opening, just big enough to roll a wine cask through, and it led to a tunnel that was about three feet wide and five feet high.

In the dim light David saw Monique bending over him. Her right arm hung limply at her side, blood dripping from the sleeve of her jacket, but her left arm was strong enough to yank him to his feet. "Follow me," she whispered, letting go of his wrist. Then, hunching low, she started running down the tunnel.

David followed her into the darkness.

WHEN NICO REACHED THE MANHOLE HE SAW ONLY THE OLD JEW, LYING faceup at the bottom of the shaft. The left side of his forehead was a bloody mess, but his eyes were open and his lips had curved into a grotesque smile. Nico was furious—his own soldiers had killed the man he'd wanted to interrogate! He took out his anger on the Jew's corpse, shooting it in the head three more times. When the gunshots ceased echoing, another noise arose from the shaft—a rapid scratching, like the sound of rats scurrying behind a wall. The Americans were trying to escape through an old smugglers' tunnel beneath the floor, whose entrance Nico could dimly see beside the dead Jew.

By this point all seven of Nico's men had rushed down the spiral stairway to the basement. He turned to Bashir, who stood at the edge of the manhole, aiming his Heckler & Koch at the corpse. Now Bashir's small size would give him an advantage. "You first," Nico ordered, pointing at the entrance to the tunnel. "Go down there and kill them."

THE TUNNEL ZIGZAGGED UNDER THE STREETS OF THE MUSLIM QUARTER. Every fifty feet or so it turned to the left or right, and because the tunnel was pitch-black there was no way to see the turns coming. David could hear Monique up ahead, cursing every time she had to change direction, and even though he could use the sound of her footsteps as a guide, he kept banging his elbows against the tunnel's rough walls and slipping in the foul puddles underfoot. Although the tunnel may have been dug by Jordanian smugglers, it now doubled as a sewer and the smell was appalling. To make matters worse, after they'd gone a few hundred feet the tunnel abruptly narrowed. David smacked his head into a stone jutting from the wall and the blow made his ears ring. He began to wonder if there was a light at the end of this tunnel. No smugglers had come this way in decades, and there was a good chance that the exit had been sealed long ago.

Then he did glimpse a light, but it wasn't ahead of them. It was behind. David looked over his shoulder and saw a flashlight beam jerkily illuminating the turn they'd just passed. At the same time, he heard footsteps behind him, clomping rapidly through the puddles. It was one of the gunmen, David thought. And the son of a bitch was moving a lot faster than they were.

David leaned forward and shouted, "Go, go!" at Monique, but she was already sprinting ahead. They ran as fast as they could, caroming painfully against the walls, but the pursuing footsteps only grew louder. Soon the light behind them was strong enough that David could see the outline of Monique's body within the tunnel, her back sharply bent to keep her head low, her legs striding furiously. She came to another turn and dashed to the left. Just as he reached the same point, their pursuer rounded the corner behind them and the walls of the tunnel turned horribly bright. For a fraction of a second David saw his own shadow looming in front of him. Then he cut to the left and a gunshot boomed down the tunnel. The bullet struck the wall where his shadow had been a moment before. Shards of stone and clods of dirt flew through the air like shrapnel. "Fuck!" David yelled. "Fuck, fuck, fuck!"

The next turn was only twenty feet ahead, and Monique had already rounded it. But when David turned the corner he saw no sign of her. The tunnel widened here and the ceiling was higher, but there was just a blank wall in front of him, a dead end. He stood there, panicking, as the clomping footsteps drew closer. Listening carefully, he could tell there was more than one gunman in the tunnel now. Several flashlight beams were approaching, casting their jiggling light on the walls.

Then he heard a loud thump and the sound of wood splintering. He looked a few feet to his right and saw Monique standing beside a door-size plywood board that she'd just slammed her left shoulder against. "Come on!" she shouted. "It's boarded up, but I think we can break through!"

She stood aside and David aimed his shoulder at the center of the board. He threw all his weight against it and to his surprise the plywood cracked and gave way. He burst through the split pieces of the board and tumbled onto the smooth floor of a long corridor.

Monique rushed over, offering her left hand to help him up, and as he rose to his feet he saw a row of giant stone blocks, running alongside the corridor like monstrous bricks. They were in the Western Wall Tunnel again, somewhere between the Holy of Holies and the emergency exit that Aryeh Goldberg had found. Then David heard another gunshot and a bullet whizzed through the split plywood board and smacked against one of the stone blocks. He dove to the side and grasped Monique's good arm and started running down the corridor, heading north toward the Holy of Holies.

"Wait! Stop!" she cried. "The emergency exit is the other way!"

David shook his head. They were at least a hundred yards from that exit, and unlike the last tunnel, this one was brightly lit and as straight as a target range. As soon as the gunmen stepped into the corridor, they'd have a clear shot. But the Holy of Holies was less than fifty feet away and there was still a crowd of *kippot srugot* praying in front of the blocked-up archway, rocking back and forth with their black prayer books in their hands and their Uzis hanging from their shoulder straps. Some of the zealots at the edge of the crowd had noticed the commotion down the corridor. They'd stopped praying to gawk at the strange man and woman running toward them. David waved at them madly.

"Hamas!" he screamed. "Hamas! They're right behind us!"

The zealots' reaction was immediate—they threw their prayer books to the ground and grabbed their Uzis. When David was ten feet away he flung himself to the floor and dragged Monique with him, rolling past the zealots' feet toward the safety of the archway. An instant later, the *kippot srugot* opened fire.

The shots thundered in the stone corridor. David and Monique huddled against the blocked-up archway, the fractured, gray wall that had absorbed so many of the zealots' prayers. Closing his eyes, David added his own plea to the Holy of Holies—God Jesus Lord, help! The juddering gunfire pounded his eardrums.

Then someone yelled something in Hebrew and the bearded Jews stopped shooting. David opened his eyes and peered down the corridor. Seven bodies, all dressed in black, lay twisted on the floor.

Miraculously, none of the *kippot srugot* were hurt. One of them, a curly-haired giant with a rainbow-colored knitted yarmulke, approached David. "Don't worry, we radioed the army," he said. Then he pointed at Monique's right arm. "We told them you'll need an ambulance."

Monique nodded. She was shivering and her lips were bluish. David grew alarmed. He wondered how much blood she'd lost. "Hey, you should lie down," he said, gently gripping her shoulder and lowering her to the floor. "Take it easy. You've earned a rest."

She didn't protest. She lay on the floor and let David put her in the shock position, elevating her legs by placing a stack of prayer books under her heels. When he was done, she let out a long breath. "I'm sorry," she said.

"Sorry? Baby, you don't have to—"

"I'm not apologizing to you. I'm apologizing to God." She shifted her head on the floor and gave him a weak smile. "And to all of His wackos."

AS SOON AS THE JEWS STARTED FIRING THEIR UZIS, NICO DOVE BACK INTO the smugglers' tunnel. He'd been so focused on chasing the Americans, he hadn't noticed the crowd of Israelis until it was too late. His stomach twisted as he lay on the tunnel's stinking floor and heard the gunshots in the corridor just a few feet away. His men were being slaughtered, all of them. Including Bashir, his friend and comrade-in-arms, whom he'd known since they were teenagers in the slums of East Beirut.

For a moment he considered joining them in death, charging down the corridor and trying to kill as many Jews as he could before they cut him down. But when he got to his feet he turned away from the broken plywood board and retraced his steps through the smugglers' tunnel, running back to the basement of Beit Shalom Yeshiva. If he hurried, he could reach the safety of the Muslim quarter's alleys before the Israeli police arrived. Then he would go to the safe house and contact Brother Cyrus.

Nico knew that Cyrus wouldn't be pleased. But he also knew that the man was relentless. Cyrus would give him new orders, a new plan. And this was the surest way for Nico to get his revenge. One way or another, he would kill the Americans. The Almighty would guide his hand as he slit their throats.

12

CAMP COBRA WAS LESS THAN TWELVE HOURS OLD, BUT IN COLONEL BRENT Ramsey's humble opinion it was already the best damn army base he'd ever seen. More than seven hundred Rangers from the 75th Regiment and two hundred pilots and crewmen from the Eighth and 160th Aviation squadrons were hidden inside a cavern in the Kopet Dag Mountains, just ten miles north of Turkmenistan's border with Iran.

Ramsey, a Special Forces man with twenty-two years in the service, stood on the granite floor of the cavern and watched his soldiers unload the trucks that had come from Afghanistan the night before. The cave was close to a Turkmen road that ran across the mountain range, and its mouth was big enough that the Rangers could drive their trucks right inside. Past the entrance, the cave widened enormously, forming a huge natural garage more than two hundred feet across. Dozens of Humvees and flatbed trucks were parked along the cavern's rocky walls. The loads on the flatbeds were covered with tarp, but Ramsey recognized them by their shapes. Each of the smaller loads was a Black Hawk helicopter. The larger loads were Ospreys, tilt-rotor aircraft that could carry twice as many men as the helicopters and fly nearly twice as fast.

And that was just the front section of the cave—the foyer, you could say. About sixty yards farther inside, the cavern's floor sloped down to an even more spacious chamber where the Rangers had erected a tent city. They'd already set up a mess hall and an armory and a field hospital, not to mention the long rows of tents that served as their barracks. Beyond this section, the cavern narrowed a bit and descended to a lower chamber and a crescent-shaped pool of greenish water, an honest-to-goodness underground lake. The water smelled sulfurous and wasn't exactly potable, but it was geothermally heated to a toasty ninety-five degrees, and some of the soldiers had already swum laps down there.

Ramsey shook his head as he thought about how goddamn perfect this base was. For one thing, it was only sixty miles north of the Iranian nuclear facility. The Black Hawks and Ospreys could reach their target in less than twenty minutes, which was a hell of lot quicker than flying from Afghanistan or the Persian Gulf. Even better, the whole operation was hidden from view. Although Iran had spy satellites that monitored military activity near the country's borders, Camp Cobra wasn't going to appear in any of their images of Turkmenistan. The Iranians wouldn't see any unusual activity on the Turkmen roads either, because the Rangers had transported everything at night. And Turkmenistan's president-for-life had sent his secret police to the area and discreetly evacuated all the nearby villages. It was a brilliant plan, and General McNair deserved a hell of a promotion for coming up with it. McNair wasn't Ramsey's favorite person in the army—the general was a straitlaced God-and-country type, whereas Ramsey was more of a hell-raiser—but the colonel had to give credit where credit was due. If Osama bin Laden and Al-Qaeda could hide in caves, then the U.S. Army damn well could, too.

After a few minutes the soldiers finished unloading the last truck and returned to their tents. Ramsey headed for the mouth of the cave, exchanging salutes with the pair of sentries posted there. McNair had gone back to Afghanistan before daybreak, leaving Ramsey in charge of the base, and now the colonel was going to stretch his legs a bit. Because of the need for secrecy, McNair had ordered everyone to stay in the cave during daylight hours, but he'd positioned a few snipers in well-camouflaged locations on the mountainsides, and Ramsey wanted to see for himself how those boys were doing. It was still early in the morning and the fog was thick in the mountain pass, so there was no chance that any satellite or spy plane would spot him. Besides, the colonel had been on duty for the past twenty-two hours, taking army-issue Dexedrine pills to stay alert, and now he needed a little exercise to calm himself down.

Outside the cave's mouth was an arid plateau covered with hard-packed dirt and prickly desert plants. The bare brown ridges of the Kopet Dag loomed all around. Ramsey liked the look of these mountains—they reminded him of his boyhood home in West Texas. The Kopet Dag weren't particularly high, but they ran straight and true like a long earthen wall, rising above the flat expanse of the Karakum Desert and forming a natural barrier between Turkmenistan and Iran. The Iranian nuclear facility was on the opposite side of the wall, inside a cavern very similar to the one that concealed Camp Cobra. As Ramsey marched across the plateau he turned his gaze in that direction. The mountains blocked his view but he kept looking anyway, feeling as cocky and eager as an eighteen-year-old recruit. Ramsey got this same feeling whenever he prepared for a mission, this powerful sense of anticipation. He knew that they wouldn't actually launch the surprise attack for at least another two days—in a final diplomatic move, the White House had given the Revolutionary Guards forty-eight hours to voluntarily surrender their nukes, which of course they would never do. But in his mind's eye Ramsey could already see the assault beginning, the Ospreys and Black Hawks rising from the plateau and racing south to their target.

Ramsey was so juiced that he walked all the way across the plateau, a brisk half mile. From this spot he could look directly south through a gap in the mountains. He couldn't glimpse Iran—the fog at the lower elevations was too thick—but in the foreground he saw a stream threading the mountain pass, flanked by junipers that looked extravagantly green against the brown surroundings. He also heard the unmistakable sound of a waterfall.

Intrigued, he made a foray down the slope, heading for the sinuous stream. He thought again of his boyhood in Brewster County, all the mornings spent exploring his father's ranch in the Del Norte Mountains, constantly scanning the ground for rattlesnakes and arrowheads. When Ramsey reached the line of junipers he started searching for the waterfall, following the sound of the plashing stream through a dense tangle of undergrowth. And then he heard someone behind him say, "Stop right there, Colonel."

It was an American voice, no foreign accent. Ramsey assumed it was one of his snipers. He raised his hands in the air and turned around, making a joke of it. "Good work, soldier," he said. "You got me, fair and square."

But when he saw the soldier he did a double take. First of all, it wasn't a man. It was a young woman, quite tall, with ample breasts and a pretty face. She wore a standard-issue army uniform, but there was no unit designation on her shoulder and no name tag on her chest. Most disturbing of all, she was pointing a Heckler & Koch nine-millimeter at his head, and there was a silencer attached to the gun's barrel. Ramsey stared at her in disbelief. "What the hell's going on?" he shouted, lowering his hands. "Put down that weapon!"

The woman frowned. "Keep your hands up, Colonel," she said. "I'm not going to warn you again."

Ramsey shook his head. One of the Rangers must've brought his goddamn girlfriend along with him. Some horny idiot had snuck this bitch onto last night's convoy and found her a hiding spot near the base. It was the only explanation that made any sense. The colonel strode toward her. "Goddamn it! I said put down that—"

She adjusted her aim and fired the nine-millimeter. Ramsey heard a muffled burst and saw his right hand explode. The bullet tore through his knuckles, nearly severing his index and middle fingers. Belatedly, Ramsey's Special Forces training kicked in. Ignoring the pain that shot up his right arm, he reached with his left hand for the M-9 pistol in his holster. But the woman shifted her aim again and fired at his left hand, tearing a ragged hole in his palm. It was goddamn fucking HUMILIAT-ING—the bitch had disabled him in less than two seconds! Enraged, Ramsey charged at her through the undergrowth, fully expecting her to shoot him again and put him out of his misery, but the bitch just stood there, smiling. Then another soldier came out of nowhere and shoved him to the ground.

The second soldier was a man at least. Ramsey opened his mouth to curse the bastard, folding his lower lip behind his teeth to shout, "Fuck you!" But then he looked up and saw the bastard's face. It was McNair. The general loomed over him, tall and gaunt, his bright blue eyes radiating fury.

Ramsey was confused as hell, and the pain in his hands wasn't help-ing any. "General?" he croaked. "I thought you went back to—"

"My orders were clear, Ramsey." McNair glowered at him. His mouth was like a minus sign. The bitch with the Heckler & Koch stood to his left. "No one was to leave the cave."

"I . . . I'm sorry, sir!" He didn't know what else to say. "I think I need to go to the field hospital!"

"No, I'm afraid not." The general stepped forward. "The Lord has different plans for you now."

Then McNair kicked him in the head and Ramsey blacked out.

13

IT WAS A PUZZLE, AND MICHAEL LIKED TO SOLVE PUZZLES. AFTER TAMARA showed him the program on the Ultra 27 workstation, he sat in front of the computer the whole night and the following morning, staring at the lines of code for sixteen hours. Then he took a nap. Tamara woke him in the evening and gave him another snack. She said she had to go away for a while to do an important job, but another of Brother Cyrus's soldiers— Angel, the man with the curved scar on his neck—would take care of him until she got back. An hour later, when the sky was fully dark, Angel led him outside and put him into the cargo hold of a big green truck, along with his computer and desk and the bare mattress.

For the next ten hours Michael sat in the cargo hold with Angel while the truck bounced on the bumpy roads. But he wasn't bored. He was still working on the puzzle, which he could do even when the workstation was turned off. The software code was in his mind now, arranged in long lines and vertiginous blocks that he could scroll up and down on the black screen of his eyelids. He wanted to spend every waking second with those lines of instructions, because when he worked on the puzzle he didn't have to think about Tamara or Brother Cyrus or Dr. Parsons. He could forget where he was and what was going to happen to him and think of nothing but the program.

At dawn the truck stopped in the middle of a desert. When Angel opened the truck's rear door, Michael saw sand dunes in every direction, rippling in great beige waves to the horizon. Angel said they were in the Karakum Desert, which stretched for hundreds of miles across the country of Turkmenistan. He helped Michael out of the truck and led him to an encampment that Cyrus's soldiers had set up amid the dunes.

Thirteen round huts were arranged in a loose cluster, and several pickup trucks and Land Cruisers were parked on the sand nearby. The huts looked like giant soup bowls turned upside down. Each was about twelve feet across and eight feet high, with a circular wall made of wooden slats and a domed roof made of felt. Angel called them yurts. He went to one of them and opened the door and led Michael inside. There was no furniture, just a big Turkish carpet spread across the floor. Two other soldiers carried Michael's mattress and desk into the yurt and began hooking up the Ultra 27 workstation, connecting its power cord to a diesel generator outside.

After Angel and the other men left, Michael sat on the folding chair in front of the computer screen and resumed working on the puzzle. He stared again at the dense blocks of code, checking each line to make sure he'd memorized it correctly. The keys to understanding the program, he'd discovered, were the equations of the unified field theory. By carefully reading the step-by-step instructions in the code, he'd found that the program performed the same tasks as the laws of physics. One part of the code determined the masses of the elementary particles—the electron, the quark, the neutrino, and so on. Another part calculated the strength of the forces between the particles. Yet another part generated the spacetime manifold, specifying the curvature and topology of the spatial dimensions as well as the direction of time. The program was radically different from conventional software because the data it handled was quantum, not binary; instead of being restricted to either zero or one, each bit could take a tremendous number of values. But the program followed the standard rules of logic, which meant that Michael could make sense of it.

The code on the screen was incomplete, though. The people who'd written it hadn't known all the equations of the *Einheitliche Feldtheorie*, so they couldn't finish the program. Michael, on the other hand, knew the entire theory, so he was able to fill in the gaps. He didn't do this work on the screen—his fingers never touched the keyboard. Instead, he extended the memorized code in his head, adding new lines of quantum variables and operators. The process involved some tricky rearrangements, but Michael was good at this. It was no more difficult than piecing together a jigsaw puzzle, and he'd spent many hours doing that when he was younger. By midmorning he could glimpse the outlines of the solution, and by noon he'd filled in the last gaps. He scrolled the finished program in his mind, seeing the blocks of code flash against his eyelids. Now they were all arranged in the correct order.

He was still double-checking the program when he heard a noise behind him. Someone had unlatched the door to the yurt. Michael expected to see Angel come inside, bringing another bag of potato chips. But when he turned around he saw it was Tamara. She still wore her desert-camouflage uniform, but now there were wet patches under her armpits. Her pistol rested in the holster on her hip, and in her right hand she held a bottle half filled with brown liquid. "Michael!" she shouted, coming toward his desk. "I'm back!"

He covered his ears. Her voice was too loud.

"Oh, sorry!" She raised her hand to her mouth and backed away. "That was stupid. Let me start over." She went to the other side of the yurt and sat down on his mattress. She set the half-full bottle on the Turkish carpet. "I got carried away. I'm just so glad to see you."

Michael waited a few seconds, then lowered his hands. "Where were you?"

"In the mountains. Southwest of here." She started fanning her hand in front of her face to cool herself. David Swift had told Michael many times that this was a dumb thing to do. Waving your hand back and forth like that just made you hotter. "I've been driving all morning. Took me five hours to go a hundred and fifty miles. The roads in this country are awful."

"You have a car?"

She nodded. "It's one of Brother Cyrus's cars. A Land Cruiser. Pretty good for off-road driving in the dunes. When I was younger I used to love to go off-roading."

"If you have a car, I want you to take me back to David Swift. I already told you his telephone number. It's 212-555-3988."

Tamara said nothing at first. Then she stood up and approached Michael's desk again. She pointed at the computer screen. "Still working on the puzzle? Have you made any progress?"

Michael sank lower in his chair. Tamara bent over him, but he refused to look at her.

"Don't be afraid, Michael." Her voice was quiet now. "You're doing a good thing, a wonderful thing. Remember what I told you? About the Kingdom of Heaven?"

He shook his head. "There's nothing in the code about heaven. It's just a simulation. The program simulates the laws of physics."

"It also shows the path to Redemption. Once we have the completed code, we'll know how to change the program."

He shook his head again, harder this time. "No one can change the laws of physics."

Tamara bent lower. Michael could feel her breath on his ear. "I bet you finished it, didn't you? You completed the program? And it's in your head now?"

He didn't answer. But when he closed his eyes he saw the code again, scrolling swiftly upward.

To Michael's great relief, Tamara stood up straight and left his side. But she returned just four seconds later and placed the half-full bottle on the desk in front of him. "We should celebrate," she said. "Let's drink a toast." Bending over again, she opened one of the desk drawers and rummaged inside until she found a couple of glasses. "It's no sin to drink if our hearts are pure, right?"

She put the glasses on the desk. Then she unscrewed the cap from the bottle and poured some of the brown liquid into each glass. Michael smelled something harsh and sweet. "What is that?"

"Jägermeister. I used to drink this stuff all the time." She picked up one of the glasses and handed it to Michael. "Brother Cyrus was right about you. He said you'd give us everything we needed." She picked up the other glass and lifted it high in the air. "You're a gift from the Almighty, Michael. The Lord has provided!" She threw her head back and drank the brown liquid in one swallow.

Michael put his own glass back on the desk. He disliked the smell. And he didn't want to celebrate anyway. Solving the puzzle hadn't made him happy. In fact, it had made him very unhappy, because now he had nothing to distract himself from the things he didn't want to think about.

"What's wrong?" Tamara asked. "You don't like Jägermeister?"

Avoiding her gaze, Michael stared at the curved wall of the hut, which was almost perfectly circular. He tried to estimate its diameter and circumference, but he couldn't focus on the problem. He kept thinking of what lay beyond the wall—the sand dunes, the trucks, the soldiers in brown uniforms.

Tamara came toward him. She stretched her arm, reaching for his shoulder, but at the last second she stopped herself. Instead, she withdrew her hand and took a step back. "Oh, Michael." She shook her head. "My brother Jack used to get that same look on his face when he was sad. And nothing I said could cheer him up."

Michael stared at her. She hadn't touched him. She'd kept her promise.

Tamara was silent for several seconds. Then she set her empty glass on the desk. "All right, enough fun and games." She reached for the computer's keyboard. "Now it's time for you to show us the solution. Go ahead, start writing the code."

She rested the keyboard in his lap. It felt very light. He looked down at the keys but didn't touch them.

"You can't keep this to yourself, Michael. It's too important. The Lord is giving us a chance to redeem the world. Don't you want to help us do that?"

He shook his head. "I can't tell you. David Swift made me promise."

"Look, I know something about David Swift. He believes in world peace, right? What's the name of his organization? The Physicists for Peace?"

Michael had seen that name on some of the papers in David Swift's apartment. Also on the front of his envelopes. One night six months ago Michael had helped David put stamps on six hundred envelopes. "It's 'Physicists for Peace.' No 'the' in front of it."

"Yes, yes, whatever. The point is, he believes in peace. And once we open the gates to the Kingdom of Heaven, all of mankind will live in peace forever. If David Swift knew that we were—"

"There's nothing in the program about heaven."

"No, that's not true! The program will tell us how to open heaven's gates." She moved a step closer. "Brother Cyrus has prepared everything. Once you give him the code, he'll take care of the rest. No more pain, no more suffering. And you'll see your mother, remember?"

"My mother is dead."

"Michael, I explained all this already! There'll be a resurrection of the dead, just as God promised. That's the task He gave Brother Cyrus, to prepare—"

"I don't believe Brother Cyrus. He wants to use the theory to make weapons."

Tamara let out a cry that made Michael cover his ears again. At the same time, she fell to her knees on the carpet. "I swear to you, Michael! I swear on everything that's holy!" She clasped her hands together. "Brother Cyrus is a man of peace! All he wants is the Redemption!"

He still didn't believe her. She was his enemy, not his friend. She'd killed Dr. Parsons. "I can't tell you!" he shouted back at her. "David Swift made me promise!"

She stopped arguing with him. Lowering her head, she pressed her hands to her face. For a long time she rocked back and forth, swaying on her knees. She made a wet, choking, groaning noise that Michael could hear even though he was still covering his ears. She was crying. He understood that much.

Finally, after about two minutes, she rose to her feet. She went to the door of the yurt and opened it. Before she stepped outside, she looked over her shoulder. "If you don't tell us the code by seven o'clock this evening, Brother Cyrus will have to speak to you. And he won't be as patient as I've been."

Then she closed the door behind her and threw the latch.

14

AFTER TREATING MONIQUE'S GUNSHOT WOUND, THE EMERGENCY-ROOM DOC-
tors at Hadassah Mount Scopus Hospital decided to keep her overnight.
It wasn't a life-threatening injury—the bullet had missed the bone and
the major artery in her upper arm—but she'd lost a fair amount of
blood, so the doctors hooked her up to an IV line and gave her a mild
sedative. She fell asleep just as Lucille arrived at the hospital, along
with a unit of Israeli Army commandos who took up positions at the
building's entrances just in case there was another attack. David gave
Lucille a rundown of everything that had happened at Beit Shalom
Yeshiva, including what he'd learned about Olam ben Z'man, whose real
name was Loebman or Loehmann or something similar. Then Lucille
returned to the Shin Bet headquarters to relay the information to her
Israeli counterparts so they could track down the former computer
scientist. Meanwhile, David went to Monique's room on the hospital's
fifth floor and fell asleep in a comfortable chair by the window, getting
his first good night's rest in three days.

He awoke at 6 A.M. The room's window faced south, toward the
Old City, and in the distance David could see the Dome of the Rock
again, now ablaze with the sunrise. Monique was still asleep, lying on
her left side in the hospital bed with a white blanket half covering her
bandaged right arm. She was in the fetal position, with her knees bent
and her hands clasped under her chin, as if she were praying. There was
no tension in her face now. In the early-morning light she looked young
and unworried, a beautiful woman blithely sleeping through the dawn.
The bustle of the day had yet to begin and the hospital seemed unusually peaceful. The room was so quiet that David could hear the drip of

saline solution through the intravenous line, which snaked downward from the plastic bag on the IV pole to the needle inserted into the back of Monique's hand.

David studied her. Whenever he looked at Monique for any length of time, he was struck by a feeling of disbelief. He was unfathomably lucky to have her as his wife. And not just because she was funny and smart and beautiful. Karen, his first wife, had been all of those things, and yet she and David had made each other miserable. The difference was that Monique understood him. She knew his reasons, his motivations—why he lost his temper over stupid things, why he sometimes retreated from the world and brooded in his office, staring at the paneled ceiling for hours. She knew his whole history—his drunk of a father, his cowering mother, his own ugly descent into alcoholism—and she didn't try to bury it. Instead she tried to understand it, because it was a part of him. She focused on him with the same intensity that she applied to physics. She considered the problem from every angle and didn't rest until she solved it.

After a while David turned away from her bed and looked out the window. The walls of the Old City were brightening as the sun rose. Closer to the hospital, half a dozen sparrows picked their way across a yellowing lawn, and as David gazed at the birds he thought of Michael again. Perhaps the most miraculous thing David had seen in the past two years was the relationship Monique had developed with the teenager. Even though she was frenetically busy these days, taking care of a demanding one-year-old daughter while doing all her research and teaching at Columbia, she always found time for Michael. She'd given him an entire library of science books to read, everything from *An Introduction to Modern Physics* to *The Fundamentals of String Theory*. At dinnertime she enjoyed quizzing the boy to see how much of the information he'd memorized. And during the day she sent him e-mails from her office, each presenting a tricky problem in geometry or calculus, which Michael would spend hours joyfully solving. David's chest tightened as he thought of those messages. They had to find the boy. They had to.

He sat by the window for another ten minutes, staring at the ancient hills of Jerusalem. Then he heard a knock on the door. He started in his chair, imagining men in black uniforms bursting into the room. Although he knew the hospital was full of soldiers assigned to protect them, he was still nervous as he rose to his feet. He tiptoed around the bed to avoid waking Monique and opened the door a crack.

Lucille stood in the hallway, holding a manila folder under her arm. Instead of her bright red suit, she wore a canary-yellow jacket and a matching skirt. Agent Parker was a big fan of primary colors.

"How is she?" Lucille whispered, craning her neck so she could look into the room. "She doin' all right?"

Her Texas accent was a bit thicker than usual and her face was creased with worry. Her reaction to the shooting had surprised the hell out of David—he'd assumed that Lucille would be furious at them for going into the yeshiva by themselves, but she hadn't uttered a word of criticism. For now, at least, she was holding back the recriminations. She stood solidly behind them, offering sympathy and support. It was hard to imagine, but David suspected that Agent Parker was growing fond of them. She was acting as if he and Monique were her real partners.

He stepped into the hallway and closed the door behind him. He noticed an Israeli soldier standing guard about ten yards away, but otherwise the corridor was empty. "She's much better. When I talked to the doctor last night, he said they'd probably release her by noon."

Lucille let out a sigh. She looked exhausted. "I still can't figure out how this happened. Why were those bastards following you in the first place?"

David saw them in his mind's eye, the assassins dressed in black, coming down the spiral stairway of Beit Shalom Yeshiva. "I think they were looking for Olam, too. They must've heard about the FBI investigation and decided to follow us just in case we found him."

"But you and Reynolds aren't FBI. How did they find out you were involved in the case?"

He shrugged. "I don't know. All I can tell you is that they had a lot of firepower." He pictured the assassins again, running through the smugglers' tunnel. Then he recalled the sight of their bodies on the floor of the Western Wall Tunnel. "Have the Israelis had any luck identifying them?"

She shook her head. "They weren't carrying any papers, so all we have are their corpses and weapons. Shin Bet is checking their fingerprints and analyzing the ballistics, but so far they haven't found a match."

And they probably won't, David thought. The assassins had been too smart to leave any evidence. They were professionals, just like the people who'd kidnapped Michael and killed Jacob. "Shit, we were lucky to survive. Or maybe God had something to do with it. I usually don't believe in Him, but every now and then I make an exception."

Lucille cocked her head and squinted, studying him carefully. And then, unexpectedly, she held out her right hand. "It wasn't luck. And it wasn't God either. You did good, Swift. You have a talent for survival."

He hesitated for a moment, surprised. Then he shook her hand. "Thank you," he said.

Despite her obvious fatigue, her grip was like iron. "Just don't get the wrong idea. You got a long way to go before you make up for all the crap you've put me through." Grinning, she squeezed his knuckles for a few more seconds. Then she let go and waved the manila folder. She lowered her voice so the soldier down the hall wouldn't overhear. "My contact at Shin Bet identified Olam ben Z'man. His real name is Oscar Loebner. Formerly a computer science professor at Hebrew University. But the university job was just a cover. He did most of his work for Aman, the intelligence division of the Israel Defense Forces."

"So Rav Kavner was right." David winced as he thought of the rabbi. He remembered the gunshot that had killed the old man, and the fountain of blood that had spurted from his forehead. "He said Olam had connections in the IDF."

"He certainly did. In his younger days Loebner belonged to *Sayeret Matkal*, the army's elite commando force. But he was injured in the early eighties, so the intelligence division sent him to school to become a computer expert. The guy turned out to be a genius at writing software." Lucille lowered her voice still further and moved her head close to David's. He could smell her perfume, a cloying lavender scent. "My contact wouldn't tell me the whole story, but it sounds like Loebner worked for Israel's nuclear program. They used his software for testing their bombs."

David nodded. Through his work with Physicists for Peace, he'd learned a few facts about Israel's nuclear arsenal. "He must've worked on supercomputer simulations. Those programs can predict the nuclear blast you'd get from a specific warhead design. The software is crucial to the Israelis because they have no other way to test their nukes. The country won't even acknowledge that it has nuclear weapons, so they can't conduct any atomic tests in the desert. They have to rely entirely on the simulations."

"Well, they can't rely on Loebner anymore. He stopped working for the IDF four years ago. He had a nervous breakdown after his son died in Lebanon." She waved the manila folder again. "But Loebner had a lot of classified information in his head, so Shin Bet kept tabs on him. According to his file, he made some friends in the settlers movement, the nationalist Israelis who are stirring up trouble on the West Bank. Beit Shalom Yeshiva is part of that network."

"Yeah, he was living at the yeshiva until last Tuesday. But where is he now?"

"Shin Bet doesn't know. Loebner went to ground and they lost track of him. The agency is checking with its informants in the West Bank settlements, but so far no one's reported anything."

David grimaced. He thought again of Michael and felt a twinge of panic. Despite all their efforts, they still had no idea who'd kidnapped the boy. Finding Loebner had become their only hope. "Jesus, what are we gonna do? Maybe we should go to the West Bank. We can look for Loebner ourselves."

Lucille shook her head. "Hold on, I'm not finished. Shin Bet's a pretty good organization, but no one beats the Bureau for good ol' American ingenuity." With a smile, she opened the folder and removed a map of Israel. Across the country's midsection was a line of red dots, each labeled with a time and date. "One of my agents in Washington sent me this an hour ago. She ran a search on Olam ben Z'man through all our databases, even though I'd told her it was just a code name. She didn't find anything at first, but last night she tried a few alternative spellings and found a cell-phone account belonging to an Israeli named Olam Bensmann." Lucille handed the map to David. "The phone company provided the tracking information for the account. These are the last known GPS coordinates."

David looked closely at the line of red dots. The first location, labeled *JUNE 7, 21:05*, was in the Old City of Jerusalem, presumably Beit Shalom Yeshiva. The owner of the phone then traveled west, following Highway 1. The last dot was on the Mediterranean coast, about twenty kilometers south of Tel Aviv. It was labeled *JUNE 7, 22:55*. David put his finger on it. "This is three days old. Don't they have anything more recent?"

"No, Loebner must've turned the phone off. But this shows where he went last Tuesday night after leaving the yeshiva. He told the rabbi he was going to visit some old friends, right?"

"Yeah, friends from the army, he said."

"He was telling the truth." Lucille took the map and pointed at the last red dot. "This location is in the middle of an Israeli military base. It's the Soreq Nuclear Research Center."

David recognized the name. Israel had two nuclear-weapons labs, Dimona and Soreq. Dimona was where the Israelis produced the plutonium fuel for their bombs. Soreq was where the nukes were designed. "That's where Loebner must've done his work for the nuclear program. The supercomputer work, I mean."

Lucille put the map back in the folder. "I'd like to know what Loebner was doing there last Tuesday. I've already asked Shin Bet for permission to visit the base and talk to their security people. Shin Bet's been cooperating with the Bureau so far, so I think they'll let me in."

"We're coming with you." David stepped toward her. "I know some of the physicists who work at Soreq. And Monique is an expert on supercomputer simulations. She uses them all the time in her research."

Lucille stared at him for a moment, appraising. Then she nodded. "Yeah, I want both of you there. Right now I need as much help as I can get."

15

THEY CAME FOR MICHAEL AT NIGHTFALL. TWO SOLDIERS IN BROWN UNI-
forms stepped into the yurt and yanked him out of his chair. Grasping his
arms, they dragged him outside to a Toyota pickup parked on the sand.
The soldiers lifted Michael off his feet and heaved him into the truck
bed, which was loaded with ammunition boxes and a belt-fed machine
gun. Despite the fact that he was screaming and flailing, he recognized
the gun right away. It was a tripod-mounted M240, the U.S. Army's
standard-issue medium-caliber machine gun. He'd seen it before in one
of his computer games.

The soldiers climbed into the truck bed with Michael and held
him down, pinning his shoulders against the tailgate. Standing beside
the M240 was a third soldier, a big man wearing a khaki uniform and
a black beret. On the beret was a patch showing a white dagger. The
man bent over Michael, watching him scream and struggle. Then the
pickup's engine started and the man sat down on one of the ammunition
boxes. The truck lurched forward, jouncing along a dirt track that twisted
between the sand dunes.

The sun had set a few minutes before, and the desert was turning
gray and featureless. Michael stopped screaming and tried to get his
bearings. The brightest part of the sky was behind them, which meant
they were heading east. The soldier in the beret continued to stare at
him. Michael glanced at the man's face, just long enough to notice his
crooked nose and brown mustache. Then he focused on the dagger
patch. After a few seconds, the man took off his beret and held it up in
the air.

"You like it?" he asked. His voice was very deep. "It's an antique.

From my days in the service." He twirled the beret on his finger, then put it back on his head. "I was a sergeant major. Sergeant Major Lukas Carter, formerly of the U.S. Army. Now a humble soldier of the Lord."

The man raised his hand to his forehead and saluted. Michael looked again at the patch and saw a yellow triangle next to the dagger. This was something else he'd seen before in his computer games. It was the insignia of the Delta Force.

Lukas pointed at the beret on his head. "You know why I still wear it? The sin of pride. I was in Delta for sixteen years. Went on missions all over the world. Won every decoration you can think of." He moved closer to Michael, leaning forward on the ammunition box. "But do you think God cares about my decorations? You think He cares how many medals I won?"

Michael didn't answer. He didn't know what to say.

"No, the Lord has more important things to worry about. Especially now." Lukas leaned still closer. His breath smelled like onions. "Judgment Day's almost here. The Almighty's finally gonna clean up this filthy world. Gonna smash Satan's armies to smithereens. And He's called on me to do my part."

The onion smell was making Michael sick. He turned his head to the side and held his breath. But he wasn't afraid of Lukas. Once again Michael had the feeling that he was inside a computer game. It was disorienting and strange, but not frightening. He wanted to see what would happen next.

"I'll be honest with you, Michael. The last days are gonna be rough. That's why they call these times the Tribulation. But Brother Cyrus will see us through. The man's got a special connection to the Lord." Lukas pointed a blunt finger at Michael's face. "You do what Cyrus tells you, you hear? Then everything'll be all right. We'll be sitting by God's throne before you know it."

Lukas wagged his finger, almost touching Michael's cheek. Then he pulled away and sat up straight. Michael coughed out a breath, but kept his head turned to the side. From the corner of his eye, he saw Lukas leaning back on the ammunition box, propped on his elbows. He was looking up at the sky, where the first stars had just appeared.

They drove about a mile across the desert. Then Michael saw

something off to the right, a big black thing half buried in the sand. He squinted, trying to identify it in the gloom. It looked like the broken shell of an oil tank. Soon he began to see other pieces of debris: rusty beams jutting from the sand, sections of pipe strewn across the desert floor. And just beyond the debris he glimpsed a deep crater, about a hundred feet across. Its walls plunged straight down, as if the hole had been made with a giant drill. Michael shivered as he stared at it.

"Impressive, huh?" Lukas had to shout over the noise of the engine, which was louder now because the truck was climbing a sandy ridge. "It happened a long time ago, when Turkmenistan was still part of the Soviet Union. One of the biggest industrial accidents in Soviet history. And that's saying something, because those commies had a lot of accidents."

"What happened?" The words sounded strange in Michael's throat. This was the first time he'd spoken since coming outside.

"The wreckage came from a Soviet drilling rig. The Karakum Desert sits on a reservoir of natural gas, see? The Russkies wanted to tap it, but they didn't understand the local geology. When they drilled into the gas just below the surface, their rigs collapsed into the sand and formed sink-holes. And some of those sinkholes were deep enough that the methane began leaking from cracks at the bottom."

A cold wind buffeted the truck and Michael shivered again. He gazed straight ahead, looking past Lukas, and saw the dirt track curving up the steep slope of the ridge. The twilight glow had nearly dissipated from the western sky behind them, but now Michael saw another glow coming from the east, illuminating the top of the ridge they were climb-ing. It was like a curtain of light filling the eastern quarter of the sky, and it grew brighter as the pickup neared the crest. He shook his head. "Is that . . . ?"

Then they reached the top of the ridge and saw the burning crater.

It was at the bottom of the slope, a quarter mile away, but it was so bright that Michael's eyes stung when he looked at it. More than twice as big as the crater they'd just passed, it was a perfect circle almost a hun-dred yards wide, and flames rose from every square foot. Gaping holes at the bottom of the crater spewed billows of burning methane. They shot fifty feet into the air like great trees of fire, roiling at the top in furi-ous eddies and surges. Smaller flames stippled the crater's rocky floor, some flickering like pilot lights, others swirling together in the updrafts. Flames even rose from the crater's steep walls, roaring up the cliffs. The fires leaped above the crater's rim and cast a yellowish sheen on the surrounding desert.

As the pickup descended the slope and approached the rim, Michael felt a gust of hot air on his face. He'd never seen so much fire before. The feeling that he was inside a computer game grew stronger. The crater was so big and bright and colorful. He turned back to Lukas. "How did it catch fire?" he asked.

Lukas shrugged. "Who knows? Could've happened when the rig collapsed. Or maybe someone threw in a match afterward, to burn the methane so it wouldn't poison the air. Either way, the fire's been going for at least thirty years. And there's enough natural gas under the desert to keep it going for centuries."

The pickup slowed as it reached the bottom of the slope and then ground to a halt about a hundred feet from the rim. The light from the fires was so blinding here that Michael didn't see the other vehicles at first. But as the pickup's engine shut off he noticed two more trucks and three Land Cruisers parked nearby. A long line of soldiers stood close to the rim, their helmets and rifle barrels silhouetted against the flames.

Lukas shouted at the soldiers, and several ran toward the pickup. The men in the truck lowered the tailgate, and Michael tumbled into the arms of the other soldiers. One man grasped his armpits and another gripped his legs. Then they carried him toward the crater.

His heart beat faster as they left the vehicles behind and moved toward the silhouettes near the rim. The air was hotter here and it pressed against his face, prickling his cheeks and pushing into his mouth. Soon they were just a dozen feet from the crater's edge. Michael could look down into the bowl and see the flames rising from every crack and rock pile. They were close, too close! The game was scaring him now and he wished he could end it, but the only thing he could do was scream.

Then he saw Tamara. She stood about six feet from the edge. The soldiers carrying Michael dropped him at her feet, and she crouched beside him. She clutched his right arm above the elbow and made a shushing noise in his ear. "It's all right, Michael, it's all right. I'm here now, see?"

He screamed louder and kicked away from her. But Tamara held on to his arm. "No, don't do that!" she yelled. "We're near the edge and it could crumble! Then we'd both fall into the crater and die!"

He looked past her, staring at the edge. It was sandy and jagged. Shadows jumped in its crevices as the flames rose and fell in the crater. He saw that Tamara was telling the truth, so he stopped kicking.

"Come on, Michael, stand up. You're getting all dirty on the ground."

She rose to her feet and pulled him up. At the same time, another soldier appeared at his left. It was Angel, the man with the curved scar on his neck, but now he seemed larger than Michael remembered because he was in full combat gear. He wore a flak jacket that bulged with half a dozen pouches for bullets and binoculars and fragmentation grenades. He grasped Michael's left arm without looking at him. His grip was tighter than Tamara's.

They turned him around until he faced away from the crater. Michael noticed that the other soldiers were backing up, moving farther from the crater's edge. He felt a stab of hope—they were leaving now! And Michael could get away from this crater and go back to the camp! But then he realized that the soldiers were simply stepping aside to make room for someone else, a man emerging from the darkness. It took Michael a few seconds to recognize the man because his black clothes blended in with the sky behind him. The only color was in his eyes, which showed clearly through the slit in his head scarf. Each of his pupils reflected the crater's yellow glow.

Brother Cyrus stopped a few feet in front of them. "Hello, Michael," he said in his muffled voice. "Do you know where we are?"

Michael didn't say anything. Now that he wasn't facing the crater, he was less afraid. He stared at the folds of Cyrus's head scarf, wishing that he could tear it off the man's head.

Cyrus pointed one of his gloved hands at the crater. "That's the Burning Gas Crater of Darvaza. The Turkmen people call it the Door to Hell. A dramatic name, don't you think?"

Again, Michael didn't answer. None of the soldiers spoke either. The only sound was the roar of the fires inside the crater.

"Unfortunately, the name isn't accurate. Hell isn't below us." Cyrus shook his masked head. Then he extended both hands and swept them in a circle. "Hell is right here. It's all around us. Our world is a slaughter-house, a foul sty of sin and death. But the Lord has promised to deliver us from this hell and lead us into the Kingdom of Heaven."

Tamara and Angel shouted, "Yes, Brother!" The other soldiers said nothing. Michael realized they were standing too far back to hear Cyrus above the noise of the gas fires.

Cyrus folded his arms across his chest. "Michael, I want to talk to you about God. I'll put it in scientific terms so it'll be easier for you to understand." He reached into his pocket and pulled out a small black book. "In scientific terms, God is the organizing principle. He's the theorem, the program, the alpha and omega. His will was made flesh in the flames of Creation, spawning stars and planets and all living things, and He speaks to us from within our minds, because our thoughts are simply manifestations of His love. And although His universe is now corrupted to its core, the beauty of God's design is that the flaws can be corrected."

Tamara and Angel shouted "Yes, Brother!" again, but Cyrus kept his eyes trained on Michael.

"God made His promise to us two thousand years ago," he said. "He promised to redeem the world at the End of Days, and to resurrect the dead from their long sleep so they could live forever in the Kingdom of Heaven. It's all written right here, for anyone to see." He waved his black book in the air. "But the sinful world forgot God's promise. Priests and ministers constructed their own idea of heaven, the place in the clouds, the so-called afterlife. They preached that a person's soul could fly to this heaven as soon as the person died, which is a doctrine that not only contradicts God's word but defies logic as well. They claim that their heaven can't be seen from earth because it exists on some mystical plane of reality. But the real reason is simpler. Their heaven is imaginary."

Brother Cyrus moved a step closer. Michael felt his courage failing.

"But God's promise isn't imaginary," Cyrus said, tapping the cover of his book. "And the True Believers haven't forgotten it. They know that the Kingdom of Heaven will be a real place, as real as the ground we're standing on, and that the Lord has called on us to hasten its coming. He's given us all the tools we need, the tools of science and mathematics, and now we don't have to wait anymore. We can cast away the sinful world and make way for God's eternal reign." He took another step toward Michael and spread his arms. "Don't be afraid, my child. Yes, we will die, but we will be born again in God's kingdom. All the clocks will stop running and time will stand still. The whole past of our universe will be compressed into one moment, and the Lord will embrace us all forever."

He took one more step forward, but Michael screamed before the man could touch him. Cyrus stood there for several seconds, his arms spread wide. Then he looked at the crater again, peering over Michael's shoulder. The yellow fires flashed in his eyes. "You must serve the Lord now, Michael. You must tell us the code. We need to know the entire program so we can unsheathe Excalibur, God's holy sword. Tamara has told me that you've refused to cooperate, so I've arranged a demonstration. I will show you what happens to those who try to stop the Almighty from fulfilling His promise."

Then he turned around to face his men and shouted, "Bring him forward!"

Michael saw some movement in the darkness beyond the crater, and after a few seconds three figures emerged from the shadows. Two of Cyrus's soldiers escorted a tall, sturdy man whose hands were tied behind his back and whose head was covered with a black hood. The soldiers held their prisoner by his elbows and he stumbled across the sand, dragging his left foot. At one point he fell to his knees and Michael saw bloody bandages on both his hands. He wore a U.S. Army uniform and as he got closer Michael saw a patch on his left shoulder saying 75-RANGER-RGT. The name tag on his chest said RAMSEY.

The soldiers stopped beside Cyrus, who placed his right hand on top of the prisoner's hood and muttered a few words that Michael didn't understand. Then Cyrus pointed at the crater again and shouted, "Go!"

Tamara and Angel turned Michael around so he could watch the soldiers drag the prisoner to the crater's edge. The man thrashed his legs and jackknifed his body, but the soldiers lifted him off the ground, raising him so high that his feet pedaled the air. For a moment Michael thought they were lifting the prisoner to give him a better view of the fires. But this couldn't be right—because of the hood, the man couldn't see a thing. Then the soldiers threw the prisoner into the crater.

Michael could still see the fires, but he couldn't see the man. It was as if the computer game had suffered a program error that froze the screen and erased all the data. He heard a noise, though, above the roar of the flames, a long tumbling wail. Then he saw a man-size cylinder of fire come to rest amid the smaller flames on the crater's floor.

"Forgive us, Lord!" Cyrus shouted. "We are coming! We will be with You soon!"

Michael wanted to cover his ears, but he couldn't—Tamara and Angel were still gripping his arms. They pulled him toward Brother Cyrus, who placed his right hand on Michael's forehead. In his left hand was a small silver device that looked a bit like an iPod. Cyrus flicked a switch on the device and held it under Michael's chin.

"Tell us the code," he said. He leaned so close that Michael could see the black threads in his head scarf. "Just speak into the recorder. I know you can see the program in your mind. The Lord has revealed the key to you, and now you must pass it on."

It was true, Michael could see the program. He didn't even have to close his eyes to see it. The lines of software code flashed within his field of vision, scrolling upward. They ascended between Michael's face and Brother Cyrus's, the quantum variables and operators gleaming brilliantly against the black scarf. But Cyrus couldn't see them. Only Michael could. It was his secret, his treasure.

"Everything has a purpose, Michael. The code will tell us how to wield Excalibur, how to aim God's sword at the weakest part of this broken world. And then, with one stroke, we will put an end to it, and the Kingdom of Heaven will take its place. Just as God promised."

Michael shook his head. He didn't care about heaven. He'd made his own promise, his promise to David Swift. And he was going to keep it.

Cyrus said nothing at first. He held his recorder under Michael's chin and waited. Then he lowered his hand and stepped backward. "All right, I'm not going to waste any more time." He turned to Tamara. "Throw him in."

She tightened her grip on Michael's right arm. "What?"

"You heard me, Sister. Throw the boy in the crater."

She made a mewling noise, like the sound a dog makes when it's hurt. Her fingers dug into Michael's biceps. "Brother, give him some more time. He'll tell us if we—"

"No! No more time!" Cyrus's voice was achingly loud. "I won't tolerate the boy's insolence any longer. His stubbornness is an affront to God."

"But how are we going to—"

"We'll find another way to make the adjustments to Excalibur. Now stop arguing and do as I say."

Michael didn't fully realize what was happening until he felt Angel yank his left arm. It was so sudden that he lost his balance. Angel was pulling him toward the crater's edge. But Tamara held on to his right arm and pulled the other way. "No, Brother!" she screamed. "Don't do this!"

Michael screamed, too. Pain flared in his shoulder sockets and ripped across his chest. He heard shouts and rapid footsteps, but the pain was so intense that everything blurred together and he had to close his eyes on the sickening whirl around him. Then he felt the grip on his right arm loosen. When he opened his eyes he saw two soldiers grappling with Tamara. One of them slammed his fist into her face while the other punched her in the stomach. She doubled over and the soldiers wrenched her arms behind her back. Her head lolled to the side as they pulled her away. Blood poured from her nostrils and coated her lips.

Then another soldier grabbed Michael's right arm. He looked almost identical to Angel and wore the same type of flak jacket, its pouches bulging with bullet clips and grenades, except that the name tag on his jacket said JORDAN. This soldier stood exactly where Tamara had been a few seconds before. Without saying a word he turned to the crater. Then he and Angel marched forward in lockstep, dragging Michael toward the edge.

Michael thrashed his legs and jackknifed his body, just like the hooded man had done, but Angel and Jordan were too strong. They pulled him forward until he stood on the crater's rim, looking straight down at the flames below. Terrified, he dug his heels into the ground, frantically trying to back away from the brink. The sandy ledge under his feet suddenly crumbled. He began to fall, his legs sliding with the sand into the crater.

Then, above the sound of his own screams, he heard Cyrus yell, "Stop!" Angel and Jordan, who still held his arms, yanked him out of the crater and threw him backward. He flew through the air and landed in the sand several feet from the crater's edge. His head rang and his heart pounded. He was still screaming, but he noticed that the screams coming out of his mouth weren't just noise anymore. They were words and numbers. He was screaming the code.

"Mixer equals Hadamard . . . qureg phase . . . qureg eigen . . . mixer phase for i equals zero . . . controlled multiply phase and eigen . . . return phase measure."

He lay there on his back for a long time, reciting the program. He wasn't hurt, but he felt nauseous and weak. Cyrus bent over him, holding his recorder above Michael's mouth to catch the flood of code. Angel and Jordan stood behind him, their faces lit by the gas fires. And way, way in the background, Michael thought he heard Tamara crying.

He finally reached the end of the program. Cyrus stood up straight and turned off his recorder. "All right, let's get back to the camp," he said. "We need to input the code and see if we have the whole thing."

Cyrus stepped away from the crater, heading back to where the pickups and Land Cruisers were parked. Angel and Jordan saluted him as he passed. Then Angel bent over Michael and offered his hand. "Come. We're leaving now."

With one more scream, Michael scrambled to his feet and flung himself at Angel, slamming into the soldier's chest and grabbing the pouches of his flak jacket. Before the man could react, Michael head-butted him, smashing his forehead into Angel's nose. Angel fell backward, stunned, and Michael landed on top of him. Then he rolled away from the soldier and curled into a ball, folding his arms across his chest and pressing his forehead to his knees.

He heard more shouts and footsteps. Other soldiers grabbed him and picked him up. But Michael kept himself curled in a tight ball as they carried him back to the pickup. He didn't relax until they'd dumped him into the truck bed. Once he was sure that the soldiers weren't watching, he moved his hands down to his navel, stretched the waistband of his pants, and slipped in the small sphere he'd removed from Angel's flak jacket. It was an M67 fragmentation grenade.

16

DAVID SAT IN THE BACKSEAT OF AN ARMORED LIMOUSINE, GAZING AT THE verdant Israeli countryside. The car belonged to Shin Bet and the driver was none other than Aryeh Goldberg, Shin Bet's telecommunications expert. He'd been assigned to help the FBI follow the cell-phone trail of Oscar Loebner, aka Olam ben Z'man. Lucille sat next to Aryeh in the front of the car, while Monique—who was feeling much better after a day and a half of rest—sat in the back with David. It was two o'clock in the afternoon and they were headed for the Soreq Nuclear Research Center, and David hoped to Christ that they would make some progress before the end of the day. He felt a panicky ache in his chest, which got worse whenever he thought of Michael.

Aryeh had tuned the limo's radio to a Tel Aviv station that played bouncy Israeli pop songs. He chatted with Lucille as he drove down Highway 1, discussing how they would handle the interview with Soreq's security chief. David glanced at Monique, but he couldn't catch her eye—she was looking out the window at the Judean Hills. She hadn't said a word since getting into the car. Lost in thought, she absentmindedly rubbed her injured arm, running her left hand over the right sleeve of her jacket to feel the bandages underneath. The light streaming through the car window illuminated half her face—one brown ear, one swooping eyebrow, one darting eye. David knew his wife well enough to recognize what was happening. She had an idea, and she was thinking it through.

After a while the highway straightened and leveled out. They left the Judean Hills behind and drove across the coastal plain. There were bright green fields on both sides of the road, some planted with crops and others strewn with wildflowers. A Hebrew version of a Michael Jackson song came on the radio and Aryeh started humming along. Then the car hit a pothole and they all bounced in their seats and Monique let out a grunt. David looked at her again. "You okay?"

She nodded blankly. Her eyes were still darting, sliding back and forth but not focusing on anything. Then she closed them and let out a long whoosh of breath. When she opened her eyes a few seconds later, they fixed on David. "I know what Olam was talking about."

"What? What do you . . . ?"

"Remember what Rav Kavner said at the yeshiva? About all the crazy Kabbalistic crap that Olam was spouting? And the idea he was so obsessed with?"

"You mean about the *Sephirot*? And *meyda*?"

"Yeah, all that bullshit. I couldn't figure it out when we were at the yeshiva, and then I forgot all about it when those assassins started shooting at us. But now I know what he meant. Olam was talking about digital physics." She moved closer to David, leaning across the limo's backseat. "In his former life as Oscar Loebner, he was a computer scientist, right? But he knew a lot of physics, too, because his specialty was developing simulations of nuclear explosions. So it's just natural that he would combine the two and—"

"Whoa, slow down!" David held up his hands. Although he was a historian of science, he didn't know as much about recent advances as Monique did. "What's digital physics?"

"Jesus, David, you gotta do a better job of keeping up. Digital physics has been hot ever since the nineties, when John Archibald Wheeler wrote his papers on it. You know about Wheeler, right?"

David nodded. "Of course. He's the guy who coined the term 'black hole.' He died just a few years ago."

"He was a professor emeritus in Princeton's department when I was teaching there. Wheeler was a great physicist, a visionary. And in the last years of his life he started going in a new direction. Some of the people in the physics department thought he was getting a little loony in his old age, but I respected him for it. He was trying to solve one of the biggest mysteries of science—why the universe is comprehensible. Why it follows orderly, mathematical laws that we can discover and understand, like Einstein's field equations or the laws of quantum theory."

He nodded again. This was starting to sound familiar. The mathematical nature of the universe was a prime topic for historians and philosophers of science. "What did Wheeler's papers say?"

"He argued that the traditional picture of the universe was outdated. Most people still think of elementary particles as tiny billiard balls, rolling around on the table of spacetime, but Wheeler knew this view was ridiculous. An elementary particle has no physical substance. It's just a collection of quantum values—energy, charge, spin, and so on—so it's more logical to think of it as a packet of information. And spacetime itself is information, too, a giant array of values specifying the curvature of the dimensions. Wheeler called this hypothesis 'It From Bit.' All physical things arise from information."

"Wait a second. I've heard of It From Bit." David searched his memory. "It's an update of an older idea, right? The theory of the computational universe?"

"Yeah, it's the same thing, more or less. When two particles collide, they exchange information. They go into the collision with one set of values—the input—and come out with another, the output. So the interactions between the particles are like the mathematical operations that take place in a computer chip. And the programs that coordinate the particle interactions are simply the laws of physics, the unified theory. You can think of the whole universe as a big computer that's been running for the past fourteen billion years. That would explain why the universe follows mathematical laws. The world is inherently mathematical because its particles are always calculating."

David gave her a skeptical look. He knew that a few physicists and computer scientists had been toying with the idea of the computational universe ever since the 1960s. But most researchers dismissed the concept, which was why David had never paid much attention to it. "It's kind of an oddball idea, though, isn't it? More of a metaphor than a real theory, don't you think? Sure, the universe may function *like* a computer, but that doesn't mean I'm really just a collection of data."

"Why not? Most of what we observe is an illusion. Objects feel solid even though their atoms are mostly empty space. Gravitational force is actually a bending of spacetime. So why can't we be composed of information?"

"So you're saying that we're all living inside someone's PC? Like in the *Matrix* movies?"

Monique shook her head. "David, please. In those movies, the people's minds are plugged into a simulation that's running on some freaky computer that took over the world. But if It From Bit is right, the whole damn universe is a kind of natural computer. You can't leave the program, because that's all there is."

David was a little surprised at how impassioned Monique was getting. He'd always considered her a fairly conservative scientist, reluctant to accept any hypothesis until there was solid evidence supporting it. The fact that she was so enthusiastic about It From Bit gave him pause. Maybe, he thought, it wasn't such a wacky idea after all. "But if the universe is a computer, who programmed it? God? You think He created the world by writing some software?"

"Well, that's obviously what Olam believed. He thought the *Sephirot* were God's programs, remember? But the It From Bit hypothesis doesn't require the existence of a divine being. The program could've evolved on its own. It could've started with a single piece of information, the primordial bit arising spontaneously from the quantum vacuum. Then the calculations proliferated, churning out scads of random data. Eventually, strings of instructions emerged from the data and became the laws of physics, the universal program that organized all the computations. This program generated the Big Bang, the expanding fireball of particles and radiation. Then more complex algorithms emerged, creating galaxies and life and consciousness."

"But what's the purpose of this computer? What's it calculating?"

"It's calculating us. The computer is all around us and we're its results. The program guided the formation of our solar system and the evolution of our species. Our brains are smaller computers that arose from the larger one. Or you can think of them as subprograms running on top of the universe's operating system, just like PowerPoint and Explorer run on top of Windows on your PC. Except the universe isn't as buggy as Windows, thank God." Monique smiled. "And there's another difference from an ordinary PC: the universe is a quantum computer. It's the particles that do the calculating, like in the quantum computers that Jacob Steele built. In essence, he was hacking into the universal computer."

She was out of breath by the time she finished. Still smiling, she reclined against the plush fabric of the backseat and waited for David to respond. He stared at her for a few seconds in silent admiration. Monique could be pretty damn persuasive. "Okay," he said, "but what about the Caduceus Array? What's the connection between that and It From Bit?"

"The purpose of the Caduceus Array was to *prove* the hypothesis, to show that it's more than just a metaphor. Oscar Loebner the computer scientist figured out a way to confirm Olam ben Z'man's crazy theory."

"But how could the Caduceus Array do that? It's just a couple of clocks linked together, right?"

"Loebner's strategy was to focus on the flow of time. Time is one of the most mysterious concepts in physics. Theorists have been speculating for decades about why time exists and why it moves in just one direction. But time's role becomes clear if you think of the universe as a computer. A computer program organizes its calculations in a step-by-step sequence, so every computer has a clock. With each tick of the clock, the calculations move another step forward—at the first tick, for instance, the program adds two numbers together, then at the second tick it multiplies the sum by a third number, and so on. A one-megahertz computer has a clock that ticks a million times per second, and a one-gigahertz computer—"

"Yes, yes, I know," David said. "Its clock ticks a billion times a second."

"Which makes it more powerful, because it can run more calculations in the same amount of time. But the clock of the universe would work a little differently, because time itself is determined by the universal program. And because the program is constantly adjusting its own run time, it would leave a telltale clue in the physical world: the flow of time would fluctuate ever so slightly from place to place. These variations wouldn't be easy to detect—you'd need a pair of very precise clocks located thousands of kilometers apart. But the discovery would prove the existence of the universal program and show that It From Bit is literally true."

"So you think that's why Jacob Steele got involved? He heard about Loebner's idea and thought he could share the Nobel Prize by building the Caduceus Array?"

"Yeah, it makes sense. Jacob would've had no trouble designing the clocks, because they used the same trapped-ion technology as his quantum computers. And he could pay for it with the money he diverted from his DARPA grant."

"And what about the disruptions they detected on the morning of the Iranian nuclear test? Have you got any ideas about what might've caused those?"

She didn't respond at first. The limo's backseat became quiet, and David heard another song on the Israeli radio station. Then Monique took a deep breath and shook her head. The passionate determination that had animated her face ever since she'd started talking now seemed to dissipate. She turned back to the car window. "No, I haven't figured out that part yet. All I know so far is that the disruptions were a surprise. But what caused them . . ." Her voice trailed off.

David looked out the other window. Panic tightened his chest again. Michael had been gone for three days now. They didn't know who his kidnappers were or why they'd taken him. The only clues came from a mentally unstable Israeli scientist who'd apparently tried to prove that the universe was a computer. And they couldn't find him either.

Pressing his forehead to the car window, David closed his eyes. Then he felt Monique's hand on his shoulder. It slid down his arm, slowly and gently. When it reached his hand he clasped it, lacing his fingers between hers. Neither said a word.

Five minutes later, the limo exited the highway and headed west on a two-lane road. Aryeh stopped humming and turned off the car radio. "Almost there," he said. "That's the gate for Palmachim Air Base."

David looked ahead and saw a landscape of sandy hillocks, dotted with thornbushes and olive trees. Running across this scrubland was a high barbed-wire fence. Beyond the fence David caught a glimpse of the Mediterranean, less than a mile away.

Aryeh drove the Shin Bet limo to a guardhouse manned by soldiers in Israeli Air Force uniforms. He spoke a few words in Hebrew to the commander, who checked Aryeh's ID and waved them through the gate. The road continued toward the sea, passing several asphalt landing zones half hidden among the dunes.

Lucille peered through the windshield, then turned to Aryeh. "This is a helicopter base, right?" she asked.

"Correct," he replied. "We station Black Hawks and Cobras here. And this is where we launch our missiles and satellites. Our country may be small, but it's full of clever people, yes? Many scientists besides Oscar Loebner have worked in this place."

"Well, let's hope Oscar talked to one of them when he came here last Tuesday. We need a lead on this guy."

As they neared the base's runway, Aryeh made a right turn and headed for a cluster of low buildings. In the middle of the complex was a structure with an oddly shaped dome. It looked like a white teacup that had been turned upside down on its saucer. David recognized the building from the work he'd done for Physicists for Peace, which had compiled a catalog of the world's nuclear facilities. It was a five-megawatt reactor, the centerpiece of the Soreq Nuclear Research Center.

Aryeh parked the car in a lot about a hundred yards from the reactor. Then he stepped outside and led them to the lab's administration building. The office of Rahm Elon, Soreq's security chief, was on the first floor.

David got a little worried when he walked into the office—Rahm was a fierce-looking soldier, tall, olive-skinned, and impressively muscled. He wore sunglasses and an air-force uniform, and he carried an oversize Desert Eagle pistol in his belt holster. Standing behind his desk, Rahm shook hands with Aryeh. Both men smiled and exchanged a few pleasantries in Hebrew. But Rahm stopped smiling when Aryeh introduced him to Lucille, David, and Monique. He clearly wasn't comfortable with the presence of the Americans on his base.

They took seats in front of Rahm's desk. Aryeh leaned back in his chair. "So we're wondering if you've made any progress," he said, switching to English. "My G-man friends are eager to find Mr. Loebner. Or Olam ben Z'man, as he now prefers to call himself."

Rahm nodded, but his expression remained cold. "We've confirmed that Loebner was on the base Tuesday night," he said. Then he closed his mouth and stared straight ahead.

Aryeh waited a few seconds, unperturbed. "Ah, that's good," he finally said. "Because Shin Bet is curious, too. They'd like to know how Loebner waltzed through the gate of an IDF installation, considering that his security credentials were revoked four years ago."

"And why is Shin Bet so curious?" Rahm asked. "This is military security, not a police matter."

"You know how it is." Aryeh shrugged. "Some big shot in the Justice Ministry gets interested and starts shouting orders at his deputies. Typical government bullshit, eh?"

"You're right, it's bullshit. You and your American friends have no business being here."

Aryeh smiled again and held out his hands in a placating gesture. "Look, Rahm, we don't want to cause you any trouble. We just want Loebner. We can't let him run around like a madman. He has too many nasty secrets in his head. So maybe you can tell us what he was doing at Soreq, yes? And maybe, please God, where he went afterward?"

Rahm said nothing at first. He just sat behind his desk, glaring at them, demonstrating his displeasure. Then he reached into one of the drawers and pulled out a folder. "Loebner didn't waltz through the gate. He cut through the fence." He handed the folder to Aryeh. "We believe he infiltrated the base at approximately ten o'clock on Tuesday evening. Unfortunately, we didn't discover the breach until midnight."

Aryeh opened the folder and leafed through it. "That's a bit slow, eh? Don't you have intrusion detectors on the perimeter?"

"We have motion sensors, infrared cameras, and closed-circuit video. But Loebner disabled the equipment in Sector 34. It's all in the report."

Lucille, who sat in the chair next to Aryeh's, craned her neck to see the folder. Then she turned to Rahm. "I guess Loebner remembered his training, huh? From *Sayeret Matkal*?"

Rahm kept his eyes on Aryeh, refusing to look at Agent Parker. "*Matkal* is our Special Forces unit assigned to counterterrorism. They're very good at infiltration."

"How do you know it was Loebner who cut through the fence if all your cameras were down?"

"Only the cameras in Sector 34 were disabled. Once Loebner was on the base, he appeared on other surveillance videos. He wore his old IDF uniform, so he didn't look suspicious to the security personnel who were monitoring the video feeds. But after we detected the perimeter breach, we reviewed the tapes and identified Loebner." Rahm reached into his desk drawer again and pulled out a computer disk. "This holds the video taken by our cameras in Building 203. That's Soreq's supply warehouse. The camera at the front door shows Loebner entering the building at ten-seventeen P.M. on Tuesday. A minute later, the camera in the basement shows him walking toward the Long-Term Storage Room and punching in the room's access code on the security panel. At ten fifty-two the cameras show Loebner coming out of the room and exiting the building. Then he left the base, presumably through the same breach in the fence."

He handed the disk to Aryeh. Lucille stared at the thing, craning her neck again. "What's in the Long-Term Storage Room?" she asked.

Rahm still wouldn't look at her. "Miscellaneous items. From projects that have been discontinued and declassified. Our classified material is stored at a more secure location in Building 101. Most of the items in the Long-Term Storage Room are at least twenty years old."

"What about Loebner's research?" David interjected. "Does the room contain any materials related to his work on warhead designs?"

Very slowly, Rahm turned his head and fixed his eyes on David. Mentioning the word "warhead" had been a mistake. The expression on Rahm's face shifted from cold to murderous. "I can't comment on Loebner's research. But I'll repeat what I said before: classified material is stored at a different location. We wouldn't keep it in the Long-Term Storage Room."

"Well, is there anything missing from the room?" Monique asked. "Have you done an inventory yet?"

"Nothing's missing," Rahm replied. "But there's been some damage."

"What kind of damage?"

With a grunt, the security chief rose to his feet. "No more questions. I'll take you to the storage room and show you. And then I very much hope that we'll be finished with this business."

NICODEMUS CROUCHED IN THE BUSHES OUTSIDE THE FENCE, ADJUSTING HIS binoculars to sharpen the focus on Soreq's administration building. He'd known in advance where the meeting would take place. Thanks to Brother Cyrus's informants in Shin Bet and the FBI, Nico had also learned Olam ben Z'man's real name. Cyrus had devised a new plan for eliminating the Jew, and Nico's job now was to shadow the Americans. He wasn't very happy with this assignment; it was infuriating to do nothing but observe these *kilab* when every cell in his body was crying out for vengeance. But Cyrus had counseled him to be patient and Nico had obeyed. They were doing the Lord's work and their reward would be in heaven.

The Americans and the Shin Bet agent came out of the administration building about fifteen minutes after they'd gone inside. Soreq's security chief, another filthy *kelb*, led them across the parking lot toward a boxy gray structure that looked like a warehouse. David Swift and Monique Reynolds walked beside the FBI agent, a fat hag with silver hair. Nico clamped his lips together as he stared through the binoculars, feeling an excruciating mix of anger and anticipation. It won't be long now, he whispered at his targets. The True Believers will pay you a visit very soon.

17

THEY SPOTTED THE DAMAGE AS SOON AS RAHM ESCORTED THEM INTO THE Long-Term Storage Room. It was a huge, well-lit, windowless space, filled with dozens of wooden crates arranged in neat rows. The crates were quite large, each big enough to hold a sofa, and they'd been stenciled with red Hebrew letters. The room's walls were an unblemished white and the linoleum floor was immaculately clean. The place was so orderly, in fact, that David was a little startled when he saw the mangled aluminum object on the floor. It lay in an aisle between two of the rows, just in front of an opened crate. The area was marked off with yellow crime-scene tape, as if the wreckage were a corpse.

He and Monique moved closer, stepping in front of Aryeh and Lucille. They reached the strip of tape that stretched across the aisle and leaned over it so they could get a better look at the object. It was a big silver cylinder, about three feet in diameter and ten feet long. Oscar Loebner had apparently wrenched open its crate, pulled the thing out, and pummeled it with a hammer. The pounding blows had crumpled the cylinder and punched a gaping hole in its midsection. Through this gap David glimpsed smaller pieces of metallic debris: shattered struts and brackets, broken rods with jagged ends. Judging from its shape, he guessed that the object might be a missile casing. Aryeh had mentioned that the IDF launched missiles and satellites from Palmachim Air Base. Perhaps this broken cylinder had once been part of an experimental rocket. Maybe one that had been designed to carry a warhead.

It looked like Lucille was thinking the same thing. After inspecting the wreckage for several seconds, she stepped back from the crime-scene tape. Aryeh also backed away from the cylinder. "Tell me something,

Rahm," he said, turning to the security chief. "There's nothing radioactive in that mess, is there?"

Rahm frowned. "I already told you, we don't store any sensitive material here. Most of the items in this room are one step away from junk. Old and declassified and good for nothing." He pointed at the Hebrew letters on the opened crate that had held the cylinder. "That shows the date when the crate was sealed—August fifth, 1989. Almost twenty-two years ago."

"Well, what is it?" Monique asked, pointing at the wreckage. "If it's declassified, you can tell us, right?"

Rahm reached into his pocket and pulled out a small notebook. He was still frowning, but now his expression seemed more perplexed than annoyed. "This item is so old, we had trouble identifying it. It came from a project called *Cherev*. That's the Hebrew word for 'sword.'" He opened his notebook and started reading from one of the pages. "The project ran from 1984 to 1989. Researchers from Soreq's Laser Science Laboratory and Satellite Development Group were involved."

"Was Oscar Loebner working on the project, too?" David asked.

Rahm shook his head. "No, he worked in the Supercomputer Laboratory during those years. But researchers from the various labs at Soreq often meet at seminars and social events, so there's a good chance that Loebner knew about *Cherev*."

Monique continued to stare at the cylinder. "So is this thing a laser?" she asked. "Or a satellite?"

"It's both." Rahm turned to another page in his notebook. "It's a laser that was supposed to be launched into orbit. But it never left the ground, obviously. The project was canceled in 1989, and the item has been sitting here ever since."

"What was it supposed to do in orbit?"

"Unfortunately, our records don't provide a complete description. Some of the documents were lost when Soreq digitized its archives in the nineties. We've tried getting in touch with the scientists who were in charge of *Cherev*, but two are dead now and the third has Alzheimer's."

Shit, David thought. Not another dead end. "Were there any younger people working on the project? Maybe research assistants?"

"We're trying to locate them. And we've requested information from the American researchers who know about *Cherev*."

This got Lucille's attention. She stepped toward Rahm, narrowing her eyes. "American researchers?"

"Yes, at the Lawrence Livermore National Laboratory in California. This was a joint project between Livermore and Soreq. The laboratories shared their results."

Lucille grimaced, evidently irked that Rahm hadn't mentioned this earlier. Livermore was one of the main nuclear-weapons labs in the United States. "Who are the American scientists?" she asked. "The Bureau can help you get in touch with them."

"I have a list of the researchers involved." Rahm flipped through his notebook until he found the page he wanted. "Yes, here it is. Livermore's code name for the project was Excalibur. Which is also the name of a sword, correct?"

David felt a burst of hope. He'd heard of Excalibur. "Wait a second. Was this part of the Star Wars program? You know, Ronald Reagan's missile-defense plan?"

Rahm shrugged. "The records don't say. But it's a good guess. The Americans and Israelis cooperated on missile-defense research during the eighties. For obvious reasons, Israel is very interested in the technology."

David looked again at the wreckage on the floor, gazing in particular at the broken rods inside the cylinder. Yes, he recognized it now. He'd seen sketches of the device in books and articles. It was a relic of the cold war, forgotten by the general public but familiar to historians. He turned to Lucille. "I know about Excalibur," he said. "It's a special kind of laser, one that can shoot beams of X-rays. It was Dr. Strangelove's last invention."

Lucille raised an eyebrow. "Dr. Strangelove?"

"Edward Teller, I mean. The father of the H-bomb. Officially, he was retired by the 1980s, but he was still running the Livermore lab. He's the guy who dreamed up Star Wars and convinced President Reagan that it could work."

"Whoa, slow down," Lucille said. "I've heard of Star Wars. But what the hell was Excalibur?"

"Excalibur was the showpiece for the whole program. Teller's idea was to combine his X-ray laser with a nuclear warhead and launch the package into orbit. In the event of a missile attack from the Soviet Union, the U.S. Air Force would send a signal to detonate the warhead in space. Excalibur would channel the bomb's energy into laser beams that would shoot down the Soviet missiles while they were arcing above the atmosphere."

Monique gripped his elbow. She was nodding vigorously. "I've heard of this, too. The device had laser rods that could absorb the X-ray radiation from the nuclear blast, right? And each rod could be pointed at a different target, so the laser beams could shoot down a whole wave of missiles at once?"

"Yeah, it was a crazy strategy, insanely ambitious. The government spent hundreds of millions on it." David leaned over the crime-scene tape and pointed at the debris inside the cylinder. "You see those jagged bits? Those are pieces of the laser rods. Each rod was about a meter long and made up of hundreds of metallic strands, all bundled together like the wires in a cable." He shifted his hand and pointed at the broken struts. "That's where the warhead would go. Just before launch, the nuke would be placed inside the cylinder, next to the laser rods. In the event of a detonation, the atoms in the metallic strands would absorb the radiation from the blast and release it in a laser beam that would travel down the length of the rod. The nuclear explosion would destroy the whole assembly, of course, but the laser beams would shoot from the ends of the rods just before the device vaporized. And because the beams would have a frequency in the X-ray range, they'd deliver much more energy than an ordinary laser, enough to bring down a Soviet missile."

Monique let out a whistle. She stared at the cylinder for a few more seconds, then turned back to David. "It might've been a crazy strategy," she said. "But as a piece of technology, it's pretty amazing."

"It was groundbreaking," he conceded. "The Livermore researchers were trying to do something that had never been attempted. And they had some success in the initial tests. They built prototypes of Excalibur and positioned the X-ray lasers next to nuclear bombs at the Nevada test site. When the bombs exploded, the researchers detected laser beams coming from the prototypes. Teller predicted that Excalibur would be ready for deployment in a few years. But the project ran into technical problems and the government cut its funding. Then the Soviet Union collapsed and the cold war ended and the U.S. banned all nuclear tests. So Excalibur was canceled." He nodded grimly. "And believe me, that was a damn good thing. We should be trying to eliminate nukes, not put them into space."

To David's surprise, no one argued with him. The room was silent. Then Aryeh stepped forward. "Okay, now we know what the thing is, yes? Livermore was sharing its information with Soreq, so the Israeli researchers must've built their own prototype laser. But why, after all these years, did Loebner come here to destroy it? Where's the sense in that?"

"Maybe Loebner's a traitor," Lucille suggested. "Maybe he's working with the Iranians. So he sabotages a defense system that could shoot down Iranian missiles."

"But Excalibur wasn't operational," Aryeh pointed out. "The IDF put it in storage and forgot about it. And Israel has other missile-defense systems that are already in place—the Patriot rockets, the Arrow interceptors. If Loebner was interested in sabotage, why didn't he go after those?"

"Because the operational systems have better security," Lucille answered. "Loebner destroyed what he could, then disappeared."

Aryeh flashed a skeptical half smile. He didn't say anything, but he clearly disagreed.

David shook his head. "No, Loebner's not the bad guy. We know he was working on an experiment with Jacob Steele. And at the moment of the Iranian nuclear test, they detected something that alarmed them. Some anomaly in the flow of time, some disruption in the workings of the—"

"You're just speculating," Lucille interrupted. "What we need is more information. We need to—"

"Loebner perceived the danger and took action." David pointed once more at the broken cylinder. "Within hours of the nuclear test, he rushed over here and demolished this prototype. So Excalibur must be related to the danger. The X-ray laser is part of the threat."

Resting her hands on her hips, Lucille gave him an incredulous look. "Excalibur is a defensive weapon, designed to shoot down missiles. How the hell could it be a threat?"

David shook his head again. He thought of what Monique had told him about It From Bit and the computational universe. He thought of the Caduceus Array, the pair of single-ion clocks hidden at Beit Shalom Yeshiva and the University of Maryland. And he remembered the last time he'd seen Jacob Steele, in the corridor outside the lecture hall at Columbia. There's something else, David thought. I'm missing something. It fluttered at the edge of his memory, just out of reach.

"I can't explain it," he said. "But I know I'm right."

THE SUN WAS SINKING TOWARD THE MEDITERRANEAN BY THE TIME THEY left Soreq. Aryeh and Lucille sat in the front of the limo, as before, and David and Monique sat in the back, but no one talked or turned on the radio. They were no closer to finding Oscar Loebner. They'd discovered a new piece of evidence, but no clues to the man's whereabouts. With enough time, perhaps, they could interview all of Loebner's colleagues and retrace his movements and unravel the mystery of his disappearance—what he detected with the Caduceus Array, why he smashed the X-ray laser, and how he was connected to Michael's kidnapping. But David knew they didn't have enough time. Time was running out.

He looked out the window as they drove back to Jerusalem. The telephone poles beside the highway cast long shadows in the late-afternoon light, which gilded the neighboring fields. His greatest fear now was that Lucille would decide to go back to America. Given their lack of progress so far, she might want to return to New York and rethink the investigation. David knew this would be a mistake, but he had little hope of changing Lucille's mind if she made that decision. Although he'd built up a good relationship with Agent Parker, in the end he was still just a civilian.

At the halfway point in the drive, where the highway climbed into the Judean Hills, Aryeh stopped for gas at a roadside station. Luckily, traffic was light and the station wasn't busy. While Aryeh went to the gas pumps, Lucille opened her enormous black purse and pulled out a tube of lipstick. David glanced nervously at Monique, then turned to Lucille, leaning forward into the gap between the car's bucket seats.

"So what happens now?" he asked. His voice was tense. "Do we stay in Israel or go back to the States?"

Lucille seemed taken aback, a little startled by his urgency. She lowered the lipstick and looked over her shoulder. "Don't worry, Swift. We still have things to do here."

He didn't know if she was telling the truth or just trying to reassure him. "Really? I get the feeling that we just hit a brick wall."

"No, you don't understand. Investigations are hard work. You can't expect a breakthrough with every interview. Most of the time, you come away with nothing. You have to try lots of approaches until you find the one that gets results."

"But what's the next step? No one knows where Loebner went after he left Soreq. He could be anywhere by now."

"I've been thinking that maybe we should stop concentrating so much on Oscar Loebner the computer scientist. He's also Olam ben Z'man the Kabbalah nut. He has ties to Beit Shalom Yeshiva and the right-wing Jewish settlers on the West Bank. And the Bureau has information on the more extreme right-wingers because they have associates in the U.S."

"You think Loebner could be hiding in one of the West Bank settlements?"

"It'd be a good place to hide. Some of the settlements are on remote hilltops surrounded by Palestinian villages. The Israeli authorities rarely go there, and the settlers are well armed because they're always fighting with the Palestinians. Here, look at this." Lucille dug into her purse and pulled out a BlackBerry. She used her thumbs to push the buttons on the device's keyboard. "I downloaded some data on the settlements this morning. We have an encrypted link to the Bureau's computers in Washington."

An alphabetical list of West Bank settlements appeared on the Black-Berry's screen. The first was Adora, the second Alei Zahav. Each name was accompanied by a satellite photo of the outpost and several links offering more information. "Wow, that's impressive," David said.

"Yeah, the Bureau spent millions on new servers and networking equipment. But at least once a month the system crashes and all the screens go black. We've had a string of bad luck with our computers."

She scrolled down the list of settlements: Alfei Menashe, Alon Shvut, Almon, Argaman, Ariel. But the names barely registered in David's mind, because Lucille had just reminded him of something. The words that had been fluttering at the edge of his memory ever since he stood in the Long-Term Storage Room suddenly swung into view. Now he remembered what Jacob Steele had said outside the lecture hall at Columbia. *A larger disruption could trigger a catastrophe. It could bring down the whole system.*

Lucille continued talking about the settlements and scrolling down her list—Dolev, Doran, Efrat, Elazar—but David was too agitated to pay attention. A horrible fear welled up inside him. He turned back to Monique and grabbed her arm. "I know why Loebner did it! Why he smashed the laser!"

She was so surprised she let out a cry. "Jesus! What the hell?"

"A crash, a computer crash! That's what Loebner was afraid of!" He pointed at the BlackBerry in Lucille's hand. "Every computer system crashes, right? There's no computer in the goddamn world that hasn't crashed at least once."

Monique stared at him, her eyes swiftly focusing. "Okay, slow down. What are you saying?"

"Can't you see? If the whole universe is a—"

At that instant all four of the limo's doors opened. A man in a black jacket appeared behind Monique and clamped a gloved hand over her mouth. Another man did the same to David, while two more assailants dove at Lucille, pinning her arms before she could reach for her gun. The men were fast and strong, and they wore black shirts and black pants under their jackets. Just like the assassins at Beit Shalom Yeshiva, David thought. They're here to finish the job.

Within seconds the four men had crowded into the car and closed the doors behind them. As the man in the driver's seat started the engine, David got a glimpse of a black van parked on the other side of the gas pumps. The van's rear doors were open, and another two assailants were shoving Aryeh inside. Then the doors slammed shut and the van peeled out of the gas station. The Shin Bet limo followed at high speed, heading back to the highway.

David's head was turned sideways, his right cheek mashed against the fabric of the backseat. He got a good look at the man behind Monique—he was bald and barrel-chested and wore a black eye patch. The man smiled at David and relaxed his hold on Monique, removing his hand from her mouth.

"*Shalom!*" he boomed. "My name is Olam ben Z'man."

18

BROTHER CYRUS'S SOLDIERS TOOK AWAY HIS COMPUTER. WHILE MICHAEL SAT on his bare mattress, the men came into the yurt and disconnected the Ultra 27 workstation. Without saying a word, they unplugged the extension cord that connected the machine to the camp's diesel generator. Then they carted the workstation outside and locked the door behind them.

Michael didn't care about the computer. He hadn't touched the machine since he'd returned from the burning crater the night before. Instead, he'd spent the whole day writing in a spiral notebook he'd found at the bottom of one of the desk drawers. Using a pencil he'd also found in the drawer, he'd written *The Discovery of Spacetime* on the notebook's first page. That was the title of chapter three of *An Introduction to Modern Physics,* another textbook that Monique Reynolds had given him for his nineteenth birthday. Michael had memorized the book and now he was copying the chapter into the spiral notebook, transcribing the text in his careful handwriting and drawing his own versions of the illustrations. He enjoyed copying books from memory. It allowed him to push all other thoughts out of his mind.

Redrawing the illustrations was the best part. Michael's favorite illustration in chapter three was the black-and-white photograph of Albert Einstein. The caption said it was taken in 1905, the year Einstein discovered the theory of relativity. Michael took special pleasure in reproducing this picture because it showed his great-great-grandfather at the age of twenty-six, only seven years older than he was. He felt a twinge, though, when he finished the drawing. Despite his best efforts, an unwanted thought had occurred to him. Looking at the picture of Einstein had reminded Michael that the physicist's greatest discovery, the unified field theory, was now in Brother Cyrus's hands. And that Michael had broken his promise to keep it secret.

It was almost six o'clock in the evening. Michael put down his pencil, which was worn down to a nub. Sitting on the edge of his mattress, he stared at the empty space on the desk where the Ultra 27 workstation had been. He knew this would be difficult, but he needed to think about the program he'd seen on that computer. He needed to figure out if Cyrus was telling the truth when he said he could use the code to remake the universe. The problem was that Michael didn't fully understand the program. He knew it was equivalent to the unified theory, and he'd formulated and memorized every line of its code, but as David Swift had told him so many times, memorizing isn't the same as understanding. David was always urging Michael to think about the textbooks he read, to run the information back and forth in his head until it made sense. So that's what Michael started to do. He closed his eyes and thought about the program.

The first thought that occurred to him was that the program had been running for a very long time. According to *An Introduction to Modern Physics,* the universe had existed in its present form since the Big Bang started nearly 14 billion years ago. If it were possible to disrupt the program, it should've happened in the first milliseconds of existence, when spacetime was densely packed with energy. Then the universe would've ended almost as soon as it began. But the program had kept running through the primordial maelstrom, and it had survived all the cataclysms of the following aeons. Michael suspected that parts of the code acted as error-correction algorithms, preventing any anomaly from queering the system. So he concluded that Brother Cyrus must be lying. Even if he built a bomb the size of the Milky Way, he couldn't generate enough energy to change the program.

But then another idea occurred to him. Maybe Cyrus didn't need quite so much energy. The fact that the universe had survived for so long didn't necessarily imply that a disruption couldn't happen; it just meant that the event had to be highly improbable. It had to be so rare that it was unlikely to spontaneously occur anywhere in the observable universe for at least 14 billion years. But it wasn't impossible. And a clever person could increase the odds by deliberately triggering it.

Scrunching his forehead to close his eyes more tightly, Michael forced himself to remember the program. Once again it flashed on the black screen of his eyelids, and he examined each line of code. At the same time, he remembered what Cyrus had said about the Kingdom of Heaven. *All the clocks will stop running,* he'd said, *and time will stand still. The whole past of our universe will be compressed into one moment, and the Lord will embrace us all forever.* And as Michael thought of those words, he focused on a block of code that stood out from the rest in his mind's eye. He saw the quantum variables and operators shift to new positions within the block, realigning themselves to form a radically different instruction. It was so simple he was amazed he hadn't seen it before. He changed his conclusion—Brother Cyrus could indeed remake the universe. A small alteration in the code could do it.

Michael had to stop thinking about it. He was shivering, even though the yurt was very hot. He opened his eyes and stared at the Turkish carpet that covered the yurt's floor. The carpet had a pattern of white and orange polygons repeating across a red background. It was a tessellation, a tiling of squares and triangles and hexagons that fit together perfectly, with no gaps or overlaps. For fifteen minutes Michael forgot about Brother Cyrus and simply studied the tessellation in the carpet, trying to identify all of its rotational symmetries. Then he took a deep breath and rose to his feet.

He went to the section of the yurt's wall behind the desk and found the small hole that had been punched through the mesh of wooden slats. The power cord for the computer had threaded through this opening, but now the computer was gone and so was the cord. Michael knelt on the carpet and peered through the hole.

He saw a large green truck parked about forty feet away. It was the same truck that had transported him to the desert camp. Two of Cyrus's soldiers were in the truck's cargo hold, and another two were on the sandy ground nearby. The men on the ground were carrying a rectangular black case and walking very slowly toward the back of the truck. The case was small, only a foot and a half long, and Michael was surprised that two men were needed to carry it. When they reached the truck they passed the case to the men in the cargo hold. Then the men on the ground picked up a section of gray pipe, about ten feet long and six inches in diameter, and put that in the truck as well. They continued loading the cargo hold for fifteen minutes, and then the soldiers closed its doors and drove the truck away, heading west on the desert trail.

Then another pair of soldiers loaded the cargo hold of a second truck and drove it away, too. Then a third truck. Four Land Cruisers and three Toyota pickups also left the camp, heading west. By seven o'clock only two Land Cruisers and one pickup remained. Michael counted seven soldiers still patrolling the area, six of them walking in pairs between the empty huts. The seventh was Angel, who was talking into his radio. He had a gauze bandage taped over his nose, and his cheeks were purple from the head butt Michael had given him.

The sight of Angel made Michael turn away from the hole and look at the pile of dirty clothes at the foot of his mattress. This was where he'd hidden the fragmentation grenade. He'd wrapped the sphere in his pee-stained underwear, reasoning that no one would want to touch such a disgusting thing. He was familiar with the M67 grenade because it was a weapon in America's Army, a computer game that the U.S. Army had developed to attract new recruits. The game had a training program that taught players how to use the grenade, so Michael knew it had a kill radius of sixteen feet. This made the M67 very effective in combat, but now it posed a problem. Michael couldn't throw the grenade at anyone entering the yurt because it would kill him, too. He'd have to wait until someone unlocked the door; then maybe he could run outside with the M67 and throw it at the soldiers. But if he wanted to escape from the camp, he had to make sure that all seven of Cyrus's men were within sixteen feet of where the grenade exploded.

Deep in thought, Michael scanned the yurt again, staring at the mattress where he slept and the desk where he worked and the plastic bucket where he went to the bathroom. From his long experience playing computer games, he knew that every program had its shortcuts, its cheats. If your character touches a secret panel, a door will unlock. If you find a hidden object—a key, a ring, a canister—your enemies will dissolve. So Michael started looking for hidden objects. First, he noticed the pad of steel wool lying next to the plastic bucket. It was for cleaning the bits of poo that stuck to the bottom of the bucket, and until now Michael hadn't touched the thing. But now he picked it up. Then he reached for the pocket flashlight on his mattress—he used this to find the bucket in the middle of the night—and removed its nine-volt battery. Last, he went to the desk and opened the top drawer. Inside were a large bag of potato chips and the bottle that Tamara had brought the day before, which was still half full of the brown alcohol she'd called Jägermeister.

He carried these four objects to the foot of his mattress and hid them under his dirty clothes. Then he turned around and went to the yurt's locked door. This is a game, he told himself. You're going to touch the secret panel.

Raising his hand over his head, Michael pounded on the door. "HELLO!" he yelled. "HELLO! WOULD SOMEBODY PLEASE COME HERE?"

He waited for an answer. There was no sound of approaching footsteps. After ten seconds he pounded on the door again. He was about to try a third time when the door swung open and Angel stepped inside, stooping low so he could fit through the doorway. He was still in the bulky flak jacket he'd worn the night before, and in the close quarters of the yurt he looked even larger. In his right hand he held a pistol, an M-9 semiautomatic.

Michael stepped backward, retreating to the center of the yurt. For a moment he wished he'd stolen a gun instead of a grenade. But Angel would've certainly noticed if his pistol was missing, whereas he hadn't noticed the theft of the M67.

Angel stared at him for six long seconds. His gun was aimed at Michael's chest. "What do you want?"

Michael focused on the crescent-shaped scar on Angel's neck. It wasn't a pleasant sight, but it was better than looking at the man's bruised face. Or at his gun. "I'd like to speak with Tamara, please," he said. "Could you ask her to come here?"

A snort came out of Angel's bandaged nose. "I'm afraid not. Tamara's a prisoner now, just like you."

"Excuse me, I don't understand."

"It was your fault. She lost her faith because of you." Angel took a step forward. He raised his pistol so that it pointed at Michael's head. "She's locked up in another yurt. The Lord may forgive her, but Brother Cyrus won't."

Michael clenched his hands to stop them from shaking. His fingernails dug into his palms. "Then I'd like to see Brother Cyrus," he said. "I'd like to talk to him as soon as possible."

"Brother Cyrus isn't here. Is there anyone else you want to see?"

"Do you know when he'll be back?"

"He's not coming back. In case you haven't noticed, we're breaking camp. We're going to the mountains. A place called Kuruzhdey."

Michael remembered something Tamara had said. She'd gone to the mountains, she'd said, to do an important job. About 150 miles to the southwest, she'd said. "Then I'd like to speak to Brother Cyrus as soon as we get to this place."

Angel shook his head. "I have some bad news for you. You're not coming with us. You've caused enough trouble already."

"Excuse me, I don't understand."

"Brother Cyrus is supposed to radio me within the hour. He's double-checking the information you gave him. As soon as he's done, we won't need you anymore."

"Excuse me, I don't—"

"Then I'll make it very clear." Angel took another step forward. He stretched his arm and pressed his M-9 against Michael's forehead. "Once I get the word from Brother Cyrus, I'm going to shoot you. The Lord wants you out of the way, and I will obey His command. You'll be the last person I put to sleep before I enter His kingdom."

Michael could feel the cold circle of the gun's muzzle. Trembling, he continued to stare at Angel's scarred neck. This is a game, he reminded himself. And he was good at games. Michael knew he couldn't outfight this man, but maybe he could outsmart him. Angel had already made one mistake. Now he might make another.

He forced himself to look at Angel's face—the gauze pad taped to his nose, the purple skin around his eyes, the dull brown pupils. And then Michael grinned, because he'd just thought of something appropriate to say. It was a line that one of the characters in Desert Commando said after he punched another character in the face during the game's hand-to-hand combat scene.

"How does your nose feel, asshole?"

Michael said it, and then the world went black. The next thing he knew, he lay on his back on the Turkish carpet. The left side of his face was hot and swollen, and he couldn't open his left eye. Angel was gone and the yurt was silent. Thin bands of evening light squeezed between the slats in the circular wall.

He turned his head from left to right. Then he flexed his arms and legs and wiggled his fingers and toes. Luckily, nothing was broken. When he clambered to his feet, the room whirled around him, but after a couple of seconds it came to rest. Then he staggered to the door and leaned beside it.

He tested the door. He applied as little pressure as possible. And it moved. The door crept forward about an inch before Michael gently pulled it back. In his fury, Angel had forgotten to lock it.

19

OLAM BEN Z'MAN SMUGGLED THEM INTO THE WEST BANK. FIRST, HIS MEN drove to an empty parking lot where they abandoned the Shin Bet limousine and transferred David, Monique, and Lucille to the black van. Aryeh was already inside, and soon all four of them were seated on the van's floor, guarded by bearded *kippot srugot* wearing black clothes and carrying Uzis. For the next hour David couldn't see anything outside, but he surmised from the frequent turns and jolts that they were navigating the West Bank's twisting back roads. He started to feel nauseous, partly from all the twists and turns, and partly from anxiety. Although he was grateful to find Olam at last, this wasn't how he'd expected it to happen.

The van finally stopped and the bearded guards opened the rear doors. The sun was setting and its last rays made David squint. One of Olam's men grasped his arm and pulled him out of the van, leading him toward a cluster of battered, beige trailers on the summit of a treeless hill. Another guard escorted Monique. More *kippot srugot* emerged from the trailers, each with an Uzi dangling from his shoulder. A white banner hung from the largest trailer, and painted on it were a pair of Jewish stars and the name of the settlement: SHALHEVET. While the guards led David and Monique toward this trailer, which seemed to be the settlement's headquarters, other settlers approached the van and grabbed Lucille and Aryeh. David noticed with some dismay that the *kippot srugot* were taking the agents to a different trailer.

The men with Uzis pushed David and Monique through the doorway of the headquarters trailer and into a windowless room. At one end of the room was a massive steel-gray cabinet, about as tall as a refrigerator and three times as wide. At the other end was an old, battered desk with one folding chair behind it and two in front. The guards pointed at the latter chairs. David and Monique nervously sat down while the *kippot srugot* stood behind them, training the Uzis at their heads. For a moment David thought they were going to execute them right there. But then Olam ben Z'man marched into the room, his black pants tucked into his combat boots and the sleeves of his black shirt rolled above his forearms.

Because of the man's bald head and eye patch, David was reminded of Moshe Dayan, the famous Israeli general, but Olam was bigger, at least six and a half feet tall, and he had the shoulders and chest of a weight lifter. He looked like he could pick up Moshe Dayan and throw him across the Jordan River. His face was dark and craggy and showed his age—he was in his fifties, David remembered—but his most remarkable feature was his uncovered eye, which had a brilliant blue iris. This eye blazed as he strode across the room. "Well, well! You're finally here!"

The muscles in his right arm bulged as he held out his hand. David started to rise, but the guards behind him gripped his shoulders and pushed him back down. So he shook hands with Olam from his chair. "Yes, I'm a friend of Jacob Steele, my name is—"

"I know who you are. Jacob told me about you. You're David Swift, professor of history at Columbia University. Also president of Physicists for Peace." He let go of David's hand and turned to Monique. "And you're Monique Reynolds, professor of physics at Columbia. Please forgive me for surprising you like this. It's not very civilized to hijack you off the highway, eh? But I had to make sure no one followed us."

David felt disoriented. He had so many questions for Olam, he didn't know where to begin. "Look, we have an urgent situation. We came to Israel with the FBI because—"

"Yes, because someone has killed Jacob and kidnapped Michael Gupta. I have contacts in the Israeli government, you see, and they told me about your investigation. The problem is that our enemies also have contacts in the government. They've infiltrated the intelligence agencies in both Israel and America." He turned around and went behind the desk, sitting down in the other folding chair. "That's why my men are interrogating Agent Parker from the FBI and Mr. Goldberg from Shin Bet."

Monique shook her head. "But they're not your enemies. They're running the investigation."

"I'm sorry, but we have to be cautious. We're fighting the *Qliphoth* and they have many spies. Look how quickly their assassins found you after you arrived in Jerusalem. They already knew that you and the agents had come to Israel to search for me."

David looked at him uneasily. "The *Qliphoth*?"

"In Kabbalah, the *Qliphoth* are the destructive forces of the universe, the opposites of the *Sephirot*. Like devils, yes? But please, don't misunderstand me. Our enemies are men, not devils."

Shit, David thought. Olam was already giving him a heavy dose of Kabbalah. David needed to steer him back to reality. "So you're saying that someone in the FBI tipped off these people?"

"Either the FBI or Shin Bet, they're both compromised. The *Qliphoth* were hoping to find me, so their assassins followed you to Beit Shalom Yeshiva. They wanted to kill me, but they killed the Rav instead." His lone eye narrowed. "They're worried because I discovered their plan. The Caduceus Array detected the disruptions from their test in the Kavir Desert."

David was relieved to hear him mention the Caduceus Array. Right now he wanted to talk to Oscar Loebner the scientist, not Olam ben Z'man the Jewish mystic. But Monique spoke first. "You mean the space-time disruptions?" she asked. "The ones that occurred when the Iranian nuke exploded?"

Olam nodded. "They spread outward from the Kavir site, hitting my clock first, then Jacob's. The anomalies were fleeting, each less than a trillionth of a second. Too brief to be detected by conventional atomic clocks, which aren't as precise as ours. And much too brief to be detected by our nervous systems, which explains why no one felt the disturbance. But during those fleeting moments the spacetime disruptions were extreme. In each instance, time was compressed so violently that it almost ceased to exist."

"But what caused the disruptions?" Monique leaned forward, balancing on the edge of her chair. "There's no way a nuclear blast could mangle spacetime like that."

Instead of answering, Olam opened one of the desk drawers. He pulled out a sheet of paper and placed it on top of the desk so David and Monique could see it. It was a satellite reconnaissance photo showing a concrete bunker in the middle of a desert. The image was so clear that David could see footprints in the sand. There was a dirt road leading to the bunker's entrance and a truck parked beside it. Between the truck and the bunker was a forklift carrying a silver cylinder.

Olam tapped the cylinder in the photo. "An Israeli satellite photographed this at Iran's Kavir site last Monday, the day before the nuclear test. None of the IDF's intelligence analysts could identify the device, so on Monday night they sent me an encrypted e-mail with a copy of the image. Although I don't work for the intelligence directorate anymore, I still help my old friends there from time to time. I recognized the device and told them what it was—a prototype of the Excalibur laser."

David leaned across the desk, trying to get a better look at the photo. He noticed that the cylinder had a sliding panel near its midpoint. That was the compartment for the nuclear warhead, the power source for the X-ray laser beams that were meant to shoot down Soviet missiles. "Jesus," he whispered. "What was it doing in Iran? Are they working on missile defense?"

"I knew the Iranians couldn't have built it themselves. The technology is far beyond them. So I assumed they stole it. I checked with an old colleague at Soreq who confirmed that the Israeli X-ray laser was still at the lab. But when I called one of my friends at Lawrence Livermore, he said their prototype had been moved out of storage two months ago. He promised he would look into the matter and find out where the laser had been taken." Olam shook his head. "The next day the Iranians exploded their bomb and the Caduceus Array detected the disruptions. Then I realized what the *Qliphoth* were doing with the prototype they'd stolen. It has nothing to do with missile defense."

Monique rose from her chair and began pacing across the room. The guards didn't stop her. "Were the Iranians trying to use Excalibur as an offensive weapon? Firing the X-ray laser to deliberately alter spacetime?"

Olam shook his head again. "I must be honest with you, Dr. Reynolds. I call them the *Qliphoth* because I don't know who they are. They're obviously working in concert with the Iranian government, but I don't believe the mullahs know what the *Qliphoth* are planning. You see, Iran wants to incinerate Israel, and maybe America, too. But the

Qliphoth want to incinerate all of Creation, and I don't think even the mullahs would go that far."

David's stomach twisted. He felt the same fear that had welled up inside him when he was in the Shin Bet limo. His suspicions had been correct. "Is it a crash? Are they trying to crash the universal program?"

"So you know about the program? Did Rav Kavner tell you?"

Monique nodded. "He told us as much as he understood. Later we realized he was talking about the It From Bit hypothesis and—"

"Ah, it's not a hypothesis anymore. Now we know beyond a doubt that It From Bit is true. The universe must be computational because we've just seen evidence of an overload. Excalibur's laser beams were powerful enough to disrupt the program."

"What?" Monique made a face. "An overload?"

"In technical terms, it was a memory buffer overflow. Every computer has a memory, yes? And the universe is no exception."

"But how could—"

"Please, let me explain. The memory of the universe is all around us, embedded in spacetime. When we fill a volume of space with particles, we're adding data to its memory. But every memory has its limits. If you pack too much matter into a small volume, the local spacetime will collapse and form a black hole. You're familiar with black holes, yes?"

"Yes, of course." She twirled her hand in a circle, urging Olam to get to the point.

"A black hole is bad for anyone living nearby, but it's not a disaster for the universe as a whole. The universal program has error-correction algorithms that stop the overload from affecting the rest of the system. The black hole bends the surrounding spacetime with its gravity, but the fundamental disruption is confined to a single point. You see?"

David was struggling to keep up. "Okay, but how does this apply to the X-ray laser?"

"A laser is an unusually orderly phenomenon. All the particles of light in the beam have the same frequency and phase, which means that the information in a laser is very repetitive. And the universal program has specialized memory caches for this repetitive data. But when—"

"Wait a second." Monique held out her hands. "Specialized memory caches? How do you know they exist?"

Olam smiled. "The universe is not only a computer, it's a very efficient computer. The specialized caches increase the efficiency of the program by compressing the repetitive data." He spoke in a pleased voice, as if he were proud of the program's ingenuity. But his smile quickly faded. "Unfortunately, there's a drawback. The specialized caches can be overloaded more easily than the ordinary ones. So if you focus intense X-ray laser beams on a very small volume of space, the surge of data can flood the memory. Ordinarily, such an event would be extremely unlikely, because natural processes rarely generate X-ray laser beams. But Excalibur makes it possible to trigger an overload. You can do it by aiming Excalibur's laser beams so that they converge in the vacuum inside the device's cylinder."

Monique stopped pacing and stood by the corner of Olam's desk. "And the overload can disrupt other parts of the universal computer? The parts that specify the structure of spacetime? Is that what the Caduceus Array detected?"

"Yes, it showed the disturbance in the time dimension, which fortunately was very brief. The disruption at the Kavir site was kept in check by the error-correction algorithms in the universal program, which isolated the memory overflow and stopped it from corrupting the rest of the system. But I fear that another test is coming. According to my calculations, if the *Qliphoth* exploded a more powerful warhead and made a few adjustments to the X-ray laser, the results could be very different. If the laser beams were more intense and converged in the right pattern, the data would overload too many caches and overwhelm the error-correction algorithms. Then spacetime would collapse at the site of the overload and the system error would spread outward at the speed of light."

Monique bit her lip. "It would expand like a bubble. And destroy everything in its path."

Olam nodded. "In a twentieth of a second the earth would be gone. In twelve hours, the entire solar system. But I don't like the word 'bubble.' This isn't a bubble, it's a crash. An error freezes the computer and the whole system goes down."

The room became so quiet that David could hear the breathing of the guards behind him. Oscar Loebner the computer scientist had just delivered some sobering news. More than twenty years ago the weapon makers of the cold war had unwittingly built a Doomsday machine. And now someone had recognized the hidden power of Excalibur, its ability to trigger an event so extraordinary that it had never occurred, not even once, in the long history of the universe. A fatal event, David thought. The ultimate fatal error. "But why would anyone want to crash the program?" he asked. "It's mass suicide."

Olam shrugged. "I don't know who the *Qliphoth* are, so I can't tell you their reasons. But I can make a guess. You see, the crash would obliterate all the matter in its path, but it wouldn't destroy the computer itself. Like when your PC crashes, yes? The screen goes black, but the program can restart. And in the same way, the universe could restart and a new Big Bang would emerge from the vacuum. But the program of this new universe might be very different from the old one. In fact, it might be possible to engineer the crash so that it makes specific changes to the software. You could change the laws of physics. Maybe adjust the speed of light and the other physical constants to create a universe that's simpler or more efficient than ours. Or you could create a new space-time with a different number of dimensions. Maybe a universe with two dimensions of time, which would allow you to travel back into the past. Or a universe with no dimension of time at all, where everything would exist in eternal stasis."

Now David rose from his chair. "So you think these people are trying to build a better universe? Maybe their own version of paradise?"

"Who knows? There are so many madmen in the world, so many false Messiahs. It might even be possible to retrieve the stored memory of the old universe and plug it into the new one. Like a resurrection, yes? Everything would be reborn in a new format, like when you convert your computer files from Windows to Mac. It wouldn't be easy to trigger this kind of restart—you'd have to adjust the angles of Excalibur's laser rods in just the right way. But if you knew the universal program in detail, you could figure it out."

David stood in front of Olam's desk and looked again at the photo of the Kavir test site. He could just imagine some arrogant idiot deciding to remake the universe. It was human nature. But then he remembered something else and felt a flash of hope. He pointed at the silver cylinder in the satellite photo. "But after the prototype from Livermore fired its beams, it must've been destroyed in the nuclear blast at the Kavir site. And you've already smashed the Israeli device that was at Soreq. So unless these *Qliphoth* can build a new X-ray laser, we should be safe, right?"

Olam frowned. "You're forgetting something. Excalibur was developed in the last years of the cold war, when the Americans and Soviets were busy spying on each other. The national laboratories were prime targets of intelligence operations in those days. If one side developed a new technology, the other side could usually copy it within a few years."

"What are you saying? The Soviets had their own X-ray laser?"

"According to my sources, they built it at the Semipalatinsk test site. But they ran into the same technical problems that stopped the Americans. So in 1990 they gave up and put the device in storage at a military depot in Turkmenistan. When the Soviet Union broke up in '91, the army didn't bother to take the laser back to Russia. They considered the thing useless, so they left it at the depot with all their other surplus equipment." He placed his hands flat on the desk and rose to his feet. "That's where we're going. Some of my old friends have agreed to lend us a transport plane. It leaves from Ramat David Air Base in two hours."

"You're planning an operation with the IDF?"

He shook his head. "I told you, we can't trust anyone in the Israeli or American governments. The *Qliphoth* have collaborators everywhere. How do you think they smuggled Excalibur out of the Livermore lab? No, I'm organizing this mission outside the official channels. Look around and you'll see the members of our strike team." He pointed at the pair of guards behind David's chair. When David turned around, he saw that the *kippot srugot* weren't aiming their Uzis at his head anymore. "Twenty men are going with us. Most are old comrades I served with in the *Sayeret Matkal*. The transport plane will take us to Baku, in Azerbaijan, and then we'll take a chartered boat across the Caspian Sea. The depot in Turkmenistan is fairly close to the seashore."

Monique looked askance. "You think the X-ray laser's still there? After all these years?"

"It's there. I confirmed it with my contacts at Mossad, which has a very good network of agents in Central Asia. And now we're going to find the device and destroy it."

David leaned across Olam's desk. "What about Michael? We have to find him, too."

Olam walked around the desk and came toward him. He towered over David. His biceps were level with David's nose, and his body odor was overpowering. "Michael is with the *Qliphoth,* I'm sure of it. And the *Qliphoth* will also be looking for the laser, so I suspect we'll find him in Turkmenistan."

"Then we're coming with you," David said. He raised his chin and looked Olam in the eye. "We have to make sure that Michael is safe."

For a moment Olam just stared at him. Then he threw one of his massive arms around David's shoulders. "Of course you're coming with us! Why do you think we brought you here?" He gave David a look that was half admiring and half amused. "Jacob told me what happened two years ago, how you and Dr. Reynolds rescued the *Einheitliche Feldtheorie*. Haven't you realized by now that you're an instrument of *Keter*?"

"*Keter*? What's that?"

"It's the highest of the *Sephirot,* the first step in the enumeration of the universe. The instrument of *Keter* has a special place in the divine plan. That's why you're here, why all these crazy things keep happening to you. *Keter* is God's most powerful tool, and now you will bring us victory!"

While Olam squeezed his shoulder, another guard came into the room and spoke a few words in Hebrew. Olam nodded, then turned back to David. "My men have finished interrogating Agent Parker and Mr. Goldberg. Neither is a spy, which is lucky. Now they can join the fight. Once I show them how deeply the *Qliphoth* have infiltrated their agencies, they'll see why we have to go off the radar." Keeping his arm around David, Olam led him across the room, stepping toward the large steel-gray cabinet. It had a pair of sliding metal doors, each five feet high and four feet wide. "I want Agent Parker to come to Turkmenistan with us. I could use another good soldier. But I have a different job for Mr. Goldberg."

"You should probably talk to them before you—"

"No, Mr. Goldberg will like this job. He's going to decode some messages for me. With a little help from this machine." Olam grasped the knob on one of the cabinet's sliding doors and pulled it open. Inside the cabinet was a crowded mass of wires and electronics. Hundreds of small glass tubes were arranged in neat rows. "The Caduceus Array isn't the only project I've been working on. I thought of a way to build something else from Jacob's trapped-ion technology."

David peered into the cabinet. He looked closer at one of the glass tubes and saw a pair of needlelike electrodes inside. It was a single-ion trap, just like the ones in the Caduceus Array, but David got the feeling that this device wasn't a clock. The tubes were connected to optical fibers that tangled together in an unruly skein. It looked a bit like the inside of a FiOS junction box, with dozens of fiber-optic lines delivering streams of data every which way.

As David studied the machine, trying to make sense of it, Monique let out a delighted gasp. "Oh my God. You've got hundreds of ions here!"

Olam nodded. "Four thousand and ninety-six, to be exact."

"And they're all linked together by fiber-optic lines!" Monique pointed at the tangle of glass fibers. "Each ion emits optical signals that travel through the lines, right? And those signals enable the ions to interact and perform calculations?"

"It was a good idea, yes? This quantum computer is the first in the world that can actually do something useful."

"But how did you do it? I thought the technology wasn't ready yet. Isn't that why Jacob gave up on quantum computing?"

Olam's face turned serious. "I succeeded because I needed to succeed. We will use this computer in our battle against the *Qliphoth*."

AFTER SUNSET NICO SWITCHED TO HIS INFRARED BINOCULARS, WHICH showed the trailers of Shalhevet as glowing white rectangles against the black hilltop. The Israelis and Americans had tried to evade his surveillance by sneaking off to this settlement on the West Bank, but Nico had followed them. Now he hid behind a boulder on a neighboring hillside, about two hundred meters away. Shalhevet was full of armed Jews, some patrolling the outpost's perimeter and others guarding the large trailer where Olam ben Z'man was conferring with his men. Nico had caught a glimpse of Olam earlier. He matched the description that Cyrus's informants had provided: a big, bald *kelb* wearing a black eye patch.

Just as Nico was about to move to a closer observation point, several figures emerged from the trailers. The infrared display in his binoculars didn't show much detail, but he saw enough to recognize two of the figures as Swift and Reynolds. A half-dozen bearded Zionists escorted them back to their van and stepped into the vehicle with them. Then Olam came out of his trailer with the silver-haired FBI agent and walked toward an identical van. Nico clenched his right hand, suppressing an impulse to grab his rifle. His orders had been clear: don't attack until you're certain you can kill all of them. So he did nothing but observe the pair of vans as they left the settlement, trundling down a dirt trail that led to the highway. Although neither driver turned on his headlights, the warm engines and exhaust pipes glowed brightly in Nico's binoculars.

After a few minutes the vans turned left on Highway 60, heading north. By that point Nico was already in his own vehicle, half a kilometer behind. As he drove past Nablus he reached for his radio. Brother Cyrus would be pleased.

20

AS DARKNESS CAME, THE PAIN IN MICHAEL'S FACE SUBSIDED. SOON HE COULD open his left eye and walk across the yurt without getting dizzy. Then he heard the sound of an engine starting and rushed to his peephole just in time to see Angel and two other soldiers get into a Toyota pickup. Michael watched the truck leave the camp and disappear down the trail, heading toward the stretch of horizon where the sun had set fifteen minutes ago.

This was a lucky thing, he thought. Now there were only four soldiers left in the camp, and Michael knew he could easily slip past them in the darkness. But he also knew he couldn't avoid leaving a trail as he fled across the desert. When Angel and his men returned to find him missing, they would quickly catch up to him by following the trail in their pickup truck. So escaping by foot was a bad idea. But there were still two Land Cruisers in the camp, and Michael realized that he could get a much longer head start on his pursuers if he commandeered one of the vehicles. He didn't know how to drive, but Tamara did. And Angel had said she was locked in one of the other yurts.

The four soldiers were still patrolling in pairs. One pair was moving in a figure-eight pattern that threaded around the yurts on the western side of the camp, while the other pair did the same thing on the eastern side. It was a good pattern because it allowed the soldiers to keep most of the camp in sight at all times. But Michael noticed that one pair was moving slightly faster than the other, and every six minutes there was a brief period when none of the soldiers could see the entrance to his yurt. He checked his watch and decided to leave at the next opportunity, which would occur at approximately 8:57. The sky was getting darker but the soldiers had not yet turned on their flashlights.

At 8:55 he opened the large bag of potato chips and poured about six ounces of Jägermeister inside, soaking the chips thoroughly. The steel-wool pad and the nine-volt battery were already in his pockets. At 8:56 he retrieved the M67 grenade from his pile of dirty clothes and went to the yurt's door. During the last minute he rehearsed the arming sequence he'd learned from America's Army. First hold the grenade's lever down, he remembered, then pull out the safety clip and pin. When the grenade is thrown, the lever will release. The fuse will burn for four seconds before detonation.

Michael held the grenade and the bag of potato chips in his right hand and the bottle of Jägermeister in his left. He waited another fifteen seconds. Then he pushed the door open and slipped outside.

It was darker than he'd expected. The yurts were black mounds against the dark gray sand. After closing the door as quietly as he could, Michael ran to the closest yurt. He tiptoed around the structure, staying close to the curving wall and on the opposite side from where he estimated the soldiers should be. As he stepped barefoot on the sand he heard a high-pitched yelp coming from inside the yurt. He recognized the voice as Tamara's, but he couldn't tell whether she was laughing or crying. Michael wanted to stop and listen, but he knew the soldiers would be coming around the perimeter any second, so he kept moving. He dashed across a clearing to the next yurt and finally to the one at the southeastern corner of the camp. He headed straight for the yurt's door, pulled it open, and dove inside.

The room was pitch-dark, but Michael felt mattresses and piles of clothes under his feet. This must be the place where the soldiers slept, he thought. He scrabbled toward the section of wall opposite the door and set the grenade, the potato-chip bag, and the bottle on the Turkish carpet. Then he removed the steel-wool pad and the nine-volt battery from his pockets.

Michael had learned the fundamentals of electricity from *The Concise Scientific Encyclopedia*. A nine-volt battery, he knew, was more powerful than a D battery or a double-A because it pushed electrons more forcefully between the battery's terminals. And if the conductor connecting the terminals is a material with high resistance—like steel wool—the electrical current will generate heat. So Michael wasn't surprised by what happened when he rubbed the steel-wool pad against the terminals on top of the battery: the mesh of wires glowed orange and burst into flames. He'd seen this done on YouTube and had always wanted to try it himself.

Once the pad was aflame, Michael placed it on the carpet next to the yurt's wall. Then he overturned the potato-chip bag and poured the Jägermeister-soaked chips on the fire. Thanks to their combination of alcohol and fat, they were very good tinder. He splattered the rest of the Jägermeister on the surrounding area, but this really wasn't necessary—the wool carpet and wooden slats were so dry, they didn't need an accelerant. By the time Michael raced out the door, the flames were spreading across the floor and climbing the wall.

He ran about thirty feet beyond the yurt and hid behind a dune, lying on his stomach in the sand. Then he waited for the soldiers to arrive, holding the fragmentation grenade in his right hand. This part of the plan had almost stumped him because he was generally unable to predict the actions of other people. How could he lure all four of the soldiers within the grenade's killing radius? He found it impossible to put himself in someone else's shoes—even the metaphor confused him—so he couldn't imagine what would cause the soldiers to draw together in such a tight grouping. But then he thought of the burning crater of Darvaza, the vast pit of flames. It was simply logical that the soldiers would respond to a fire, especially if it was big enough. They would come to the burning yurt and try to put out the fire before it destroyed their possessions.

And that was exactly what happened. First one pair of soldiers arrived, then the other. They shouted and stamped their boots on the flames. Their actions were as logical and predictable and inevitable as the trajectory of the grenade after it left Michael's hand.

21

ANGEL WAS ANNOYED. ONE OF THE TRUCKS IN THE CONVOY HEADING FOR Kuruzhdey had veered off the trail and gotten stuck in a ditch about ten kilometers west of the Darvaza camp. Because Angel's pickup was the only vehicle with enough horsepower to tow the truck out of the sand, he'd had to leave the camp with two of his soldiers and drive to the accident site. He found this assignment a little demeaning—he was a Soldier of God, not a tow jockey!—but there was no getting around it. The convoy was carrying important materials for Brother Cyrus.

Luckily, he and his men finished the task quickly, pulling the truck out of the ditch on the first try. They were unhooking the towline when Angel received a transmission from Brother Cyrus. "Headquarters to Angel. Are you there, Angel?"

He fumbled for his radio and pressed the talk button. This was the call he'd been waiting for. "This is Angel," he said. "Ready for instructions. Over."

"The Lord has provided, Angel. We will meet in heaven. Over."

He grinned. The message meant that everything was ready. Brother Cyrus had finished double-checking the code, running the program on his powerful computers to confirm that it was consistent and complete. Now the Lord's plan was in its final stage. The Redemption was less than forty-eight hours away.

"Roger," Angel said into the radio. "Requesting permission to proceed with the cleanup. Over."

"Permission granted. Peace be with you, Angel. Over and out."

Angel hooked the radio to his belt and ordered his men into the pickup. Then he got in the driver's seat and turned the truck around and headed back to the Darvaza camp. He usually wasn't fond of cleanup operations, and he wasn't looking forward to shooting Tamara—until her loss of faith, she'd been an excellent soldier—but he knew he'd get some satisfaction from killing the boy. He was a stubborn child who needed to be taught a lesson. As Angel drove east, gripping the pickup's steering wheel, he imagined that his hands were around the boy's throat. He wouldn't even have to waste any bullets.

TAMARA JUMPED WHEN SHE HEARD THE EXPLOSION. IT HAPPENED ONLY A few seconds after she smelled the smoke, and at first she assumed that a crate of ammunition had exploded because of a fire in one of the other yurts. But there was a terrible silence after the blast, no shouting soldiers or squawking radios or clumping footsteps in the sand. She listened carefully and heard the distant crackling of a fire, but nothing else. Then she heard something much closer, the sound of her door being unlocked. Tamara stood up, ready to pounce on whoever stepped inside. When the door opened she saw a tall, barefoot nineteen-year-old with matted hair and a swollen black eye.

"Michael!" she shouted. "What happened to you?" She rushed toward him with her arms spread wide, but at the last moment she stopped herself. He didn't like to be touched.

He took a step backward. "Excuse me," he said. "We should leave the camp as quickly as possible."

She looked him over. It had never been easy to read Michael's expression, but now he seemed blanker than ever. Aside from the contusion around his left eye, his face was pale. "Oh God!" she cried. "Did Angel do that? Or one of the other soldiers?"

"Four of the soldiers are dead. I recovered two weapons from their flak jackets."

He raised his hands and for the first time Tamara noticed what he was holding. In his right hand was an M-9 pistol and in his left was an MK3A2 concussion grenade. "Michael, give me that thing!" she yelled, reaching for the grenade. "It's dangerous!"

But Michael took another step backward and held the grenade away from her. "I know how to use this weapon," he said.

His voice was slow and monotone. Tamara stared at him and shook her head. Something terrible had happened to the boy. Something had changed him. She felt a chill as she looked at his bruised face.

"We should leave the camp as quickly as possible," he repeated. "Angel and the two other soldiers will return very soon." He tucked the pistol in his pants and put the grenade in one of his pockets. Then he turned around and walked out of the yurt.

Tamara followed him outside. The sky was black and moonless but the light from the burning yurt flickered across the camp. Within ten seconds they reached the pair of Land Cruisers. Tamara peered through the window of the nearer car and saw that the keys were in the ignition, thank the Lord. She got into the driver's seat and started the engine. Michael opened the passenger-side door but didn't get in.

"Come on!" Tamara yelled. "What are you waiting for?"

He was staring at something in the distance. He raised his arm and pointed. "Headlights," he said. "In the west."

ANGEL COULDN'T BELIEVE IT. ONE OF THE YURTS WAS BURNING OUT OF CONtrol. And none of the soldiers at the camp had radioed him. It didn't make sense. Unless his men had deserted, which was very unlikely, they would've contacted him in this kind of emergency.

His eyes were focused on the fire, so he almost didn't notice the movement to the left. One of the Land Cruisers was hurtling across the camp. Its headlights were off, but Angel could see the firelight reflected off its body. The vehicle got on the trail and headed east, toward the burning crater.

Angel floored the gas pedal and his pickup lunged over the sand. As he got closer to the camp he saw bodies near the flaming yurt. No, not bodies—pieces of bodies. Torsos and arms and legs, still wrapped in khaki. Four of his soldiers were dead. And the prisoners who'd killed them were trying to escape.

Keeping one hand on the steering wheel, he looked over his shoulder at the truck bed. His two remaining men sat on ammunition crates next to the tripod-mounted M240. One of them, Angel thought, could jump out of the pickup and get into the Land Cruiser that was still parked at the center of the camp, a hundred yards ahead. The other could open the crates and start feeding the machine gun.

TAMARA KEPT HER HEADLIGHTS OFF AS SHE DROVE OUT OF THE CAMP, HOPing to plunge unseen into the vast black desert, but Angel spotted her too fast. He headed straight for her in his pickup, his high beams glaring in her rearview mirror. Her only chance now was to outrun the bastard, so she stomped the gas pedal. She'd gone off-roading in Land Cruisers many times before, and she knew all the pluses and minuses of the car. It had a big V-8 engine, but it handled like a fucking elephant. And the pickup behind her was a Toyota Tundra, which had the same damn V-8. To make matters worse, another pair of headlights soon appeared behind her—the second Land Cruiser. Shit, she thought, what the hell was I thinking? She should've punctured its tires before they left the camp.

The trail ran up the slope of a long ridge, skirting sand dunes to the left and right. The pickup and the other Land Cruiser were about two hundred yards behind. At first the pursuing vehicles drove in tandem, but then the two pairs of headlights diverged, with the pickup moving to the right and following a second trail that ran parallel to the first. She worried now that the parallel trail was slightly shorter, which would allow the bastards to cut her off. For a moment she considered leaving the trail altogether, but she knew this was the riskiest option—if she got stuck in the sand, she and Michael were as good as dead. And while she was thinking about all this and trying to drive as fast as she could without flipping the car or diving into a sand dune, she heard a distant, chugging noise. Then she remembered what Angel carried in the truck bed of his pickup.

She turned to Michael, who sat rigidly in the passenger seat. "GET DOWN!" she screamed. "GET—"

One of the bullets from the M240 smashed into the Land Cruiser's rear window. The safety glass shattered and Tamara felt a sudden blast to the left side of her face. Pain shot across her ear and scalp, and blood streamed down the side of her neck. She panicked, assuming the bullet had hit her, and almost let go of the steering wheel, but then she noticed that the driver-side window was gone. She touched the left side of her head and felt bits of safety glass embedded in her skin, but no bullet wound. The round had missed her and hit the driver-side window instead. She glanced to her right and saw Michael huddled in a ball under the glove compartment.

"Michael!" she screamed. "Are you all right?"

He didn't reply. Her left ear was ringing and wind was rushing into the car through the shattered windows. "Michael! MICHAEL!"

"Yes, I'm all right." His voice was low. "You should drive faster."

She pressed the pedal to the floor. The Land Cruiser bellowed and tore up the trail, leaping through the air and bouncing hard against the sand. They flew past the field of industrial debris and the first crater, the smaller one that hadn't caught fire, a yawning pit of blackness on their right. The machine gun in the pickup stopped chugging; because the parallel trail ran around the other side of the crater, the debris and sand dunes blocked the gunner's line of fire. But soon they would reach the crest of the ridge and come down the other side and the two trails would converge at the burning crater. The other Land Cruiser and the pickup were working as a team, the Cruiser lighting them up with its high beams so the gunner in the pickup could target them. Sooner or later another bullet would streak into the car and the race would be over.

"Michael!" she yelled. "Do you still have that pistol?"

"Yes," he replied.

"I'm going to tell you how to use it. First you have to—"

"I know how to use this weapon. It's a nine-millimeter M-9, the standard sidearm in America's Army."

"Okay, great. I want you to fire it at the headlights of the car behind us."

"The vehicle behind us is approximately a hundred yards away. The maximum effective range of the M-9 is fifty-five yards."

"What? What are you—"

"The weapon isn't accurate enough to hit the headlights, especially when fired from a moving vehicle."

"I just want you to try—"

The Land Cruiser suddenly jumped over the crest. They were airborne for what seemed like an eternity and then the front wheels hit the trail and they were speeding down the other side of the ridge.

The burning crater was straight ahead, a bowl of fire in the center of the windshield, growing larger as they barreled downhill. Tamara saw the junction where the trails came together, only a hundred yards away, and when she looked in the rearview she saw the pickup truck closing in from the southwest. Its machine gun chugged again and the bullets hit the sand behind them. There was no point, she realized now, in shooting out the headlights. The gunner could see them by the light from the crater.

The terrain flattened near the crater's rim. After they passed the junction Tamara made a hard left, trying to put as much distance as possible between her and the pickup. Then she felt a tap on her shoulder. Michael was climbing through the gap between the bucket seats, heading for the back of the car. "Go over there," he said, pointing through the windshield at the northern end of the crater. "Close to the edge."

"Michael, get the fuck down!"

"The other weapon I took from the soldiers is a concussion grenade. I'm going to throw it behind us. But first you need to get closer to the crater."

She glanced over her shoulder. Michael was in the backseat now, holding the grenade in his right hand. "Oh Jesus. Be careful with that . . ."

"I can time the throw so that the grenade explodes near the vehicles. But they're far apart and I need to disable both of them. So you have to drive near the edge."

This is insane, Tamara thought. But she didn't argue. She was out of ideas and willing to consider anything. She cut the wheel to the right, aiming for the crater's northern end.

She looked in the rearview again. The pickup and the other Land Cruiser had passed the junction and were less than fifty yards behind. They were trying to catch up to her by rounding the crater as quickly as possible, veering to the right and driving within twenty feet of the crater's edge. Michael turned around and looked through the space where the rear window used to be. He knelt on the backseat, clutching his grenade and silently moving his lips, probably counting in his head. But Tamara saw it was hopeless. The other Land Cruiser was about forty feet ahead of the pickup. If Michael was lucky he could knock out the Cruiser, but not the truck. And then the gunner in the truck bed would start firing at them again.

Then Michael yelled, "Turn left!" and threw the grenade.

Without thinking, Tamara cut hard to the left. An instant later she heard the explosion. In the rearview mirror she saw the other Land Cruiser jump off the ground, as if it had just hit a tremendous speed bump. The car bounced on the sand and the pickup swerved to avoid hitting it. And then the crater's edge fractured. A thousand cracks spread from the rim, and the sandy ground buckled. The Cruiser and the pickup plowed into the sand and began to slide sideways. Tamara stepped harder on the gas and turned away from the rearview, but as she sped from the rim she heard a low-pitched groan behind her. When she looked in the mirror again the vehicles were gone. The burning crater had grown still larger, with a new jagged edge at its northern end, and she saw nothing inside it but the insatiable flames.

22

"WHERE THE HELL HAVE YOU BEEN, LUCY?"

The director was pissed. Although he was more than five thousand miles away, in his corner office at the FBI headquarters in Washington, his disapproval registered loud and clear over the phone. Lucille had to hold her BlackBerry a couple of inches from her eardrum. "I'm still in Israel, sir," she said. "At a location on the West Bank." Specifically, she was in a van belonging to Olam ben Z'man, speeding north toward Ramat David Air Base, but the director didn't need to know this detail. If spies had infiltrated the Bureau, as Olam claimed, it would be unwise to reveal too much. "And I'm still working the kidnapping case. But we've run into a few complications."

"The West Bank? I thought you were in Jerusalem."

"Yes, sir, let me explain. I told you this case might have implications for national security and I was right. The guy we were looking for turned out to be a computer scientist who did classified work for the IDF. And he found evidence of a theft from the Lawrence Livermore nuclear-weapons lab. The stolen device is called an X-ray laser. The code name of the project is Excalibur."

There was a pause, a long one. The director's silence confirmed Lucille's suspicions. She knew he had to be aware of the situation because the Bureau was in charge of investigating security lapses at the national labs. "I heard about that report," he finally said. "The Israeli government contacted us last Tuesday and said they had satellite images showing Excalibur at the Iranian test site. But when we called the Livermore director, he said the X-ray laser had been dismantled and sold for scrap two months ago. And he had the records to prove it. So we told the

Israelis they were wrong. Their analysts must've misidentified the object in the image."

"Sir, if I may ask, where did those records come from?"

"From the contractor that did the dismantling. A small company in Sacramento called Logos Enterprises."

"And is this a reliable source?"

"We have no reason not to believe them. What's going on, Lucy? Spit it out."

Lucille took a deep breath. "My contacts here have given me a piece of intelligence that they haven't officially shared with Washington yet. The Israeli listening stations have been working overtime ever since the nuclear test, monitoring all communications in and out of Iran. Two days ago they intercepted a message from California to a location in western Afghanistan, close to the Iranian border. The message had U.S. military encryption, but the Israelis managed to break it."

"What?" The director raised his voice, forcing Lucille to move her BlackBerry a little farther from her ear. "They can't break our codes. That's impossible."

He was right—the Israeli intelligence agencies couldn't do it. But Olam ben Z'man had deciphered the message with that fancy quantum computer of his. He'd tried to explain the technology to Lucille before they left Shalhevet, but it was all gobbledygook to her. "Whoever sent the message must've screwed up the encryption," she said, sidestepping the truth for now. "Anyway, here's what it said: 'RECEIVED INQUIRY ABOUT REMOVAL OF EXCALIBUR. GAVE THE PREPARED ANSWER. AWAITING FURTHER INSTRUCTIONS.' As you can see, sir, the message suggests that some kind of cover-up may be going on."

"Who sent this? And who received it?"

"Both the sender and the receiver used unregistered wireless devices. But the sender's signal went through a cell tower in Sacramento, which is why I think you should take a closer look at Logos Enterprises. The receiver's signal went through a tower in the Afghan city of Herat. I checked with a contact at the National Security Agency who said the Taliban in that part of the country sometimes use cell phones, but they've never encrypted their messages this way."

There was another long pause. The director said nothing, but in the background Lucille heard him tapping his fingernail on his desk, which was something he always did when he was agitated. "This isn't good, Lucy. At the very least, this is an unauthorized use of military encryption. And if there's a connection to the Taliban or the Iranian nuclear program, we could have a real problem here."

Lucille agreed. She'd been worried as hell ever since Olam told her about Excalibur. She hadn't understood much of what he'd said, and she was reluctant to tell the director the crazier parts of the story—the data overloads, the memory caches, the universal program. He would say she was talking nonsense and dismiss her warnings altogether. But the intercepted message was solid evidence. It was proof that foreign operatives had stolen U.S. military codes and infiltrated a nuclear-weapons lab, which was a pretty goddamn serious security breach. And that was why Lucille had agreed to tag along on Olam's unauthorized mission. There was a nest of rats in Washington, and some of them had burrowed their way into the Bureau. She needed to convince the director to start flushing them out.

"Sir, if I may offer a suggestion? When you assign the team that's going to interview the folks at Logos Enterprises, instruct the agents not to reveal anything about the encrypted communications. They should just ask for more details about the dismantling of Excalibur. Then the contractor might get nervous and send another message we can intercept. If we're lucky we'll figure out who's on the receiving end in Afghanistan, and then we can get the Pentagon to track them down."

"Good idea. I'll set the wheels in motion." He coughed and started tapping his desk again. "Where exactly on the West Bank are you?"

Lucille looked out the van's window. They were less than ten miles from the airport. If she boarded Olam's plane, she would be violating every rule in the Bureau's manual. But that was okay, she thought. She was planning to retire soon anyway. "I'm sorry, sir, your signal's breaking up. I'll contact you again when I'm back in range."

23

BROTHER CYRUS REMOVED HIS GLOVES SO HE COULD HOLD THE DISK OF URA-
nium in his bare hands. It was only four inches wide and less than an inch
thick, but it was heavy for its size, almost ten pounds. Dull silver in color,
it looked like an oversize coin. Five identical disks lay inside the black
case in front of him, each nestled in its own lead-lined compartment.
Another case contained nine more pieces of uranium that had been fashioned into rings that would fit neatly around the disks. Individually, each
piece was safe to handle. Because U-235 decayed so slowly, the disks and
rings emitted little radiation. In fact, they didn't even feel warm to the
touch. The danger came from putting the pieces together.

In all, Cyrus had two hundred pounds of highly enriched uranium,
which was far more than the critical mass he needed. He'd obtained
the fuel from a research reactor in Kazakhstan. Despite all the American efforts to stop nuclear smuggling, tons of old Soviet uranium were
still stored in lightly defended facilities in Central Asia. For the sake of
simplicity, Cyrus had decided to build a "gun-type" device to trigger the
explosion, the same design used in the Little Boy bomb that destroyed
Hiroshima. He was familiar with the technology; during the early part of
his career he'd learned the basics of nuclear weapons so he could better
oversee the development of new ones. He'd been a cocky young man
in those days, obsessed with earthly wants and ambitions, but God had
been preparing him all along. He saw now that the Lord had guided his
life from the start, giving him all the tools he would need to bring about
the Redemption.

Cyrus put the disk of uranium back into its compartment, then rose
from his chair. He was inside a DRASH, a Deployable Rapid Assembly

Shelter, which was a fancy name for a large military tent, about twenty feet wide and forty feet long. At the center of the tent stood the ten-foot-high gun tube, which was anchored vertically into the ground. The uranium disks would be lowered to the bottom of the tube in a loose stack. The rings would be positioned near the top of the tube, held in a bullet-like canister. Bags of cordite would be stuffed into the tube just above this bullet. When everything was ready, Cyrus would order his men to detonate the cordite. The explosion would propel the bullet down the tube at a thousand feet per second, smashing it into the stack of uranium disks at the bottom. The rings would encircle the disks and the U-235 would go critical. The uranium's slow decay would accelerate in a chain reaction, releasing the energy from trillions and trillions of atoms at once.

He stepped toward the gun tube and ran his hand along the steel. The design had already proved itself at the Kavir test site. Cyrus had given the Iranians everything they needed, including another hundred pounds of the enriched uranium taken from the Kazakh reactor. In return, the Revolutionary Guards had allowed Cyrus to test the Excalibur prototype he'd stolen from Livermore. The Iranian nuke had fit neatly inside Excalibur, the gun tube slipping into the fat silver cylinder like a pencil inserted in a soda can. When the bomb went off, Excalibur's laser rods absorbed the X-ray radiation from the explosion and channeled billions of joules of energy into twelve powerful beams that converged inside the cylinder. By focusing on a tiny area, the X-ray lasers had challenged the limits of the universal program, pouring intense streams of data into specialized memory caches that had never handled so much information before. The resulting disruptions hadn't been severe enough to crash the program—the universe, like man, was a stubborn creature, unwilling to accept the light of God's love. But thanks to the code Michael had provided, Cyrus now knew the ideal beam configuration for overcoming the error-correction algorithms. Just as important, he planned to set off a bigger blast this time, which would intensify the flood of data into the caches. The explosion would be a hundred times more powerful than the Kavir test. It would guarantee the coming of the Kingdom of Heaven.

Keeping his hand on the gun tube, Cyrus closed his eyes. He'd sacrificed so much to reach this point. And one last sacrifice was still to come. The world had such a long history of suffering, it seemed cruel to add any more in its final hours. Yet it was necessary. It was brutal and ruthless and cold-blooded, but it was the only way to end the suffering once and for all. A flaw in the program had corrupted the universe, and this flaw was the dimension of time, which was the wellspring of evil and sin and death. By offering the infinite choices of the future, time destroyed the perfection of the present, just as Adam destroyed the Garden of Eden when he chose to eat the fruit from the Tree of Knowledge. But now the Redemption was at hand, and the True Believers would correct the flaw. They would eliminate the dimension of time and make God's kingdom unchanging and eternal.

Cyrus unwrapped his head scarf so he could stand face-to-face with the Almighty. "Oh Lord," he whispered. "Keep my will strong. Let me not be distracted by the wickedness of this world as we near the end. Let me think only of You. Soon I will lead Your subjects into the kingdom, and our resurrected thoughts will meld with Yours forever. Your Creation will be a flawless gem, fixed in the bliss of Eternal Life! From beginning to end, from alpha to omega!"

He continued praying for several more minutes, his hand on the steel column that pointed toward heaven. When he opened his eyes he saw General McNair in front of him, standing with his head bowed and waiting patiently for him to finish.

"Ah, Samuel!" Cyrus cried. "Have you been praying with me?"

"Yes, Brother," the general replied, raising his head. His face was long and gaunt, but his eyes were a vibrant blue. "As it says in the Book of Ruth, *Whither thou goest, I will go.*"

Cyrus wasn't wearing his head scarf, but it didn't matter. McNair had seen Cyrus's repellent face many times before. The two men had known each other for twenty-five years. More important, it was McNair and his Special Forces team who'd rescued Cyrus from the cave in Gazarak Mountain after he'd been tortured for three days by Satan's foot soldiers. The general had seen Cyrus's degradation and disfigurement, but the sight hadn't made him flinch. Instead, it had strengthened the bond between them.

"This is a glorious moment," Cyrus exulted. "After all our years of effort, we're standing on the Lord's doorstep! Very soon we will see His blessed face!"

McNair nodded. "Yes, Brother, I long to see Him." His voice was fervent but his eyes wouldn't meet Cyrus's. He kept licking his lips and opening and closing his hands. His combat uniform smelled strongly of perspiration.

"What's wrong, Samuel? You look troubled."

McNair was silent. Although he had a reputation as one of the toughest generals in the U.S. Army, he was often hesitant in front of Cyrus. He'd done more than any other True Believer to pave the way for God's Eternal Reign, and yet he needed constant reassurance.

Cyrus gave him a smile. "Are you having doubts?" he asked. "About your sacrifice?"

The general shook his head firmly. "No, Brother. No doubts at all."

"Then perhaps you're concerned about your troops? Maybe because they don't know what will happen to them?"

McNair shook his head again. "No, it's better this way. The burden of decision would've been too great, so I've made it for them. I can think of no finer mission for my men than opening the gates to God's kingdom." He closed his right hand into a fist and held it high. Then his arm fell to his side, slapping against his fatigues. "But the nearer we get, the more I worry. My superiors at Central Command are watching me closely. And the Joint Chiefs are demanding updates on Cobra every hour. My faith is still rock solid, Brother, but I'm worried that the unbelievers will discover our operation and shut it down."

"Be calm, Samuel." Cyrus rested his hand on McNair's shoulder. "You must always remember that God is on our side. Hasn't He given us everything we need?" He gestured at the gun tube standing in the center of the tent. "Even the unbelievers in Washington are playing their part, advancing the Lord's plans without knowing it. Speaking of which, what's the latest word on the timing of the Ranger assault?"

"The Iranians haven't responded to the president's ultimatum, but no one expected them to. Now that they have the bomb, they're not going to give it up without a fight. The president is going to give them another twenty-four hours, and if they don't respond by then, we'll get the green light. That means we're scheduled to launch the surprise attack after nightfall tomorrow."

Cyrus smiled again. "You see? We have plenty of time to put everything in place."

McNair nodded, but he still wouldn't look Cyrus in the eye. "Brother,

I spoke with Lukas a few minutes ago. He was in the convoy that just arrived from the Darvaza camp. He told me that Tamara was no longer a Believer. He said you cast her out because she disobeyed your orders."

Cyrus stopped smiling. It was painful to remember the incident. And he suspected that it was distressing for McNair, too. The general had become quite fond of Tamara. Cyrus squeezed the man's shoulder. "Yes, she weakened. Because of her sympathy for the boy. I had to order Angel to put her to sleep. But listen to me, Samuel—her rest will be brief. In just a matter of hours, she'll be resurrected along with the rest of us and we'll see her again in the eternal kingdom."

"No, she's still alive. Lukas told me that the convoy lost radio contact with Angel, so they sent a couple of men back to the camp. The men found four dead soldiers and no sign of Tamara or the boy. It looks like they escaped. One of the Land Cruisers was missing and the charred wrecks of two other vehicles were at the bottom of the burning crater."

Cyrus felt a twisting in his chest, a coil of righteous anger. "What? Why wasn't I informed of this?"

"Lukas said he just received the news. He was afraid to tell you, so he asked me to do it."

The coil of anger tightened. Cyrus closed his eyes. The corruption of the world never ceased to amaze him. It was so deeply embedded in the fabric of the universe that he sometimes felt as if every particle was conspiring against him. Now Tamara had put their entire operation in jeopardy. Cyrus knew that as soon as she reached the nearest town, she would try to contact the American authorities. Although the officials might not believe her story at first, they would certainly make inquiries. The woman had to be stopped.

Cyrus tilted his head back and took a deep breath. He followed the same advice he'd just given McNair—he reminded himself that God was on their side. Then he opened his eyes and pointed at the general. "All right, we're going to take care of this. We're going to organize a search party. Does Lukas have any idea where the prisoners might've gone?"

"He said the men who went back to the Darvaza camp found Land Cruiser tracks leading away from the crater. The men followed the tracks northeast through the desert, but they estimate that the prisoners are several hours ahead."

"Good, very good. I'll send Lukas and another team to Dashoguz so they can approach the prisoners from the opposite direction. With the Lord's help, we'll cut them off before they can reach any of the oasis villages."

"Is there anything I can do, Brother?"

Cyrus nodded. "I want to you to take advantage of the connections you've made with the Turkmen government. Get in touch with your new friend, the president-for-life, and tell him to mobilize his internal security forces. We may need their help to clean up this mess."

24

AN IDF TRANSPORT PLANE HOLDING FOURTEEN PASSENGERS—OLAM, DAVID, Monique, Lucille, and ten heavily armed *kippot srugot*—landed at the airport near Baku, Azerbaijan, at 2 A.M. on June 12. The pilot, an old friend of Olam's from his days in the *Sayeret Matkal,* taxied the plane to an empty hangar. They rendezvoused there with another of Olam's former *Sayeret* comrades, now a Mossad agent who ran Israel's intelligence operations in the region. David was surprised at first that Loebner had so many useful contacts, but Olam explained that the *Sayeret Matkal* was a fraternity of sorts. Veterans of the commando unit held influential positions in Israel's government ministries and intelligence agencies. Over the years, Olam said, he'd done many favors for his old colleagues, and now they were paying him back.

Inside the hangar Olam's team exited the plane and transferred to a minibus. They left the airport without any trouble—the Mossad agent had already bribed the Azerbaijani officials—and the minibus sped to Pirallahi, a grim petroleum depot on the Caspian Sea. When they reached the waterside Olam ordered everyone out of the bus, and they ran in the darkness toward a decrepit wooden pier. At the end of the pier was a rusty fishing trawler, about ninety feet long, with a tall mast near the bow and a two-story deckhouse at the stern. A dozen more *kippot srugot* who'd come to Azerbaijan on an earlier flight were already on the trawler. Once everyone was aboard, Olam started the boat's engines and within minutes they were gliding across the Caspian. David leaned against the deck rail as they headed east toward Turkmenistan. He saw nothing on the horizon but the distant lights of the offshore oil derricks.

The deckhouse had two cabins, a small one intended for the boat's captain and a much larger one for the crew. Olam assigned the smaller cabin to Lucille and Monique, and everyone else piled into the bunks in the larger room. David stretched out on an upper bunk and closed his eyes. Exhausted, he fell asleep almost immediately, but as he drifted off he pictured a long silver cylinder, lying on its side like a cannon. Its aluminum skin glinted under fluorescent lights. It was the X-ray laser, he realized as he slipped into unconsciousness. The Russian copy of Excalibur was waiting for them in the Turkmen depot on the other side of the sea.

David was so tired he could've slept for twelve hours, but at seven in the morning he awoke to the sound of off-key chanting. Olam's men stood in a circle, rocking back and forth as they read from their prayer books. Each man wore tefillin, the small black boxes that religious Jews strap to their foreheads and arms during morning prayers. For several minutes David lay in his bunk with one eye open, secretly watching the *kippot srugot* pray. As their singsong voices rose and fell, he wondered what Olam had told them about the universal program.

In a way, the program was a confirmation of their faith: the devout had always believed that God had a plan for the world, and now they could view His actual instructions, written in the divine language of quantum code. But it was still unclear, at least to David, exactly who had written the thing. As Monique had said, the universal program could've evolved on its own, emerging from randomness at the beginning of time and surviving to this day simply because it was more robust than any of the alternatives. So faith remained a choice, or perhaps more accurately, a predilection, and David was jealous of these *kippot srugot* who were blessed with the predilection for belief. For a moment he longed to join them, to grab a prayer book and sing a hymn to the Almighty. But the feeling didn't last long. The prayers went on and on, and after a while David lost interest. He quietly got dressed and slipped out of the cabin.

On the deck, the morning light was blinding. The Caspian Sea was still, its gray surface broken only by oil derricks and channel buoys. The boat smelled strongly of anchovies, which wasn't David's favorite aroma, so he walked toward the bow, hoping to get a bit of fresh air. Then he heard a distinctive clicking noise, the muffled bang of a pistol fitted with a silencer.

He ran toward the noise, then froze. Agent Parker stood next to the boat's railing, pointing her Glock at an abandoned derrick about a hundred yards off the starboard bow. The derrick's platform was unoccupied and David couldn't understand why Lucille was shooting at it. Then he realized she was practicing her marksmanship. She held the gun at eye level, clutching it with both hands, and took another shot. The bullet pinged off one of the derrick's struts.

Satisfied, she lowered her gun and replaced its empty magazine with a full one. She wasn't wearing her bright red suit anymore, nor the bright yellow one; she'd changed into a pair of bulky camouflage pants and a black turtleneck. Her shoulder holster hung from straps that looked like suspenders, running down to a belt cinched around her thick waist.

He stepped forward, moving slowly so as not to startle her. "Nice shot," he said. "I'm glad you're not one of the bad guys."

Lucille holstered the Glock and turned around. She looked different in the early-morning light—younger, fresher, healthier. Her face was pinkish, and the wrinkles under her eyes didn't seem quite so deep. She looked more like the Lucille whom David remembered from two years ago, the implacable FBI agent who'd chased him across thirteen states.

"Morning, Swift," she drawled. "You couldn't sleep either?"

"Olam's soldiers woke me up. They start their praying early."

She chuckled. "Well, let's hope they can fight as well as they pray. If the Turkmen Army catches us sneaking into their country, there's gonna be some shooting."

David nodded. He felt a wash of uneasiness in his gut. Until now he'd been so focused on finding Michael that he hadn't really thought about the dangers to Monique and himself. "What'll happen if they arrest us? You know anything about the prisons in Turkmenistan?"

"Prison? We'd be lucky to go to prison." She leaned against the boat's railing, propping her elbows on the top bar. "Far as I know, relations between America and Turkmenistan aren't so great. There's a good chance they'd hang us as spies. And the State Department wouldn't be able to do a damn thing about it." She shook her head. "No, we're on our own now. The only person who can help us is old Mr. Glock here."

She raised her right hand to her shoulder holster and patted the butt of her pistol. She was scaring the hell out of David with her dire warnings, but she didn't seem too concerned herself. She looked happy. David pointed at her gun. "Is that why you're doing target practice?"

"Yeah, it's been a while." She stretched her right arm, opening and closing the hand. "I was feeling a little stiff this morning, so I thought I'd give it a go. I figured if I used the silencer I wouldn't attract too much attention."

"You don't have to worry. There's no one else around for miles."

"You're right about that. I've been out here for almost an hour now and I haven't seen another boat. I suppose the fishing ain't so good around here."

"Well, the Caspian has a lot of environmental problems. It used to have tons of sturgeon, but the poachers killed almost all of them for their caviar. Now there's only smaller fish and those are disappearing, too."

Lucille cocked her head and smiled. "That's what I like about you, Swift. Your head's full of facts. And some of them are even useful."

She chuckled again, then removed her Glock from its holster. David thought she was going to resume her target practice, but instead she offered the gun to him. She held it by the barrel, pointing downward. "You should get some practice, too. You've fired a Glock before, right?"

David nodded. This was something else that had happened two years ago. "Yeah, but I was firing wild. I wasn't trying to hit anything."

"Okay, I'll teach you how to hit something. Go on, take the gun."

He hesitated. He wasn't sure he wanted to learn this.

Lucille frowned. "Look, Swift, you signed up for this job. And you're a danger to everyone if you don't know how to shoot. Now take the damn gun."

He grasped the handle. It was warm and a little slick from Lucille's sweat. She let go of the barrel and David felt the weight of the gun in his hand.

"It's loaded," she said. "So keep it pointed downrange. First thing you do is pull back the slide to put the round in the chamber. But you already know that, right?"

David cocked the gun. "What's my target?"

She pointed at a channel buoy about twenty-five yards from the boat. "Try hitting that thing. Now remember, the boat's moving, so you gotta track the target and aim a little behind. Keep your right arm straight and in line with the barrel. Wrap your left hand around your right, with the thumbs crossed. Line up the front sight inside the rear sight and the target just above. And squeeze the trigger nice and slow."

Trying to keep all these instructions in mind, David aimed at the buoy. It was a pretty big target, a bobbing cylinder about the size of an oil drum, and he didn't think he'd have any trouble hitting it. But when he pulled the trigger, the bullet dove into the water about five feet to the side.

"Wrong," Lucille said. "You screwed up the trigger pull. The Glock's got a heavy trigger, and if you jerk it back you'll throw off the aim. Don't worry about speed now. Just do it nice and steady."

David found another buoy to target. But he missed this one, too, by about the same margin. He tried and missed a third time and was about to try once more when Lucille said, "Wait," and stepped behind him.

"You're all tense and you're not breathing right," she said. She placed her right hand on the small of his back and her left on his chest, just below his collarbone. Then she straightened his spine. Her hands were fantastically strong. "Don't lean over so much. Now forget about the gun for a second and take three deep breaths."

He did as he was told. He was afraid not to. He breathed in the brackish air of the Caspian.

"Now take a few shallow breaths, baby breaths," she said. "Calm down, then take the shot. It's easy if you don't tense up."

Baby breaths. David liked that phrase. He took a few baby breaths and willed himself into stillness.

After several seconds he spotted another buoy. He lined up the sights and tracked the target. Then he squeezed the trigger nice and slow. The bullet clanged against the metal.

"There you go!" Lucille cried. "Don't stop now, keep shooting!"

He held the gun steady and pumped the trigger, adjusting his aim as the buoy slipped past. He counted nine more clangs before he ran out of ammunition. Nine hits out of the thirteen remaining bullets. Almost 70 percent, he calculated as he lowered the gun.

Lucille smiled and clapped him on the shoulder. "You see, I told you it was easy! And once you learn the trick, you never forget it. It's like riding a bicycle."

David smiled back at her, although he wasn't feeling quite so triumphant. He'd just learned that there was a trick to killing people, which wasn't a happy thought. "Well, you're a good instructor. Thank you."

"When all this is over, you can enroll at the FBI Academy. I'll even write you a letter of recommendation. It's never too late to serve your country, you know."

He handed her the Glock, glad to be rid of its weight. She ejected the empty clip and put in another full one. Then David heard footsteps behind them. He turned around and saw Monique on the trawler's foredeck, looking strong and beautiful in her own turtleneck and camouflage pants. Lucille waved at her cheerily. "Hey, come on over! I'm teaching combat skills to the peace activist."

Monique came toward them but didn't return the greeting. Her face was sober, her mouth a grim line. She's worried, David guessed. She's thinking about their mission.

Lucille pointed at her. "I'd give you a few tips, too, but I know you don't need 'em. I remember your dossier. You owned a Smith and Wesson before you moved in with Swift, right? Went to the shooting range once a month, if I'm not mistaken."

Monique nodded but didn't say anything. David could tell she was quite upset. Her eyes were glassy.

Lucille noticed, too. She holstered her gun and started walking away. "Well, I better get going. I'm gonna see if there's anything to eat on this boat besides anchovies."

David waited until Lucille reached the stern and entered the deckhouse. Then he slipped his arm around Monique's waist. "Hey, what's wrong? What—"

"Shhh." She put her index finger on his lips. "Don't talk, baby. Just hold me."

They stood by the boat's railing, neither saying a word. David smiled and caressed her cheek with the backs of his fingers, which she usually liked, but her worried expression didn't ease. Instead, it grew more severe. Her brow furrowed and she bit her lip. Turning away from him, she stared at the eastern horizon, where the coastline of Turkmenistan had yet to appear. It was more than worry, David thought. It was a premonition. Monique had a terrible look of despair on her face, as if she'd just foreseen her own death.

He couldn't stand to see that look. He wanted to erase it, expunge it, expel the evil thing forever. So he pulled her close and pressed his lips against hers. They were moist and warm and salty from the sea spray. She leaned into him, opening her mouth and closing her eyes. He closed his eyes, too, and felt her fingers on the back of his neck. The boat rocked under their feet but they were in perfect balance. David had the sensation that time itself was slowing down, each second stretching and stretching until everything stood still, his whole life contained in a single bright moment.

Monique moved her lips close to his ear. "I'm scared," she whispered. "I'm scared and I need you. Right now."

"Where should we—"

"The smaller cabin. While Lucille's eating breakfast, we'll have the room to ourselves." Then she took David's hand and led him toward the deckhouse.

25

AFTER THEY LEFT THE BURNING CRATER, TAMARA SPENT THE NEXT EIGHT hours driving through the Karakum Desert in pitch-black darkness. She refused to turn on the Land Cruiser's headlights because she was certain that Brother Cyrus would order the True Believers to search for her, and she knew they could spot her from miles away if the car's lights were on. So she crept along at a walking pace, judging the location of the sand dunes by the tilt of the Cruiser and steering blindly around them. Because Cyrus's convoy had gone southwest toward Kuruzhdey, she figured it would be safest to go in the opposite direction. Luckily, Michael was able to help her with the navigation. He'd apparently memorized a bunch of star charts, and by looking at the sky and checking his watch every ten minutes he was able to keep them on a northeasterly path.

The sun came up at 5:30 A.M. and Tamara stopped to refill the Cruiser's tank from the big jugs of gasoline stored in the back of the car. Now that it was daytime she could drive much faster, going up to thirty miles an hour in some stretches, but it was still a grueling, bumpy ride. By 9 A.M. the car was blazingly hot, and although they'd driven more than a hundred miles since leaving the Darvaza camp, they were still surrounded by sand dunes. The desert seemed endless. Every ten minutes Michael checked his watch and pointed out the correct direction, now judging by the position of the sun, but otherwise the boy was unresponsive. He hadn't said a word for hours. Tamara was getting worried about him—there was no food in the car and only one bottle of water. Every now and then he let out a low moan, which Tamara assumed was from hunger pains.

And then, shortly after ten o'clock, Michael said, "Look," and pointed to the right. Tamara thought at first that he was correcting their heading again, but this time he seemed to have made a mistake.

"Michael, are you sure that's northeast? It seems too close to the sun to be—"

"No," he said, still pointing. "A village."

Tamara leaned forward, squinting. She saw a cluster of gray shacks on the horizon. She immediately steered the Land Cruiser toward it, driving as fast as she could. To the left of the village she noticed tall poles sticking out of the sandy ground, a whole line of them stretching eastward. They were telephone poles.

She stepped on the gas. She needed to find a telephone in that village and place a call to the U.S. embassy. If she could talk to the American ambassador and explain the situation, maybe he could help them get out of Turkmenistan before the True Believers tracked them down. She didn't care about her own life, but she was determined to save Michael, even if it meant blowing the whistle on Brother Cyrus. Ever since she'd joined the True Believers she'd clung to Cyrus's prophecies, his promise that she would see her brother Jack again. But now she saw that Cyrus had been wrong—the promise had been fulfilled on earth, and not in the Kingdom of Heaven. Tamara saw her brother's spirit inside Michael. Jack's helpless eyes stared at her from the boy's blank face. Saving him was more important to her now than redeeming the universe.

After a few minutes she reached the edge of the village. Calling it a village was really an overstatement—there were only a dozen crude shacks built from sheets of rusted metal. The shacks leaned against one another in a crooked jumble, and several cooking fires smoldered in blackened pits nearby. The village lay at the end of a long sandy trail, but Tamara didn't see any cars or trucks. The only motor vehicle in sight was a dusty motorcycle parked behind a blocklike concrete structure, which was by far the biggest building in town. There was also a camel tethered to a pole, a mangy dromedary standing in a patch of sand littered with its droppings. But no people were outside. The hottest part of the day was approaching, and the village's residents were probably sweating inside their shacks.

Tamara stopped near the settlement, wondering what to do. Then she spotted two children carrying a tin washtub, one at each handle, like a Turkmen version of Jack and Jill. They were about six years old and quite adorable. The boy wore shorts and a striped T-shirt, and the girl wore a long colorful dress and a flowered kerchief. They were carrying water from the village pump to one of the shacks, but they slowed once they saw the Land Cruiser. They seemed more curious than afraid. Tamara stepped out of the car and walked toward them.

The children stood very still, looking her over. They'd probably never seen a woman in a uniform before. Tamara gave them a smile. "Hi, kids! I'm looking for a telephone." She said "telephone" loud and slow, hoping the Turkmen language had a similar word for it. "Do you know where I can find a *telephone*?"

They stared at her, intrigued but uncomprehending. Then Michael got out of the car and the children seemed to get nervous. They stepped backward and some water sloshed out of their washtub. Their eyes were fixed on the M-9 pistol tucked into the waistband of Michael's pants. Tamara went over to him and pulled the bottom of his T-shirt out of his pants so that it hid the gun. Then she turned back to the kids. "You know what a *telephone* is, right? Do your parents have a *telephone*?"

But the children continued to stare at Michael. Something about him fascinated them. He turned to the side, averting his eyes, but after a few seconds he stepped forward and knelt on the sand next to them. Then he pursed his lips and made a ringing noise. Tamara was dumbfounded—it sounded exactly like the ring of an old-fashioned, rotary-dial phone. Then Michael flattened his lips and let out a warble that sounded just like a cell phone's ring.

The children finally understood. The girl nodded and laughed. The boy shouted, "*Hanha!*" and pointed at the blocklike concrete building.

Tamara felt stupid. She should've realized this from the start. Although the concrete building was ugly, it was a lot nicer than the metal shacks, so it probably belonged to the richest family in town, the only residents who could afford phone service. "Thank you," she told the children. Then she turned to Michael. "Come, we're going to make a call."

Taking a shortcut, they approached the building from behind, striding past the motorcycle parked by the back door. It was a Ural, a rugged, well-made Russian bike with a sidecar. Tamara gave it a quick once-over as she walked by, but Michael stopped and stared. His face was so rapt, Tamara had to smile. "You like motorcycles?" she asked.

He pointed at the Ural. "This looks like the motorcycle that Monique Reynolds let me ride."

"Monique Reynolds? She's your adopted mom, right?"

He nodded. "We were on the beach. She let me ride in the sidecar. And she showed me how to start the engine and work the controls."

Tamara waited a few seconds, letting the teenager examine the bike. Then she said, "Come on," and Michael reluctantly followed her.

They walked around the building to the front door, which was painted black. Tamara knocked on it, and when the door opened she felt even stupider than before. The man in the doorway wore a green uniform with red epaulets, and behind him was a dark, grim room with the green-and-red flag of Turkmenistan hanging on the wall. Shit, she thought, this isn't a private residence. It's the local police station. And judging from what she knew about third-world policemen, she sensed that this officer would be more of a hindrance than a help.

The man said nothing. He simply narrowed his eyes. His face was square and swarthy and suspicious.

"We're *Americans*," Tamara said, pointing at herself and Michael. "And we're very lost. We were wondering if we could borrow your *telephone*."

The officer remained silent. He poked his head out the door and looked behind them, probably wondering how the hell they got there. Then he spotted the Land Cruiser, which was parked about two hundred feet to the right of the police station.

"Yes, that's our car," Tamara said, playing the hapless tourist. "And we're almost out of gas. We really need to make a *telephone* call."

The man frowned and stuck his hand out. "Passport!" he barked.

Tamara put on an abject expression, tilting her head in a hangdog way. "And that's another problem! Someone stole our passports and all our money! We have absolutely nothing!"

"Passport!" he barked again, louder this time. It was apparently the only English word he knew. When she didn't respond, he leaned toward her and shouted in Turkmen, spraying her cheeks with saliva.

She gritted her teeth and looked the guy over. He had a semiautomatic in the holster hanging from his belt. A Russian Makarov, by the looks of it. Tamara had seen Makarovs before. A few of the True Believers carried them. "We just need to make one phone call, all right? Then we'll explain everything."

The officer turned sideways and pointed at the grim room inside the station. He shouted more incomprehensible Turkmen, but the message was clear: he was ordering her and Michael to go inside, and she doubted very much that it was an invitation to use the phone. She took a step toward the doorway and peered into the darkness. She saw a cracked cement floor and a couple of desks and an empty jail cell with rusty iron bars. But no other police. Officer Spittle was alone.

She looked over her shoulder at Michael. "I want you to do something for me, okay? Pretend to trip on the doorstep."

"Excuse me," Michael said, "I don't—"

"You don't have to understand. Just pretend to fall down."

She stepped inside the station and positioned herself next to the Turkmen officer. Then Michael surprised her again. Staring straight ahead, he banged his foot against the doorstep and fell sprawling to the floor. When the officer shouted at him, he let out a convincing groan. And when the man bent over to grab him by the elbow, Tamara pulled the Makarov out of his holster and cocked the pistol. Before the officer could turn around, she fired a warning shot into the ceiling. The man stumbled backward, his arms flailing.

"OVER THERE!" Tamara shouted, pointing at the jail cell.

She kept the gun aimed at the officer's forehead until he stepped inside the cell and closed the door behind him. She tested the bars to make sure it was locked. Then she started looking for the telephone. "Shut the front door," she told Michael. "And lock it."

The phone was on one of the desks. She picked up the receiver and heard a dial tone.

"Tamara?" Michael stood in the doorway, gazing outside. "Someone's coming."

"Who? Another officer?"

"No, another Land Cruiser."

26

LUKAS LEANED FORWARD IN THE PASSENGER SEAT. HE SAW THE CAR THE prisoners had taken, parked in the dunes next to an oasis village, about a quarter mile ahead. "That's them!" he shouted at Jordan, the lanky, red-haired True Believer who was driving their Land Cruiser. Jordan stepped on the gas and the car rocketed down the trail. They would make contact in fifteen seconds, Lukas estimated. He turned to the two soldiers in the backseat.

"Remember my orders," he warned. "Shoot the tires, but not the passenger compartment. I need to interrogate Tamara before we execute her. Understand?"

He pulled back the slide on his Heckler & Koch. Lukas didn't really need to interrogate the bitch. He wanted her to survive the firefight so he could shoot her in the guts afterward and watch her die. He wanted her to die a slow, painful death, to suffer as much as Angel had suffered after his pickup fell into the burning crater. Although the Redemption was fast approaching, there was still a little time left for payback.

THE LAND CRUISER WAS GOING AT LEAST SEVENTY MILES AN HOUR, ITS wheels hurling long rooster tails of sand. At first the car followed the trail toward the police station, but when it was about two hundred feet away it veered off the path and started leaping through the dunes. Tamara saw it was heading straight for *her* car. The idiots probably thought she and Michael were still in the vehicle.

The Makarov was still in her hand, still cocked. She put herself in the shooting stance she'd learned seven years ago in basic training, planting her feet squarely in the doorway of the police station. The Land Cruiser was passing from left to right, about a hundred feet away. She closed her left eye and sighted down the barrel. Then she started firing at the car's right front tire.

After the second shot, the tire exploded and the car swerved. She shifted her aim, firing at the rear tire now, but the car tilted on the edge of a dune and toppled over, rolling down the sandy slope and coming to rest on its roof. She targeted the windows, trying to hit the car's occupants before they could crawl out of the upside-down vehicle, but the front half of the Land Cruiser had slid behind a sand dune, so she had to pour all her fire into the backseat. Then she saw some movement behind the car. An instant later, a bullet hit the police station's doorframe, just inches above her head. She scrambled back inside the station, crouching on the floor beside Michael. More bullets whizzed through the doorway. They slammed into the desks and chipped the cement floor and ricocheted off the iron bars of the jail cell. The Turkmen police officer let out a yelp and backed into the corner of the cell, trying to get out of the line of fire.

The shooting continued for about fifteen seconds, then abruptly ceased. Shuffling closer to the doorframe, Tamara peeked around its edge and spotted two figures behind the overturned Land Cruiser. A soldier with flaming-red hair aimed his rifle at the police station, and a big, ugly lummox pointed his handgun in the same direction. Tamara recognized them—Jordan and Lukas, two of her least favorite True Believers. They were former Delta Force commandos who'd been recruited to the cause by Brother Cyrus and General McNair, and both were excellent marksmen. Tamara quickly withdrew into the station.

Michael tugged on her sleeve. He looked scared but not panicky, which was damn good under the circumstances. "Are they Brother Cyrus's soldiers?"

She nodded. "I got some of them, but two are still standing."

She heard a gunshot, but no bullet hit the police station. Then she heard another shot, followed by the sound of a distant ricochet. Tamara peeked around the doorframe again and saw Lukas aiming his pistol at her Land Cruiser. One of its front tires was already flat. Lukas fired again and burst the other front tire. He'd obviously realized by now that she and Michael weren't in the car, but he was shooting at it anyway to eliminate their means of escape. Feeling a surge of anger, Tamara started to aim her Makarov at him, but as she pointed the gun through the doorway a bullet from Jordan's M-16 whistled past her right ear.

"Goddamn it!" she screamed, falling backward on her ass. "I can't get a shot! That redheaded asshole is covering the door!"

Michael bit his lower lip and stared at the floor. For a moment Tamara thought he was going to start crying. Then he pointed to the back of the police station. Past the desks and the jail cell and the Turkmen flag was another door, the station's back door. "We can go out that way," he said. "And ride the motorcycle that's parked behind the building. The Ural, the one with the sidecar."

Shit, Tamara thought, why didn't she think of that? She felt a burst of relief so strong she laughed out loud. But then she pictured the area behind the police station and shook her head. The shacks behind the station were too tightly clustered. She knew she couldn't maneuver the Ural motorcycle between them. She'd have to go around the shacks, and that meant they'd be exposed. They'd have to ride across Jordan's line of fire, less than a hundred feet from his position. The bastard could easily pick them off.

Unless he was distracted by something else. As Tamara crouched on the cement floor of the police station, a plan began to form in her mind. It wasn't a perfect plan. But in combat, there was no such thing as perfect.

She gazed at Michael. She wanted to grab his shoulders and look him in the eye, but she knew it would upset him. Instead she spoke softly and slowly. "Michael, how much do you know about the Ural? You said your mom showed you how to start the engine, right?"

He nodded. "Yes, and how to work the controls. The throttle and the brake are on the right handle, and the clutch is on the left. The gears—"

"Do you think you can ride it by yourself?"

He nodded again, smiling. "Yes, I can ride it. Monique Reynolds said the sidecar gives the motorcycle more stability. She was going to let me drive it on the beach, but then David Swift came running toward us and said it wasn't safe to—"

"Okay, Michael, listen up. I want you to go out the back door and get on the Ural and start it up. Then turn the bike to the south and ride as fast as you can. You got that?"

"And you're going to sit in the sidecar?"

Tamara shook her head. "No, I'm going to stay here. Cyrus's soldiers will try to shoot you while you're riding away. But I'm going to shoot them first. I'll run out the door and fire so many bullets at them that they won't be able to aim at you."

"Do you want me to come back here later? To pick you up?"

"No, I want you to keep going. Ride south until you come to another village. Then find a telephone and call David Swift. Tell him what Brother Cyrus is planning to do. You know David Swift's phone number, right?"

He nodded a third time. "Yes, it's 212-555-3988."

Tamara smiled. She wanted so much to hug the boy, but she kept her hands to herself. Her stomach churned as she looked at Michael, knowing she would never see him again. But it was the only way. She had to save him. "Okay, go!" she said, pointing at the station's back door. "Don't forget what I told you!"

Obediently, he turned around and dashed across the room. While he opened the back door and ran outside, Tamara peeked around the frame of the front doorway again. The two gray Land Cruisers glared in the sunlight, the farther one kneeling on its flat tires and the closer one lying on its back like a beetle. Lukas and Jordan crouched behind the overturned car, looking for signs of movement. Beyond them, the sand dunes stretched to the horizon.

A moment later, Tamara heard the rumble of the Ural's engine. The True Believers heard it, too. Jordan lifted his head from his rifle's scope and Lukas turned toward the noise. Tamara waited until the engine's rumble rose in pitch and volume, indicating that Michael had started his dash to the south. She saw Jordan swing his M-16 away from her, aiming it in a new direction. Then Tamara charged out of the doorway, screaming at the top of her lungs and firing the Makarov at the soldiers.

Jordan's head swiveled and his eyes widened and he started to point his rifle at her, but she shot him in the throat before he could pull the trigger. Then she aimed her gun at Lukas, but he ducked behind the Land Cruiser and her shot passed over his shoulder. Tamara charged forward and fired at him again, trying to get between Lukas and the motor-cycle. If she could find some cover behind a sand dune, she could pin him down and stop him from taking a shot at Michael. From the corner of her eye she saw the boy on the Ural, barreling over the sand about a hundred feet away.

But then Lukas did something she hadn't expected: he came around the back of the overturned car and shot her from behind. Tamara felt a jolt between her shoulder blades and another in the small of her back. The bullets pushed her forward and made her drop her pistol, but she felt no pain at first. She even managed to take a few more steps before falling. As she tipped forward she turned her head, hoping to see Michael again, but instead she saw Lukas kneeling on the lip of a dune and point-ing his handgun at the motorcycle. Then the pain tore into her, ripping through her whole body, because she knew Michael wouldn't make it. Lukas would shoot him and he would die in agony. And it was her fault.

She landed facedown, splashing into the sand. More pain shot through her torso and her vision blurred. She heard more gunshots, a great many gunshots, but she didn't hear what she expected next, the sound of the motorcycle crashing. With great difficulty she lifted her head and tried to focus.

The gunshots were coming from the Ural. Michael had taken his M-9 out of his pants while riding the motorcycle and fired at Lukas. The big, ugly True Believer lay behind the dune now, clutching his right arm. Tamara felt a bolt of joy that was even more intense than her pain. Michael fired three more bullets that flew over Lukas's head. Then she heard nothing but the blessed roar of the Ural's engine, which grew steadily fainter as the boy sped away.

Lukas staggered to his feet. He found his pistol and tried to fire it at Michael with his left hand, but the motorcycle was out of range now. Tamara lowered her forehead to the sand and whispered, "Thank you." Then she began creeping toward the upside-down Land Cruiser. She was dying, but there was one more thing she could do. She couldn't move her legs, so she clawed the ground with both hands and dragged the rest of her body forward, leaving a trail of thickened, reddish sand behind her.

She didn't stop until she reached Jordan's body. There was a bloody hole in his neck, just above the collar of his flak jacket. Tamara used the last of her strength to fling herself on top of the corpse. She felt unbearably dizzy and was desperate to close her eyes. But she bit her tongue to stay conscious and hung on to the dead soldier, her hands groping.

Then she heard Lukas's voice above her. "You stupid bitch!" he yelled. "You think you can stop us?"

Before she could reply, he stomped on her back. The heel of his boot smashed into her ribs. Then he grabbed a fistful of her hair and pulled back her head. "Answer me, bitch! You think you can stop us?"

"No," she gasped. "I can't. But Michael will."

"No, he fucking won't!" he screamed into her ear. "I'm gonna get on the radio and report his position to the other units. And then we'll have twenty soldiers coming at him from all sides. So you haven't accomplished a fucking thing. You've just prolonged his suffering! And now you're gonna suffer, too!"

He grasped her shoulder and flipped her onto her back. But she'd already removed one of the M67 grenades from the pouch in Jordan's flak jacket. While Lukas had been screaming at her, she'd pulled the safety clip and the pin and released the lever.

Tamara clasped her hands around the grenade, hiding it from view. Lukas stared at her, puzzled, as the four-second fuse burned down between her palms. She didn't know if she would ever see the Kingdom of Heaven, but that didn't matter now. She smiled at Lukas. "You're wrong," she whispered. "Our suffering is over."

27

AS NIGHT FELL ON THE EASTERN SHORE OF THE CASPIAN SEA, OLAM'S
assault team departed from the fishing trawler in three Zodiacs. Each of
the inflatable boats held eight commandos and a sixty-horsepower outboard, equipped with heavy-duty mufflers to minimize the engine noise.
The Zodiacs cruised in a long line, spaced about a hundred yards apart.
Olam rode in the first boat with David, Monique, and Lucille. They wore
black pants and black shirts, and their faces and necks and hands were
smeared with black paint. Most of the *kippot srugot* in the Zodiacs carried Galil rifles, the standard infantry weapon of the IDF, but Olam had
slung an M24 sniper rifle over his shoulder. Lucille carried her Glock
and wore a black wool cap over her mass of platinum hair. David and
Monique carried Desert Eagle pistols that Olam had given them. David's
gun, tucked in a shoulder holster, pressed against his ribs, impossible to
ignore.

They were approaching the strait that led to the Kara-Bogaz, a shallow gulf of the Caspian. A bridge ran over the strait, but luckily it wasn't
carrying any traffic at the moment. This stretch of the Turkmen coastline
was deserted. Nevertheless, the commandos were silent as they drifted
under the causeway, letting the current sweep them past the concrete
pylons. Within twenty minutes they'd passed through the strait and into
the vast darkness of the Kara-Bogaz. The gulf stretched a hundred miles
inland but was only a few yards deep. Because they were now very far
from the nearest habitation, they could rev up the outboards. Soon they
were heading full speed toward their landing point, which was directly
north of their ultimate objective, the Turkmen military depot.

Olam sat between David and Monique, his muscled torso straining against the rubber side of the Zodiac. He nudged David with his elbow. "What do you think?" he said, gesturing at the blackness all around them. "It's like the universe before the Creation, eh? *'And the earth was without form, and void, and darkness was upon the face of the deep.'* And we are like the spirit of God, yes? Moving upon the face of the waters?"

David frowned. He wished he was sitting next to Monique. After they'd made love in the trawler's cabin, she'd fallen into her somber mood again. They'd hardly talked at all as they'd changed into their black clothes and smeared paint on their faces. Now David tried to look past Olam and catch Monique's eye, but it was so dark he could see only her profile. He shook his head and turned back to Olam. "We're not the spirit of God," he said.

"What's wrong, my friend? Are you nervous? I told you, you shouldn't worry. We will destroy the X-ray laser before the *Qliphoth* can use it. You will bring us victory because you're the instrument of—"

"Yes, you told me, the instrument of *Keter,* the first step in the enumeration of the universe, whatever that means."

Olam seemed amused. He cocked his head and pointed at David. "You don't like to talk about God, do you? You'd prefer to avoid it, eh? You'd rather talk about forces and particles and dimensions."

"No, that's not it. I just don't like it when people think they're acting on God's behalf. Acting as if God told them what to do, and now they think it's their job to tell everyone else. And that's the whole history of religion, pretty much."

Olam laughed, a low rumble in his chest. "For a historian, you're playing very loose with the facts. Not every religion is so demanding. In my version of Judaism, God doesn't give orders. He simply exists. He's a presence in us and in everything around us." He gestured at the darkness again, raising his right hand and tracing a circle with his finger.

David stared at the surrounding waters, looking past the silhouettes of the commandos sitting on the other side of the boat. He turned toward Monique again, just to reassure himself that she was still there, but Olam's broad shoulders blocked her from view. The man's mysticism was starting to annoy him. "If it's just a presence, why not call it 'reality'? Why create this concept of God at all?"

"Perhaps I'm not explaining so well. The universe is information, yes? I think we can agree on that. And God is the idea that connects the information. The program that brings everything together."

"But why call it God? When you use that name, you're implying the presence of a heavenly father figure, some benevolent old man who watches over the universe and cares about us. And that kind of God doesn't exist."

"Are you sure?" He leaned a little closer to David. His body odor mixed with the brackish scent of the gulf. "What do you think protects us from chaos? If there were no program, the universe would be a mishmash. Everything would happen at once and nothing would make sense. But the program chooses one thing out of all the quantum possibilities and says, 'So be it!' And though the choice might seem random to us, it is anything but. You, of all people, should remember what Einstein said: God doesn't play dice with the universe. The program coordinates everything."

"So what are you saying? That the program is conscious? That it has our best interests at heart?"

Olam shook his head. "All I'm saying is that everything is chosen according to a plan. Every movement of every particle. And in that sense, the universe cares about us. Everything and everyone is important. And that's reassuring, yes?"

David shrugged. He couldn't think about this right now. He was sweaty and disoriented and very frightened. He wished Olam would just stop talking.

The man patted his shoulder. "I need to speak to Agent Parker for a moment. Slide down here and take my place."

He stood up and made his way to the stern, where Lucille sat next to the Zodiac's coxswain. As soon as Olam left, David gratefully slid next to Monique. She didn't say anything. She didn't even turn her head. But she stretched her hand toward his and clasped it.

Thirty minutes later, the coxswain throttled back the engine and the Zodiac slowed. David gazed ahead and saw a long black ridge on the southern horizon, running between the surface of the gulf and the starry sky. After ten more minutes the coxswain shut off the outboard and raised the propeller, and the commandos jumped out of the boat and began dragging it to shore. David and Monique got out, too, first splashing in the shallow water and then walking on a salt flat that crunched under their boots. Soon the commandos beached all three Zodiacs and headed for the ridge.

A narrow trail climbed the steep slope. David was scrambling up the trail, behind Olam and Lucille and ahead of Monique, when he saw a flashing light. Someone was signaling to them. This man was yet another of Olam's *Sayeret Matkal* comrades, a Mossad agent who'd worked for several years in Central Asia. Olam had already briefed the assault team about the purpose of this rendezvous, but David was still impressed when he reached the top of the trail and saw what was waiting there. A herd of twenty-two horses stood near the edge of the ridge, their bridles held by local Turkmen boys hired by the Mossad agent.

Monique caught up to David and stood beside him. "They're beautiful," she whispered.

"They're Akhal-Tekes, the golden horses of Turkmenistan," he whispered back. "They're supposed to have fantastic speed and stamina."

Monique approached one of the animals, holding out her hand and speaking to it gently. Although she was a city girl, she'd done some weekend horseback riding when she was a professor at Princeton. David's experience was more limited—he'd gone on a pony ride when he was seven and spent a day and a half at a dude ranch with his first wife ten years ago. But Olam had assured him that the Akhal-Tekes were gentle creatures and that David's horse would instinctively follow the others in the herd. One of the Turkmen boys helped David into the saddle and held the bridle while he got the horse under control.

Olam ordered two of the commandos to stay behind to guard the Zodiacs. Another six were assigned to reconnaissance: riding the fastest horses, they would venture several miles ahead of the main party and screen its flanks, ready to radio a warning if they spotted any threat. That left Olam, David, Monique, Lucille, and twelve others in the main group. They trotted off to the south, heading across an arid plain toward the military depot.

It was the emptiest country David had ever seen. The landscape was relentlessly flat and the only lights were the stars overhead. He could hear his horse's hooves striking hard-packed sand, but he couldn't see the ground or any of the other Akhal-Tekes. It was amazing that the horses could find their way in the dark. Their night vision was clearly better than his. After a while he started to enjoy the ride, the sensation of flying through the darkness with the cool wind buffeting his face. The other horses trotted ahead and behind him, their hooves pummeling the plain, and he wondered which one was Monique's. It was so exhilarating that for a few seconds he forgot all about the X-ray laser and what they were planning to do.

After an hour, though, David started to get saddle sore, and the ride became a lot less exhilarating. But Olam didn't stop. At 2 A.M. a crescent moon rose above the horizon, and its light seemed almost blinding compared with the darkness they'd been traveling through. David could suddenly see the other horses and riders beside him and the sweat streaming down his own horse's neck. And in the distance, about half a mile ahead, he saw a sinuous stretch of cliffs gleaming in the moonlight. It was an enormous, jagged wall of rock looming over the plain like the cliffs of the Grand Canyon. The moonlight illuminated the strata running across the rock face, broad bands of lighter-colored stone alternating with darker layers.

"Yangykala," Olam muttered. He was riding a few feet to David's left.

"What? Is that the name of the canyon?"

Olam nodded. "It means 'burning fortress.' Come, let's hurry. Now that the moon is up, anyone can see us. Head for the shadows below the cliffs."

A minute later they cantered into the shadowed area at the base of the rock wall. They rode single file, with Olam in the lead, entering a ravine that twisted deeper into the canyon. David saw towering rock formations on all sides, shaped like castles and temples and spires and prows. It made him feel a bit claustrophobic—the cliffs had an angry, menacing look, as if they were just waiting to slide forward and crush the life out of him. He was starting to wonder if maybe they'd taken a wrong turn when Olam gave a signal to halt the column. The commandos dismounted and David clumsily did the same.

Olam scrambled up to a rock shelf, then lay on his stomach and peered through his binoculars, which were equipped with an infrared display. To David's surprise, Lucille followed right behind him, moving as nimbly as a mountain goat, and took out her own pair of binoculars. After several seconds Olam waved at David and Monique, signaling them to come forward. They joined him on the shelf, crawling on all fours. Olam passed his binoculars to David. "Take a look at the depot," he whispered. "And tell me what you think."

David fitted the binoculars to his eyes and adjusted the focus. He saw a building that looked like a small warehouse, maybe a hundred feet long and fifty feet wide, sitting at the head of the ravine where the canyon dead-ended. The building was surrounded by sheer cliffs on three sides. For extra protection it was enclosed in a rectangle of chain-link fencing, about twenty feet high. "It's a good location," David said. "Very defensible."

Olam nodded. "What do you think of the security?"

"I don't see any guards or sentries. But I suppose they could be somewhere inside the building."

Olam took the binoculars from David and handed them to Monique. "What about you? You see anything unusual?"

"The lights are out," she said from behind the binoculars. "The compound has floodlights, but they're turned off. Without the lights, they can't see if anyone's approaching. Which suggests that either they're very stupid or no one's there."

"Correct." Olam smiled at her. "It looks like the soldiers locked up the place and went home. While we were on the trawler we scanned the radio bands used by the Turkmen military and overheard some unusual messages. It appears that the country's president ordered his internal security forces to pull back to the capital for some reason. This might be a very lucky thing for us."

"Or it might be a trap." This warning came from Lucille, who'd just lowered her binoculars. "The soldiers could be hiding in the building, waiting to ambush us."

Olam nodded. "Correct again. We must be cautious."

He turned around and went back to confer with his commandos. Two of them detached from the group and headed for the storage depot, one carrying a pair of bolt cutters and the other holding a sledgehammer and a Halligan bar. Four other commandos took up positions on the ledges of the surrounding cliffs and pointed their rifles at the compound. Then Olam returned to the rock shelf carrying two more pairs of binoculars. He gave one to David and kept one for himself. "Now we can all see what happens."

David trained his binoculars on the two commandos approaching the depot. Because the infrared scope captured heat emissions, the heads and hands of the men glowed brightly on the display. The commandos crept up to the fence and sliced through the chain-link with the bolt cutters. Then they slipped into the compound and scuttled toward the building's entrance. Working together, they inserted the Halligan bar between the door and the frame and pounded it with the sledgehammer. The noise echoed in the ravine. In a few seconds the commandos pried the door open and rushed into the building.

The echoes died and the canyon was silent again. David couldn't see the commandos anymore. His stomach clenched as the silence went on. Then Olam's radio crackled with a spurt of Hebrew words. Olam responded in Hebrew, then turned to David and Monique. "There are no Turkmen soldiers in the building. But my men have found an aluminum cylinder. About three meters long and one meter in diameter."

David nodded. "Those are the dimensions of Excalibur. It must be the Russian copy of the laser."

"Not so fast," Olam said. "I want you and Dr. Reynolds to go to the building and see if it's really the X-ray laser. You saw the damaged laser in the storage room at Soreq, so you know what to look for. It should have a sliding panel at the midpoint of the cylinder, and the twelve laser rods should be inside. Once you confirm that it's the laser, tell the men to begin placing the C-4 charges." He turned around and pointed at the six remaining commandos, each of whom carried a munitions bag. "That's the ordnance team. They have enough explosives to level the building."

Lucille rose to her feet. "Wait a second," she said. "If Swift and Reynolds are going in, I'm going with them."

Olam nodded. "Understood. I'll stay outside and keep watch with the other men on the cliffs. Just in case the *Qliphoth* decide to sneak up on us. Because they want the laser, too, yes?" Smiling, he patted the sniper rifle slung over his shoulder.

"All right," Lucille said. "We'll be back in a few minutes." Then she and David and Monique followed the men in the ordnance team, who were already jogging toward the depot.

They ducked through the cut in the fence, then ran to the door that had been pried open. Inside the warehouse, David saw flashlight beams crisscrossing the darkness, illuminating dozens of old crates stamped with Cyrillic letters. The ordnance team opened their munitions bags and pulled out spools of wire and yellow bricks of C-4, which looked like blocks of cheese wrapped in cellophane. Meanwhile, the two commandos who'd broken into the building stood in the center of the room, pointing their flashlights at a long aluminum cylinder resting on wooden trestles. As David approached the device he saw the sliding panel, which curved around the cylinder's waist. It resembled the sliding cover of a rolltop desk, and was just big enough for the insertion of a nuclear warhead. The design allowed the warhead to be placed next to the laser rods. Once the bomb was in position, the panel would be closed and the air pumped out of the cylinder so the radiation from the nuclear blast could travel unimpeded to the lasers.

The panel was closed now. Tentatively, David grasped its upper edge. He needed to slide the panel down to see if the laser rods were inside the cylinder. He was half afraid that an old nuclear warhead would also be in there, but he knew this was absurd. The Russians wouldn't have left *that* behind.

He tried to slide the panel down but it didn't move. He tried again, putting a little more muscle into it. Still it wouldn't budge.

Monique came over to him. "What's wrong? It won't open?"

"It hasn't been opened in twenty years. It's probably rusty."

Now Lucille stepped forward. "Here, let me give you a hand."

David moved over and Lucille gripped the panel's edge. She whispered, "One, two, three," and on "three" they both yanked on the panel and it came sliding down. David saw, to his relief, that there was no nuclear warhead inside. But there were also no laser rods. The cylinder was empty except for a stack of yellow bricks, each impaled by a slender metal plug that was connected to a tangle of wires. They looked like the bricks that the Israelis had just taken out of their munitions bags, the blocks of C-4. This confused David—how did they get in here already? But Lucille saw the reason right away.

"BOMB!" she yelled. She turned around to face Olam's commandos, who stopped what they were doing. "THE CYLINDER'S RIGGED! EVERYONE GET OUT!"

Then Lucille turned toward the door and lowered her torso like a linebacker. Hooking David with her right arm and Monique with her left, she shoved them across the warehouse, still yelling, "BOMB! BOMB! BOMB!" They'd just reached the door, a few steps ahead of the commandos, when the C-4 exploded.

28

ARYEH GOLDBERG WAS AN EXPERT CODE BREAKER. BEFORE HE'D JOINED SHIN Bet, he'd done his army service in Unit 8200, the famed IDF division that deciphered the communications of Israel's enemies. For three years he'd decrypted the coded radio messages of the Syrian and Lebanese armies, which were picked up by the Israeli listening station on Mount Avital in the Golan Heights. And in the years since then, Aryeh had improved his code-breaking skills, learning new cryptographic techniques while working for Shin Bet. But when he saw Olam ben Z'man's quantum computer, he knew everything had changed. Thanks to this cabinet full of glass tubes and optical fibers, all his hard-earned expertise was obsolete.

Now Aryeh sat at a desk in Olam's trailer in Shalhevet, feeding data to the computer. The data came, coincidentally enough, from Unit 8200; Olam was an old friend of General Yaron, the unit's commander. Shortly before Olam left for Turkmenistan with the Americans, he'd quietly made an arrangement with Yaron, offering to decrypt any coded messages that Unit 8200 couldn't break. So on the morning of June 13, one of the settlement's *kippot srugot*—a young, slender zealot named Ehud ben Ezra—picked up a stack of computer disks from the Unit 8200 headquarters in Herzliya and delivered them to Shalhevet. The disks, which now lay on the desk in front of Aryeh, contained all the encrypted communications that had been intercepted by Israeli listening stations over the past three days.

Aryeh hadn't contacted his superiors at Shin Bet since coming to Shalhevet. The messages previously deciphered by Olam's computer had revealed that foreign operatives had infiltrated the Israeli intelligence agency, as well as the FBI, the CIA, the National Security Agency, and the Pentagon. Aryeh was so alarmed by the situation that he couldn't sleep. Slumped in his chair, he stared groggily at Ehud ben Ezra, who was inserting the newly delivered disks into the quantum computer's optical drive. Olam had taught Ehud how to run the computer; the young zealot had formerly been a student at Hebrew University, and he seemed a little brighter than the other settlers in Shalhevet. As Ehud started the decryption program, he struck up a conversation with Aryeh, asking a flurry of questions about cryptography. Wearily, the Shin Bet agent tried to explain the basics.

"Okay, it's very simple," he said. "The cipher is the sequence of steps for coding and decoding a message. You use the cipher to turn a message into gobbledygook and then back into readable text."

Ehud nodded. He had a wispy, reddish beard and wore a black yarmulke. "And is the cipher the same thing as the key?"

"No, the key is a big number that plugs into the cipher and specifies the coding. So if a general at army headquarters uses a key to encode a message, the poor schmuck in his foxhole needs the same key for decoding it. But if you use the same key too many times, an enemy can figure out what it is, yes? So the army has to change its codes every day, always introducing new keys before its enemies can break the old ones."

"But how does—"

"Yes, I know what you're going to ask. How does the general distribute the new keys to all those poor schmucks in their foxholes? That's a big problem in military communications, keeping track of all the keys and making sure that your enemies don't steal them when they're in transit. But you can solve the problem by using public-key cryptography, which is the kind of encryption you see on the Internet."

"I think I read something about that, but it didn't make—"

"Forget what you read. Just listen to me. Instead of using one key, this system has two. Every user has his own public key for encoding messages and his own private key for decoding them. It's like having a lockbox with two keyholes, one for locking, the other for unlocking. If you want to send a secret message to a friend, you say to him, 'Hey, give me your public key.' So your friend sends his public key over the Internet, and you use it to encode your message, which is like putting the message in the box and locking it. Then you send the encoded message to your friend, who uses his private key to unlock the box. Because the private key never leaves his possession, no one else can decode the message."

"And that's how the military distributes new encryption keys for its communications?"

"Yes, it's much safer than distributing them on paper. The IDF and the Pentagon use public-key systems to secure their classified data networks. The Pentagon's network is the one that carried the message about Excalibur that Olam decoded a few days ago. You know, the message that was sent from California to Afghanistan after the Iranian nuclear test."

"But if the public-key system is so safe, how did Olam decode that message?"

Aryeh smiled. Despite his fatigue, he was enjoying this. "Ah, here's the trick. Because the private key decodes what the public key has encrypted, the two keys have to be mathematically related, correct? The private key is usually based on a pair of prime numbers, and the public key is the number you get when you multiply the two primes together. So if the private key is based on seven and nineteen, the public key is one hundred thirty-three, yes?"

Ehud had to think about it for a second. Aryeh got the feeling that math hadn't been the boy's best subject at Hebrew University. "Yes, seven times nineteen is one hundred thirty-three."

"But if this is true, the private key isn't so private, eh? Because if you know the public key, all you have to do is find the prime factors of one hundred thirty-three and you'll know the private key, too. But when you get to large numbers, numbers with hundreds and hundreds of digits, finding the prime factors becomes very difficult. You can easily multiply two large primes together, but if you give the resulting number to a computer and say, 'Tell me which primes I multiplied,' it can take the computer a thousand years to figure out the answer. That's why it's hard to break the encryption. Finding the private key isn't impossible, but you'll have to wait a long time if you use an ordinary computer."

Now Ehud smiled, too. He finally understood. "But Olam's computer is different? It's good at finding the prime factors of large numbers?"

"Yes, exactly. Because a quantum computer can perform trillions and trillions of calculations at once, it can test many numbers at the same time to see which one is the prime factor. If you know the message's public key, which is easy to intercept, the quantum computer will quickly figure out the private key and decode the message for you. That's what the machine is doing right now." Aryeh pointed at the computer inside the gray cabinet, which made a low, humming noise as it performed its calculations. "You just inputted three days' worth of encrypted communications, but the computer will decipher them all in about an hour."

Ehud stared at the machine for a few seconds, still smiling. He seemed to have gained a new appreciation for the computer. Then he turned back to Aryeh. "Well, that gives me enough time for morning prayers. Do you want me to bring you some breakfast when I come back?"

Aryeh shook his head. His anxiety had also affected his appetite. "No, I'm not hungry."

"I'll bring you something anyway. You need to eat, Mr. Goldberg."

After Ehud left the room, Aryeh took off his glasses and rubbed his eyes. Maybe he should find a place to lie down, he thought. He should try to take a nap while the computer was working. But he suspected that he wouldn't be able to sleep. It would be like trying to doze off in a burning house. All his instincts were telling him that something was wrong. And he was very worried about his American friends, who were probably somewhere in the deserts of Turkmenistan by now. He wished he could contact them, but he knew that Olam and his commandos wouldn't use their radios unless they had to. And besides, Aryeh had nothing useful to give them yet. He needed to analyze the intercepted communications first. Then, with any luck, he could identify the people who Olam called the *Qliphoth*, the ones who'd placed Excalibur at the nuclear test site in Iran.

Aryeh folded his arms across the desk and rested his head on them. Lucille had told him before she left Shalhevet that she had a plan for getting the *Qliphoth* to reveal themselves. She was going to persuade the FBI to pay a visit to Logos Enterprises, the California defense contractor that had removed Excalibur from the Livermore lab and supposedly dismantled it. The idea was to make the people at Logos so nervous that they'd send another message to their contact in Afghanistan. It was possible that Logos had already sent this message, and that Unit 8200 had already intercepted it. In fact, Aryeh hoped that the message was on one of the disks that were now feeding their data to the quantum computer. In his mind's eye, he saw the computer spit out a name, the name of the Afghan contact, but the letters were blurred and Aryeh couldn't read it.

The next thing he knew, Ehud was shaking him awake. The boy's left hand was on Aryeh's shoulder, and his right hand held a plate of Israeli salad. "Mr. Goldberg?" he said, resting the plate on the desk. "Look, I brought you some food."

For several seconds Aryeh just stared at the jumble of diced cucumbers and tomatoes. Then he remembered where he was. He stretched his arms and arched his back and let out a yawn. When he looked at his watch, he saw that he'd been asleep for ninety minutes.

"Ach!" he cried, turning to Ehud. "Did the computer finish its run?"

The young man nodded, but he didn't look pleased. "Yes, it's done. And one of the deciphered messages has the word 'Excalibur.' But there's no—"

Aryeh jumped to his feet. "Where is it? Let me see!"

Ehud placed a sheet of paper on the desk and pointed at a line of text near the top. Aryeh hunched over the document. First he saw the decoded information about the sender and the receiver. The signal had come from California, from the same unregistered wireless device used in the previous message, and it had been relayed by the same cell-phone tower in Sacramento. But this time the message hadn't traveled to western Afghanistan. It had gone to a tower in southern Turkmenistan before being shunted to the receiver. The message itself was short, just seven words: MORE INQUIRIES ABOUT EXCALIBUR. MUST TALK ASAP.

Aryeh felt the disappointment in his stomach. He'd hoped for more. "Is that it? Nothing else?"

Ehud tapped a line near the bottom of the page. "The computer also decoded a second message, which was sent from Turkmenistan to Sacramento about thirty seconds after the first. But I don't understand this one at all."

Aryeh saw the words next to Ehud's index finger. Just six of them: SWITCH TO DRSN. I'LL CALL IMMEDIATELY.

He grimaced. "Ah, this is bad. DRSN stands for the Pentagon's Defense Red Switch Network. It's for transmitting voice communications, not data. Our friend in Turkmenistan obviously agreed to have a conversation with his contacts in California. Unfortunately, we won't be able to decipher it."

"Why not?" Ehud asked. "I thought we had the world's best code-breaking machine."

"DRSN is more secure than the Pentagon's data networks. Because the system has a separate infrastructure of secure lines and terminals, our listening stations can't eavesdrop on it as easily. It's supposed to be reserved for the top officials at the Pentagon. The fact that our Afghan friends are using this network is very surprising. They must have some highly placed informants." Aryeh shook his head. Damn it to hell, he thought. And they were so close.

Ehud kept his finger on the page. "But if the network is only for the highest officials, there must be someone who controls access to it, right? Like a telephone operator?"

"Not necessarily. It could be automated."

"But either way, you'd probably need a code to get access. And someone must keep records, right? Records of who got on the network and when?"

Aryeh stared at the boy. He was right—on a network that was as secure as DRSN, you couldn't get access with an unregistered device. You'd need to input a personal code assigned by the network. And if Aryeh could look at the DRSN call logs and the records of the code assignments, he could determine who made the mysterious call from Turkmenistan to California. Those records would be classified, of course. But Aryeh had a source in the Pentagon.

He stepped toward Ehud and hugged him, kissing the boy's fore-head. "You should go back to school, you know that? You're too smart to be in a place like this."

"What? I don't—"

"Now get out of here." Aryeh let go of him and pointed at the door. "I have some calls to make."

29

DAVID OPENED HIS EYES. HE SAW A THIN STRIP OF SKY ABOVE HIM, RUNNING between two jagged cliffs. It was a dim grayish blue, the color of dawn. He lay on his back and a circle of men looked down at him. They wore mud-caked boots and ragged brown uniforms, but his vision was blurry and he couldn't make out their faces. They were carrying rifles, though, he could see that much. And although he was bleeding from cuts on his head and neck and arms, no one was rushing to treat his wounds or even help him to his feet. So the men probably weren't his friends. Shit, he thought, who the hell are these guys?

Then he noticed that one of them wasn't a man. It was a heavyset woman with disheveled white hair, standing on one leg. She was being held upright by the men on either side of her, who gripped her arms and dragged her forward. Her injured leg was bent sideways and the pants were ripped at the knee and damp below it. David squinted at her face and saw her open her mouth, but he couldn't hear what she said—something was wrong with his ears. Then she opened her mouth again and he did hear something, very faint. It was Agent Lucille Parker saying his name.

The men threw her to the ground next to David and in that instant everything came back to him: the Zodiacs, the Akhal-Tekes, the storage depot, the C-4. Lucille clutched his arm. Her gun and shoulder holster were gone, he noticed, and so were his. She had a deep gash that slanted across her chin and another that ran from her cheekbone to the corner of her mouth. She was crying and her tears were seeping into her cuts. He groaned, "Lucille!" and his own voice sounded strange and distant. "What happened? Where's Monique?"

She closed her eyes and shook her head. "We were just outside the door. The blast pushed us away."

"But where's . . . ?"

Then David looked past her and saw the bodies on the ground. They lay faceup in a long line, obviously dragged out of the wreckage by the soldiers in brown uniforms. Heart pounding, David sat up and looked at their dead faces. He counted twelve of them, all bearded men in black clothes. Neither Monique nor Olam was among them. At first David felt relief, but as he stared at the corpses of the *kippot srugot* he was overcome with horror. He'd listened to these men's prayers just twenty-four hours ago.

Propping himself on one elbow, David pointed his other hand at the soldiers standing around him. "Who are you?" he yelled. "WHO THE FUCK ARE YOU?"

The soldiers said nothing. David couldn't tell if they even understood English. But while he waited for them to answer, the circle parted and a tall, wiry man stepped into the gap. This one looked different from the others. His uniform was dark green instead of brown, and he wore a checkered keffiyeh that draped his shoulders and the back of his neck. Also, his face looked oddly familiar. It was swarthy and stubbled and painfully thin. After a few seconds David remembered. Pointing at the man, he turned to Lucille. "That's the pilgrim! The one with the cross, the one who followed us to the yeshiva in Jerusalem!"

The man nodded. "My name is Nicodemus. And yes, I followed you to Beit Shalom. That was another good day for killing Jews." He smiled. "How many did we kill there? Thirteen? Fourteen? Funny, it's about the same number we killed today."

Lucille glared at him. "Don't forget, the Jews killed some of your men, too."

His upper lip twitched, but he kept smiling. "No, I haven't forgotten. That's why I arranged this operation. When I discovered you were going to Turkmenistan, I rushed here to join my fellow True Believers. They'd already removed the X-ray laser from this depot, but there was another one that was damaged beyond repair, so we used the spare cylinder as a decoy and filled it with C-4. Then we found a hiding spot in the ravine and waited for you to arrive." He pointed at the line of corpses. "It worked quite well, don't you think? We killed nearly all of you. Olam ben Z'man and Monique Reynolds slipped away, but they won't get far. They'll try to regroup with the six Israelis who were riding reconnaissance, then head back to the Zodiacs. But we have a squadron waiting for them there."

Lucille tightened her grip on David's arm. But it wasn't fear, he sensed—it was hope. Monique and Olam were still alive. And this surge of hope reminded David of the reason he was here, why he'd traveled so many thousands of miles to this awful place. "Where's my son?" he demanded, looking Nicodemus in the eye. "Where's Michael Gupta?"

"Oh, he's dead, too. We killed him after he gave Brother Cyrus the information we needed. But I can assure you that it was done in the most humane way. Brother Cyrus is the Redeemer, holy and compassionate. Much more compassionate than I am."

David faltered for a moment, but he kept staring at Nicodemus. The man's eyes slid to the left and his lip twitched again. And David felt another surge of hope, because he knew that the man was lying. "No, Michael's not dead," he said firmly. "Maybe you wanted to kill him. Maybe you were planning to. But it didn't happen."

Nicodemus stopped smiling. He gave up all pretense and glowered at David, widening his nostrils. Then he turned to his men and shouted, "Get them up!"

A pair of soldiers grabbed David and lifted him to his feet. Another pair lifted Lucille. Nicodemus reached for his belt and removed a long knife from a leather sheath. He stepped forward and held the knife a few inches in front of David's eyes. The blade shone in the strengthening light of dawn. "You killed my friend Bashir and for that I should slit your throat. But Brother Cyrus wants to speak to you, so it will have to wait."

David felt dizzy but he clenched his teeth. "That's too bad. My heart is breaking for you."

"Yes, it's very funny. I must obey Brother Cyrus, so I can't kill you." He clasped the knife's handle and drew his hand back. "But I can kill this one."

In one quick motion, he stepped toward Lucille and cut her throat. She looked at David for an instant, her wet eyes beseeching him, her mouth opening and closing soundlessly. He saw the slit across her neck, a bright red line. Then the blood streamed down and her head fell forward.

30

MICHAEL DID EXACTLY WHAT TAMARA HAD TOLD HIM TO DO. HE KEPT RIDING south on the Ural motorcycle, looking for another village where he could make a telephone call. He rode through the desert until the late afternoon, constantly scanning the horizon. He saw sand dunes, of course, and some scraggly bushes with leafless white branches, and at one point he saw a pair of camels walking across a stretch of hard, flat ground. But he saw no villages, no trails, and no telephone poles. And then at four o'clock, after he'd traveled 181 kilometers (Michael checked the odometer), the motorcycle sputtered to a halt. He'd run out of gas.

For the next three hours he tried to push the Ural south, but he didn't get very far. As the sun began to set, he rolled the bike into a sandy trough between two dunes, where there was some shelter from the wind. He was very thirsty, but he had no water. When he opened the storage compartment at the back of the sidecar, he found only a can of peaches and a rolled-up magazine with pictures of naked women on the cover. He managed to puncture the can by ramming it against the Ural's fender, and he sucked the peach syrup out of the hole, swallowing every drop. But when he was finished, he was thirstier than ever. He tried to ignore it by looking at the pictures of the naked women, which he studied until it was too dark to see.

The wind grew stronger after sunset, and sand blew into Michael's eyes. It also got colder. He climbed into the Ural's sidecar and curled up inside the padded space. Even though he was still cold, he managed to sleep for a few hours. Then the sun rose, and by eight o'clock the sidecar was too hot. He took off his shirt and created a sunshade by tying the sleeves to the Ural's handlebars. But it was hot even in the shade, and

Michael's lips were dry and cracked. He remembered that a human being could live for three to seven days without water. But *The Concise Scientific Encyclopedia* had also mentioned that the survival time decreased significantly when the air temperature was high. Because more moisture evaporated from the body. And you couldn't stop evaporation.

Michael tried to focus on the magazine again, but his vision had become blurry. When he raised his head and looked at the sand dunes, they seemed to move across his field of vision, flowing like waves on the ocean. He thought he could also hear the sloshing of the waves, but he knew this was just the sound of his own pulse, which he could hear very clearly when he clamped his hands over his ears. David Swift had once told him that there were six quarts of blood in his body, and when Michael had first heard this fact he'd imagined storing his blood in three half-gallon milk cartons, which would take up most of the space on the top shelf of their refrigerator. But now he pictured his blood soaking into the sand, binding the loose grains into thick reddish clumps, like the ones he'd seen the last time he'd looked at Tamara.

He closed his eyes so he wouldn't have to look at the dunes anymore. Tamara was dead, he knew that. And he'd failed to do what she'd told him. He hadn't found a village or a telephone, and he'd never gotten a chance to talk to David Swift. His eyes stung and his stomach ached as he thought about all the things he'd done wrong. You're a failure, he told himself. You've failed in every way.

And then he heard David Swift's voice. It sounded as if it were coming from just behind him.

You're not a failure, Michael. You're a wonderful boy.

Michael turned around. There was nothing behind him but the Ural motorcycle. But he spoke to David anyway. "No, I'm not. I broke my promise. I told Cyrus the code."

It's not your fault. You held out for as long as you could. I'm proud of you, Michael. Very proud.

His eyes stung but he couldn't cry. He was too dehydrated. "But it doesn't matter! I broke my promise and now Cyrus is going to alter the program. He's going to kill the world!"

No, he can't do that. He can't kill the world. Just look at it, Michael. Look how beautiful it is.

Michael looked up. He saw nothing but sand dunes. And in his mind's eye he saw things that were worse. The man falling into the burning crater. The soldiers blown apart by the grenade he'd thrown. "It's already dead," he told David. "There's nothing alive here."

What about those birds?

At first Michael didn't understand. The sky was a blank, searing sheet of blue. But a moment later he spotted them: two big black birds flying over the dunes. Except they weren't flapping their wings. And they seemed to be getting larger. Then Michael heard a distant thumping, percussive and deep, like the sound of a giant beating his club against the great bass drum of the desert.

"They're not birds," he whispered. "They're helicopters."

31

THEY DIDN'T EVEN BURY HER. AFTER NICODEMUS CUT LUCILLE'S THROAT, HIS soldiers dumped her on top of the corpses of the Israeli commandos. David got one last look at Agent Parker—her eyes wide open, her head tilted back, her shirt smeared with blood—before the soldiers threw him down and pushed his face into the dirt. One of them tied his hands behind his back and another bound his legs at the ankles and a third gagged him with a strip of cloth that tasted of motor oil. Then they dragged him to a convoy of gray Land Cruisers and tossed him into the back of one of the cars.

He thrashed on the floor of the Cruiser's cargo area, banging his head against the folded seats. Three soldiers in brown fatigues got into the car, two settling in the front seats and one climbing into the cargo area with David. This soldier had a face like a hatchet, with a sharp chin and a long nose. As the convoy started moving, the soldier grinned at David and asked, "Are you comfortable, Brother?" David let out a roar and tried to stomp his bound feet into the bastard's face, but the soldier punched him in the stomach. Then he tied another rope around David's knees and anchored it to a bolt protruding from the floor. David kept thrashing for several minutes, straining against the rope while the soldiers laughed. Finally, he lay still and closed his eyes, but his torment continued. In his mind's eye he saw Lucille after her throat had been slashed, opening and closing her mouth as the blood poured out of her. As if she were trying to tell him something.

He wanted to die. But first he wanted to kill everyone around him.

The road they were traveling on was in terrible shape. The car bumped over ruts and ridges and potholes, reducing their speed to about thirty miles per hour. But David didn't feel any turns, so he knew the road ran straight. After a while he opened one eye and saw the morning sunlight illuminating the hatchet face of the soldier sitting beside him. They were moving southeast.

Slowly, he began to recover. He thought of Monique and Michael and Olam. Despite everything, they were still alive. By some miracle, they'd beaten the odds and escaped, and that meant David shouldn't give up hope. But then he thought of Excalibur and his heart sank again. Nicodemus said his so-called True Believers had removed the Russian laser from the depot. And because they'd already tested the American prototype in Iran, exploding a nuclear bomb to power the device, they knew what it could do. David didn't know why they wanted to crash the universe, but in the end it didn't matter. Fanatics didn't need reasons. Their leader was obviously this Brother Cyrus, whom Nicodemus had called the Redeemer. David assumed he was a religious leader of some kind, a messianic cult figure, but one who was rich enough to equip a small army and powerful enough to collaborate with the Iranians. That was the worst kind of fanatic, he thought—a smart, disciplined madman with power.

After about four hours of driving, the True Believers ate their lunch in the car. The soldiers in the front seats passed a hunk of bread and a crooked black sausage to Hatchet Face. They didn't offer any food to David, and he wouldn't have accepted it if they had. They traveled for another hour on a smoother highway, then made a right turn. After a while David sensed that the road was sloping upward. He craned his neck to look through the car windows and saw mountains looming on either side. The convoy of Land Cruisers was leaving the desert behind and entering a mountain pass. The road snaked between steep, brown slopes sprinkled with loose stones. David's ears popped from the change in altitude. In less than ten minutes they rose thousands of feet.

As they ascended, David tried to determine where they were. Thirty-six hours before, back when he was on the transport plane flying from Israel to Azerbaijan, he'd studied one of Olam's maps of Turkmenistan. Now he pictured the map in his head and drew a diagonal line across the country, starting at Yangykala Canyon. He estimated that they'd driven about two hundred miles southeast. Extending the line on his mental map, he saw that it stretched to the Kopet Dag, the mountain range that ran along Turkmenistan's southern border. David's stomach clenched— they were on a road that crossed the mountains, heading straight for the Islamic Republic of Iran.

He started thrashing again, trying to snap the rope that tied him down. Once they crossed the border there would be no chance of escape. Brother Cyrus was probably waiting for them at the Kavir test site, along with the Russian laser and another nuclear bomb. They were driving toward Armageddon, the final battle, where the human race would prove its ingenuity by triggering the quantum crash.

Then the Land Cruiser pulled off the road and stopped. David jerked his head from side to side, looking for signs of a border crossing—a guardhouse, a pair of flags, a lowered gate. He screamed behind his gag, hoping to attract the attention of the border guards, although Brother Cyrus had probably bribed them to look the other way. The other Land Cruisers in the convoy also pulled off the road and parked nearby.

The two soldiers in the front seats stepped out of the car, walked to the back of the vehicle, and opened the rear door. Meanwhile, Hatchet Face pulled a knife out of the sheath on his belt. David froze and thought of Lucille again, remembering the look on her face after her throat was slit. But the soldier simply cut the rope that tied David to the car's floor, then grasped his ankles and pulled him out of the Land Cruiser. The other two soldiers grabbed his arms.

David twisted his body, trying to squirm out of their grasp, but he was weaker now—he hadn't eaten in sixteen hours. The three True Believers carried him away from the car, walking across a stretch of flat, dusty ground at the foot of a steep slope. As he struggled vainly to free himself, David saw other soldiers emerging from their Land Cruisers and lining up in front of the cars. But he saw no gates or flags or guardhouses. It wasn't a border crossing—the convoy had stopped in the middle of nowhere.

Then the three soldiers carrying David stopped in their tracks. He turned his head and saw Nicodemus approaching. The man draped his checkered keffiyeh over his shoulders, then bent over David's suspended body and smiled. "Did you enjoy the drive, Professor Swift?"

David yelled, "Fuck you," behind his gag. It came out as a pair of grunts, but Nicodemus seemed to catch the meaning. His smile broadened. "I have some news for you. Before leaving Yangykala, we informed the Turkmen Army that several Israeli commandos had slipped into their country. Now a Turkmen helicopter division is hunting down the intruders. Do you think your wife and your friend Olam will surrender? Or will they go down shooting?"

David roared again and jackknifed his body, hoping to fling himself at the bastard, but all he managed to do was make Hatchet Face stumble. Nicodemus laughed. "All right, enough gossip. You have an appointment with Brother Cyrus. Come this way."

He marched toward the slope and the soldiers followed, swinging David like a side of beef. At the base of the mountain was a jagged hole, about six feet high and four feet wide. It was the mouth of a cave, utterly dark. Nicodemus removed a flashlight from his belt and stepped inside, lowering his head with practiced familiarity, as if he'd done this many times before. Hatchet Face backed into the cave, tightening his grip on David's ankles, and the two soldiers holding his arms moved closer together and shuffled into the darkness.

David was reminded of the smugglers' tunnel under Jerusalem's Old City. The cave was long and narrow and musty, its limestone walls slick with bat droppings. The floor was level for the first hundred feet or so, then began to descend. Nicodemus slowed his pace and turned around, pointing his flashlight at the stony ground to help the soldiers find their footing.

"A nice place, don't you think?" he said, looking at David. "This mountain is like Swiss cheese, full of holes. And all the passages come together at the bottom. We call this tunnel 'the back door' because it's much narrower than the main entrance. Wait a moment and you'll see."

The soldiers slipped and slid down the sloping tunnel, almost dropping David a couple of times. He'd stopped struggling by this point and just stared at the cave's walls, which flickered with the shadows cast by the flashlight. He could sense the mountain above him, the billions of tons of rock and dirt, and the air seemed to get warmer and damper as they descended. It was suffocating, the closeness and the darkness, and he started hyperventilating through his gag. This was a one-way trip, he thought. The soldiers were taking him to his grave.

Then the tunnel leveled out and they stepped into a subterranean chamber. A smooth shelf of limestone ran alongside an oval pool of greenish water, about fifty feet across. The rocky ceiling of the chamber arched overhead, studded with stalactites. Water dripped from the ceiling into the pool, making circles on its surface. The air was very warm and smelled like rotten eggs. David knew right away it was a geothermal spring. The Kopet Dag was a tectonically active area—below the mountain were molten rocks that heated the water in the underground chambers. The rotten-egg smell was hydrogen sulfide, which was produced when the hot water dissolved sulfur-bearing minerals.

Nicodemus and his soldiers walked along the limestone shelf to the other side of the chamber. As they carried David down the path, he noticed a shaft of light coming through a hole in the chamber's far wall. His heart leaped for a moment because he thought it was sunlight, but then he realized that the color was wrong. It was bluish, artificial light coming from an adjacent chamber on the other side of the wall. The passageway between the chambers was less than three feet wide, just big enough to crawl through, and as they got closer David saw a large man standing in front of it. He was a soldier, too, with a rifle slung over his shoulder, and he saluted Nicodemus as they came near. But this soldier's uniform was different from the ragged brown fatigues of the True Believers. It had a pale green camouflage pattern and looked crisp and new.

Nicodemus returned the man's salute. "We found him, Sergeant. So now you owe us an apology. Didn't I tell you that my men would track him down?"

The sergeant stared at David. "This is the guy?" he said, raising an eyebrow.

"I know, he doesn't look like much. But he's clever."

Shaking his head, the sergeant bent over to get a closer look. He had a blond buzz cut and bad razor burn on his cheeks. The sleeves of his combat uniform were rolled up to his elbows, revealing muscular forearms covered with tattoos. In the strong light coming through the passageway, David could read what was written on the front of his uniform. On the right side of his chest was the name MORRISON; on the left, U.S. ARMY. On his left shoulder was a patch with the name of his regiment: 75-RANGER-RGT.

David started screaming again behind his gag. This man wasn't some ragtag True Believer—he was a U.S. Army Ranger, a Special Operations soldier! David yelled, "Help me!" but of course the gag made his words unintelligible. Sergeant Morrison glared at him, then stood up straight and turned back to Nicodemus. "How the hell did this guy get the jump on Colonel Ramsey? He's a goddamn runt."

"We think he's a spy, but we're not sure who he works for. He may have ambushed Ramsey after the colonel walked out of the cavern. Our interrogators will find out exactly what happened. That's why we brought him here. So please, let us through."

The sergeant moved aside. Nicodemus crawled through the passageway first, then Hatchet Face. The two soldiers behind David lowered him to the ground and stuck his bound legs into the hole, but just as Hatchet Face grabbed his ankles and started to pull, Sergeant Morrison stepped forward.

"This is for Ramsey, you scumbag!" Then the sergeant delivered a swift kick to David's ribs.

The pain shot through his chest. Closing his eyes, he went into a fetal curl. Hatchet Face pulled him through the passageway and David took an aching gulp of air. Then he opened his eyes and the pain turned to shock as he stared at the chamber he'd just entered. It was as big as an arena, as big as Madison Square Garden. The ceiling was at least a hundred feet high, lit by powerful floodlights on tall steel poles. To his left was another pool of greenish water, but this one was a genuine underground lake, stretching to recesses at the back of the cave that were so far away even the floodlights couldn't reach them. Straight ahead was a rock shelf where two tents had been erected, a large one that was at least forty feet long and a smaller one behind it. And to his right was a natural staircase of limestone slabs, climbing about fifty feet to an immense upper chamber. David saw dozens of tents up there, and that was only in the area closest to the staircase. The cavern extended way beyond and seemed to hold an entire military camp. He could hear the voices of hundreds of soldiers echoing against the rocky walls. Jesus, he thought, what the hell is going on?

He was still gasping when the True Believers picked him up from the ground. They carried him toward the large tent just ahead, where two more Army Rangers guarded the entrance. The guards saluted Nicodemus as if he were an old friend, as if it were perfectly normal for a band of religious fanatics to come waltzing into a hidden U.S. Army camp. The True Believers brought David inside the tent and deposited him, faceup, on a plain wooden bench, the kind you'd see in an army mess hall. Nicodemus came forward with another length of rope and tied David to the bench. He wrapped the cord around David's knees, waist, and chest, binding his whole body to the long wooden plank.

"You must be confused, eh?" Nicodemus said as he worked. "Well, I have just enough time to give you an explanation. You're in Camp Cobra, which is a cavern occupied by nine hundred and sixty American soldiers. Most of them are Army Rangers preparing for a surprise attack on Iran. And their commander is General McNair, who happens to be a friend of Brother Cyrus." He tightened the rope, making David wince. "McNair invited Cyrus and the True Believers to Camp Cobra, but there was a problem. The general had to explain to his Rangers why all these unfamiliar men were coming to their cave. So he invented a little story. He said he'd ordered an undercover Special Forces team to find Colonel Ramsey, a very unlucky Ranger who wandered out of the cavern and went missing a few days ago." He gave the rope a final tug and tied the knot. "Then the story took a tragic turn. The Special Forces team discovered that Ramsey was dead. But they found his killer at least. And that's you!"

Nicodemus pointed at him and grinned. "It's a good story, eh? But now we're close to the ending. Good-bye, Professor Swift." His grin vanished as he spoke David's name. Then he and his men left the tent, exiting the same way they'd come in.

The ropes were so tight, David could hardly breathe. He turned his head and surveyed the tent, which was shadowy and silent. Peering into the darkness, he saw electronic equipment—computers, radios, map displays—resting on tables that ran along the canvas walls. It looked like a command-and-control center, the kind of place where army generals could monitor the battlefield and issue orders to their troops. But besides David, there was only one person in the tent, a man dressed in black pants, a black jacket, and black gloves. He stood about twenty feet away, in the center of the tent, with his back turned. One of his gloved hands touched a steel pipe that stood on its end, anchored in the ground. About ten feet high and six inches in diameter, the pipe loomed over the man's head, which was wrapped in a black scarf.

"Hello, David," the man said without turning around. "I'm Brother Cyrus." He tapped the pipe. "And this is Little Boy."

THE PAIR OF HELICOPTERS LANDED IN THE DESERT, TOUCHING DOWN between the dunes. Michael was more than a hundred feet away, but the rotors kicked up the sand so violently that it stung his skin and pelted the stranded motorcycle. Blown free of the dunes, the sand grains whirled in a huge dust devil that obscured the helicopters, blurring them into vague black shapes. They didn't look like birds anymore, Michael thought. They looked like giant tadpoles with propeller beanies on their heads.

He laughed. It was a funny sight. He had no idea why the helicopters had landed here, or who was inside them. They might be carrying Brother Cyrus's soldiers, he thought, and the soldiers might try to shoot him again. But he wasn't afraid anymore. Dying from a gunshot was better than dying of thirst. The soldiers would be doing him a favor.

He stood up and squinted, trying to see through the whirling cloud of sand. A man jumped out of one of the helicopters and started jogging toward him. He was a big man, that was all Michael could tell at first. And he was holding a rifle. A second soldier jumped out of the helicopter, and this one was shorter and slimmer than the first. They ran through the sand cloud and when they emerged Michael noticed two things. The first soldier had a black eye patch. And the second soldier was a woman. It was Monique Reynolds.

"Michael!" she shouted, throwing her arms around him.

32

ARYEH GOLDBERG'S CONTACT IN THE PENTAGON WASN'T JEWISH. HE WAS AN Irish Catholic named Joe Dowling who worked as a telecommunications specialist in the Defense Information Systems Agency. Dowling had no particular affinity for Israel, and no ideological desire to help the country. He'd become a source for Israel's intelligence agencies simply because he felt that the U.S. Defense Department wasn't paying him well enough. So he supplemented his income by selling tidbits he gleaned from the Pentagon's communication networks, usually news of American troop deployments in the Middle East. Aryeh didn't like the man personally, but his information was always reliable.

"I have a job for you," Aryeh told him over the phone. He used a customized satellite phone issued by Shin Bet. It had enough encryption to frustrate any eavesdropper who wasn't in possession of a quantum computer. "And I need it done quickly."

"No problem," Dowling replied. "But I charge an extra fee for fast service. You know that, right?"

"Yes, I'm familiar with your fee schedule. You'll find the work order at the usual place." Aryeh had already sent the order to a Mossad colleague in Washington, who'd hidden the packet at the dead drop where Dowling picked up his clandestine assignments. The packet contained information on the DRSN call from Turkmenistan to California, including the estimated time of the call and the approximate locations of the sender and receiver. Once Dowling had this information, he'd be able to find the call in the system's records and identify the personal codes that had been used to access the network. "It's a simple job, really. We're just looking for a name. The name of the person who placed the call."

"Hey, I'm good with names. So when do I get paid?"

Aryeh thought about it for a moment. He hadn't cleared this assignment with anyone in Shin Bet. He couldn't share his suspicions with his superiors because one of them might be a spy for the *Qliphoth*. But Aryeh felt certain that once the mess was cleaned up and the traitors were exposed, Shin Bet would retroactively approve the expense.

"The cash will be there tomorrow, at the usual place. But only if you're quick."

"Don't worry. I'll call back in an hour."

DAVID RECOGNIZED IT, OF COURSE. EVERY HISTORIAN OF TWENTIETH-CENTURY physics knew about Little Boy, the fifteen-kiloton bomb that destroyed Hiroshima. It was the simplest possible design for a nuclear weapon: just shoot a chunk of uranium down a ten-foot-long gun tube and smash it into a second chunk at the bottom. It was cruder and less efficient than the bombs that were built afterward, but it was such a surefire device that the researchers in the Manhattan Project had never even bothered to test it. They knew without a doubt that Little Boy would work.

As soon as David saw what it was, he started screaming through his gag. He strained against the ropes that tied him to the bench and yelled, "BOMB! BOMB! BOMB!" just as Lucille had done when she'd spotted the C-4 in the Turkmen depot. He screamed until he felt his vocal cords tearing, and then he screamed some more, hoping that maybe one of the hundreds of Rangers in the underground camp would become curious or concerned. But the gag muffled his voice and garbled his words, and no one rushed into the tent.

Brother Cyrus turned away from the gun tube and walked slowly toward him. David noticed that Cyrus's head scarf covered his whole face. Only his eyes were visible through a narrow slit in the black fabric. He came to the bench and looked down at David. "It's all right," he said, his voice muffled by the scarf. "You can scream if you like. It doesn't bother me. And it won't disturb anyone else in the camp either. The Rangers believe you killed their Colonel Ramsey, and he was a well-liked man. They also believe that I'm here to interrogate you, so they're expecting you to scream."

To David's surprise, Cyrus's voice wasn't cruel. It was calm and reasonable, even sympathetic. He was simply stating the facts.

"And maybe it's good for you to scream a little," he continued. "Maybe you need to purify your spirit. Purge your anger and fear, and think only of the Lord. We can take a special joy now in turning toward God because these are the last hours of the corrupt world. Very soon, His love will flood the universe." He spread his arms wide in a benedictory gesture. "And you, of all people, should be joyful, David. The Redemption is just as much your doing as mine. The Lord called you to this task and you performed it well. That's why I brought you here, to give thanks and rejoice with you!"

David shook his head. Who the hell was this guy? It was maddening to listen to him and not be able to respond. He wanted to grab Cyrus by the neck and turn him toward the gun tube and shout, *Jesus Christ, what the fuck are you doing?* But with his hands tied and his mouth gagged, all he could do was shake his head and scream.

"Think about it for a moment, David. Two years ago, when you uncovered Einstein's unified theory, you gave us the first glimpse of God's plan. I know you tried to hide the theory again, but while you went back to New York and your job at Columbia, intelligence agencies around the world began investigating the incident. I would've liked to talk to you then, but you and your family were under FBI surveillance. So I started doing some research of my own. I knew a few scientists who could help me make sense of the intelligence reports. And I knew that sooner or later the Lord would provide." He held out his gloved hands as if preparing to accept a gift. "And He did. Within a year we'd assembled half the equations in the theory. What's more, my scientists discovered that the equations flowed from a universal program that had been running since the Big Bang. They even managed to reconstruct a good chunk of that program. And I saw—praise God!—that the program had a weakness. The Lord showed me the flaw and told me what to do."

Brother Cyrus sat down on the bench, his rear end a couple of feet from David's head. He lowered himself carefully, as if his joints were hurting him. He wasn't a young man, David realized. He was probably in his sixties. A good, hard punch to the solar plexus would be enough to take care of him. David jerked his arms, trying to loosen his bindings, but his hands were going numb now, pinned between the bench and the small of his back.

"The next step was to gather the tools I needed, but the Almighty had already provided most of those. I knew we could use Excalibur to exploit the weakness in the program because in my younger days I'd worked on the X-ray laser project at Livermore. I also knew we could steal the uranium from one of the reactors in Kazakhstan, and I was certain that the Iranians would let us test Excalibur at the Kavir site if we gave them some of the nuclear fuel. And after Michael Gupta joined our party and filled in the gaps in the code, we could determine how to properly adjust the Russian laser we'd acquired. Michael showed us not only how to overload the flawed program, but how to remake the universe as God intended, a perfect and timeless Kingdom of Heaven where we will all be resurrected and live in eternal peace. And you assisted us, too, David. Our operation had two loose ends—Jacob Steele and Olam ben Z'man—and you helped us eliminate both of them."

Cyrus leaned closer as he said this and rested his gloved hand on David's shoulder. The gesture surprised and sickened David. He twisted his body, writhing so violently that he would've toppled the bench if Cyrus hadn't been sitting on it. The man retracted his hand but stayed bent over David, lowering his voice almost to a whisper.

"There was one last obstacle. To trigger the memory overload, we needed to intensify the laser beams. And the only way to pump more power to the beams was to explode a more powerful weapon. We needed at least five hundred kilotons, which is beyond what a simple uranium bomb can generate. An American thermonuclear warhead could do it, but how could we arrange to detonate the bomb next to the X-ray laser? Because of the Comprehensive Test Ban Treaty, neither America nor Russia explodes nuclear weapons in underground tests anymore. And even if we could steal a warhead from one of the nuclear arsenals, we wouldn't be able to detonate it. The permissive action links lock the bomb's firing mechanism, and only the president can release those codes. So we faced a problem, a serious problem that threatened to derail all our efforts."

He stood up, rising with a grunt, and walked back to the gun tube. He spread his arms again, standing with his back to David and gesturing at the weapon as if he were blessing it.

"But the Lord provided once again. He spoke to me in my thoughts, where He is always present. I knew I had to force America to deploy one of its nuclear weapons. And I knew the president had promised never to do that unless another country launched a nuclear attack first. So the only option was to meet the president's condition." He pointed his gloved hand at the bottom of the tube. "My Little Boy will explode at two o'clock this afternoon, incinerating and burying this camp. And because the uranium in this device comes from the same stockpile as the U-235 we gave to the Iranians, the debris from the blast will have the exact same radioisotope signatures as the debris from the Kavir test. The CIA will quickly send reconnaissance drones here to investigate the nuclear catastrophe, and when they analyze the fallout debris they'll conclude that this was another Iranian bomb. Which is perfectly logical, of course. Wouldn't it make sense for Iran's Revolutionary Guards to use one of their nuclear weapons to eliminate the Ranger battalion that was preparing to attack them?"

David closed his eyes. The horror pressed down on him, close and suffocating. The nuclear explosion would collapse the cavern. The American soldiers would be crushed under tons of rock and dirt. And in response, the United States would launch a nuclear attack of its own.

"The target of the American retaliatory strike will be a facility near the Iranian town of Ashkhaneh. That's where the Revolutionary Guards are storing the rest of the U-235 we gave them. The facility is located in a cavern much like this one, deep underground. So the U.S. Air Force will send a B-2 bomber to deliver its strongest bunker buster, a modified B83 nuclear warhead. The bomb is attached to a precise guidance system and designed to burrow twenty feet into the ground before exploding. And it has a yield of twelve hundred kilotons, which is more than enough for our purposes. We know the coordinates of the target, and in a few minutes my True Believers and I will go to Ashkhaneh to deliver the X-ray laser. We'll position the device at the target point so that the laser rods will be close to the warhead when it detonates."

Cyrus's calm, reasonable voice droned on. He sounded as if he were reciting a shopping list instead of the preparations for Doomsday. David kept his eyes closed, too appalled to even look at the man. Jesus, he thought, how the hell did Cyrus acquire all this classified information?

How did he know so much about the air force's warheads and targets? It couldn't have all come from General McNair. David couldn't begin to fathom it. In frustration, he gave up thinking and started banging the back of his head against the bench. It was the only response that made any sense.

He soon felt Cyrus's gloved hand on his forehead, holding him still. David opened his eyes and saw the man kneeling on the floor. "I understand, David. I've felt this pain, too. I was also a prisoner once, in the mountains of the Hindu Kush. I'd come to Afghanistan to field-test a new reconnaissance drone. An infantry platoon was escorting me to an airfield near Jalalabad when the Taliban ambushed us." He lowered his head and stared at the ground. "Satan's foot soldiers captured me and took me to a cave in Gazarak Mountain. Then the interrogations began. Satan's men took turns, torturing and mutilating me. And then, three days later, I was rescued. My old friend Sam McNair led a Special Forces team that raided the hideout and killed my captors. But the Lord had already saved me, David. I saw His blessed face for the first time on that mountain. And now the same thing can happen to you. All you need to do is turn to Him."

David pushed his forehead against the gloved hand, trying to shake it off, but Cyrus pressed down firmly. Then, with his other hand, he began to take off his head scarf. He gripped the end of the black fabric and carefully unwound it, moving his hand in slow circles around his head. "I'm going to show you something now. I was once a sinful man, proud and arrogant in my corruption. And I still live in that man's body and speak profanities with his tongue. And I still wear his hideous face. I've endured it like a deadweight for the past seven years while I hid my true self and my knowledge of the Lord. But in just a few hours I will cast it off. I will give up this mutilated flesh and deliver my soul to heaven, where my thoughts will rest eternally with God." His hand went around his head one more time, pulling the last band of fabric from his face. The scarf fell to the ground. "Pray with me now, David. Let us show our true selves to the Lord."

David stared at him. Cyrus had a square, pinkish face. His lips were slender, his eyes were gray, and his forehead was topped with thinning white hair. His face wasn't hideous or mutilated. It was unscarred and perfectly ordinary, the face of a mild-mannered sixty-something-year-old man.

He smiled. "You've seen me before, haven't you?"

It was true. David had seen him before.

JOE DOWLING OF THE DEFENSE INFORMATION SYSTEMS AGENCY CALLED BACK after fifty-eight minutes. "Aryeh? I got the information you wanted. I'll put it in a packet and leave it for you at the usual place."

Aryeh squeezed his phone. He couldn't wait for the information. He needed to know this instant. "No, tell me now. Tell me the name."

"Over the phone? Are you sure—"

"Yes, over the phone! Do you want to get paid or not?"

There was a pause. "Okay, here goes. The network access code used by the contact in Turkmenistan belongs to a director at DARPA, the Pentagon's research agency. The name is Adam Cyrus Bennett."

33

MICHAEL WAS CRYING, BUT THERE WERE STILL NO TEARS. MONIQUE HANDED him a canteen and told him to take a small sip of water. Then she helped him stand up and led him to one of the helicopters. Halfway there, his knees buckled and he started to fall, but the big soldier with the eye patch grasped his arm. He was one of the biggest men Michael had ever seen. He had a terrible smell, like an old sneaker.

"Shalom!" he boomed. "My name is Olam." His voice was loud, but Michael didn't mind so much. It was better than listening to the pounding of his own pulse.

When they reached the helicopter, another soldier helped Michael climb aboard. Two more soldiers gripped his elbows and guided him to a bench seat on the left side of the cabin. They were odd-looking soldiers—they had long, scruffy beards and wore black uniforms and knitted skullcaps. But Michael didn't care. He'd never been inside a helicopter before and he was eager to look around. The cabin was about seven feet wide and fifteen feet long, with bench seats on both sides. He craned his neck to see the cockpit, but Monique stopped him from getting up to take a closer look. She sat beside him on the bench seat and made him take another sip of water from the canteen, a bigger sip this time. Then she hugged him.

"Oh, Michael! Thank God! Thank God!"

He would've screamed if anyone else had hugged him. But for some reason Monique's touch felt different—not as alien or jarring. It had been the same way with his mother. Michael didn't really like the hug, but he could tolerate it.

"How long were you in the desert?" she asked. "And how did you get here? What were you doing with that motorcycle?"

He didn't answer. He didn't want to talk about Tamara or how he got the Ural. He took another sip from the canteen instead.

She pulled back and looked at his face. Then she nodded. "It's all right, Michael. I'm just glad we found you."

"Yes, it's a miracle," said Olam. The one-eyed soldier stood beside the bench seat, bending over so his head wouldn't hit the cabin's ceiling. "Like a story from the Bible, yes? The well in the middle of the desert? The God of Abraham has given us a hard time, but He hasn't abandoned us."

A thought occurred to Michael. He looked around the cabin again, counting all the people inside. "Where's David Swift?" he asked. "Is he in the other helicopter?"

Monique lowered her head. Her cheeks were wet. She wasn't dehydrated, so there were tears when she cried.

Olam patted her arm. "Don't worry," he told her. "He's alive." Then he turned to Michael. "David was with us until eight hours ago, when we were ambushed in Yangykala Canyon. I saw the bastards capture him and kill Agent Parker, but they didn't kill David. They put him in one of their Land Cruisers and headed southeast."

Michael dared to glance at the man's lone eye. It looked very big for an eye, as big as a golf ball. Its iris was bright blue. "Is this your helicopter?"

"It is now!" Olam laughed, and the sound echoed in the cabin. "After we escaped from Yangykala, we regrouped with the six men I'd sent on reconnaissance. Then the Turkmen Army sent their MI-8s after us."

Michael knew what an MI-8 was. He'd seen them in his computer games. The helicopter he was sitting in, he realized, was an MI-8. He would've recognized it earlier if he hadn't been so woozy. "The MI-8 is a Russian-made troop-transport helicopter," he told Olam. "It can also be used as a gunship."

"Yes, the Turkmen Army inherited some of them after the Soviet Union broke up. I have to tell you, they're not very good. I like to fly the Yanshuf, the Israeli version of the Black Hawk. Compared to the Yanshuf, this is a piece of garbage." He banged his fist on the wall of the cabin. "And these particular MI-8s have no rockets or missiles on their racks. The only armaments are the built-in machine guns."

Michael smiled. He liked talking to this soldier. "But if these helicopters belong to the Turkmen Army, how did you—"

"Ah, yes, we played a little trick on them. When the helicopters approached, we put down our guns and surrendered. But once they landed, we changed our minds about surrendering." He let out another booming laugh. Then he reached into the pocket of his fatigues and removed a piece of paper. "We found these orders on the helicopter pilots. Someone had told them where we were. And the same orders instructed the pilots to search for you, too." He pointed at Michael. "This paper said you were headed south from an oasis village in Dashoguz province. That's how we found you."

Monique raised her head. She'd wiped the tears from her cheeks. "The Turkmen Army is cooperating with the soldiers who attacked us. Whoever's in charge of the operation must've—"

"His name is Brother Cyrus," Michael said. "I was in his camp near Darvaza."

Monique stared at him. "Brother Cyrus? Is that his real name?"

"That's what his soldiers call him. He wears a head scarf over his face."

Very gently, Monique grasped his shoulder. "This is important. Michael. How many soldiers does he have?"

Michael closed his eyes and searched his memory. "I counted a total of fifty-two soldiers in the camp. Twenty-five of them wore Special Operations insignia. I also saw seven Land Cruisers, six Tundra pickups, and four Kamaz trucks."

"What else? Did this Brother Cyrus have something called Excalibur? Did he ever mention that name, Michael?"

He turned away from her. He remembered the name. "He said he was going to unsheathe Excalibur. He said the code would tell them how to aim God's sword at the weakest part of this broken world."

"What did he mean by 'the code'? Did he mean a program?"

Michael nodded. His eyes stung, and now he felt hot tears on his cheeks. "I broke my promise. I told him the code."

"And this program embodies the laws of physics?" Her voice was softer now, no more than a whisper. "And shows how to remake the universe?"

His tears blurred his vision. Monique's face shifted and dissolved. "I'm sorry! I'm sorry! It's my fault! I'm sorry!"

Monique pulled him close and hugged him again. Crying hard, he rested his forehead in the crook of her neck. Until it actually happened, he didn't think Monique would forgive him. How could you forgive someone for killing the world? But she wouldn't be holding him right now, he thought, if she'd hadn't forgiven him.

He sat there for almost a minute while Monique patted and rubbed his back, making circular "there, there" motions. Finally she said, "It's all right, Michael. We're going to sort this out." Then she turned to Olam. "Should we contact the Americans in Afghanistan?" she asked. "This helicopter has a radio, doesn't it?"

"And what will we tell them?" Olam's brow wrinkled below his skull-cap. "That a man named Brother Cyrus is planning to crash the universe? Even if they believed us, they couldn't act fast enough. First they'd start their own investigation. Then they'd send diplomatic cables to the Turkmen president. Then they'd wait for him to reply." He shook his head. "No, it's too late for that. Cyrus is ready to strike."

"Well, what can we do about it? We don't know where he is!"

Olam pulled another sheet of paper from his pocket. "We know that the convoy of Land Cruisers headed southeast from Yangykala Canyon." He unfolded the paper and tapped the top left corner. "We could fly back there and try to retrace the convoy's route."

Monique leaned forward to look at the paper, and so did Michael. It was a map of Turkmenistan. The country was shaped like a shoe, with the heel and sole pressing down on Iran and the toe digging into Afghanistan. And in the part of the sole where it arched most sharply, Michael saw a familiar name. He pointed at it. "Kuruzhdey," he said.

"What?" Monique looked at him. "Did you say something, Michael?"

"Kuruzhdey," he repeated. "That's where Angel said Brother Cyrus's trucks were going."

Olam brought the map closer to his face. Then he spun around and said something in Hebrew to his men. Two of the soldiers dashed out of the helicopter and raced across the dunes to the other MI-8. Another two men rushed forward to the cockpit and began flipping switches on the control panels. In a few seconds Michael heard the whine of the helicopter's turboshaft engines.

Olam looked over his shoulder as he stepped into the cockpit. "It's two hundred fifty kilometers away," he said. "We'll be there in an hour."

34

BROTHER CYRUS DEPARTED FROM CAMP COBRA BY WAY OF THE BACKDOOR tunnel that bypassed the main entrance. Nicodemus and most of the other True Believers went with him, shining their flashlights on the tunnel's rocky walls. Cyrus had left a dozen men behind to guard the tent that held Little Boy. These holy martyrs would remain in the cavern's lower chamber to make sure that no one interfered with the nuclear device. It was probably an unnecessary precaution; none of the Rangers in the camp knew about the bomb, and General McNair had already ordered his men to stay away from the tent. But the Lord, Cyrus knew, always rewarded the prudent. McNair would also stay behind in Camp Cobra while Cyrus and his followers crossed into Iran. Little Boy's detonator was set to go off at two o'clock, which gave them nearly an hour to get clear.

Cyrus's knees ached as he climbed the dark, narrow path. It would've been more comfortable to leave the cavern by the main entrance, passing the long rows of tents in the upper chamber and the dozens of aircraft parked just inside the cave's mouth. But he couldn't walk through Camp Cobra wearing his head scarf, and if he went unmasked one of the Rangers might recognize him. Although Adam Cyrus Bennett was a civilian, he was well known in the U.S. Army. He'd started his career in 1969 as a researcher at the Livermore lab, where he'd learned about nuclear warheads and X-ray lasers. When the cold war ended he became a director at DARPA, in charge of awarding Defense Department grants to researchers developing new military technologies. For the next twelve years he was a dedicated civil servant, frequently visiting the front lines to field-test new weapons and determine what the soldiers needed. It was during one of those visits, a trip to eastern Afghanistan in 2004, that the Taliban ambushed his army escorts and took him to the cave in Gazarak Mountain. Then Adam Cyrus Bennett saw the Lord's face and realized that he'd been serving the wrong master.

After McNair's troops rescued him, he was flown back to Washington and spent the next three months recuperating at Walter Reed Army Medical Center. The doctors said he made a remarkable recovery, especially considering the severity of his wounds. After another month of rest, he returned to his office at DARPA and his job of sustaining America's military superiority. By that point, however, he wasn't Adam Cyrus Bennett anymore. Satan's foot soldiers had torn his spirit from his body, yanking his corrupted soul through the carvings they'd made in his chest and back and crotch. But the Lord, in His infinite wisdom, had filled his body with a new spirit. He was Brother Cyrus now, God's humble servant. "Adam Cyrus Bennett" was nothing more than a disguise, a way to secretly fulfill the Lord's plans.

And it was a good disguise, ideally suited for his new mission. Every year Cyrus's office distributed $500 million of research grants. About a third of the funding came from the Pentagon's classified "black budget." Because the Defense Department didn't have to disclose the details of these appropriations, it was easy for Cyrus to secretly funnel a sizable amount to the Redemption. He'd used the classified funds to hire experts to study the intelligence reports about the unified field theory. The black budget had also financed the clandestine activities of the True Believers—the fleet of trucks and Land Cruisers, the camp in the Turkmen desert—as well as the theft of the enriched uranium from the reactor in Kazakhstan. Cyrus had used another chunk of money to establish Logos Enterprises, the shell company that whisked Excalibur out of the Livermore lab. And he'd spent $10 million on the construction of Jacob Steele's Caduceus Array.

This was the trickiest part of the operation. Jacob had come to DARPA with the proposal of building single-ion clocks to prove the computational nature of spacetime. Cyrus saw right away that such an instrument would be useful to his cause. By measuring the fleeting time disruptions caused by the Excalibur test in Iran, the Caduceus Array would show whether the laser could really trigger the Redemption.

Keeping his true purpose a secret, Cyrus allowed Jacob to divert his DARPA grant to the experiment. After the Iranian nuclear test, Cyrus's men went to Jacob's lab and downloaded the data on the disruptions, then blew up the place to destroy the evidence. But the reclusive physicist had a secret of his own—from the very beginning Jacob had refused to reveal the name of his Israeli collaborator. Cyrus ultimately sent one of the True Believers to pry the information from him, but Jacob said nothing even when Lukas held a nine-millimeter pistol to his head. Fortunately, Cyrus had a few clues to the Israeli's identity, which he passed on to Special Agent Lucille Parker when she came to investigate the lab explosion. He knew she could locate the mysterious Olam ben Z'man. And when she did find him, Cyrus arranged the ambush in Yangykala Canyon to eliminate the threat.

As he looked back on it now, Cyrus couldn't help but marvel at his success. He felt no personal pride, however; all the credit belonged to the Lord, who'd blessed him with so many ardent followers. General McNair was the first, and Cyrus soon found others who hated the corrupt world and yearned for God's kingdom. He and McNair focused their efforts on their colleagues in the Defense Department, recruiting two more general officers and several dozen lower-ranking soldiers. These True Believers were all too familiar with the world's corruption, having seen it firsthand in Iraq and Afghanistan. Their souls had been lacerated by war and its atrocities. Before meeting Cyrus, many of the soldiers had contemplated suicide. But once they realized that Cyrus could extinguish the evil and open the gates to heaven—a *real* heaven, not some childish fantasy—they pledged themselves to the Lord. At the same time, Cyrus assembled his network of paid informants, using the DARPA funds to infiltrate government agencies in the United States and Israel. In addition to providing valuable intelligence, these informants helped Cyrus shield his operation from the scrutiny of federal bureaucrats and inspectors.

The only difficulty, Cyrus discovered, was a personal one: as his efforts accelerated, he grew more and more impatient. He was so eager to enter the Kingdom of Heaven that he began to loathe his old life and his repellent body. Every time he looked in the mirror he thought of the Book of Joshua, chapter seven, verse thirteen: *There is an accursed thing in the midst of thee.* Cyrus started to wear a head scarf when he was with his True Believers, and soon his self-loathing grew so intense that he wore the scarf even when he was alone. The corruption of the universe was written on his face, and he longed to be rid of it.

Now, after several minutes of hard climbing, Cyrus glimpsed the mouth of the backdoor tunnel. Nicodemus and a few other soldiers rushed ahead, cradling their rifles, just in case there were any enemies standing outside. The True Believers quickly secured the area and Cyrus stepped into the sunlight. Its rays warmed the fabric of his head scarf, which he'd donned again after praying with David Swift. Turning around, he gazed at the mountain from which he'd just emerged, and in his mind's eye he pictured the 960 solders inside the cavern, ignorant of what awaited them. Cyrus's eyes filled with tears—all those marvelous young men, so steadfast and trusting! He imagined the soldiers looking at him as if he were their father, and Cyrus—who had no children of his own—was overwhelmed with love.

He wished he could take the men aside and rejoice in the wonder of their sacrifice. With one grand gesture they would erase all their sins. The light of God's love would flash through the cavern, and thunder would echo in the bowels of the earth. Satan's minions in America and Russia and China would see the flash and hear the thunder, but they wouldn't recognize God's hand. Steeped in darkness, the leaders of the corrupt world would see only death. The president, the most powerful leader of them all, would respond by hurling more death at his foes. But his warhead would strike Excalibur, God's mighty sword, buried at the foot of an Iranian mountain. And Excalibur would resurrect the universe, turning death into life eternal.

Cyrus and his True Believers turned left, heading for the wide plateau that lay in front of the cavern's main entrance. After two minutes they came close enough to see the pair of CV-22 Ospreys that had just been rolled out of the cave's mouth. McNair's soldiers had unfolded the wings of the aircraft and rotated the tilt rotors to their vertical takeoff positions. Under the original plans for Operation Cobra, the tilt-rotor aircraft were supposed to spearhead the Ranger assault on the Iranian nuclear facility in Ashkhaneh. But that attack would never happen, of course. The assault wasn't scheduled to begin until well after nightfall, whereas Little Boy would detonate in just fifty-two minutes.

The soldiers who'd fueled and prepared the Ospreys had already returned to the cave. Cyrus didn't need any aviators from the Special Forces to fly the craft; he had his own pilots and navigators. But a lone man came toward them, a tall, gaunt soldier in a combat uniform with three black stars arranged in a vertical line below the collar. It was Lieutenant General Sam McNair. He spread his arms.

"I came to see you off, Brother," he said. "And wish you Godspeed."

The general seemed much cheerier now than the last time he and Cyrus had talked. He doesn't have to worry anymore, Cyrus thought. Even if McNair's superiors at Central Command discovered what he was doing, they couldn't stop him now. There wasn't enough time. "Thank you for readying the aircraft," Cyrus said. "How did you explain the situation to your soldiers?"

"I told them that Operation Cobra was canceled because the Iranians had agreed to surrender their nukes. It's a fairly preposterous lie, but my men accepted it." He pointed at the Ospreys. "They believe these aircraft will transport a special delegation to the Ashkhaneh facility to supervise the destruction of the Iranian nuclear devices. Again, it's not the most believable story, but we only need to buy a little more time."

"And what happens when the Pentagon's airborne radar detects the Ospreys flying into Iran? Have you prepared for that possibility?"

"Yes, Brother. I've shut down all communications in and out of the cavern. I've told my men we need to stay inside and go radio dark for the next hour."

Cyrus nodded, satisfied. McNair had done his job well. Not only had he finalized the arrangements at Camp Cobra, but he'd prepared Cyrus for the last stage of his journey. Because each Osprey held up to thirty-two soldiers, Cyrus could take all his True Believers with him to Ashkhaneh and still have room left over for the Russian X-ray laser. Flying across the border wouldn't be a problem either, because the Iranians were expecting them—Cyrus had promised the Revolutionary Guards another shipment of U-235. And the flight would take less than half an hour, so they should reach the Ashkhaneh facility just before Little Boy went off. The plan was perfect, he thought. Just as the Lord had promised.

"Then there's nothing left to do," Cyrus said. "Except bid each other good-bye." He stepped toward McNair and placed a gloved hand on the general's forehead. "The Lord is well pleased with your sacrifice, Samuel. And we will make sure that your sleep lasts only a few hours. The air force will retaliate swiftly, as soon as night falls. And then you and I will step into God's kingdom together."

Brother Cyrus prepared to give McNair a final blessing, but the general didn't lower his head. Instead he looked Cyrus in the eye. "Brother, one more question. Have you eliminated David Swift?"

"No, I left him in the lower chamber of the cavern. Under heavy guard, of course. Fifty minutes from now, he'll make the same sacrifice as you and your men. Let's hope that in his last moments he contemplates the Lord and sees the error of his ways."

McNair frowned. "Swift is an unbeliever. He doesn't deserve to be with us at the end."

"Even the unbelievers serve God. And soon we will all be together in the Kingdom of Heaven. So let us be generous." He stared at McNair for a few seconds to drive the point home. Then he nudged the general's head downward and delivered the final blessing, rushing a bit through the Latin. Cyrus still had many things to do, and he was anxious to get going. He needed to disable the transponders on the Ospreys and send a radio transmission to the Iranians. And once he reached Ashkhaneh he needed to place the X-ray laser at the target coordinates.

Taking a deep breath, he left McNair and walked with his men to the Ospreys. They were odd-looking, hybrid aircraft. They had wings like an airplane, but at each wingtip was an enormous three-bladed rotor attached to a turboprop engine. When the rotors pointed up, the Osprey could take off like a helicopter, but once the craft was in the air, the rotors tilted forward and functioned as propellers. As Brother Cyrus stared at the ungainly things, a group of True Believers approached the nearer of the two craft. His men held the Russian X-ray laser, carrying the long aluminum cylinder as pallbearers would carry a heavy coffin, with three men on one side and three on the other. The cargo door at the back of the Osprey dropped open, and the soldiers carefully slid the laser into the fuselage. Then the aircraft's turboprops started up and the rotors began to turn, their black blades cutting the sky.

35

THE SLOW, LOGICAL VOICE OF GENERAL YARON, COMMANDER OF UNIT 8200, came over the phone. "I'm sorry, Aryeh. I relayed your information to the IDF General Staff, but that's all I can do."

Aryeh had known Yaron for a long time—they'd once worked side by side in the army's code-breaking unit—but he'd never realized until now how much he disliked the man's voice. In America, Yaron would be considered emotionless, but for an Israeli he was positively robotic.

"I don't believe this!" Aryeh shouted. "Don't they see how dangerous the situation is? This Bennett schmuck is cooperating with the Iranians! Didn't the General Staff look at the messages we decoded?"

"Yes, they saw the messages. But the evidence is sketchy."

"Sketchy? The messages are crystal clear! Bennett stole Excalibur from the Livermore lab and installed it at the Kavir site just before the Iranian nuclear test! And now he's making his next move in Turkmenistan!" Aryeh realized he was losing control, but he couldn't help it. He was overcompensating for Yaron's lack of emotion. "At the very least, couldn't the IDF inform the Americans that one of their Pentagon officials has gone berserk?"

The line was silent for a few seconds. This was another infuriating thing about Yaron: he always thought before he spoke. "The General Staff has already contacted their liaisons in the U.S. Defense Department."

"And what did the Americans say?"

Another aggravating pause. "They said nothing. They simply thanked us for the information."

"Ach, don't you see what's happening? Bennett has a whole goddamn brotherhood of spies. They've infiltrated the Pentagon and the FBI and even Shin Bet. Bennett's friends are protecting him, you see? They're covering up his plans until it's too late!"

This time the silence lasted a full twenty seconds. Yaron was thinking very carefully. Aryeh suspected that the general was trying to determine how much he could safely reveal. "There's another possible explanation," he finally said. "As you know, the Americans have tried to restrain us from striking Iran's nuclear facilities. They've insisted on taking care of the problem themselves. It's possible that the decoded messages are connected to that effort. Turkmenistan, you see, is one of Iran's neighbors."

It took Aryeh a little while to catch Yaron's meaning. "You think the Americans are planning an assault? They're going to attack Iran from Turkmenistan?"

"I'm just speculating. I have no evidence."

"But that makes the situation even more dangerous! This Bennett schmuck is out of his mind, but the scientific theory he's—"

"Aryeh, I'm sorry, but I have to end this call. I recommend that you continue your work on the intercepted communications. If you uncover any more relevant information, please let me know."

Then the line went dead.

DAVID LAY IN THE DARKNESS, SCREAMING BEHIND HIS GAG. HIS ARMS WERE still tied behind his back and his ankles were bound together, and a third rope tethered him to a spike lodged in the ground. About half an hour had passed since Cyrus ordered his men to remove him from the large tent where Little Boy was and bring him to this smaller, darker tent. He wasn't sure of the time—with his hands behind his back, he couldn't look at his watch—but his best guess was that it was between one and two o'clock. Which meant that the bomb could explode at any moment.

Then the tent flaps opened and a pair of Army Rangers stepped inside. David's heart leaped—he'd finally gotten someone's attention!—and he screamed even louder, still yelling "BOMB! BOMB! BOMB!" even though he knew it sounded more like a stream of muffled *Ahs*. But his hopes sank once he got a good look at the soldiers. One of them was the guy who'd kicked him in the ribs, the giant with the buzz cut and the razor burn, Sergeant Morrison. The other was an older man, tall and thin. His uniform had three small black stars under the collar and the name MCNAIR on the right side of the chest. This was Brother Cyrus's accomplice, David remembered, the general who commanded the Ranger camp. The man looked at him with undisguised hatred.

Morrison stepped forward. "That's him, sir," he said, pointing at David. "That's the son of a bitch who killed Colonel Ramsey."

McNair nodded. "He doesn't look like an Iranian, does he? Or like a Turkmen either."

"I heard a rumor he was American, sir. A fucking traitor."

David shook his head violently. McNair knew exactly who he was. The general was just feigning ignorance now, the same way he pretended to be ignorant of the nuclear device in the middle of his camp. David felt sick as he stared at the man. McNair was going to sacrifice his own soldiers. He'd condemned them to death without a second thought.

The general grunted. "Well, whoever he is, he understands English. Get him up, Sergeant."

Morrison removed a combat knife from his belt and cut the rope that tethered David to the ground. But he didn't cut the bindings on David's ankles or wrists, and worse, he didn't remove the gag. Instead, he and McNair grabbed his arms and dragged him out of the tent.

The floodlights in the lower chamber of the cavern made it almost as bright as day. David squinted as McNair and Morrison pulled him through the tent flaps. Two more Rangers who were stationed in front of the tent snapped to attention. "Sir!" one of them shouted. "Do you want us to transfer the prisoner? We can—"

"At ease, gentlemen," McNair replied. "I just want to have a chat with him. He didn't answer a few questions in his last interrogation, so I thought I'd take another crack at it."

The guards nodded, glaring at David. "You need any help, sir?" one of them asked. "I'd love to ask this bastard a few questions."

"No thank you. Sergeant Morrison and I can take care of it."

As they hauled David away, dragging him across the rock shelf toward the underground lake, he spotted the larger tent where he'd seen Brother Cyrus, the tent that held Little Boy. It was surrounded by soldiers now, at least a dozen, all carrying assault rifles. David jerked his head in that direction, screaming, "OVER THERE! OVER THERE!" behind his gag. But McNair and Morrison took him the other way.

Soon they reached the edge of the lake, where the greenish water lapped against the shelf of gray limestone. The rotten-egg smell of hydrogen sulfide was stronger here, and columns of bubbles rose to the surface. David looked up and saw bats flitting near the cavern's ceiling, heading toward the black grottoes at the far side of the lake. The soldiers moved along the lake's edge, dragging David farther away from the tents and the illumination of the floodlights. They finally stopped at a shallow pool that was adjacent to the lake. A narrow channel connected the two, but the pool was frothier than the lake and the water in it was a brighter green. The sight of it made David uneasy. It reminded him of the hot springs at Yellowstone Park, which he'd visited several years before.

McNair and Morrison dropped him on the muddy ground near the edge of the pool. "We call this the Sour Tub," McNair said, pointing at the bright green water. "When we set up camp in this cave a few days ago, some of our boys decided to go swimming in the lake down here. But they noticed that if anyone swam too close to this pool, their skin would start to burn. Here, let me show you."

The general stepped forward and dipped the toe of his boot in the pool. He let only a couple of inches get damp, but David heard a hissing noise and saw bubbles appear on the tan cowhide. And now he remembered something else from his visit to Yellowstone: when he'd sat on a wet rock next to one of the springs, the moisture had burned a hole in his pants. The shallow pool contained high concentrations of sulfuric acid, which formed in the water when hydrogen sulfide combined with oxygen.

McNair smiled at David for a moment, then turned to Morrison. "Sergeant, please step back twenty paces. I want to have a private conversation with the prisoner."

Morrison looked uneasy. The giant soldier sucked in his razor-burned cheeks. "Sir, are you sure you—"

"You know my motto, Sergeant: no one left behind. This man killed Colonel Ramsey, and now he's going to tell me where he left Ramsey's body. One way or another, I'm going to get the information from him. So please step back."

Reluctantly, Morrison retreated into the shadows. McNair waited until the sergeant was well out of earshot. Then he bent over David and grasped the front of his shirt, balling the fabric in his fists. "As you may have guessed, I don't really care about Ramsey," he whispered. "Brother Cyrus ordered the colonel's execution, and I know exactly where his bones lie."

David thrashed on his back, trying to wriggle free, but McNair held on to his shirt and dragged him toward the pool. Standing at the edge, the general suspended David's head and shoulders over the water. "Ramsey was executed at the burning crater. A very painful death, but at least it was quick. Your death will be a little slower. We have twenty-five minutes until the moment of our sacrifice."

Then McNair dipped him in the pool. He carefully lowered David into the water, as if he were baptizing him. The general didn't let him go under—the water touched only the back of his head and the tops of his ears—but it felt like a swarm of bees was stinging his scalp. David screamed behind his gag again and struggled to lift his head.

After a few seconds McNair pulled him out of the water and threw him into the mud. "It hurts, doesn't it?" McNair said. "But you hurt us, too. You and the Israelis nearly upset our plans. And your idiot son corrupted Tamara, and she was a woman I held very dear."

David lay on his back, nauseous from the pain. He realized that McNair had just been talking about Michael, but he was too terrified and confused to make any sense of it.

The general rested his hands on his hips. "I've never understood unbelievers like you. Do you think it's funny to scoff at God? To laugh at things like faith and patriotism?" He curled his lip. "It's all just a joke to you, isn't it? Something you can snicker about with your friends in New York City?"

Weakly, David shook his head.

"Did it ever occur to you that while you were laughing at us, my men were risking their lives to protect you? That you were slandering the very soldiers who kept you safe?" McNair came closer, crouching beside David. His voice was thick with contempt. "No, you didn't care. Because you're an ungrateful sinner. But now it's time for you to make amends." He reached for the damp gag that covered David's mouth. "I want you to apologize, before God and my men. Apologize for your whole filthy exis-tence. If you don't, you're going back into the tub."

Using both hands, McNair pulled the gag off. David felt a rush of adrenaline—here was his chance! But when he tried to yell, "BOMB!" again, he could barely make a sound. His jaw ached from being propped open for so long, and his throat was raw from all the screaming he'd done already. "Please," he managed to gasp. "Don't do this . . . to your men . . ."

"No, wrong answer. There's something called belief, Mr. Swift, and I believe in the Redemption."

"There's still time . . . to evacuate the cave . . . and disable the—"

McNair punched him in the face, just below his left eye. The gen-eral's knuckles smashed into his cheekbone. David heard the smack, then felt a sharp arrow of pain. His ears rang and his skull rattled. The pain quickly spread to his eye socket and forehead, and he felt a fresh, blister-ing agony in his fingers as well. Trapped between his back and the muddy ground, his hands felt like they were burning. There was sulfuric acid in the mud, too.

McNair bent over him, rubbing his knuckles. "You're the most stub-born sinner I've ever met. Even now at the very end you won't admit you're wrong."

"Please . . . please listen . . ."

Before he could say another word, McNair grabbed the front of his shirt and dipped him in the pool again. David tucked his chin against his chest, trying to keep his head as high as possible, but his back touched the surface and the water engulfed his hands and forearms. The pain was tremendous, as bad as submerging them in boiling water. He flailed desperately, screaming, "NO, NO, STOP!" But McNair wouldn't lift him out of the pool.

David must've lost consciousness for a few seconds, because the next thing he remembered was being dropped into the mud again. His arms were jerking uncontrollably. He frantically tried to pull them out of the burning mud, straining so hard he thought his bones would snap. And then he felt something else, something that instantly focused his mind and tamped down the pain. The rope that bound his wrists together had loosened. When he pulled his arms now, he could feel the cord stretching. He remembered Yellowstone again and the hole in his pants. The same thing was happening now to the rope around his wrists. The sulfuric acid was burning through it.

McNair grabbed the front of his shirt once more. "All right, this is your last chance. If you won't open your eyes, I'll take them away from you. You understand, Swift? If the next thing that comes out of your mouth isn't a plea for forgiveness, I'll put your head under the water and you'll have a couple of bloody holes where your eyes used to be."

David nodded. At the same time, he continued jerking his arms. His hands squirmed under his back, tugging at the cords and pushing them deeper into the burning mud. "Okay," he gasped. "I'm sorry. Very sorry. Please forgive me."

The general leaned closer, lowering his face until it was right above David's. "Are you mocking me?"

David shook his head. The pain was making him nauseous again. But the cords were loosening. Just a little more. "No, I swear! Please, God, forgive me!"

McNair stared at him, wrinkling his nose in disgust. Then he turned away from David and called out to Morrison, who stood in the shadows thirty feet away. "Sergeant! The prisoner has apologized for what he's done. Do you think we should forgive him?"

And while McNair waited for an answer, David's right hand slid free. The pain in his fingers was excruciating, but he managed to dig them into the mud beneath his back. He grasped a burning handful and flung it in the general's face.

McNair fell backward, his hands covering his eyes. Morrison shouted, "Hey!" and started running toward them. David's legs were still bound at the ankles, so he stayed on the ground and rolled like a barrel, moving away from the shallow Sour Tub and toward the edge of the deep underground lake. Then he tumbled into the water and began to swim.

36

MONIQUE STOOD BEHIND THE PILOT'S SEAT IN THE HELICOPTER'S COCKPIT, leaning over Olam's shoulder. For most of the flight Michael had stood beside her, eagerly inspecting all the dials and switches on the MI-8's instrument panels, but a few minutes ago he'd gone back to the cabin to look at something else. Now Monique gazed out the cockpit window at the Kopet Dag, which stood like a dark wall at the southern edge of the desert. As the helicopter flew closer, she could see the gray flanks of the mountains, the ridges that rose precipitously from the desert floor. She also saw the massive spurs jutting sideways, and the rock slides that fanned down the slopes. And when they were quite close, less than a mile away, she saw the breach in the wall. A paved road climbed from the desert to a narrow gap between two ridges. This was the mountain pass that led to Kuruzhdey.

"Interesting," Olam observed. His grasped the MI-8's control stick with his right hand and flipped a switch on the overhead panel with his left. "The road is empty. And it's almost two o'clock in the afternoon. You'd usually see at least a few cars or trucks at this time of day, yes?"

Monique gazed at the highway below. Olam was right, there was no traffic whatsoever. "What do you think? Someone's blocking the roads?"

"It looks like the whole area has been evacuated. There was no movement in the village we just passed."

"Well, if the Turkmen Army is cooperating with Brother Cyrus now, they could easily clear the area. But why the hell would they agree to do it? What's in it for them?"

Olam shrugged. "Money, I suppose. Or maybe they were intimidated. The *Qliphoth* are very powerful. They seem to have friends everywhere."

Monique recalled her first conversation with Olam, back in Shalhevet, when he'd warned them about the *Qliphoth*. "Devils, right? That's what the word means in Hebrew?"

"Literally, it means 'shells' or 'husks.' The *Sephirot* shine God's light on the universe, and the *Qliphoth* block the light." He extended his hand toward the cockpit window, pointing at the mountains up ahead and the deep shadows between them. "But the Kabbalah tells us that even the *Qliphoth* are part of God. They serve a purpose, too. When we break the *Qliphoth,* when we crack open the shells, God's light shines even more strongly, yes?"

Monique nodded, although she didn't really understand him. She'd never had much use for religion. The concept of God had always seemed unnecessary to her, like the luminiferous ether that was once believed to pervade the universe. She'd learned to make her own way in life, without help from God or anyone else. But now her atheism was starting to waver. At this point she was willing to accept help from any corner. So as Olam guided the helicopter into the mountains and the other MI-8 trailed a quarter mile behind, Monique offered a silent prayer. If anyone's up there, she thought, now's the time to show Your face. Stop this crazy fuck Cyrus from destroying Your Creation. And please save David. Please save David.

THE WATER WAS WARM AND DARK. DAVID SWAM DOWN TO THE ROCKY BOT-tom of the lake, sweeping his arms in long, powerful strokes, his muscles remembering the long-ago days when he'd swum for the Stuyvesant High School team. His burned forearms hurt like hell, but the pain eased as he glided underwater and put some distance between himself and the Sour Tub. The sulfuric acid was so diluted in the lake that he could even open his eyes, although he couldn't see anything in the dark water. He kept swimming in the same direction, heading toward the grottoes on the far side of the lake. His feet were still bound, so he pumped his legs like a mermaid's tail and pulled himself forward with cupped hands. He stayed underwater until his lungs were bursting, then quietly surfaced and took a quick breath. Then he dove again.

The second time he surfaced he found himself inside one of the grottoes. It was so dark in there, he could hide in the recesses and no one would see him. He heard water lapping against a rock wall, so he headed for the noise and bumped against a ledge that was a couple of feet below the surface. He clambered onto the ledge and pulled up his knees so he could tug at the rope around his ankles. Luckily, these cords had also gotten splashed with sulfuric acid, and after several seconds he was able to loosen them and slip his feet out. Then the pain in his arms returned with a vengeance. He held them above the water, glad that he couldn't see his burned skin in the darkness. But he could see the glowing hands of his watch, which was still ticking. It was 1:49. Eleven minutes until detonation.

He heard shouting from the other side of the lake, about two hundred feet away. In the glare from the floodlights he saw soldiers running toward the Sour Tub, where McNair and Morrison were still crouched. The soldiers huddled around them, some of them talking into their radios. Then three of the soldiers removed their boots and began taking off their uniforms. They're going to dive into the lake and come after me, David thought. The only question is whether they'll find me before the bomb goes off.

He pushed himself away from the rock wall and started swimming diagonally across the lake, heading for the tent where Little Boy was. He knew it was insane—the tent was surrounded by armed guards. And now that he'd assaulted General McNair, it was even less likely that any of the soldiers would listen to him. But he didn't know what else to do. He swam as fast as he could, and in two minutes he was treading water in the part of the lake that was closest to the tent. He was about thirty feet offshore and the tent was another forty feet from the lake's edge. He was close enough that he could see the faces of the soldiers.

"Hey!" he shouted. "There's a bomb in that tent! Do you hear me?"

The soldiers saw him. They stood there for a moment, just staring. Then six of them started jogging toward the lake's edge.

"No, you have to get out of here!" David shouted. "Everyone has to get out! There's a goddamn nuke in that tent and it's gonna—"

A bullet streaked into the water a few feet to his left. David ducked below the surface and dove to the lake bottom, swimming away again.

Jesus, he thought, it's hopeless. All the soldiers would die in the blast, and he would, too. Cyrus had planned the operation too well. It was impossible to stop it now.

David stayed under as long as he could. He knew the soldiers were waiting for him to come up and would probably blow his head off when he did. But no shots rang out when he finally surfaced. Instead, he saw Sergeant Morrison swimming toward him, very fast. The soldier's tattooed arms stroked furiously, slapping the water, and his blond head skimmed the surface like a bullet.

David dove again, heading for the dark grottoes. He went deep and glided underwater for at least half a minute. Then he rose to take a breath, but at the point where he thought he would break the surface he banged his head against something. The blow disoriented him. Twisting in the pitch-black water, he raised his hands and felt slippery limestone above him. He'd swum into an underwater cave. He turned around and tried to swim out, but he immediately smacked into a rocky wall. Clawing at the rock, he turned parallel to the wall and swam alongside it. He tried to rise to the surface and bumped his head against the cave's ceiling again. Panicking, he swam in the opposite direction, his arms flailing. He couldn't hold his breath much longer. His chest was tight and dense and burning and he felt an overwhelming urge to open his mouth and let the black water rush in. His whole body convulsed with horror.

Then he raised his head one more time and broke free of the water.

He took several sputtering breaths. Then he noticed that Sergeant Morrison wasn't anywhere nearby. And there were no soldiers shooting at him from the lake's edge. In fact, he wasn't in the underground lake at all. He was in the oval pool in the adjacent chamber, the one he'd seen after coming down the backdoor tunnel with Nicodemus. David realized he must've gone through an underwater tunnel that connected the oval pool to the lake in the larger chamber. Turning to the left now, he saw the shaft of light from the circular passageway between the chambers, where Sergeant Morrison had kicked him in the ribs. But the sergeant was no longer at his post, of course.

David swam to the rock shelf at the edge of the pool and heaved himself out of the water. Then he looked at his watch, but its face was cracked—he must've smashed it against the limestone while he was struggling underwater. The glowing hands had stopped at 1:54.

Breathing fast, he peered into the darkness, looking for the backdoor tunnel. Jesus, what he wouldn't give for a flashlight! After a few seconds, though, he felt a cool draft in the chamber and followed it to a five-foot-high opening in the rock wall. He stepped into the tunnel and was about to begin the long, dark climb to the surface when he heard a shout behind him. He turned around and in the dim light he saw Sergeant Morrison in the oval pool, swimming toward the rock shelf.

"HEY!" Morrison shouted. "HEY! HE'S ESCAPING!"

OLAM WAS GETTING FRUSTRATED. HE FLEW THE MI-8 DIRECTLY ABOVE THE Kuruzhdey district, but neither he nor Monique saw any trucks or Land Cruisers in the mountain pass below. There were wooded ravines and arid plateaus between the steep ridges and even a few concrete structures scattered along the paved road, but no vehicles or people or movement of any kind. Olam spotted a radio tower on a summit a few miles away, but when he flew closer to investigate he saw only a small shed at the base of the tower, too small to hold Excalibur. So he circled back to Kuruzhdey and inspected the mountain pass again, flying below the ridges and inside the ravines and checking every cliff and promontory. Monique got a sinking feeling in her stomach. Maybe Michael had misheard Angel when he'd revealed the name of the True Believers' destination. Or maybe Angel had lied to Michael, or just said the wrong name by mistake.

Then Olam pointed at the ground. "Ah, look over there! You see the tracks?"

Monique looked down at a sandy plateau between two parallel ridges. She saw a few brown clumps of vegetation on the ground, but nothing else. "What tracks?"

"It's a landing zone! It looks like a pair of large helicopters took off from there not long ago."

She leaned a little closer to the cockpit window. Near the middle of the plateau was a circle of ground where the sand had been disturbed. No, two circles. And several converging tracks led from the circles to an indentation at the base of one of the ridges. "You're right," she said. "Something happened here."

"Let's take a look, yes?" Olam picked up the radio transmitter and said something in Hebrew to Lieutenant Halutz, the pilot of the helicopter behind them. Then they started to descend.

DAVID SCRAMBLED UP THE SLOPING TUNNEL. THERE WAS NO LIGHT AT ALL and the tunnel's floor was a rocky chute, covered with shifting slabs and stones, but he lowered his head and pumped his legs and leaped forward into the darkness. He planted his feet blindly and groped the tunnel's walls. Every ten yards or so he stumbled to the ground and yelped in pain as his burned forearms scraped against the rock, but he didn't stop, he couldn't stop. He thought of his journey down this tunnel with Nicodemus and Hatchet Face and tried like hell to remember how long it was. A thousand feet? Two thousand? And he thought of his broken watch, the hands stopped at 1:54. He had no idea how much time had passed since then.

Then he heard shouts again, echoing up the tunnel. The rocky walls suddenly turned visible, catching the stray light from the flashlight beams that were lancing behind him. He ran faster now because he could see the stones underfoot, and he wasn't afraid of the soldiers anymore, he wasn't afraid of anything except that gun tube at the bottom of the cavern, the steel pipe filled with fifty kilograms of uranium. And as he ran he shouted, "BOMB! BOMB! BOMB!" and he thought again of Lucille rushing out of the Turkmen depot, hooking one arm around him and the other around Monique and shoving them both out the door. Then he saw the mouth of the tunnel, the blessed circle of light, and with a great yell he charged forward and burst into the open air.

But he didn't stop running. He dashed across the flat ground at the foot of the mountain, heading for the shelter of a ravine on the other side of the road. He crossed the strip of asphalt and hurtled down a sandy slope. Then he felt a push from behind, and a pair of tattooed arms encircled his waist. Sergeant Morrison tackled him and they tumbled into the ravine together, jouncing along the ground until they crashed into a clump of dry bushes. David landed on his back, the wind knocked out of him, but Morrison clambered to his knees and raised his fist. His blond head was silhouetted against the sky, and above the sergeant's shoulder David could see the top of the mountain they'd just escaped. Morrison pulled back his arm, aiming carefully. But before he could throw the punch, a vast rumble shook the roots of the Kopet Dag, and the mountain behind him began to fall.

37

THE PRESIDENT WAS SLEEPING SOUNDLY IN THE WHITE HOUSE MASTER BED-room when the Secret Service agents burst in and turned on the lights. Agent Thompson—the president's favorite night-shift agent—came to the bed holding a maroon bathrobe. The other agent threw off the bed-covers.

"I'm sorry, Mr. President," Agent Thompson said. "We have to leave right now." He grasped the president's elbow and lifted him off the mat-tress.

"What?" He was groggy and confused. He wondered where his wife was, then remembered she was at Camp David with the girls. Jesus, he thought, what time was it? "Come on, guys, I'm in my boxers. Let me get—"

"We have clothes for you on *Marine One,* sir." Thompson and his partner helped the president put on the bathrobe, guiding his arms through the sleeves. Then the agents hustled him out of the bedroom and down the hallway.

As they quickstepped toward the stairs, Thompson raised his left hand to his mouth. "Thompson to Blowtorch," he said into the micro-phone on his shirt cuff. "We have Renegade. Heading for the South Lawn. Over."

The president was wide-awake now and starting to worry. There had been false alarms before, when the Secret Service had rushed him out of the White House because some idiot in a private plane had flown into the protected airspace. But never in the middle of the night like this. "What's going on?" he asked.

"Don't know, sir," Thompson replied. "But we're taking you to Andy."

Shit, he thought. This was no false alarm. Andy was the code name for Andrews Air Force Base, the field where *Air Force One* was stationed. Whatever the nature of this emergency, the Pentagon had deemed it serious enough to warrant moving the commander in chief out of Washington.

The president and his Secret Service agents made their way to the South Lawn, where *Marine One* had just touched down. Bracing themselves against the rotor wash, they jogged across the grass and boarded the helicopter. Within seconds they were in the air, heading southeast toward Andrews. The agents handed the president a gray suit, a white shirt, and a pair of black shoes, and he quickly got dressed in the helicopter's lavatory. Then he entered the main cabin and took his usual seat.

The cabin was crowded. Sitting across from the president were the chairman of the Joint Chiefs of Staff, the national security adviser, the national director of intelligence, and the defense secretary. At the other end of the cabin were several generals from Central Command, which controlled military operations in the Middle East, and Special Operations Command, which oversaw all Special Forces units. And sitting all by himself in the cabin's far corner was a young air-force major whose sole duty was to carry the black briefcase known as the Football. It looked very much like an ordinary briefcase, except that it had an antenna near the handle.

The president waited a moment, composing himself. Then he turned to the chairman of the Joint Chiefs. "What's the situation?"

The chairman's face, usually ruddy and fierce, was now pale and unshaven. He held a manila folder in his lap. "About an hour ago we detected a seismic event that had all the characteristics of an underground nuclear explosion. We thought at first that the Iranians had conducted another test, but the epicenter was north of Iran's border. It was in the Kuruzhdey district of Turkmenistan, where our Ranger battalion is positioned." He paused, his eyes avoiding the president's. "We tried to contact the unit, but we couldn't raise them on the radio. So we instructed our reconnaissance satellites to train their cameras on Kuruzhdey during their next pass of the region." He opened his folder and removed a stack of photographs. "These images were taken thirty minutes ago. They show the area outside the entrance to Camp Cobra."

The president inspected the photos. He'd seen earlier satellite images of the Camp Cobra site and remembered the topography: a band of flat ground running between two parallel ridges. But in the photographs the president was viewing now, one of the ridges had collapsed. A vast fan of rocky debris had spilled through a gap in the line of cliffs.

For about ten seconds he couldn't breathe. When he finally did, he felt an ache in his chest. "Jesus," he whispered. "Are there any survivors?"

The Joint chairman grimaced. "We're preparing to send a search-and-rescue team from Afghanistan, but first we need to measure the radiation levels in the area. We've already dispatched a pair of reconnaissance drones to collect samples of the radioactive debris from the explosion."

The president nodded, trying to stay calm. That was his job, to analyze the situation in a rational way and consider the appropriate response. But he was feeling anything but rational at the moment. It took all of his willpower to remain in his seat and nod at the general. He wanted to rush into the helicopter's cockpit and grab the controls of *Marine One* and fly it directly to Turkmenistan. He wanted to land on the pile of debris he'd seen in the photograph and start digging through the rocks with his bare hands. "How could this happen? Was it an accident? The Rangers didn't have any tactical warheads, did they?"

"No, sir, they didn't. And this wasn't an accident. About twenty minutes before the explosion, our radar systems detected two aircraft traveling south from Kuruzhdey to the Iranian border. And we intercepted a brief message that was sent from one of the aircraft to the Ashkhaneh nuclear facility."

"They were communicating with the Iranians? With the Revolutionary Guards?"

"Yes, sir. The message was in Farsi. The English translation is, 'Detonation in nineteen minutes.'"

The president nodded again. Now he understood why the Pentagon was rushing him out of the capital. Nearly a thousand American soldiers had just been killed in a nuclear attack. And more attacks could be coming. This possibility scared the hell out of him, but it also focused his mind. Get your shit together, he told himself. Step up and take control. He pointed at the Joint chairman. "Did the radar systems track the two aircraft?"

"They landed near the Ashkhaneh facility. By the time our satellites passed over the area, the Revolutionary Guards had hidden the aircraft, most likely inside the bunker. But the images show a company of armed men, which is probably the Iranian strike team. They must've discovered the location of the Ranger camp and launched a preemptive attack against it."

"Mr. President." A gray-haired, jug-eared army general raised his hand to get his attention. It was General Philip Estey of Special Operations Command. "Our analysts have come up with a possible scenario to explain what happened. The Camp Cobra site was a cavern with many passageways and entrances. The Iranian commandos must've discovered a tunnel that the Rangers weren't guarding. And then all they had to do was place one of their nuclear devices inside the mountain."

Again, the president wanted to jump out of his seat. He was enraged— no one in the Pentagon had mentioned this vulnerability before! How could all their strategists and experts have overlooked such an obvious thing? "Christ!" he yelled. "I don't believe this! You didn't—" But he stopped when he saw General Estey's stricken face. He'd just remembered that Estey had been a close friend of McNair. "Hold on, I'm sorry. Was General McNair at Camp Cobra at the time of the explosion?"

Estey nodded. His face was as pained and sober as a preacher's. "Yes, sir, he was there. McNair was strongly committed to the mission's success and took a hands-on role." He bowed his head and stared at the cabin's floor. "I'm not giving up hope until we hear from the search-and-rescue team. But in all likelihood, Samuel is gone."

Several other generals bowed their heads, too. For a few seconds the cabin was silent except for the thumping of the helicopter's rotors. But the president had no time to mourn. He was still enraged, and now all his fury was directed at the Iranians. "All right, our first priority is defending against further attacks. Our forces in the Middle East should go on highest alert. All units return to their bases and hunker down." He turned to the national director of intelligence. "Is there any evidence that the Iranians are preparing another nuclear strike? Either in the Middle East or here in the U.S.?"

The NDI shook his head. "No, sir. We still believe that their nuclear devices are inside the Revolutionary Guard's Ashkhaneh facility."

"Well, we're not going to give them a chance to use another one. We're going to destroy that facility. We're going to make it disappear." He turned back to the Joint chairman. "Get the stealth bombers in the air. Loaded with the B83, the bunker-busting nuke. As soon as we confirm that the Iranians were behind the attack on Camp Cobra, I'll give you the authorization to deploy the warhead." He jerked his head toward the air-force major who held the Football, the black briefcase containing the nuclear attack plans.

"How are we going to get confirmation?" the chairman asked. "If you ask the Iranians, they'll just deny any involvement."

General Estey raised his hand again. "Mr. President, in a few hours we should be able to analyze the radioactive debris collected by our reconnaissance drones. If the radioisotope signatures from the Camp Cobra explosion are similar to those from the Iranian test in the Kavir Desert, we can conclude that the same nuclear fuel was used in both cases."

The president took a deep breath. It was a grave decision, with terrible consequences either way. But as commander in chief, his primary responsibility was to his troops. And he had to stop the Iranians immediately, before they could attack again. "That's good enough for me. If we get confirmation from the debris analysis, we'll launch the nuclear strike on Ashkhaneh. And then we'll destroy the rest of the Iranian military with our conventional forces. I assume those plans are already in place?"

The Joint chairman saluted. "Yes, sir!"

By this point, *Marine One* was descending. The president gazed out the helicopter's porthole window and saw the runways of Andrews Air Force Base. About a hundred yards away was a 747 with the words UNITED STATES OF AMERICA written in gray letters along the fuselage. The plane looked similar to the other 747s in the *Air Force One* fleet, but the president knew it was very different on the inside. It was an E-4B, specially modified for use as a mobile command post, with hardened electronics that could withstand the electromagnetic pulses caused by high-altitude nuclear explosions. The Pentagon had given this aircraft the code name of Nightwatch. But it was better known as the Doomsday Plane.

38

AS BROTHER CYRUS HAD EXPECTED, THE IRANIANS AT THE ASHKHANEH nuclear facility weren't happy. They didn't like the fact that Cyrus had broken radio silence with his cryptic message in Farsi. And they were even more displeased when Cyrus and his men arrived in two Osprey tilt-rotor craft that looked like they'd just been stolen from the Marine Corps. The Iranian soldiers were scared enough already of an American attack, and they knew that the U.S. Air Force's reconnaissance satellites were passing over the area every thirty minutes. So they rushed out of their bunker and quickly towed the suspicious aircraft into a hangar that the Revolutionary Guards had carved into the mountainside. The hangar was essentially a large cave with a wide mouth and an arched ceiling. The bunker was a separate network of caverns that had a concrete pillbox at its entrance and a spiderweb of sloping tunnels that ran twelve hundred feet below the mountain.

Inside the hangar, Cyrus's soldiers unloaded the promised shipment of enriched uranium, hauling the heavy, lead-lined cases out of the Ospreys. The Iranians carried the U-235 back to their bunker, eager to return to the depths of the cavern where they'd stored the previous shipments of nuclear fuel. Then General Jannati, the commander of the Ashkhaneh facility, entered the hangar with two of his lieutenants. Cyrus had met Jannati before. Because the general spoke English well, he'd become Cyrus's main contact in the Revolutionary Guards. He was a short, skinny man in a ridiculous-looking uniform. He frowned as he approached Cyrus. "Good afternoon, Mr. Black," he said.

Cyrus hadn't revealed his true identity to the Iranians. They knew him as Cyrus Black, the masked leader of an international smuggling ring. "A pleasure to see you again, General. Please excuse us for violating your security rules, but we had to leave Turkmenistan on short notice."

Jannati kept frowning. "You were supposed to arrive at night. And travel by car, not aircraft. Our agreement was very clear on that point."

"A thousand apologies. But now you have the last shipment of U-235. And I brought a little something extra for you."

The general glanced nervously at his lieutenants. Then he leaned closer to Cyrus. "Is it in the aircraft?" he whispered. "The Courvoisier?"

Cyrus nodded. Jannati had a taste for cognac, which was illegal in the Islamic Republic of Iran. But the general had found ways to privately indulge.

Jannati turned to his lieutenants and barked an order in Farsi. The two men saluted and marched out of the hangar. Once they were gone, the general grasped Cyrus's arm and headed for the Ospreys. "You were lucky to get out of Turkmenistan," Jannati said. "I just heard a report of an earthquake there."

"Really?"

"Yes, just across the border. Less than a hundred kilometers north of here."

Brother Cyrus smiled. Praise the Lord, he thought. Praise Him in His mighty heaven.

While General Jannati found the case of Courvoisier and opened a two-hundred-dollar bottle of XO Imperial, Cyrus took Nicodemus aside and told him the good news. Then he quietly ordered the True Believers to remove the X-ray laser from the Osprey, carry it out of the hangar, and put it in position at the target point. He reminded them to do the job slowly and carefully. There was no need to rush, he said. The U.S. Air Force wouldn't launch its retaliatory strike until nightfall, when the B-2 Stealth bombers would become impossible to detect.

After an hour and a half, the True Believers completed their task and returned to the hangar. By this point, General Jannati was stone drunk. He sprawled on a wooden crate, his head drooping as he clutched the bottle of cognac with both hands. Cyrus stood nearby, keeping a watchful eye on the general and smiling behind his head scarf. They were on the threshold of the kingdom now, just inches away. Cyrus reviewed his preparations one last time to make sure he hadn't forgotten anything.

The only flaw in their plans was the fact that the Turkmen Army hadn't captured Olam ben Z'man yet. But Cyrus didn't consider Olam a serious threat. Even if the Israeli tried to warn the Americans, it was very unlikely that anyone at the Pentagon would take him seriously.

As General Jannati took another swig from his cognac bottle, the radio on his belt let out a squawk. A tentative voice came out of the radio's speaker, posing a question in Farsi. After a few seconds, the voice repeated its question. The Revolutionary Guards were obviously wondering when their commander would return to the bunker. Jannati ignored the radio transmissions for as long as he could, then groped for the handset and began shouting into it. When he was finished, he tossed the radio aside and turned to Cyrus. "Idiots," he muttered. "They can't do anything on their own. Always waiting for my orders." He shook his head. "I told them I'd shoot the next person who radios me. Maybe I'll get a little peace now."

Cyrus nodded. "A wise move. You're teaching them discipline."

"Exactly! Every army must have discipline." Jannati pointed at the True Believers who stood at attention on the other side of the hangar. "Look at your men, how dutiful they are. How do you manage it? I suppose you pay them well enough, eh?"

Cyrus nodded again. To convince the Iranians that he was a smuggler, he'd demanded $15 million for the uranium. "The money helps," he said. "But the most important thing is belief. Your men must believe in you."

Jannati leaned forward and narrowed his eyes. "You and your men are religious, yes? Faithful Christians of some type?"

Cyrus stared at the general, who perched precariously on the edge of the crate. The Iranian was more perceptive than he'd realized. "That's correct," Cyrus replied. "We believe in God."

"Yes, I suspected as much." Jannati raised the bottle of cognac and took another swig. "Tell me something else, Mr. Black. What's in the aluminum cylinder that your men unloaded from the aircraft a while ago?"

Cyrus jumped. The question had come out of nowhere. "Excuse me?"

"I didn't get a very good look at the thing, but it seemed familiar. You placed a similar device at the Kavir site before the nuclear test, didn't you?"

Damnation, Cyrus thought. He'd hoped that the Courvoisier would distract Jannati from any discussion of Excalibur. "My apologies. I thought I explained all this in our previous meetings. I have another client I'm not at liberty to reveal, another government that's very interested in nuclear testing. They paid me to install and monitor the scientific instruments at the test site. The data collected by the instruments will help this client advance its own nuclear program. Your commander in chief approved this provision when we made our agreement."

"Yes, he was a bit desperate, wasn't he? He would've agreed to anything as long as you gave him the uranium. Our own enrichment plants weren't producing the fuel fast enough, and he was under a great deal of pressure to conduct a test this year." Jannati covered his mouth and belched. "But now the situation is changed. My superiors have instructed me to ask a few questions about your scientific instruments."

Cyrus was alarmed, but he kept his voice steady. "Certainly. What would you like to know?"

"Well, first off, why are you installing additional instruments now? We're not planning any more nuclear tests."

Cyrus nodded. He'd hoped to avoid this confrontation, but that was impossible. General Jannati had become a threat, and all threats to the Redemption had to be eliminated. Cyrus stepped toward him. "The explanation is simple." He extended a gloved hand. "Come with me, General. I think you'll find this fascinating."

Jannati swayed on his crate, grinning blearily. "What? You want to go somewhere?"

"Not very far. Just a few steps outside." Cyrus placed his hand on Jannati's back. After a moment's hesitation, the general shrugged and let Cyrus guide him out of the hangar.

Once they were outside, they turned left and walked alongside the foot of the mountain. About four hundred yards west of the hangar was a stretch of flat, sandy ground. Several weeks ago, while the True Believers had been preparing Excalibur for the Kavir test, some of Cyrus's men had borrowed a bulldozer from the Iranians and dug a thirty-foot-deep hole in the sand near the base of the mountain. Then they'd borrowed a crane to lower a large steel chamber into the cavity. Finally, they'd refilled the hole, but left a tunnel in place so they would still have access to the buried chamber. Cyrus had told the Iranians that he was installing a monitoring device that would measure the seismic echoes from the Kavir test, but that was a lie. The impact chamber would be the final resting place for the Russian X-ray laser.

Cyrus escorted Jannati into a trench that ran down to the mouth of the tunnel. The entrance was a rectangle braced with timbers, about twelve feet high and eighteen feet wide. It looked like the entrance to a two-car garage, except for the low wall of sandbags. Nicodemus and two other True Believers stood in front of the dark rectangle, cradling their carbines. Cyrus gave a signal to Nico, raising two fingers in the air. Then he turned back to Jannati. "This X-ray laser is almost identical to the one we placed at the Kavir site, but it was built by the Russians. They copied the American prototype."

The general nodded drunkenly. "What did you say? A laser?"

They walked into the tunnel, which sloped downward like a steep ramp. Nico followed them, turning on his flashlight. "An X-ray laser," Cyrus repeated. "It converts the radiation from a nuclear explosion into high-energy laser beams."

"But I told you, we're not planning any more—"

"Wait just a moment, General. Then everything will become clear."

The tunnel was less than a hundred feet long, so they soon reached the impact chamber. It was fitted with a large viewing window, about the same size as one of the windows in a public aquarium. Cyrus and Jannati stopped in front of the window and Nico shone his flashlight at the thick sheet of glass. Inside the chamber was the long aluminum cylinder that Cyrus's men had just positioned. The sliding panel on the cylinder was open, and Cyrus could see the twelve laser rods inside, each four feet long and composed of hundreds of slender strands that had been bundled together. The rods were held in place by struts projecting from a central pole. The assembly resembled the skeleton of a folded umbrella, with the rods corresponding to the umbrella's ribs, all of them aimed at a focal point inside the cylinder. The Omega Point.

Cyrus stared for a moment at the laser rods, enraptured by their beauty. Then he turned back to Jannati. "Are you familiar with the B83 warhead?" he asked.

"B83?" The general looked befuddled. His eyes darted back and forth between Cyrus and the window of the impact chamber. "Isn't that an American nuclear bomb?"

Cyrus nodded. "It was originally a gravity bomb, but the air force gave it a GPS guidance system and turned it into a bunker buster. It's designed to burrow below the surface before exploding, so it can maximize the damage to an underground facility. To destroy an installation like yours, located in a cavern under a mountain, the best target would be a patch of sandy ground next to the mountain's base."

"I'm sorry, but I don't see what this—"

"We're standing at the target right now. In a few hours a Stealth bomber will deliver a B83 that will strike the ground directly above this chamber and burrow twenty feet through the sand. The target was preplanned, you see, and I already knew the coordinates when we dug this pit. And military GPS is very precise. Any targeting error would be less than a meter."

Jannati was silent for a few seconds. Then he burst out laughing. "Very good, Mr. Black! And now you're going to tell me that you're an American spy? And you delivered the uranium to the Revolutionary Guards just to give the U.S. Air Force an excuse to blow us up?"

"No, not quite. I had to arrange a more significant provocation to ensure that the president would retaliate with the B83. The earthquake in Turkmenistan was actually a nuclear explosion that incinerated a hidden army base called Camp Cobra. And I planted very convincing evidence of Iranian involvement in Cobra's destruction."

The general stopped laughing. He rocked unsteadily on the balls of his feet. "All right, enough of this nonsense. What's going on?"

"The policy of deterrence requires the Pentagon to respond with a nuclear strike. And I have followers in Washington who'll make sure that the president launches the attack on this facility. General Bolger of Global Strike Command is a True Believer, and so is General Estey of Special Operations Command." Cyrus pointed at the top of the impact chamber, which was covered with a steel grate. "The warhead will enter the chamber there. Its nose will lodge in the grate and the bomb will explode. We've already pumped the air out of the chamber, so the radiation can travel through the vacuum to the laser rods. And because the warhead will be so close to the rods when it explodes, the energy delivered to them will be tremendous."

Jannati stared at the chamber. A spark of fear belatedly flashed in his bloodshot eyes. "You're serious, aren't you?" he shouted, turning to Cyrus. "What the hell have you done?"

"You see how the laser rods are angled toward a focal point? The beams will converge inside the cylinder, in a specific pattern that will maximize the flow of data to the memory caches in that tiny volume of space. And when those caches overload—"

"Damn it, answer me! What have you done?"

"I'm trying to explain, General. We're going to open the gates to the kingdom."

Curling his lip, Jannati reached for his pistol. At the same moment, Nico slammed his flashlight into the back of the general's head. As Jannati staggered, Nico removed the SIG Sauer nine-millimeter from the man's holster. Then he grabbed Jannati's hair, pulled back his head, and used a combat knife to sever the general's throat.

Jannati landed on his back. He clamped a hand over his neck but the blood spewed between his fingers. Cyrus bent over him. "Well, we won't have time for the full explanation. But we will meet again, General. In the Kingdom of Heaven, the Lord will gather all of us in His arms, every creature He ever—"

Jannati arched his back and spat a mouthful of blood at Cyrus. Then the general's hand slid off his throat and the rest of his blood poured out of him.

Cyrus removed a handkerchief from his pocket and dabbed his clothes. The corruption of the world never ceased to amaze him. But it would be over soon.

He turned to Nico. "Go back to the hangar and retrieve the general's radio. If his soldiers try to contact him again, tell them that their commander is indisposed." He put the bloody handkerchief back in his pocket. "I don't think the Iranians will give us any trouble before nightfall. But just in case they do, order our men to dig defensive positions around this tunnel."

39

DAVID OPENED HIS EYES AND SAW MONIQUE. HE COULDN'T SEE HER FACE SO well—his eyes were full of grit and stung like crazy—but he noticed that her cornrow braids were speckled with sand. It actually looked sort of cute, although he knew she'd be mortified if she saw her hair in the mirror. She bent over him, biting her lip and wiping tears from her eyes, and he wanted to say something about her hair, something that would make her laugh, but his throat was so sore he could barely swallow. Then he looked a little closer at her face and saw a jagged cut on her left cheek and another on her chin. And he started crying, too, partly because he hated to see her hurt, and partly because he was so glad she was alive.

He was inside some kind of vehicle, in a gray and boxy cabin, lying on a stretcher that jutted from the steel wall like a shelf. He tried to prop himself up and noticed that his forearms were covered in bandages. Because of the burns, he remembered, the sulfuric acid burns. Agitated, he sat up and grasped Monique's shoulders.

"The mountain," he gasped. "The soldiers. In the mountain. We have to go back. We have to see . . ."

Monique shook her head. "No, David. We can't go back. The mountain collapsed. And there's radioactive debris." More tears leaked from the corners of her eyes. "I saw it from the air. Fire shot from the mouth of the cave. Then the cliff crumbled. And everything slid down."

"Wait. You saw it from the air?"

"We're in a helicopter." She pointed to the front of the cabin, and David saw the cockpit. But there was no rotor noise, and they didn't seem to be moving. "That's how we spotted you. After we pulled away from the explosion, we saw movement in the ravine. We picked up you and seven other men, U.S. Army soldiers. It looks like they belong to a Special Operations unit."

"Yes, they were getting ready to attack Iran. But there were hundreds of men in that cavern! You found only seven?"

"Those were the only survivors. Four of them were snipers posted on the slopes near the cavern and three said they left the cave because they were chasing you. We searched the rubble for a long time, and so did the pilots in the other helicopter. Then we flew about ten miles west and landed on this mountaintop. The wind is blowing east, so we should be safe from the fallout here. And now we—"

"Shalom!" boomed a familiar voice. "Is the instrument of *Keter* awake yet?"

Olam ben Z'man stepped into the helicopter's cabin, still wearing the black clothes he'd put on for the raid at Yangykala. But before David could react to this remarkable sight, he saw someone else standing beside Olam. It was a tall, young man with unkempt hair and a bruised face. The young man turned his head slightly to the left, his eyes avoiding David's, but he walked over to the stretcher without any hesitation and raised his right hand as if he were taking an oath. "Where were you?" he asked in an even voice. "I was looking for you."

David also raised his right hand. This was the greeting he always used with Michael. The boy didn't like to be touched. "I'm here now," David said. "And I'm so happy to see you." Then he turned his head away and covered his eyes. Emotion squeezed his chest and throat. He held still and waited until he could breathe again. The tears made his eyes sting even worse, but he didn't care. He was so grateful.

The cabin was silent for a few seconds. By the time David removed his hand from his eyes, Michael had gone to one of the helicopter's port-hole windows and started tracing figures in the condensation on the glass. Monique touched David's shoulder. "Six of Olam's men are still alive," she said. "Shomron, the radioman, was injured at Yangykala, but the rest are all right. They're outside now, trying to send a radio message to the American bases in Afghanistan. There's a transmission tower on this mountain."

"Yes, that's why we landed here," Olam said. "The radios on the helicopters weren't strong enough. It's strange, but someone seems to be jamming the military frequencies in this area."

No, it's not strange, David thought. "It's the U.S. Air Force," he said. "They're probably following orders from one of Cyrus's True Believers. They're jamming the airwaves because Cyrus doesn't want anyone to know what really happened at Camp Cobra." He remembered Cyrus's round, pink face, so ordinary and familiar. "I saw him take off his head scarf before he left the camp. It's Adam Bennett."

Monique stared at David, her mouth half open. She raised her fingers to her lips. "What? The DARPA director?"

He nodded. "His whole confession in Jacob's lab was an act. He just wanted us to find Olam for him. The guy's crazy, but he has an impressive organization, probably funded with all the money he siphoned off from DARPA. And some of his followers have important jobs in the military. Like the Special Operations general who let him put a nuke inside that cavern."

"Charah!" Olam cursed. He turned his head toward the cockpit, his lone eye blazing. "I told you these *Qliphoth* were powerful! This is how they infiltrated so many agencies!"

"But this is insane!" Monique stood up suddenly. "Why would they blow up an American base?"

"Cyrus needed a more powerful explosion," David answered. "To give the X-ray laser enough energy to trigger the quantum crash."

"I still don't—"

"He destroyed Camp Cobra to provoke a response. He knows the president will order a nuclear strike on the Iranians now. So Cyrus is going to put the X-ray laser at the target coordinates."

The cabin went silent again. Monique scrunched her eyebrows together, and a vertical line appeared on her forehead, above the bridge of her nose. David knew exactly what it meant. She wasn't scared or confused anymore. She was pissed. "Where's the son of a bitch now?"

"Cyrus said he was going to a Revolutionary Guard facility near the Iranian town of Ashkhaneh. That's the target for the American nuke."

Olam pulled a map out of his pocket and unfolded it. After a few seconds he poked the center of the page. "Yes, Ashkhaneh. It's about a hundred kilometers south of here. Also in the mountains, the southernmost ridges of the Kopet Dag."

Monique grabbed Olam's arm. "We have to stop this! We gotta get on the radio and call the fucking White House!"

Olam shook his head. "Even if we can manage to get a signal through all the jamming, how do we know that anyone will listen? If these True Believers have infiltrated the Pentagon, they're not going to let us communicate with the president."

"Well, what are we gonna do? Just wait here on this mountain until the universe crashes?"

"No. We're not going to wait." Olam folded his map and put it back in his pocket. "Five of my men can still fight, and we have seven Army Rangers. We also have two built-in machine guns on each of our helicopters. And we have enough fuel to fly to Ashkhaneh." Turning around, he marched to the helicopter's doorway and shouted at his men in Hebrew. Then he turned back to David and Monique. "Shomron will stay here and continue working on the radio tower. So you have a choice to make. Will you stay here or come with me?"

David heaved himself off the stretcher and rose to his feet. He felt a little rocky and his arms were bandaged and stiff, but he could still fire a pistol. He turned to Monique and she nodded—they were both going with Olam. But they would have to leave Michael behind.

David stepped toward the teenager, who was still tracing figures on the porthole window. "Michael?" he said. "Listen, you're going to stay here with one of the Israelis, okay? Monique and I are going away, but we'll come back as soon as we can. We'll leave you some food and water, and maybe Shomron can give you a puzzle to work on. All right, buddy? You think you can handle that?"

The boy grimaced but kept his eyes on the window. David noticed that he was drawing a picture of a fire, with dozens of squiggly flames rising from a large bowl.

"I promise I'll come back, Michael. You hear me? I promise." And David raised his right hand again, as if taking an oath.

40

THE PRESIDENT SAT ALONE IN HIS OFFICE ON THE E-4B, WHICH WAS FLYING
somewhere over the Midwest. It was midmorning in the United States
and early evening in Iran. The sun shone through the aircraft's windows,
casting shadows across the president's desk. His office here was small,
about the size of a walk-in closet. Most of the E-4B's middle deck was
occupied by the air-force communications specialists, who kept the plane
in touch with the rest of the military. The chairman of the Joint Chiefs
was also on the plane, along with the director of national intelligence
and the secretary of defense. But none of the White House staffers who
usually advised the president had come on board, and there were no
congressmen or reporters or political aides either. He was surrounded by
men in uniforms now.

His desk was covered with classified documents. Every ten minutes
or so, an air-force colonel knocked on his door and delivered another
report on the Camp Cobra explosion. The first search-and-rescue teams
had arrived at the site, garbed in Hazmat suits, and started looking for
survivors. So far, they hadn't found any. The State Department had contacted the Iranian government and demanded information on the two
aircraft that had flown across the border to the Ashkhaneh facility, but
the officials in Teheran denied any knowledge of the flights. The news
services were reporting an earthquake in southern Turkmenistan, and
the Pentagon had refrained from correcting them. At some point the
president would have to address the nation and reveal the awful dimensions of the tragedy. But not yet.

After a while he realized that the air-force colonel was wasting his
time. The president couldn't read the reports. He couldn't do anything

except think about the moment when the bomb exploded. He thought of the soldiers at Camp Cobra preparing for their mission—cleaning their rifles, loading their packs, maybe writing letters to their parents or wives or girlfriends. Then he pictured the explosion, the sudden flash of light, incinerating everything in the cavern. And then he saw the mountain falling, burying their ashes.

If the Iranians did it, they had to be punished. Nine hundred and sixty American soldiers were dead, and one of them was a lieutenant general. More important, it was a nuclear attack, the first ever against the United States. The country was obligated to retaliate in an overwhelming way, with its own nuclear weapons. Still, the president felt uneasy. Talking about deterrence was one thing, but actually dropping the bomb was another. It would change the world, and not for the better.

He heard another knock at his door. He said, "Come in," but this time it wasn't the air-force colonel. The director of national intelligence stood in the doorway.

"Sir, we've finished analyzing the debris from the Camp Cobra explosion," the DNI said. "The radioisotope signature is identical to the fallout from the Iranian nuclear test."

It felt like a kick to the stomach. Wincing, he stared at the reports on his desk. "Are you sure? Absolutely sure?"

"The percentages of U-235 and U-232 in the fallout are the same. We also found identical amounts of beryllium, a rare element that's used in the structure of uranium bombs."

The president said nothing. He knew what he had to do, yet he remained silent.

"This is solid proof, Mr. President," the DNI added. "The radioisotope signatures are as unique as fingerprints. We know that the uranium in the weapon that destroyed Camp Cobra came from the same stockpile that supplied the fuel for the Iranian nuke tested in the Kavir Desert. And the beryllium results indicate that the two bombs also had the same design and structure."

The president stared at the man for a few more seconds. Then he shook his head. He couldn't put it off any longer. It was time. "Tell everyone to gather in the conference room. We'll open the Football there."

41

SWEATING INSIDE THE WINDOWLESS TRAILER IN SHALHEVET, ARYEH GOLD-
berg continued to decipher encrypted messages using Olam ben Z'man's
quantum computer. He began analyzing the communications intercepted
by Israeli listening stations earlier in the year and found additional
evidence of Adam Cyrus Bennett's plot. Since January, Bennett had
exchanged dozens of messages with Lieutenant General Samuel McNair,
a U.S. Army Special Operations commander, and Nicodemus Aoun, a
Lebanese terrorist well known to the IDF. Aryeh didn't understand the
how and why of Bennett's plan yet, but he felt he had enough proof now
to persuade the IDF General Staff to take action. At 5 P.M. he was about
to call the Unit 8200 headquarters in Herzliya and ask to speak to the
unit's commander again. But General Yaron called him first.

"Aryeh? You need to come here at once. I assume you remember
where the division headquarters is?"

Aryeh was more surprised by Yaron's tone than by what he'd just
said. The normally emotionless general sounded worried. "What is it?
Why do you need me?"

"We've heard some very strange things. And we think they might be
related to the communications you deciphered."

"What things?"

Yaron paused, but only for a second. "There are news reports of an
earthquake in southern Turkmenistan. Not a very big earthquake. But
the epicenter is close to the radio tower that carried one of the messages
about Excalibur."

"What's strange about that? The area is tectonically active, yes?"

"The strange thing is that the IDF doesn't think it's an earthquake.

Our seismic monitors indicate that it was an underground nuclear explosion. When our intelligence division contacted the Americans to see if they came to the same conclusion, none of the Pentagon officials would talk about it. But they've gone to DEFCON 1, the highest level of alert."

Aryeh bit his lip. He remembered what Olam had said before he'd gone to Turkmenistan. Excalibur channeled the energy from nuclear explosions. And the more powerful the explosion, the more damage the X-ray laser could do. "You think the Iranians detonated another nuke? And now the Americans are going to retaliate?"

"Listen carefully, Aryeh. When the Iranian crisis started, Unit 8200 deployed several boats in the Arabian Sea to monitor radio communications in the region. About an hour ago one of our boats picked up an encrypted signal that was sent from an American Milstar satellite in a narrow spotlight beam. But there were no American ships within the beam's range, and our boat's radar didn't find any aircraft nearby."

"I'm sorry, I don't—"

"Half an hour later, another of our boats detected a second spotlight beam from the same satellite. This boat was five hundred kilometers north of the first one. So now our analysts had a track to follow, and they came to a reasonable conclusion. The Milstar satellite is communicating with an American B-2 bomber. You see, the plane has stealth technology, which explains why it didn't show up on our radar. And a B-2 squadron is based about two thousand kilometers south of our boats, on the island of Diego Garcia in the Indian Ocean."

Aryeh was familiar with stealth bombers, of course. He'd even seen one a few years ago at an air show in America, a sleek, black plane shaped like a bat's wing. "Those aircraft can carry nuclear weapons, yes?"

"Correct. And the track indicates that the B-2 is heading for Iran."

Aryeh shook his head. His neck was cold with sweat and his gut was cramping. He scooped up his papers, all the transcripts of the intercepted messages, and stuffed them into his shoulder bag. "I'm coming to Herzliya," he said. "I'll be there in half an hour."

42

MICHAEL WAS IN THE SHACK AT THE BASE OF THE RADIO TOWER, SITTING cross-legged on the wooden floor. David Swift had left him a bottle of water and a chocolate bar with a picture of a cow on the wrapper. It was an Israeli candy, David had told him, a gift from one of the soldiers dressed in black. David had said it would taste just like a Milky Way bar, but Michael was reluctant to try it.

Shomron, the Israeli radioman, sat on the floor, too, with his back against the opposite wall and his bandaged leg stretched out in front of him. There were also bandages on the soldier's face, covering everything except his mouth and one of his eyes. At first the bandages reminded Michael of Cyrus's head scarf, and he didn't like this memory. But after several minutes he grew more comfortable with Shomron. The fact that most of the soldier's face was covered was actually a relief. When Michael looked at the man he didn't have to follow all the intricate movements of the facial muscles and agonize over what they meant. The soldier's face was fixed in a single expression, so Michael never had to worry that he was missing something.

Shomron pointed at him. "Olam told me that you're a clever boy. Very good at mathematics and physics, he said. Is that true?"

Michael nodded. He was happy that Olam had complimented him. He liked the big bald soldier with the eye patch. "Yes, it's true. My great-great-grandfather was Albert Einstein."

"Really? Then I'm very fortunate to have you here. I might be able to use some of your skills right now." He shifted on the floor and pointed at a gray console in the corner of the shack. "Those are the controls for the radio tower. And I have to use those controls to solve a puzzle. Do you like to solve puzzles?"

Michael nodded again.

"Good," Shomron said. "This puzzle involves radio jamming. Do you know what that is?"

Michael scrolled through his memory of *The Concise Scientific Encyclopedia*. "Jamming is the intentional disruption of a radio signal. To stop someone from receiving the signal, a jamming device transmits noise on the same frequency."

"Yes, correct. That's what our enemies are doing to us right now. They have an EA-18 Growler aircraft that's transmitting large amounts of noise on the military frequencies. So even though we have this very nice radio tower, all our signals are being drowned out."

Michael thought about it for a moment. "Do you know where this aircraft is located?"

"Ah, very good! I can see you're already working on the puzzle. I'm going to explain something else to you now. It's called a countermeasure."

THE PAIR OF MI-8S DOVE ACROSS THE BORDER, FLYING JUST THIRTY FEET OFF the ground to avoid being spotted on the Iranian radar. David's stomach did somersaults as the helicopter pitched up and down. Gripping the edge of his seat in the cabin, he twisted around so he could look out one of the porthole windows. The MI-8s were following the contours of the Kopet Dag, hiding behind each ridge for as long as possible before popping over the crest and descending into the next valley. They cruised over cliffs and canyons and rock slides, all brilliantly lit by the setting sun. A herd of wild goats scattered below them as the helicopters hurtled south, but David saw no villages or roads or people. The landscape was arid and strangely empty, as if the apocalypse had already happened.

Monique sat to his right. She was inspecting the Desert Eagle semi-automatic that Olam had given her, hefting the pistol to feel its weight in her hand. She practiced loading the weapon, slamming the magazine into the gun's handle and popping it out, doing it over and over until it was second nature, and as David watched her he thought of Lucille. He quickly shook his head to dispel the memory—he couldn't bear to think of Lucille now—but the feeling stayed with him, an odd disorientation. The two women were different in so many ways, but both of them knew how to handle a gun.

Olam was piloting their MI-8 but the rest of the Israelis were in the helicopter flown by Lieutenant Halutz. David and Monique shared their cabin with the seven Rangers, the survivors of Camp Cobra. Six of them sat on the opposite side of the cabin, the four snipers who'd been posted outside the cave and the two soldiers who'd come out the backdoor tunnel with Sergeant Morrison. Morrison himself sat a couple of feet to David's left. Because the sergeant had come out of Camp Cobra without a weapon, Olam had given him one of the AK-47s he'd acquired from the Turkmen helicopter crew.

At first Morrison studiously avoided eye contact with David. But about twenty minutes into the flight, while Olam was putting the MI-8 through a particularly violent series of maneuvers, the back of David's head banged against the cabin wall and Morrison turned to him. "Are you all right, sir?" he shouted above the rotor noise.

David rubbed his scalp. It was a little strange to hear that "sir." This was the same guy who'd kicked him in the ribs and helped General McNair drag him to the Sour Tub. But that was before Little Boy exploded. "I'm fine," he replied. "Thanks."

Morrison kept staring at him. The sergeant clearly wanted to say something else, but he couldn't bring himself to do it. After a while David got tired of waiting, so he held out his right hand. "You don't have to call me 'sir.' My name's David."

He grabbed David's hand and squeezed it tightly. His eyes were bloodshot and full of remorse. "I'm so fucking sorry, man. I wish I'd listened to you. I wish to Christ I'd listened."

Morrison seemed absolutely sincere. He held on to David's hand as if it were a lifeline, refusing to let go. But David wasn't ready to forgive him yet. "Yeah, I wish you'd listened, too."

The sergeant shook his head. "I still can't believe it. How the hell could McNair do it? It's fucking unbelievable."

"He thought he was carrying out God's plan. But his instructions were coming from Cyrus, not God."

"And that guy works in the Pentagon, too, right? Another fucking monster."

"No, he's not a monster." David remembered Cyrus's face, so ordinary and calm. "He's just deluded. He thinks he's doing us all a favor."

Morrison tightened his grip. He was hurting David again, but not intentionally this time. "Whatever he is, he's gonna die. I can promise you that." He let go of David's hand and pointed at the bandages on his forearms. "How are the burns? Did that Israeli medic give you anything for the pain?"

David nodded. "Yeah, they dosed me up."

Then Morrison pointed at the Desert Eagle in David's hand. "And what about that? You think you can handle it?"

He nodded again. "I've had some practice with the Glock. This gun's heavier, but I think I'll be all right."

"I tried the Eagle once. It's a hell of a good piece." He leaned a bit closer and patted the barrel of his AK-47. "And I'm gonna stay right with you, okay? Me and my buddies are gonna watch your back. I can't change what I did before, all the shit that went down in the cave. But I can help you now."

David nodded a third time. He still wasn't ready to forgive Morrison, but he'd rather fight alongside the sergeant than against him.

Then he felt a tap on his right shoulder and turned back to Monique, who was gazing out the porthole window. She pointed at another ridge, about two miles farther south. Nestled within the folds of the mountainside was a concrete pillbox, barely visible in the twilight. That was the entrance to the Iranian bunker. The mountain curved inward to the right of the structure, and in the semicircle of flat ground at the foot of the slope were banks of fresh earth, newly dug fortifications.

"One minute to landing!" Olam's voice boomed from the cockpit. "Prepare to move out!"

THE *SPIRIT OF AMERICA*, A B-2 STEALTH BOMBER STATIONED AT DIEGO GARCIA, was already flying over southeastern Iran when it received the Emergency Action Message from the Milstar satellite. The message had been coded by the air force's Global Strike Command, which changed its encryption keys every hour. The keys themselves had been transmitted to the B-2 in another encrypted message sent previously, when the bomber was still cruising over the Arabian Sea. Over the bomber's radio came the tense voice of an air-force communications specialist, repeating the message's six-character preamble three times.

"Lima Three Foxtrot Hotel Seven Romeo."

"Lima Three Foxtrot Hotel Seven Romeo."

"Lima Three Foxtrot Hotel Seven Romeo."

Colonel George Ashley, the mission commander, turned around in his seat and unlocked the safe in the bomber's two-man cockpit. He pulled out the June 13 codebook and turned to the EAM authentication tables. The first two characters of the preamble specified which table Ashley should use, and the next four characters were the authentication code. Colonel Ashley consulted the Lima Three table and looked up the proper code for the current hour. It was Foxtrot Hotel Seven Romeo.

"The Emergency Action Message is authenticated," the colonel said, reciting the words he'd memorized long ago and hoped never to utter. "This message is a valid nuclear-control order."

He passed the codebook to Major Wilcox, the bomber's pilot. Wilcox looked at the page and nodded. "I concur."

Colonel Ashley then turned to the screen on his cockpit display, which showed the rest of the message that followed the authentication code. The order directed them to proceed to the preplanned target and deliver the B83 earth-penetrating warhead. It also contained the permissive action links that would unlock the warhead's detonator.

The colonel swallowed hard. "How long till we reach Ashkhaneh, Major?"

"About thirty-five minutes, sir."

43

BROTHER CYRUS SPOTTED THE PAIR OF HELICOPTERS THROUGH HIS BINOCU-lars while they were still several miles away. At first he felt a stab of despair. It was the first wave of an American assault group, he thought. Somehow his plans had been discovered and the president had ordered an airborne attack against him. After half a minute, though, Cyrus got a better look at the helicopters and realized they weren't American. They were Russian-made MI-8s, old-fashioned transport helicopters that were designed more than forty years ago. What's more, there seemed to be only two of them—no other aircraft or vehicles were approaching the Ashkhaneh facility. Best of all, Cyrus saw no rockets or missiles hanging from the helicopters' weapons racks. The markings on the craft identified them as belonging to the Turkmen Army's aviation division, the unit that had been dispatched to hunt down Olam ben Z'man and his remaining commandos. Olam had obviously taken control of the MI-8s and decided to challenge Cyrus again.

Cyrus smiled, ecstatic with relief. Olam and his helicopters didn't worry him. The Israeli's armaments were laughably feeble: a couple of medium-caliber machine guns mounted on each MI-8 and, at most, an assortment of small arms carried by his commandos. Cyrus's men, in contrast, had the most advanced machine gun in the U.S. Army's arsenal, the XM-806. Four of these guns were positioned in foxholes around the entrance to the tunnel, ready to shred any aircraft or vehicle that came near. In addition, the True Believers carried Stinger surface-to-air missiles and rocket-propelled grenade launchers. The helicopters were fly-ing too low to be hit by the Stingers, but they would make perfect targets for the RPGs, which were loaded with a new type of explosive called the thermobaric grenade. This projectile was designed to blow up concrete buildings, so it could certainly demolish an MI-8.

Cyrus whispered a prayer to the Almighty, apologizing for his momentary lapse of faith. As he finished, the radio hanging from his belt let out a squawk. He reached for the thing and saw that the transmission was from the Revolutionary Guards inside the caverns of the Ashkhaneh facility. One of General Jannati's lieutenants was yelling in broken English.

"Attention . . . Mr. Black . . . observing two helicopters . . . from north approaching . . . must speaking with . . . Commander Jannati . . . further orders . . . requiring."

Cyrus pressed the talk button on the radio. "General Jannati is well aware of the situation. Those helicopters are piloted by Israeli commandos, and we intend to destroy them as soon as they come within range. Your commander is helping us coordinate the operation."

The word "Israeli" caused great consternation on the other end of the line. Cyrus could hear terrified shouts in Farsi. *"Khoda! Khoda! Chi kar konim?"*

"Please stay calm," Cyrus said. "General Jannati wants you to remain in your bunker. We have enough antiaircraft weapons to handle the threat. Repeat, remain in your bunker."

"Yes . . . yes, acknowledging."

Cyrus smiled again as the radio went silent. The last hour of the corrupted universe had indeed turned joyful, just as he'd hoped. He checked one more time with Nicodemus to make sure that his soldiers were properly dug in. He couldn't see the MI-8s now—the helicopters had ducked behind one of the spurs along the ridge—but very soon Olam would launch his attack, and the True Believers would be ready to destroy him.

After taking one last look at the darkening sky, Cyrus entered the tunnel that led to the impact chamber. He'd decided to stand in front of the chamber's viewing window during the final minutes, staring at the wondrous laser that would open the gates to God's kingdom. He knew he wouldn't be able to see the warhead entering the chamber, or the laser beams generated by the blast of radiation—his sinful body would be vaporized before that information could enter his brain. Nevertheless, he wanted to stand as close as possible to the Omega Point, where

Time would end and the Redemption would begin. Perhaps it was self-ish of him, but he wanted to be the first person to enter the Kingdom of Heaven.

THE MI-8 TOUCHED DOWN NEAR THE BASE OF THE MOUNTAIN AND DAVID jumped out of the helicopter. He followed the lead of the six Rangers in front of him, running away from the flat, sandy ground of the landing zone and heading for the shelter of the mountainside. Monique was right behind him and Sergeant Morrison brought up the rear. The helicopter took off as soon as they'd exited, but the sand still whirled around them. The soldiers became dark blurs in the purple light of dusk, all running toward a great black wall that blocked half the sky.

Once they reached the slope, they regrouped under a granite over-hang. David leaned against the rock wall, his heart hammering. Monique panted beside him, leaning forward slightly as she caught her breath. It reminded David of the times when they went jogging together, except now they wore black fatigues instead of tracksuits and carried four-pound Desert Eagles in their hands. In the distance David could hear the thumping rotors of the MI-8s. Olam's helicopter was somewhere above them, flying close to the mountain and reconnoitering the area. Lieuten-ant Halutz's MI-8 had gone farther west to drop off the Israeli comman-dos on the other side of Cyrus's position.

The Rangers headed in that direction, jogging single file and staying close to the mountainside. A few hundred yards ahead was a rocky spur that jutted north from the ridge. David remembered seeing it from the air—the spur marked the eastern edge of the semicircle where Cyrus's men were dug in. The Rangers crept forward to take a peek around the rock pile at the end of the spur. Then the ground erupted under their feet.

The boom echoed against the mountain. One of the Rangers flew upward in a fountain of sand.

David froze. It's a mine, he thought. We're walking through a mine-field.

The soldier's body landed a few feet away. He was clearly dead. Both his legs and the bottom part of his torso were missing. In shock, David stared at the dark puddle that covered the soldier's last footprints. But the other Rangers remained calm and carefully moved backward, retracing their steps. Their faces were grim, but they didn't stop for a moment. Instead, they turned away from the minefield and began scaling the steep eastern wall of the spur.

David followed them, eager to get away from the flat ground now. He clambered to a narrow ledge, then reached for Monique's hand and pulled her up. Groping for handholds, they scrambled up the slope, kicking stones down the mountain with every step. They kept climbing until they reached a rock shelf at the top of the spur. The Rangers were already lined up along the shelf, kneeling behind a natural parapet of granite slabs. David joined them and peered over the edge.

Although the last remnants of daylight were fading from the sky, he could see the earthen fortifications, which were about sixty feet below them and a hundred yards to the west. Cyrus's men had dug four foxholes and placed a big machine gun in each one. Narrow trenches ran between the foxholes, forming a rough square. At the center of the square was a wider trench leading to a tunnel entrance that was partially blocked by sandbags. That's where the X-ray laser is, David guessed. He remembered what Cyrus had told him at Camp Cobra, about the bunker-busting warhead that would burrow into the ground before exploding. So the laser would have to be positioned underground, at the end of that tunnel.

He turned to Sergeant Morrison and pointed at the tunnel entrance. "Over there," he whispered. "That's the target. We have to get inside that tunnel and destroy the laser."

Morrison shook his head. "Shit, you gotta be kidding. They got at least forty men in those trenches. And you'd need a fucking tank to get past those machine guns."

"Then radio the helicopters. Tell them to concentrate their fire on the tunnel entrance."

"Look, you're not getting it. The guns in those foxholes shoot fifty-caliber armor-piercing rounds. They can take out a helicopter at two thousand yards. That's way past the range of the fucking peashooters in the MI-8s."

"No, *you're* not getting it!" David pointed at the sky, which was filling with stars as it darkened. "Any minute now a B-2 bomber is gonna drop a warhead on that laser. And when that happens, it's gonna kill *everyone*. It's good-bye to the whole fucking universe!"

"Keep your voice down!" Morrison reached for the radio on his belt. "We're gonna coordinate an attack with the choppers. Just stay low, all right? And hold your fire until I give the order."

Clutching his radio, Morrison moved toward the other Rangers. Meanwhile, David scuttled over to Monique, who lay on her stomach about twenty feet away, pointing her Desert Eagle through a gap in the granite slabs. She glanced at him, keeping one eye on her gun sights. "Jesus. This doesn't look good."

"Don't worry, we can do it."

"There's only eight of us. And four Israelis somewhere on the other side. It's not enough."

"We have the helicopters, too. They're moving into position now."

Monique didn't respond. She didn't believe him, he thought. She'd analyzed their situation and calculated the odds and concluded that they didn't have a prayer. It was a logical conclusion, a solid scientific prediction backed up by all the facts. But David refused to think that way now. He thought of Michael and Jonah and Baby Lisa, his three perfect children, sitting on opposite sides of the globe. He wasn't going to let them die. He didn't know how, but he was going to save them.

After about a minute, the beating of the rotors grew louder. The MI-8s had turned off their running lights and now they thudded in the darkness. David lay on the rock shelf not far from Monique and held his gun with both hands, pointing it at the trenches and foxholes. Off to his right, he heard the Rangers chamber their rounds into their rifles. Then Sergeant Morrison shouted, "Fire!" and David started shooting.

The barrage was deafening. The Desert Eagle kicked in his hands and the rock shelf rumbled underneath him. The Rangers strafed the foxholes and trenches, and the helicopters dove toward the fortifications, their machine guns chugging. But an instant later, David heard an even louder noise, an impossibly fast sequence of booms, like never-ending thunder. The machine guns in the foxholes opened up on the MI-8s, and David saw the tracer rounds lance across the sky. He glimpsed the outlines of the helicopters, banking wildly to get out of the line of fire. Then he looked down at the foxholes again and saw one of the machine guns turn toward their position on the spur.

"GET DOWN!" Morrison yelled. "GET—"

The armor-piercing rounds smashed into the mountain. Rock chips sprayed from the granite slabs and rained down on the slopes. David and Monique rolled to the left, tumbling behind a large boulder. But the Rangers kept shooting. The whole mountainside was exploding around them but they stayed in their positions and returned fire.

David and Monique moved farther to the left, scrabbling up the slope. They found another boulder to hide behind and David peeked around its edge. In one of the trenches, Cyrus's men had turned on a searchlight and trained it on the spur. Another searchlight was aimed at the Israeli commandos who were shooting at the fortifications from the other side. And in the center of the camp, near the entrance to the tunnel, David saw a man kneeling on the ground, with a long tube resting on his shoulder. He couldn't see the man's face—he was too far away—but he noticed the checkered keffiyeh draped over the man's shoulders.

Just as David recognized him, a rocket shot out of the tube on the man's shoulder. Trailing a long tail of fire, it flew straight toward one of the MI-8s, which was just pulling up from its dive. The rocket hit the helicopter's nose and there was a tremendous explosion. Then David saw nothing but the fireball.

NICODEMUS SHOUTED "HALLELUJAH!" AS THE THERMOBARIC GRENADE exploded. The blast roared against the mountainside and illuminated the sandy ground below, bathing all the True Believers in its holy light. This is the face of God, Nico exulted, the dazzling countenance of the Almighty! He's gazing down on us now as the gates of heaven start to open. And He's telling His loyal servants that He is well pleased.

The wreckage of the helicopter dropped like a stone, crashing to the ground about a hundred meters away. Nico threw the empty launcher aside and picked up a loaded one. There was one more MI-8, one more satanic insect to be swatted. Then the path to the Redemption would be clear. He rested the launch tube on his shoulder and pointed it at the sky.

•   •   •

JUST BEFORE ARYEH ARRIVED AT THE UNIT 8200 HEADQUARTERS, THE DIVI-
sion received a radio transmission from Turkmenistan. The signal was
picked up by one of the IDF's antennas on Mount Avital in the Golan
Heights, and the source was identified as a ship on the Caspian Sea, an
old fishing trawler that the Israeli intelligence agencies sometimes used
to surreptitiously intercept Iranian communications. Because the boat's
captain reported directly to General Yaron, the transmission was routed
to the general's office. But the captain said he was simply relaying a signal
that had originated from a radio tower in the Kopet Dag, a signal sent by
someone named Mordecai Shomron.

By the time Aryeh rushed into Yaron's office, the general was deep
in conversation with Shomron, who turned out to be a *Sayeret Matkal*
veteran and a comrade of Olam ben Z'man. Yaron—who'd gained some
weight and lost some hair since the last time Aryeh had seen him—sat
behind a desk crowded with communications equipment, including a
console with a pair of speakers and a gooseneck microphone. Shomron's
voice streamed out of the speakers in a mad rush.

"Do you understand now, General?" the voice said. "This is a threat
to the existence of the State of Israel. It's a threat to the existence of the
whole world, actually, but you can stress the danger to Israel if you think
that's the best way to get the attention of the General Staff."

Yaron pressed a switch and leaned toward the microphone. His
console was apparently connected to the antennas on Mount Avital.
"Unfortunately, there's nothing the IDF can do," he said. "The Pentagon has broken off communications with us. And even if the lines were
open, I doubt we could convince them to halt a nuclear strike against
the Iranians."

"Is there some way to contact the White House directly? Although
the people who organized this plot have collaborators in the American
government, we don't believe the president is involved."

Aryeh's gut cramped again. He thought of the B-2 bomber getting signals from the Milstar satellites as it cruised toward Iran. And he
thought of all the crazy things Olam ben Z'man had said—about warheads and X-ray lasers and memory overloads and universal programs—
and began to wonder if they just might be true.

He approached General Yaron's desk and pointed at the console. "May I respond, sir?"

The general said, "Go ahead," and pressed the switch for him.

Aryeh spoke into the microphone. "This is Agent Goldberg of Shin Bet. I've been deciphering the communications between Adam Cyrus Bennett and his collaborators. Bennett has infiltrated the Pentagon so thoroughly that I believe it would be difficult to warn the president through the usual military channels."

The radio was silent for several seconds. "Well, what do you suggest we do?"

Aryeh rubbed the stubble on his chin. For a telecommunications expert, this was an interesting problem. What would be the best way to send a message directly to the president? "What kind of station are you transmitting from?" he asked Shomron.

"It's a radio tower normally used by the Turkmen Army, I believe. The equipment is old but functional. We were able to circumvent the U.S. Air Force's jamming devices by generating a spotlight radio beam that focused the signal on the Israeli ship to the west of us."

Aryeh smiled. "That's good. I want you to prepare to send another spotlight beam. This one pointing south." Then he turned to Yaron. "General, could I have access to the satellite communications that your boats in the Arabian Sea intercepted? The signals sent to the B-2 bombers, I mean. I want to try to decipher them."

Yaron looked at him gravely. Under ordinary circumstances he would've categorically denied the request. Aryeh was asking him to divulge the most sensitive communications of Israel's closest ally, the signals from Global Strike Command that carried nuclear-control orders to America's bombers. But after a couple of seconds Yaron nodded. Shomron had obviously done a good job of opening the general's eyes. "We intercepted another Milstar signal sent to the B-2 twenty minutes ago, while it was over southeastern Iran," Yaron said. "We have a few clandestine antennas inside the country, you see."

"Yes, I'll need that, too," Aryeh said. "Please transmit all the intercepted communications to Olam's headquarters in Shalhevet. I'll tell the *kippot srugot* to fire up the computer."

• • •

OLAM BEN Z'MAN SAW THE FIREBALL AND SAID A PRAYER FOR LIEUTENANT
Halutz. He recited the Kaddish, the mourner's prayer, while struggling to
evade the machine-gun fire, yanking the MI-8's control stick to pull the
helicopter skyward. As the .50-caliber rounds slammed into the fuselage
and shattered the porthole windows, he muttered the Hebrew words
under his breath: *Yit'gadal v'yit'kadash sh'mei raba . . .*

By the time he finished the prayer, he was out of the line of fire,
soaring through the darkness that surrounded the mountain. But the
machine-gun rounds must've hit the MI-8's fuel tanks, because the
gauges showed they were nearly empty. Olam shook his head. This helicopter was a piece of junk anyway, he thought. And now there was only
one thing left to do with it.

With the remaining fuel he throttled up the engines, climbing in a
wide arc until he was four hundred meters above the ground. Then he
tilted the nose downward and started his dive.

JUST SECONDS AFTER HALUTZ'S MI-8 EXPLODED, A GRENADE HIT THE RANG-
ers. David and Monique were more than a hundred feet away, crouched
behind a boulder farther up the mountainside, but the shock wave from
the blast nearly knocked them over. The searchlight beams illuminated
a cloud of dust above the granite slabs that the Rangers had been hiding behind. Below the cloud, half a dozen bodies lay motionless on the
rock shelf. Sergeant Morrison's corpse sprawled on top of two others. It
looked like he'd tried to shield them at the last moment.

David leaned his forehead against the rough face of the boulder.
They were done, he thought. They were finished. All the fighting and
struggling had been for nothing. And soon the whole world would turn
to nothing, devoured by a great expanding hole of nothingness. David
tried to picture it, the overload that would freeze the universal computer, halting the trillions of calculations taking place every nanosecond
in every minuscule volume of space. Then the long silence would begin.
Cyrus had called it the Kingdom of Heaven, and maybe he was right.
The new universe would be without time or change, an eternal resting
place. A place of peace, certainly. But only because nothing could ever
happen.

Then David heard a furious whine of protest. It was the rotor noise from the surviving MI-8, but louder and higher-pitched than before, wailing from above. He peered around the edge of the boulder and looked up, trying to spot the helicopter. Cyrus's men did the same thing, aiming their searchlights at the noise. The converging beams found the MI-8, which was still hundreds of yards away but coming in fast. All the machines guns in the foxholes quickly turned in that direction and fired at the helicopter, shooting streams of tracer rounds into its bulky fuselage. And then David saw Nicodemus again, kneeling in front of the tunnel entrance with another grenade launcher on his shoulder, its tube pointed at the helicopter's nose.

David stepped away from the boulder, moving into the open. There was nothing inside him now but pure unholy rage. Before the world ended, he wanted to kill this man. He *needed* to kill this man. He held the Desert Eagle in front of him and it shook in his hands.

And then he heard Lucille's voice. He heard it in his mind and heart and stomach. He felt one of her hands on the small of his back and the other on his chest, just below his collarbone. She stood right behind him, bringing her lips close to his ear.

Keep your right arm straight, she said. *Wrap your left hand around your right, with the thumbs crossed. Line up the front sight inside the rear sight and the target just above. Then squeeze the trigger nice and slow.*

OLAM AIMED FOR THE TUNNEL. THE ROUNDS FROM THE MACHINE GUNS TORE dozens of holes in his MI-8, but they couldn't stop the helicopter's descent. When he was a hundred and fifty meters away he saw a man in a checkered keffiyeh in front of the tunnel entrance, holding a grenade launcher on his shoulder. Olam's heart clenched—this was the one thing that could stop him. But then the man shuddered and dropped the launch tube. He fell sideways and lay on the sand. A dark red splotch spread across his keffiyeh.

Ah, Olam thought, this is the instrument of *Keter*! The Crown of the Universe has guided David's hand!

Laughing now, Olam rolled the MI-8 counterclockwise, turning the helicopter on its side so it would fit through the tunnel. He hit the entrance at more than three hundred kilometers per hour, and the rotor sheared cleanly off the fuselage. The helicopter plowed right through the sandbags and careened down the steeply sloping tunnel, hardly slowing at all as it slid toward the bottom. Olam had time to offer just one more prayer, a hymn of praise to the *Sephirot* that had created the universe.

Keter. Chokhmah. Binah. Chesed. Gevurah. Tiferet. Netzach. Hod. Yesod. Malkuth.

The last thing Olam saw was Adam Cyrus Bennett, standing with his back against a large viewing window. The plump leader of the *Qliphoth* held out his arms, as if he thought he could stop the ten-ton fuselage from smashing into his X-ray laser. But no one can change the laws of physics. The helicopter rammed into the glass and exploded, and as Olam died he saw the husks of the *Qliphoth* split open to let the light of God shine through.

ARYEH CHECKED HIS WATCH FOR THE FORTIETH TIME. BASED ON THE FLIGHT path and speed of the B-2 bomber, General Yaron had estimated that it would arrive at Ashkhaneh at approximately 9 P.M. local time. It was now 7:25 in Israel, which meant that it was 8:55 in Iran. But while Aryeh paced across Yaron's office, the general sat calmly behind his desk and studied a printout of the message they'd just received from Shalhevet.

Ehud ben Ezra, the young zealot in charge of running Olam's quantum computer, had inputted the data from the intercepted Milstar communications and sent the results of the calculations back to Yaron. The general grinned as he stared at the printout. He'd become so intrigued by the computer's capabilities that it seemed as if he'd forgotten all about the stealth bomber. "Fascinating," he muttered. "This machine changes everything. They'll have to rewrite all the cryptography textbooks."

Aryeh clenched his hands. "General, how much longer—"

"This is the private key!" Yaron showed him the printout, which was covered with hundreds of digits. "Thanks to that crazy man Loebner, no public-key encryption system is safe anymore. My specialists are using this key right now to decode all the Emergency Action Messages that Global Strike Command sent to the B-2. And EAMs are considered to be the most secure communications in the world!"

"Yes, but how much longer will it take?"

"Soon, soon. There are several steps, you see. This private key will unlock the first message sent to the bomber, the one the air force used to distribute the other keys. Then we have to use one of *those* keys to decipher the Emergency Action Message that our antennas inside Iran picked up. And then we have to code a new EAM using all the same keys so that it looks like it came from the proper authorities at Global Strike Command. It has to have exactly the same TRANSEC and COMSEC encryption and—"

One of the general's aides burst into the office. "Sir, we have it! We're ready to transmit!"

Aryeh rushed to Yaron's desk. He hit the switch on the radio console and leaned over the microphone. "Shomron? This is Goldberg. We have the message we want you to relay. As soon as you receive it, transmit the signal in a spotlight beam, pointed directly south. It's time for your tower to start broadcasting."

CROUCHED ON THE MOUNTAINSIDE, DAVID SAW OLAM'S HELICOPTER PLUNGE into the tunnel. Then he saw the flames and smoke burst out of the tunnel's mouth. A moment later the tunnel collapsed, snuffing the fire. The sand poured into the underground space, and soon there was a shallow crater above the spot where the X-ray laser had been. Even if David hadn't seen the helicopter's tail number, he could've guessed that it was Olam, and not Lieutenant Halutz, who'd piloted the MI-8 that dove into the tunnel. You had to be a little crazy to think of a stunt like that. David's eyes stung as he imagined the man's last moments. He'd saved the world, but it was a poorer place without him.

Cyrus's soldiers stopped firing their machine guns. About half of them ran over to the collapsed tunnel and stared blankly at the ground. Some fell to their knees, screaming. Others tried digging holes in the sand with their bare hands. But they quickly gave up.

And then, one by one, they started running away. Throwing down their packs and weapons, they leaped over the trenches and charged into the darkness. They went in random directions, some north, some east, some west. They didn't have a particular destination, David realized. They were simply running away from the target where the war-head was going to explode. With their leader dead and the X-ray laser destroyed, they knew that the Kingdom of Heaven—or at least the version Cyrus had promised them—wouldn't be opening for them any time soon. What they faced now was plain old death, ordinary oblivion. And this prospect scared the shit out of them, as it does to most people, so they reverted to their baser instincts and tried to get the hell out of there.

But David didn't join them. He knew that you couldn't outrun a megaton blast. It was going to scorch the area for ten miles around and spread radioactive fallout even farther. Exhausted, he stumbled over to Monique, who was perched on the stony slope a few feet away, watching the last of Cyrus's soldiers abandon their foxholes. She was a physicist, so she knew the futility of running even better than David did. With a tired groan, he sat down next to her.

"Is this spot taken?" he asked.

She leaned against him, resting her head on his shoulder. He put his arm around her waist.

"You know what's funny?" she said. "It's a lovely night."

It was true. He looked up at the sky and saw a glorious swath of stars shining over the Kopet Dag. He hadn't seen such a beautiful sight in years. It was so easy to forget how wondrous the world is, he thought.

He squeezed the soft flesh just above Monique's hip. He loved that part of her. "I feel bad about breaking my promise to Michael. I promised we'd come back for him."

"It's all right, David. He'll be all right."

"And Jonah. And Lisa. Jesus, this is going to be hard on them. I don't know how they'll—"

"Shhh." She stretched her hand toward him and put her index and middle fingers over his lips. "Let's not talk about that."

Before she could move her hand away, he clasped her wrist. Then he kissed her fingers, the underside of each knuckle. "I love you, Monique. I just wish we could've spent more time together."

She moved her face closer to his. "We're together now."

• • •

TWO MINUTES BEFORE THE *SPIRIT OF AMERICA* ARRIVED AT THE TARGET COOR-dinates, another voice came over the bomber's radio. This voice, Colonel Ashley thought, wasn't as tense as the one that had delivered the last Emergency Action Message. It was an older man's voice, with a trace of an accent.

"Lima Three Foxtrot Hotel Seven Romeo."

"Lima Three Foxtrot Hotel Seven Romeo."

"Lima Three Foxtrot Hotel Seven Romeo."

Ashley checked his watch. The authentication code was still valid. Nevertheless, he went through the motions of unlocking the safe and opening the codebook and checking the authentication tables again. The procedures had to be followed.

"The Emergency Action Message is authenticated," he said. "This message is a valid nuclear-control order."

He passed the codebook to the pilot. Major Wilcox looked jumpy as hell. "I concur, I concur. What's the message?"

The colonel smiled as he read the first words on the cockpit display. "Mission aborted," he said. "Return to base."

"WOOOO-HOOOO!" Wilcox yelled. "Hell yeah!"

"Wait, there's more. They want us to disable the detonator on the warhead. And then transmit a confirmation that we've disabled it. To make sure that the nuke can't be deployed."

Wilcox shook his head. "Someone must've seriously fucked up."

"We have to send the confirmation via satellite to the E-4B Night-watch plane. And there's an attached message here for the president. His eyes only."

"You know what this means, don't you? They're going straight to the top to get around the Defense Department brass. Someone at the Penta-gon fucked up big-time. And now Global Strike Command is blowing the whistle on them."

"Look, we don't know—"

"Well, how else would you explain it? We were two minutes away from deploying a nuke, for Christ's sake! I think that qualifies as a serious fuckup."

Colonel Ashley agreed. But he didn't like to encourage speculation. "Let's just follow our orders, Major."

"Yes, sir!" Wilcox banked the B-2, putting the bomber into a wide right turn.

The colonel reached for the armaments panel and punched in the code for disabling the detonator. Then he took a moment to look through the cockpit window at the darkened landscape below, the mountains they came so close to bombing. Thank God, he whispered. Thank God.

EPILOGUE

SIX U.S. ARMY RANGERS WEARING WHITE GLOVES AND TAN BERETS CARRIED a flag-draped coffin down the cargo ramp of the C-17 transport plane. Marching in slow, measured steps, they crossed the tarmac of Dover Air Force Base, the sprawling airfield in Delaware that was the receiving point for the bodies of American troops killed overseas.

David watched the solemn ritual from thirty feet away, standing at the end of a long line of officials from the Defense Department and the FBI. It was a hot, humid afternoon in late July, the temperature near ninety degrees. The stolid faces of the Rangers glistened with sweat as they carried the coffin toward a panel truck parked near the C-17. They halted at the truck's rear door, which was open, and remained motionless for several seconds. As if on cue, all the officials on the tarmac raised their arms in a slow salute, and the soldiers slid the coffin into the truck. Then the carry team did a crisp about-face and returned to the C-17's cargo hold. There were seven more bodies in the plane.

David raised his right hand to his heart. Monique, who stood beside him, did the same. They'd driven down from New York City that morning, invited to the ceremony by the FBI director, who stood at the other end of the line of officials. Aryeh Goldberg was there, too, having flown in from Israel especially for the ceremony. It was a bittersweet reunion. The airfield was silent as the soldiers unloaded the plane, slowly carrying the coffins to the panel truck.

David glanced at Monique to see how she was doing. She gave him a quick, reassuring nod. For the past five weeks they'd done nothing but try to recover. Luckily, neither of them had any summer classes to teach or major research projects to pursue. They could spend all their time with their children and each other. *Every hour on this earth is a gift,*

David thought. But the odd thing about the gift of life is that you can't truly appreciate it until you come close to dying.

After the battle outside the Ashkhaneh facility, he and Monique had sat under the stars for half an hour, calmly waiting for the stealth bomber to deliver its warhead. As the minutes passed, though, it became clear that the bomber had been diverted and they weren't going to be incinerated after all. So they regrouped with the Israeli commandos—three of them had survived the Ashkhaneh battle—and made radio contact with General Yaron of the Israeli signals-intelligence corps. Yaron ordered them to hike several miles south to a remote highway where they could rendezvous with one of his Iranian spies. Over the next forty-eight hours Yaron's spy managed to smuggle them from the Kopet Dag to the Alborz Mountains, then across the border to Azerbaijan, and finally to Israel. Meanwhile, Michael and Shomron were picked up by the American search-and-rescue team that had been dispatched to southern Turkmenistan. Thanks to Aryeh's message to the president, relayed via the stealth bomber, the White House had shelved its plans for attacking Iran and begun dismantling Adam Cyrus Bennett's secret network.

By the time David and Monique got back to the United States, the newspapers were filled with stories about the nuclear catastrophe at Camp Cobra. The FBI had already rounded up the remaining True Believers, although some of them, including General Estey of Special Operations Command, committed suicide before they could be arrested. Then the president gave a prime-time speech explaining how a top Defense Department official had betrayed the nation. He revealed that Bennett had led a group of fanatics who'd collaborated with Iran's Revolutionary Guard, using funds from the Pentagon's classified budget to collect enriched uranium and build nuclear devices. But he didn't mention Excalibur. He said Bennett had destroyed Camp Cobra to instigate a nuclear war between America and Iran, but he didn't say anything about X-ray lasers or the universal program or the threat of a quantum crash. The White House had decided not to reveal this vulnerability in the grand design of Creation. If it were well known, another madman might try to exploit it.

For the same reason, the president didn't reveal the involvement of David, Monique, or Michael. He gave the full credit for stopping Brother

Cyrus to the Israeli and American soldiers who'd fought the True Believers at Ashkhaneh. Seven of the coffins in the C-17 contained the bodies of the Rangers who'd died in that firefight. The Pentagon had retrieved their remains after several weeks of diplomatic wrangling, and now the secretary of defense and the chairman of the Joint Chiefs of Staff were at Dover Air Force Base to honor their homecoming. They stood at the midpoint of the line of officials, holding their right arms in stiff salutes until the soldiers in tan berets unloaded the next-to-last coffin from the transport plane. Then another carry team headed for the C-17, a non-military team this time, consisting of four men and two women wearing identical gray suits. A minute later they came down the cargo ramp with the last coffin, which held the body of Special Agent Lucille Parker.

The FBI director stepped forward. So did David, Monique, and Aryeh. They advanced across the tarmac, heading for a shiny black hearse parked next to the panel truck. The carry team of FBI agents also headed for the hearse, marching slowly. David's throat tightened as he stared at the flag-draped coffin. It was no different from the other coffins that had been taken out of the C-17, but he couldn't bear to look at it. He turned away and looked at the FBI director, who'd lowered his head and closed his eyes. His lips moved, but he spoke so softly David couldn't make out what he was saying. Maybe it was a prayer, he thought. Or an apology. David closed his own eyes and remembered seeing Lucille on the deck of the fishing trawler, pointing her Glock at one of the oil derricks in the Caspian Sea. She'd been happy that morning. David wanted to remember her that way.

He opened his eyes just as the six FBI agents slid the coffin into the hearse. Once they closed the vehicle's rear door, the FBI director shook hands with the carry team, muttering a quiet thank you to each agent. Then David heard the sound of more cars approaching. He turned around and saw three black limousines drive across the airport's apron and stop near the line of Pentagon officials. More men in dark suits emerged from the cars and briskly reconnoitered the area, positioning themselves around the limousines. They were Secret Service agents, David realized. After another few seconds the agents opened the back door of the middle car, and the president of the United States stepped onto the tarmac.

The officials saluted him, of course. The president saluted back, but he didn't stop to chat with the secretary of defense or any of his deputies. Instead, he walked straight toward the hearse. David had never seen the president in person before, and he was a bit surprised by the man's appearance—he looked older and sadder than David had expected. There were patches of gray in his close-cropped hair.

He stepped toward the FBI director and shook his hand. "I'm very sorry for your loss," he said in a low voice.

The director raised his head. His eyes were wet. "Thank you, sir."

"I know this is small consolation, but I'm going to award Agent Parker the Presidential Medal of Valor. The country owes her a great debt."

"That's for damn sure. She was brave as hell."

There was an awkward silence. The president waited a few seconds, looking uncomfortable. Then he turned to Monique. "Thank you for your service, Dr. Reynolds. And thank you for not revealing the existence of the universal program. It must be difficult for a scientist to hide the truth, but in this case I don't think we have a choice."

Monique shook the president's hand, but said nothing. For the first time since David had met her, she seemed at a loss for words. After a few seconds the president let go of her hand and reached for David's. "And you must be Dr. Swift?" he said. "Your name came up a few times in the FBI reports I read."

David felt disoriented. He watched himself shake hands with the president. "Uh, yeah, that's right," he said. "The FBI loves to write reports about me." He stood there with his mouth open. He couldn't think of anything intelligent to say. "I've got this bad habit of being in the wrong place at the wrong time."

"We were all in the wrong place, I'm afraid. But you helped us put things right." He gave David a sober look. Then he smiled. "So I assume you're back at Columbia now? And still running Physicists for Peace?"

Jesus, David thought. He couldn't believe it. The president was making small talk with him. "Yeah, we're still fighting the good fight. We have another conference scheduled for this fall."

"Glad to hear it. You're doing important work. We have to find new ways to reach across borders. Because the old ways aren't working anymore."

David nodded. It was true: the need for peace activism was greater than ever. The United States had managed to avoid war with Iran—after Bennett's treachery was revealed, the Revolutionary Guards surrendered all the U-235 that Cyrus had given them—but the Iranian government was still producing its own enriched uranium at the centrifuge complex in Natanz. Another conflict was sure to break out unless the citizens of both countries came to their senses.

The president moved a step closer. He put one hand on Monique's shoulder and the other on David's. "I have a proposal for both of you. I've been thinking about this tragedy we've suffered and what we could've done to prevent it. And I've decided that I need better information from the scientific community."

Monique finally found her voice. "What do you mean?"

"There's an imbalance. I have hundreds of people giving me advice on military, diplomatic, and economic issues. But my contact with scientists is limited. They're either buried in the federal bureaucracy or isolated on the college campuses. What I need is a liaison. Someone who could put me in touch with the best minds in each field, particularly during a crisis." He gazed intently at Monique, then at David. "You think you could do something like that?"

David smiled. This had to be a joke. "You want us to work for you?"

"You wouldn't have official positions. You'd be more like consultants. I'd call on you only when we need your help."

"But neither of us is qualified. We have no government experience and no—"

"I don't need more bureaucrats. I need smart people who have plenty of contacts in the scientific community. You two would be perfect for the job."

Slowly, David realized that the president was serious. The commander in chief was asking for their help

"You don't have to answer right away," the president added. "Just think about it. My chief of staff will be in touch."

DAVID WAS STILL THINKING ABOUT IT FOUR HOURS LATER WHEN HE returned to New York City. In a daze, he dropped off Monique at their apartment, then drove to the Upper Manhattan Autism Center to pick up Michael. The past few weeks had been difficult for the teenager; he was still suffering from the trauma of the kidnapping and the terrible things that had happened afterward. Two weeks after coming back to the United States he threw a punch at one of his teachers at the autism center. The next week he smashed one of the center's computers. David had arranged extra therapy sessions for the boy, but his progress had been slow.

Michael was waiting for him in the center's recreation room, sitting at a square table under the watchful eyes of the staff members. He was hunched over a sheaf of papers and writing something with a ballpoint pen. Probably copying the words from another science textbook he'd memorized. David watched him for a few seconds, marveling at the look of concentration on the teenager's face. Then he gently tapped the table. "I'm here, Michael. It's time to go home."

The boy stopped writing and put down his pen. But he didn't look at David. He kept his eyes on his papers. "You're late," he said. "You were supposed to pick me up at five o'clock. The time is now five-oh-seven."

"I'm sorry. There was traffic on the interstate. Come on, let's go."

Michael didn't move. David could tell there was something else on his mind. In these situations he'd learned that it was better not to rush the boy. So David stood by the table and waited him out.

"I don't like this school anymore," Michael finally said.

David took a deep breath. This wasn't the first time they'd had this conversation. "We've talked about this, Michael. I think the teachers here are helping you a lot."

"No, they're not. I'm not learning anything here."

"You're learning how to get along with other people. And that's very important."

Michael shook his head. "I don't like this school. I want to go to a different one."

The boy's voice was calm, but David noticed that the staff members were watching them carefully. He needed to end this argument before it escalated. "All right, I understand. Let me do a little research, okay? Maybe I can find another center where—"

"You don't have to do that." Michael picked up the sheaf of papers. "I already found another school and downloaded the application."

He handed the papers to David, who began leafing through them. It was a long application, with half a dozen pages of essay questions. The pages were out of order, but David could see that Michael had answered each question in his beautifully neat handwriting. He'd written essays about his personal goals and favorite hobbies and fondest memories. He'd even attached the application fee, five twenty-dollar bills he'd saved from his allowance. David finally found the first page of the application and saw the name of the school written at the top. It was Columbia University.

"I want to study physics," Michael said. "I'm going to become a physicist."

David's eyes welled. Of course, he thought. It was the perfect choice.

Michael pointed at a box at the bottom of the last page. "This application requires your signature. Where it says 'Parent or Guardian.'"

David wiped his eyes. Then he picked up the pen and placed the page on the table so he could sign it.

"It's my pleasure," he said. "You'll make a great physicist, Michael."

AUTHOR'S NOTE

Part of the fun of writing science thrillers is putting real technologies and scientific principles into the fiction. Here are some of the facts and theories that I incorporated into *The Omega Theory:*

QUANTUM COMPUTERS. I became interested in this field in 2008 when I edited an article written by two leading experts on quantum computing—Christopher R. Monroe of the University of Maryland and David J. Wineland of the National Institute of Standards and Technology. Monroe invited me to his lab at Maryland's College Park campus, where researchers are taking the first steps toward building ultrafast computers that use ions to perform calculations. The code-breaking computer in *The Omega Theory* is based on the ingenious devices I saw during that visit. (I simplified some of the details; real ion traps, for instance, require additional electrodes and oscillating electric fields.) You can read more about the technology in "Quantum Computing with Ions" (*Scientific American,* August 2008).

IT FROM BIT. For decades theorists have kicked around the idea that the universe is a computer, running a program that put the Big Bang in motion. The eminent physicist John Archibald Wheeler put it this way in his autobiography, *Geons, Black Holes, and Quantum Foam: A Life in Physics* (1998): "Now I am in the grip of a new vision, that Everything is Information. The more I have pondered the mystery of the quantum and our strange ability to comprehend this world in which we live, the more I see possible fundamental roles for logic and information as the bedrock of physical theory." In the 2006 book *Programming the Universe,* MIT researcher Seth Lloyd described how quantum fluctuations at the beginning of time could have generated simple programs that organized the universe, laying down the physical laws that would govern all of the subsequent calculations. My own contribution to this topic is to pose the question: If the universe is a computer, what could make it crash?

EXCALIBUR. During the 1980s, Edward Teller—father of the H-bomb—promoted a radical idea for missile defense: shoot down Soviet ICBMs using high-energy X-ray lasers powered by a nuclear explosion in space. After researchers tested the concept in underground nuclear blasts in Nevada, the project—first dubbed Excalibur, then Super Excalibur—became the centerpiece of the Star Wars program. Later tests showed, however, that the technology wasn't as promising as advertised, and the government abandoned it. Excalibur never became a weapon, but it was a step into the unknown, and it's easy to imagine that this unprecedented physical phenomenon could have unforeseen effects. An excellent book about the project is *Teller's War* by William J. Broad.

TURKMENISTAN GEOLOGY. A catastrophic accident at a Soviet drilling site in Turkmenistan's Karakum Desert left a sinkhole that became the burning crater of Darvaza, where the natural-gas fires have been raging for decades. Yangykala is also a real place in Turkmenistan, as beautiful as the Grand Canyon but with far fewer tourists. The Camp Cobra cavern is similar to Kow Ata, a huge cave at the foot of a mountain in the Kopet Dag range. And yes, Kow Ata has an underground lake. You can go swimming there, but it's a little spooky.

The same people who helped me polish *Final Theory*, the first book in the David Swift series, came to my aid again while I was writing *The Omega Theory*. My friends at *Scientific American* were generous with their support and encouragement. The members of my writing group—Rick Eisenberg, Johanna Fiedler, Steve Goldstone, Dave King, Melissa Knox, and Eva Mekler—plowed through stacks of manuscript pages and patiently pointed out my mistakes. My agent, Dan Lazar of Writers House, made sure that I met my deadlines, and Sulay Hernandez of Touchstone edited the book with care and imagination. And once again I owe a great debt to my wife for reminding me how lucky I am.